ALSO BY CHUCK BARRIS

Confessions of a Dangerous Mind

Bad Grass Never Dies: More Confessions of a Dangerous Mind

The Game Show King

You and Me, Babe: A Novel

THE BIG QUESTION

Chuck Barris

Simon & Schuster

NEW YORK • LONDON • TORONTO • SYDNEY

SIMON & SCHUSTER
Rockefeller Center
1230 Avenue of the Americas
New York, NY 10020

For information about special discounts for bulk purchases, please contact
Simon & Schuster Special Sales at 1-800-456-6798 or
business@simonandschuster.com.

Designed by Paul Dippolito

Manufactured in the United States of America

1 3 5 7 9 10 8 6 4 2

Library of Congress Cataloging-in-Publication Data
Barris, Chuck.
The big question : a novel / Chuck Barris.
p. cm.
1. Reality television programs—Fiction. 2. Game shows—Fiction. I. Title.
PS3552.A7367B54 2007
813'.54—dc22
2006052617

ISBN-13: 978-1-4165-3525-6
ISBN-10: 1-4165-3525-X

for my dear wife, Mary

No matter how much time I have left with you,
it isn't enough.

and for my dear friend Reuven Frank

Referring to television, Reuven once told me,
"In the kingdom of the blind, the one-eyed man
is a consultant."
I was never quite sure what Reuven meant by that,
but I believed him.

You never know what worse luck your bad luck has saved you from.

—CORMAC MCCARTHY

I

It happened on a bleak Friday afternoon in late November . . .

It happened on a bleak Friday afternoon in late November in the year 2011. That's when the hand shot out and grabbed him.

The assault took place during one of those cold spells that occur with regularity between Thanksgiving and Christmas. A blustery wind whipped around street corners and made life miserable. It was the kind of cold New Yorkers say goes right through you. The streets were filled with bundled-up shoppers in overcoats and scarves, executives wearing dark blue cashmere topcoats, tourists shivering in mackinaws, earmuffs, and Yankee baseball caps just purchased from street vendors.

The fingers that took hold of him were so strong he could feel the pressure through his fur-lined raincoat, sport coat, turtleneck sweater, and the two undershirts beneath. The man had been lost in thought walking along the east side of Madison Avenue when the attack took place. He experienced a thick feeling of terror grip his chest like an iron vise. He was sure he would soon be fighting for his life against a demented lunatic right there in the middle of the pavement. He could see tomorrow morning's *Post* headline:

CRAZE-O MURDERS FAMOUS TV PRODUCER ON UPPER EAST SIDE

The hand spun him around. As the producer came face-to-face with his assailant, he couldn't believe his eyes. The hand with the powerful grip belonged to a pathetic old cripple!

The producer was relieved.

He wouldn't have to physically defend himself against a crazed maniac after all. Quite the contrary. His assailant was powerless and disabled, old and sickly to boot. The geezer had to be in his eighties, guessed the producer. The old man's strong grip came from years of supporting himself on a crutch. He had been frightened by a lame, emaciated bum, frail and misshapen.

The cripple had a face full of liver spots. He hadn't shaved in days. His sparse beard was filthy. Crumbs of food were embedded in it. His lips were chapped, split in some places, with several sores on them. The old cripple's entire right side was tilted down toward the street. His right arm hung limply by his side. His right leg appeared to be almost useless. It was obvious he'd suffered a stroke. The cripple wore a seedy, weather-beaten fedora and a torn and stained overcoat worn more for protection than looks, like a turtle's carapace. The coat was held together by one button and several large safety pins. Portions of dirty socks protruded through the sides of his old, cracked shoes.

The producer's relief turned immediately to violent machismo. He pulled away from the filthy clutching fingers with a violent jerk. When he did, the old cripple stumbled backward one or two steps. Several passersby scowled at the man for being so arrogant and physical with someone so old and less fortunate than himself.

The cripple seemed unperturbed.

The producer was furious. Goddamn it, he thought, why do I always attract the lunatic fringe? Why does every panhandler follow me down the entire length of the street asking for money, waving his filthy paper cup in my face? How come every hobo carrying a billboard on his back shoves his flyers into my stomach and every pedestrian with the flu coughs and sneezes in my direction when he walks by? And why does every nitwit in Manhattan stop me to give me his god-awful television ideas? As sure as I'm standing here, this derelict has the best television show ever created by man.

"What do you think you're doing?" hissed the producer.

"Aren't you . . . aren't you the guy who—?"

"I'm not anyone you should be the least bit concerned about."

"But you *are,* aren't you? You're the famous—"

The cripple slurred his words when he talked. Yellowish spittle gathered in the corners of his mouth and saliva drippings covered his chin. Nothing about the poor soul was the least bit appealing.

"I'm not famous."

"Yes, you are."

"Just go away, you son of a bitch, and leave me alone."

"Easy now, mister. There's no need for that kind of language. Show a little respect for your elders. Just tell me whether you are or are not the big-shot television producer who had all those game and reality shows on the air. The one I've been wanting to talk to for an entire year. No, more like *praying* to talk to. Well, come on, you are, aren't you?"

"I'm a television producer, but I'm not famous. Now go away."

"*Ha!* I knew you were famous and I know who you are. You're—"

"Didn't I just tell you to go away? Where do you get off grabbing my shoulder, anybody's shoulder, you bent and misshapen piece of *scheise*."

"I *must* talk to you," said the cripple, immune to slurs. "I'm sure you won't believe your ears when I tell you what I'm going to tell you. Or your eyes when you see what I have to show you. You'll—"

"You're not going to show me a damn thing. Now go away, do you hear?"

"Like I was saying, you'll want to hear what I have to say because . . . because . . ." The cripple suddenly stopped speaking and started coughing. Violently. The spasms turned his white face red as the poor man gasped for breath. The cripple's helpless coughing momentarily mesmerized the producer. It caused him to stare at the sick shell of a man and wonder when he would quit his awful hacking. Other pedestrians stopped walking and regarded the cripple as they passed. Eventually the cripple was able to get his coughing under control, and when he did he continued speaking as if nothing had happened. ". . . because it's important I speak with you. Very very very important. Three verys." The cripple cackled.

"I'm sure what you have to discuss is important," said the producer. "Every misfit walking the streets of this city always wants to talk to me about something important, usually some incredible television idea, the best ever created by man. Or the beggar wants money for something. Okay, okay, I'll give you a couple of dol—"

"I don't want your goddamn money!" snapped the cripple, fuming. He took a deep breath. "God knows I can use it, but I don't want it. I didn't stop you to ask for money. I stopped you because I want to

offer you something that I am sure will *make* you money. Tons of it. And some most assuredly for me too. I just want you to come to my room and hear what I have to say and see what I have to show you. I can explain everything . . . and . . . and you know . . . a picture is worth a thousand words, right? When I show you my video you'll see what I mean. I need you to come to my apartment because I don't want to take the video out into the street. You'll understand why when you see it. It's the most incredible television idea—"

"*See!* Of course it's an incredible television idea. Didn't I tell you every miscreant on the street has an incredible television idea? It's always an incredible television idea. Not just a *good* television idea but an *incredible* television idea. Do you have any idea how many times I am approached with incredible television ideas in a given week?" The producer shook his head, taking a moment to think angry thoughts. "Besides, I don't develop television program ideas anymore, Bozo, especially someone else's television idea. I *never* did that. I only develop my own ideas. Besides, I quit the damn television business long ago, and—"

"Not that long ago. Not really. What's it been? Five years?"

"Ten."

"Okay, ten. If it's been ten years, then it's time for you to get back into the fray." The cripple smiled.

"Don't you presume to tell me—"

"You won't believe this idea of mine," continued the cripple. "You *must* hear what I have to explain to you and see what I have to show you in private. It's extremely important you see the videotape. It's also important that it be just the two of us. After you hear what I have to say and see the tape, you'll understand. I promise you, I absolutely promise you, you'll beg me to let you do my program idea posthaste. You're the one person alive who's smart enough to understand what I intend to show you and *do* something about it."

A passing ambulance's screaming siren momentarily stopped the two men's exchange. During the lull, the producer thought to himself, maybe this creep will go away peacefully if I just speak calmly and nicely to him.

"Look, old man," he said calmly and nicely, even trying to smile a bit, which was difficult, for the producer never smiled, "you've got the wrong guy. I don't have all the contacts with the networks and syndicators I used to have. I would have a hard time getting an idea *of my own* done these days. Believe me, that's true. Good-bye, old man."

The producer turned and started to walk away.

"That's *bullshit*," yelled the old cripple, limping after him.

Vera Bundle decided to make herself a cup of afternoon tea in the kitchen of her home in Steubenville, Ohio.

Steubenville's just across the Ohio-Pennsylvania border on the Ohio side, a bit west of Pittsburgh, Pennsylvania, and north of Wheeling, West Virginia. Like Pittsburgh, Steubenville's a steel town. They make a lot of it there. Or used to. They also have some fairly large paper mills in Steubenville and more whorehouses than most cities of comparable size. Steubenville's a gray, depressing city. Its population has been trending downward since 1980. Roughly twenty thousand people live there now.

Dean Martin grew up in Steubenville.

Vera Bundle did too.

Short and plump, Vera Bundle was in her midseventies and still relatively spry for her age. She was never seriously sick and had good color. Her hair was frizzy and naturally brown. She kept it cut short and worn in a pageboy. The bangs running across her forehead resembled dead weeds, making Vera appear even more dowdy than she was, which was seriously dowdy. Vera Bundle tended to wear plain, formless dresses, usually under an apron tied in the back. She always wore sensible shoes on her slightly large feet and favored small hats when she went out. Vera had a nice smile but didn't use it often. That's because Vera Bundle rarely had a lot to smile about.

Vera always wore a pair of granny spectacles that rested on the bridge of her red and veiny nose. The hundreds of tiny purple veins came from years of drinking "occasional" glasses of sherry and frequent shots of J&B scotch. She drank mostly out of boredom and more now than she had in the past. Even Vera noticed how her drinking had increased. She guessed it was due to her becoming more and more uninterested and listless about life. She often wondered why over the past few years a gray curtain seemed to have dropped down in front of her. Why, the first word she said every morning when she woke was "damn." Vera never used to wake up and say that. She used to be happy in the morning. It was the start of a brand-new day.

Now she said damn.

Vera missed her dear husband, Norville. More now than she had in the past. Perhaps that was the root of her unhappiness. Prolonged life without Norville—it had been almost fifty years—might very well be the cause of her depression. Well, it made sense, didn't it? For one thing, she and Norville had done so many things together. Their daily breakfast ritual, going to the movies, reading in bed before going to sleep. The simple life. It was so much fun. And Norville was so funny! He could make Vera Bundle laugh louder and longer than anyone else she knew. But for so long now, Norville had been just plain dead Norville, a pile of bones in a beat-up casket in the cold, hard ground out there in Memorial Park Cemetery.

"I know this is a touchy subject, Vera, but you haven't laughed or done much of anything since Norville passed," said her friend Esther Wigton over tea one afternoon at the Conrad Hotel. The Conrad was the only hotel in Steubenville that served high tea at four P.M. "Norville died fifty years ago, Vera. Isn't that time enough to mourn someone? You should have moved on years ago."

Vera sighed. She had heard that speech maybe a thousand times from Esther.

Vera Bundle was retired now. She used to teach geography at PS 13, the grammar school in downtown Steubenville. Vera knew she would miss teaching after she retired, but enough was enough. At her farewell lunch she told the crowd as much. Actually it wasn't exactly a crowd. Only four friends came to Vera's retirement party.

"I think forty-five years is plenty of teaching for one person," she told them.

The four friends nodded.

At the end of her short speech Vera thanked her friends for her going-away present. It was a Timex wristwatch they had all chipped in to buy her. "It's something I will always cherish," she said.

The four friends nodded.

Vera loved being retired. She finally had the time to concentrate on furthering her own education in her own way. It was something she had been doing part-time her entire life. Now she would be able to do it full-time. What that meant was she could study her *Encyclopaedia Britannicas* and *National Geographics* all day, all afternoon, and all night, if she so desired.

And she so desired.

Vera Bundle owned a complete set of the *Encyclopaedia Britannica,* all twenty-five volumes. Vera's encyclopedia covers were made of imitation leather with gold-flecked borders. The twenty-five volumes were housed in a special custom-made bookcase that came with the set. It had taken Vera three years of saving from her bimonthly teaching paychecks and some of the money her husband Norville left her to purchase the set of encyclopedias complete with its own bookcase. It was an extravagance, but so what? Vera considered the investment the best she'd ever made. She adored her *Encyclopaedia Britannicas*.

Vera Bundle had her own special routine prior to perusing a volume of the *Britannicas*. First she made herself a cup of tea. She would pour the hot water into her cup, dip her tea bag once or twice (she didn't like her tea too strong), add quite a bit of milk and two heaping teaspoons of sugar, and stir. Every time Vera made a cup of tea—every single time—she thought of her late husband Norville. How he used to say, "I like my tea like I like my women, Vera, hot and sweet."

"Now you stop that, Norville Bundle," Vera would reply, pretending to be angry.

"Aw, I'm only teasing you, Vera baby," Norville always said, tickling her ribs with his index fingers, Vera wiggling around, trying to dodge his fingers but not trying to dodge his fingers. "Vera, you know you're the only one I've ever loved."

They'd joke around talking silly like that for a spell and then they'd hug and kiss . . . and . . .

God, she missed him.

After Vera Bundle finished stirring her tea, she added a shot glass, filled to the top, of J&B scotch. Vera never stirred the tea once the scotch was in the cup.

When her tea was prepared, Vera took two vanilla sugar wafers from the cookie tin in the cupboard and carried the tea and wafers on a small tray to her favorite armchair in the living room. She placed the tray on a tea table that was her mother's, and her mother's mother's before that, going back maybe a hundred years or so. Once in the armchair, Vera pulled the chain that turned on the floor lamp with the imitation Tiffany shade. Vera used a hundred-watt bulb in the lamp. In the past she'd used lesser-watt bulbs, but in the last five years her eyes had become worse and worse. Now she was forced to wear store-bought glasses for reading, and her lightbulbs had increased from forty watts to sixty watts to the present hundred watts.

When Vera needed to buy store-bought glasses with a higher magnification or if she were compelled to go to a one-hundred-and-fifty-watt bulb, she vowed she would make an appointment with Dr. Duane Carper, the cute young eye doctor in Wheeling. Vera's friend Esther Wigton constantly raved about Dr. Carper since seeing him a month ago. Vera was sure Esther had a crush on the eye doctor. When Vera was a young girl she could never have imagined a woman of sixty-plus years having a crush on anyone. She still couldn't imagine it. Women of her age and Esther's were much too old for those kinds of shenanigans. True, Esther Wigton was younger than she. Esther was in her midsixties. About the age Vera was when she met John. But Vera got over it real quick and Esther hadn't gotten over anything. In fact, she was *still* acting downright childish. An example of this had happened just the other day at the Inn of the Sixth Happiness Tea & Sandwich Shop.

Esther said to Vera, "God, Dr. Carper's sexy."

"My goodness, Esther, Dr. Carper must be half your age!" said Vera.

"What's age have to do with it? Duane's a man and I'm a woman, for God's sake."

"Now it's Duane, is it?"

"Oh, control yourself, Vera. I know how the subject of sex gets you all riled up."

"No, you control *yourself,* Esther," whispered Vera. "People at the other tables can hear you."

"Oh, Vera, for heaven's sake. You're such a prude. So someone overhears us. So what?"

"So what?"

"Yes, so what? What's wrong with getting a little at our age? Or at least *dreaming* about getting a little?"

"This entire conversation is absurd."

"It'll all stop being absurd, Vera, when you get the hots for some young man."

"Get the hots. Honestly, Esther."

Was that it? Had she gotten "the hots" for John?

"You'll see, Vera. You'll find yourself doing things you never imagined you would do in your life. That is, if you ever meet a younger man who gets your blood boiling."

"Honestly, Esther. Gets my blood boiling. You are something."

After making herself comfortable in her armchair, with a cup of tea sitting on the table beside her, Vera would take an encyclopedia from the bookcase, sniff its leather cover, then open the book and sniff the first page. She never tired of these delicious and familiar smells. After her sniffs, she usually examined the entire volume from cover to cover, riffling through its pages, lost in a wonderful world of facts and figures, historical data, exotic photographs, and maps and charts until something caught her eye. Then she would stop and read and read and read. She daydreamed of the faraway cities and countries she came across that she would never see, places with magical names like Al Jizah, Timbuktu, and Kilimanjaro.

"So much to read, so little time to do it," Vera often said aloud.

Along with her beloved *Encyclopaedia Britannica*s, Vera had a subscription to *National Geographic* dating back to 1941, the year Vera started elementary school. The subscription was a gift from her Uncle Conrad Finley. Uncle Conrad would tell Vera, "You'll get more out of one *National Geographic* than all the other textbooks you'll ever read."

Now, seventy years later, there were so many *Geographic*s piled up in nice yellow stacks on her bedroom floor that sometimes she couldn't move around. Occasionally a handyman friend of hers had to come to the house and make passageways to allow Vera to walk to bed at night or to the bathroom when she had to go.

Vera would be the first to admit that even with her *Encyclopaedia Britannica*s and *National Geographic*s, not a day went by when she wasn't deeply discouraged and lonely. The few friends Vera had believed that her inability to get over her husband Norville's passing was the reason behind Vera's depression. They begged her over and over again to go out and find a man.

"At *my* age?" she often replied. "What a thought."

Vera hadn't lived with another man in fifty years. Maybe she should have looked for a husband right away like everyone told her to do. She was only twenty-seven back then, still young and good-looking, not all fat and dumpy the way she was now.

Heck, she thought, even in my sixties when I met John, I was still a fine-looking lady.

Daniel Patrick Brady was born in a row house on Stoneway Lane across the Philadelphia city line in a suburb called Bala Cynwyd, Pennsylvania. All the houses on Stoneway Lane had slate roofs, stone sidings, steps of stone, and little windows. Brady attended Bala Grammar School, which went as far as the sixth grade. It was there his schoolmates first called him DP.

In the fall the so-called varsity football team of little Bala Grammar School played St. Matthias Catholic. St. Matt's was a large, gray building with a massive bell tower over the impressive wooden doors of its main entrance. St. Matt's went as far as the eighth grade; consequently, the Catholic boys were two years older and much bigger than the Bala school twerps. With this advantage, the parochial school creamed the secular kids every year on the rocky field adjacent to the school. And by embarrassing scores too, like 84–0.

One evening at the dinner table, after a St. Matt's–Bala football game, a young and bruised DP Brady asked his father whether he could continue his next two years of school at St. Matthias instead of the public junior high school.

"Why?" asked his father, a muscular, short-tempered, unsympathetic man named Flynn Brady. DP's father owned a small appliance business in West Philadelphia. Flynn Brady wasn't an easy man to live with. He didn't involve himself with family problems. Just yelled a lot and drank a lot. "Those Catholic boys beat the shit out of you guys again?" he asked.

"Language," said DP's mother, a frail, short, thin, flat, sickly woman who tended to wear a lot of black.

"We're Catholics, aren't we?" asked Daniel Patrick. "So why can't I go to a Catholic school?"

"All this because of a football game." Flynn Brady shook his head. "Don't worry, you'll fill out. Right now you take after your mother, but you'll fill out. Now shut up and eat your dinner," said DP's father, pointing a long finger with a dirty fingernail at the kid's food. DP's father was not very understanding.

Turning to his mother, DP asked, "We're good Catholics, aren't we?"

"Of course we are," snapped DP's father. He sat at the head of the table, his suit coat hanging from the back of his chair, his shirt collar open, his tie pulled down a notch or two, and his suspenders dangling by the sides of his pants.

"We don't go to church every Sunday," said his twelve-year-old son. "I don't, and I don't see the two of you going very much."

"I'm tired on Sundays," muttered DP's father, not enjoying his son's interrogation. "I work hard during the week, and—"

"We're *not* very good Catholics," said DP's mother softly.

"Jesus Christ, Emma . . ." snorted Flynn Brady.

"Well, we're not. God knows we're going to pay for it too."

"Why, if we're Catholic," asked young DP, "am I going to Bala Grammar School and not St. Matthias?"

"Answer him, Mother," ordered Flynn Brady.

"I have nothing to say," said Emma Brady.

DP's father said, "They expect a yearly contribution to the church fund if your kid goes to St. Matt's, that's why."

"That's not true," sighed DP's mother.

DP's father shook his head.

DP wasn't always sure why his father shook his head. Discouraged? Disappointed? Something his mother said?

"I want to go to St. Matthias," said the boy.

And so he did, completing his seventh and eighth grades there. And then on to high school at St. Joseph Prep School, not far from St. Matthias. It was at St. Joe Prep that Daniel Patrick Brady began his Jesuit education. When DP graduated from St. Joseph Prep

School, he continued to stay in the neighborhood, entering St. Joseph College, a few blocks away.

DP Brady loved St. Joe. He lived with three classmates in a small apartment not far from school on City Line Avenue. He worked lunch and dinner behind the cash register in the college cafeteria to pay for some of his tuition expenses. Young DP Brady hadn't "filled out" yet, as his father had promised, and though he couldn't make any varsity team, DP was one of the school's most popular students.

Senior year, he became the basketball team's mascot.

St. Joe was a big-time basketball power and its mascot was a hawk. Being the hawk mascot called for someone with a lot of nervous and frenetic energy, more important than agility and athletic prowess. If you were chosen as the school's hawk, you were awarded a full scholarship for your senior year along with a hawk costume, and were required to run around flapping the hawk's wings for the entire game. The hawk was allowed to rest during halftime. Many tried out for the honored position, but only one was chosen.

Daniel Patrick Brady was chosen.

As the St. Joe hawk, DP traveled with the basketball team to Madison Square Garden for the National Invitation Basketball Tournament.

At the beginning of his senior year, DP Brady received a scholarship from the Jesuit Society of Philadelphia that would cover his senior year's tuition. The society was investing in DP because they saw in him the makings of a profound Jesuit priest. Under Daniel Patrick Brady's photo in the St. Joseph College yearbook it said: "A born leader."

During DP's last year at St. Joseph, he decided to become a priest. But not a Jesuit priest. A priest of the Catholic church. DP's father wasn't thrilled. His appliance business was growing and he was hoping his son would join him after he finished his education.

DP's father was convinced this religious thing of his son's would blow over like a nasty summer heat wave when DP was handed his diploma. Flynn Brady had already painted a sign saying BRADY & SON as a surprise graduation present for Daniel Patrick and bought him a nice Bulova wristwatch. DP accepted the watch but not the sign, and consequently the **BRADY & SON** unveiling on the roof of the store never happened.

It broke Flynn Brady's heart.

He stored the sign in the basement of his appliance store.

Daniel Patrick Brady was accepted at St. Charles Borromeo Seminary on Lancaster Avenue and City Line, again not far from the family's row house on Stoneway Lane. St. Charles Borromeo resembled Versailles. The seminary was an impressive collection of immaculate white stone buildings surrounded by a high black wrought-iron gate. St. Charles Borromeo stretched across acres and acres of well-kept formal gardens and hundreds of healthy and well-kept oak and maple trees.

Young Brady was one of one hundred students to enter the seminary. In one of the books he was given to study was written:

> *The Lord has sworn, and he will not repent:*
> *"You are a priest forever . . ."*
>
> PSALM 110:4

DP Brady turned himself into a dedicated seminarian.

He graduated from St. Charles Borromeo with honors.

In 1999, when Billy Constable was eight years old, he walked over to the Bowling Green, Kentucky, fairgrounds, where the annual county fair was in progress. Billy roamed around watching the rides and listening to the calliope music. He was mesmerized by the Ferris wheel, the merry-go-round, the flying saucers, the loop-the-loop, and the many exciting booths.

All of a sudden something stopped Billy Constable dead in his tracks. It was the big hunting knife he noticed hanging above what turned out to be a very large roulette wheel. Billy didn't know the first thing about roulette wheels or that the knife was a prize. All he knew was he wanted that hunting knife more than life itself.

Little Billy walked up to the man behind the roulette wheel counter and said, "Can I buy that there knife for fifty cent?"

Billy held up his half-dollar to show the man.

"No you can't, sonny, you can't buy it. But you can try and win it with your half-dollar."

"How do I do that?"

"What you do is give me your fifty-cent piece and I'll give you a chip. You put the chip on your favorite number on that there board over there. I spin this here wheel and when the wheel stops spinnin' an' the little rubber arrow ends up pointin' at your number you get to keep that big ol' huntin' knife."

"And if it don't end up pointin' at my number?"

"You lose your fifty-cent piece."

"I wouldn't want a do that. A fifty-cent piece's a lotta money," said Billy.

"Yeah, it is. Your ma and pa know you're wanderin' around this park wavin' a fifty-cent piece around, sonny?"

"Nope. But they don't much care what I do. An' my house ain't that far away. So should I give you my fifty-cent piece?"

"Don't know what to tell you, sonny."

"It's the last fifty-cent piece I have from all the dollars I made mowin' lawns this week."

"How many dollars you make?"

"Three dollar. An' sixty cent too. I bought myself some things yesterday. This is all I have left, this here fifty-cent piece. But I want that there knife real bad."

"Don't know what to tell you, sonny."

"They don't make fifty-cent pieces no more," said little Billy.

"I know."

"Someone give this to me. He said keep it for good luck."

"So you gonna keep it?"

"No. I'm gonna put it on number twenty-two."

"Why twenty-two?"

"Dunno."

"Okay, give me your fifty-cent piece, sonny, and I'll give you this blue chip. You go over there an' put the chip on the number twenty-two. See where the numbers are?"

"Yeah, I see 'em," said Billy.

Some grown-up people were standing around the numbers, not

paying much attention to an eight-year-old kid with a blue chip. The grown-up people were too busy concentrating on the serious business of choosing their own numbers. Billy wiggled into where he could put his chip on number twenty-two.

When everybody had their bets down, the man spun the big roulette wheel. Billy shut his eyes, put his dirty hands over them, and held his breath until he heard the wheel come to a stop. When Billy opened his eyes, he saw the rubber arrow pointing directly at number twenty-two. The man behind the counter grinned from ear to ear, reached up and grabbed the big, scary-looking hunting knife, and handed it to Billy.

The knife measured about ten inches from the top of the handle to the tip of the blade. It came complete with a leather holster with a loop on the back that Billy could slide his belt through. Billy Constable strutted around town wearing that knife, the holster banging against his hip, for weeks and weeks. He even slept with it belted around the waist of his jammies.

When Billy Constable was eight years old he was a good-looking kid. Unfortunately, he wasn't nearly as good-looking when he grew up. For one thing, Billy's chin stopped growing. Also his freckles disappeared and he began losing his mop of dusty brown hair. He didn't gain any weight. He just grew. Billy became tall and skinny and almost bald and chinless and bony and shy and introverted and I don't know what else.

One day in late December 2011, Billy Constable turned nineteen and decided to leave his home in Bowling Green, Kentucky. "I'm gonna seek my fortune in New York City," he told his parents the night before he left. Billy's mother said just about the same thing his father had said, which was basically, "That's nice."

Billy couldn't explain why he picked New York City or why he decided to leave home so close to Christmas. He just did. Billy's folks didn't care where he went or what he did when he got there. Ma and Pa Constable never gave a good goddamn what any of their nine kids did. They weren't what you'd call loving or caring parents. They never beat their kids but they never hugged them, either. They just never paid them any attention.

So Billy Constable grabbed a Greyhound bus heading north. It was raining when Billy boarded the bus. It rained all that day and well into the night. The constant rain would have driven Billy crazy and the ride would have bored him to death if he wasn't sitting next to a young stranger who seemed friendly.

Billy Constable was seated by the window. The stranger, who was one of the last to board the bus, sat next to him on the aisle.

They didn't know it yet, but the stranger and Billy Constable were the same age, easygoing, and fun to be around. They were skinny as sticks with maybe a total of two hundred and fifty pounds between them. Both were from the South, heading north to start anew. Both were young and hadn't done much with their lives so far. And neither one of the boys was afraid to risk some of his loose change on various wagers. This last trait quickly endeared them to each other.

But that's where the similarities ended.

The stranger was outgoing and extroverted. Billy Constable was shy and mostly kept to himself. The stranger had lots of red hair. Billy was going bald. The stranger was dressed like a country bumpkin. He wore a leather porkpie hat and a torn denim jacket and jeans. His T-shirt advertised the John Deere Company. His jeans were cut so high above his ankles you could see his skin over the tops of his socks. Billy had on his best (and only) sport coat, tie, and dress shirt. Stuff he wore to church.

"You from Bowling Green?" asked the young stranger shortly after they were seated.

"Yep. You too?" asked Billy, looking out his window even though the bus was still in the terminal.

"No. I'm from Knoxville. Hitched a ride to Bowling Green. What's your name?"

"Name's Billy. Billy Constable. What's yours?"

"Jimmy Joel Jenks," he told Billy's back. "Where you headin', Billy?"

"New York City," he answered, still staring out the window. Billy preferred to look out his window rather than into the stranger's eyes. Billy didn't like to look into a stranger's eyes. In fact, Billy didn't like to look into anybody's eyes. Not at first. "Where *you* goin', Jimmy Joel?" he asked the window.

"Anywhere that suits me."

"How will you know when you find a place that suits you?"

"I'll know."

"Have any idea where that might be?"

"Don't know the answer to that question," replied Jimmy Joel Jenks, his warm smile wasted on the back of Billy's head. "You say you're goin' to New York City?"

"Yep."

"Reckon I'll go there too."

That's when Billy Constable turned from the window and faced Jimmy Joel Jenks. "*Reckon* you'll go there too?" he asked, his eyes all squinty with seriousness, which was what happened when Billy talked serious.

"Yeah. Why not?" said Jimmy Joel Jenks.

"You're goin' to New York City just 'cause I said I was goin' to New York City?"

"It's as good a reason as any."

During their rainy ride north, Billy Constable pocketed a little over a dollar of Jimmy Joel Jenks's loose change betting on raindrops. Billy chose one raindrop up at the top of their window and Jimmy Joel another. The winner was the one whose raindrop arrived at the bottom of the window first. Sometimes the boys got to yelling and rooting so hard for their raindrop they'd wake up other passengers who were sleeping. Or trying to. Some of the passengers would curse and say nasty things to the boys, but they continued betting on raindrops anyway.

"Lord Almighty, Billy," said Jimmy Joel Jenks when he was finally out of change. "How you always know which damn raindrop's goin' to get down to the bottom first?"

"Just lucky, I guess," answered Billy Constable.

It was snowing and very cold in Manhattan. There were Christmas decorations already on storefronts, Christmas trees on traffic islands, and wreaths on lampposts.

The boys split up at the main entrance to the Port Authority bus depot on Eighth Avenue. They understood they had been through a baptism of sorts, leaving home close to Christmas and coming to New York together like they did.

"Take care, Jimmy Joel, y'hear?" said Billy Constable.

"You take care a yourself too," said Jimmy Joel, the condensation coming out of both their mouths when they talked, as if they were smoking cigarettes.

They hugged each other fondly in parting, smacking each other's back.

Billy Constable checked into the McBurney YMCA at 125 West 14th Street. The room was cheap and clean. The next day he began pounding the streets looking for a job. When he wasn't looking for a job in the newspapers' want ads, he was drinking coffee and eating doughnuts in a corner coffee shop named Benny's Downtown Diner.

Eventually Billy found a position as a boxer. Not a prizefighter; Billy folded men's suits and packed the suits into boxes in a clothing factory's shipping department. He was taught how to fold the suits in a special way by another boxer, a black man named Luther something-or-other. Luther something-or-other showed Billy how to fold a suit so the suit could travel clear across the country and arrive at its destination without a single crease.

Soon after Billy was established as a boxer in the clothing factory, he found and rented a small one-room apartment in the basement of a West Village brownstone. The apartment had some furniture in it already, including a bed. The rent was reasonable.

Billy felt lucky.

Everything seemed to be falling into place easier than he'd expected. He had a decent job, money in his pocket, and a place to live. He had a new friend named Jimmy Joel Jenks.

And then Billy met Sonny Lieberman.

The cripple refused to let the producer get away. Not after finally finding the bastard and getting within speaking distance. He wasn't the least bit concerned that he was causing a disturbance, standing on Madison Avenue in the middle of the pavement with tons of shoppers about, yelling at this guy like he was. Hell, they could have been arguing in the Macy's Department Store front window for all he cared. The cripple was convinced the fate of his entire project rested in this man's hands, and he absolutely could not allow the lucky happenstance to fail.

"You still have programs on the air in reruns, don't you?" asked the cripple. "Plenty of them. You haven't been out of the business like you say you have. Your saying you've been out of business is unadulterated malarkey. All the network honchos and syndicators remember your name. I wouldn't be surprised if some of the network honchos and syndicators still know you personally. You still have clout. Plenty of it. So don't give me that crap about your contacts drying up."

The producer stopped walking. He had to. The cripple was limping after him, shouting his accusations, making an embarrassing scene. The producer hated embarrassing scenes.

The producer turned and said, "Look here, you ignorant fool, just—"

"Hell, if it wasn't for your programs," shouted the cripple, "they wouldn't have anything to run on the Game Show Channel, would they? As I see it, you really haven't left the business at all. Your star hasn't diminished and neither has your pull. Not as much as you say."

"Listen," said the producer, unable to believe he was still having a conversation with this lowlife, "I left the business because I was sick of it. I'm still sick of it. My feelings haven't changed one iota."

"I beg to differ," sneered the cripple. "I don't think you left *the business*, as you call it, because you were sick of it. I think you left *the business* because you were able to put a zillion dollars in your pocket. I read all about your big killing in the trades." The cripple started coughing again. New spasms, more savage and more uncontrollable than before, turned the sorrowful old soul into someone more helpless and pitiful. His arms waved about like a puppet's. His back was hunched. Once again pedestrians watched as they walked by. The producer, his eyes riveted on the cripple, waited for what seemed like an eternity for the old fool to stop coughing.

When the cripple finally finished hacking, his hand shot out like a striking snake and stuffed a piece of paper into the producer's coat pocket. As soon as the paper was safely tucked away, the cripple quickly retracted his hand and smiled.

The producer was appalled. When he got home he would send the coat to the cleaners immediately. "Damn him," the producer said under his breath, feeling more and more queasy as he looked at the smiling bum's infected gums and yellow teeth, teeth that were still in his mouth.

"When you sold your company, how long were you contractually not allowed back into television?" asked the relentless cripple.

"Five years," mumbled the producer.

"It's 2011 now, so your banishment's over with. God, I have a toothache. Hurts like hell. Do you know a good dentist?" The cripple rubbed his left cheek. "So now you can come back to television, right? Could have come back years ago if you wanted to."

"Yes, I could have come back years ago," allowed the producer, "and no, I don't know a dentist."

"I don't have a phone in my room," explained the cripple. "But my name and the number of a pay phone down the hall are on the piece of paper I just put into your raincoat pocket."

The cripple coughed several times quite loudly but quickly recovered. The cripple seemed to understand that what little hope he had of the famous producer coming to see him depended upon stopping the coughing immediately.

"It takes me a while to get to the pay phone," said the cripple, trying to clear his throat. "This damn leg, you know." The cripple presented a paralyzed leg with a flourish of his left hand as if introducing a vaudeville act. "So let the phone ring. There's nobody on my floor during the day but me. They're all working." He took a deep breath, struggling to prevent another coughing attack. He inhaled deeply, gulping air like a drowning man. "Damn emphysema. Thank you, R. J. Reynolds and Company," he whispered.

When the cripple regained control of himself, he said as calmly as he could, "I never thought I'd find you. You're not listed in the phone book and I don't know anyone who knows where you live. You keep your life extremely private, don't you? Fate has brought us together so that we both can become rich and famous. In my case, rich and famous *again.* In your case, richer and more famous." The cripple gave a quick cackle, then said, "You've got to come to my apartment and let me show you my videotape." In desperation, the cripple grabbed a handful of the producer's overcoat and pleaded, "You've just got to."

The producer yanked his coat away from the cripple with such a burst of violence it caused the bum to almost fall once again, and his coughing to return, outbursts so explosive they made the cripple's eyes water and his nose run. Once again the cripple found himself spraying his revolting spittle about, this time more heavily than before. He tried to stop scattering phlegm by coughing into the crook of his arm. It helped.

The cripple's horrible hacking wasn't helping the producer's disposition. He considered the cripple the most revolting person he'd ever met. He wondered if this panhandler, coughing as violently as he was, might expire right there in front of him on Madison Avenue. He hoped so.

"Enough of this," hissed the producer. "Enough! I don't want to look at you or listen to you anymore. And blow your goddamn nose. Snot's running down your upper lip, for Christ sake."

The cripple was quite aware the producer had had about as much as he could take. He could only shrug his shoulders and say, "I'm pathetic, I know that. You think I don't know that? I know, but what can I do? As Popeye said, 'I yam what I yam.'" The cripple cackled.

The producer said nothing.

The cripple smiled, pulled a filthy handkerchief from an overcoat pocket, and blew his nose. Out of courtesy the cripple turned his head when he did. He blew his nose loudly. And while he was at it he hacked a glob of spit into the handkerchief for good measure. The cripple studied the spew to see if it was green, yellow, or white.

"My doctor told me to check out what I cough up. He said if my sputum was white, it was okay. If it was yellowish, he said it was not great but not real bad. If it was green, it was bad. Mine's yellow."

"I'm thrilled to hear that," said the producer.

The old cripple put the handkerchief back in his coat pocket.

"Handkerchiefs are revolting relics of bygone times," he commented. "They just don't make sense. Sneeze and cough into them, then put them back in your pocket only to sneeze and cough into them a few minutes later. Walk around with a collection of your entire day's snot in your pocket. On the other hand, one doesn't have to carry a handkerchief anymore, does one? They've got Kleenex now. But would you believe I can't afford Kleenex? I go through box after box. Doesn't pay. Better to carry a handkerchief. A footnote on my fall from grace. Can't even afford Kleenex anymore. You're absolutely sure you can't recommend a dentist?"

"Good-bye, Mr. . . ."

"Hey!" shouted the cripple, taking a few limps forward. "I know I'm not a very pleasant person to look at, let alone talk to. I also know you won't believe me when I tell you this, but I used to be respected and rich. That was many years ago. I'm eighty-one. Be eighty-two next June. Old age sucks. The only good thing about it is, it doesn't last very long. Me, I'm just about worn-out now, but back then, back in the sixties and seventies, I was hot as a pistol. Had more energy than ten of you combined. And enough money to live happily ever after. But times change. Things happen. Now I can't even afford Kleenex. Now I'm not worth a fart in a wind tunnel. Shit. Life's funny, isn't it? 'All the best days of life slip away first. Illness and dreary old age and pain sneak up, and the fierceness of harsh death snatches us away.' Virgil." The cripple shook his head despondently. "I can tell you my life story some other time. Virgil gave you the short version. As if you're interested in my life story."

The slovenly geezer started coughing again.

When he stopped, he said, "Listen, I've got to speak to you. You won't be sorry to hear what I have to say nor sorry to see what I have to show you. And more important, the timing is perfect. *Perfect!*"

"Perfect for what?"

"Perfect for making it happen."

"Making *what* happen?"

"Trust me, it will be worth it," said the cripple. "My father used to say never trust someone who says 'trust me.' But trust me."

The producer said nothing.

"Listen. That piece of paper I stuck in your coat pocket with my name and number on it? I carry it in case I drop dead. That way at least somebody will know who I am and they can notify my family. No. No. Just joking. I don't have any family left to telephone. I always carry the paper with my name and telephone number on it on the off chance I'll bump into you. You think you can force yourself to believe that? So please call me."

"I'll call you," said the producer, willing to say anything to get rid of the walking pestilence.

The cripple knew chances were slim that the producer would truly telephone. "I hope you do call," the cripple told the producer. "I hope you do. I hope you're not saying that just to, you know, just to get rid of me. I really hope you do call."

The cripple shifted his crutch into a more comfortable position under his left arm. He fixed his filthy hat so that it sat on his head more securely and, saying something the producer didn't hear, limped away.

"What?" yelled the producer to the departing cripple, surprising himself for wanting to prolong talking to the lowlife. "You said something. What did you just say?"

The cripple had gone only a short distance down the pavement. He turned and yelled back. "I said come see me before it's too late."

The producer said, "Before it's too late? Too late for what?"

But the cripple was gone, lost in a crowd of pedestrians.

That night the producer sat in his armchair ignoring the important investment documents he should have been studying. He could do nothing but think about the goddamn cripple. The old vagrant's last statement, "Before it's too late," played over and over in his head. Too late for what? The cripple *is* knowledgeable, thought the producer, and he does know about me. What if the guy does have a bizarre idea that's really good? What if . . .

Eventually the producer got out of his art deco armchair, walked across the long, wide living room of his luxury duplex apartment, opened the hall closet, and dug out the crumpled piece of paper from his raincoat pocket.

On the dirty piece of paper was scribbled:

Chuck Barris 212 555 5872

Steve Beastie was born in either Chicago or Cleveland, he couldn't remember which. Why Beastie didn't know where he was born is complicated. But it makes sense, I guess.

Anyway, in 1974, when Steve was seventeen, he left Chicago for New York City to live with his grandmother. In his early Bronx days

Beastie was just another skinny, scuzzy black kid with perhaps more bravado than most of the gangbangers he hung out with. He, like the rest of his gang, wore a lot of gold chains around his neck and earned money moving drugs. Beastie sold anything he could get his hands on: decks of heroin, nickel and dime bags of weed, vials of cocaine.

Beastie's granny, while working at Lerners Department Store, tried her best to take care of her only grandson and keep him out of trouble. It wasn't easy. She gave it her best shot until the day they sent Steve Beastie to Rikers Island for armed robbery. Beastie was eighteen years old when they collared him for a stickup gone wrong. That's about when Steve's granny washed her hands of him.

Steve Beastie had scoped out the liquor store for about a week. He thought he'd prepared "one hundred percent perfect," only to find out later that he hadn't, that he wasn't even close. Over the years, Beastie would chalk off his botched robbery to inexperience. He promised himself that it wouldn't happen again.

He was right. It wouldn't.

The store Beastie chose to rob was located in the Brighton Beach area of Brooklyn. It was a liquor store on a desolate corner of Ocean Parkway and Surf Avenue. Goldstein's Liquor was the name of the place.

"It said so on the sign over the storefront," Beastie told some of his gangbanger friends. "Being that Goldstein's a Jew name, I figure a Jew family runs the store. And a Jew owner has to be a long-nosed pansy scared a his own shadow, know what I mean? So I go into the store an' try to buy a bottle of bourbon. I can tell right away the Goldsteins are a bunch a kiss-ass kikes right off the boat if ever I seen any, know what I mean? They wouldn't sell me anythin' 'cause they say I'm underage. I was pissed at them cocksuckers throwin' me outta the place like they did but I felt good about the way I was checkin' it out. Like it's all part of the process, know what I'm sayin'?"

Beastie's gangbanger friends liked what he was saying, agreed he had balls, and gave Beastie a bunch of high fives.

Three days later on a Thursday evening, Beastie entered Goldstein's Liquor store at eleven twenty in the evening. He wore a bandanna tied around his nose and mouth like an outlaw out of the Wild Wild West and an Oakland Raiders baseball hat with the brim over his right ear. He held a Saturday night special in his right hand. The special was a cheap handgun that had a tendency to explode when fired, something the smart kid from Chicago or Cleveland or wherever the hell he was from didn't know. Beastie walked into the liquor store and confronted the Goldstein family's twenty-one-year-old daughter, Dora, standing behind the counter. Dora, the youngest of the four Goldstein siblings, was afraid of her own shadow. Only when it was an emergency did the Goldstein family let Dora work the night shift, and rarely alone.

The night of the robbery, Dora Goldstein wasn't working and wasn't alone. She was keeping her oldest brother, Jacob, company. Jacob Goldstein was an ex–Delta Force fighter and a veteran of the first Gulf War (something else Beastie didn't know). Jacob was a tough cookie and quite adept at breaking necks along with knowing how to use the double-barreled shotgun that was bracketed under the store's cash register (more facts Beastie didn't know). Unfortunately, Jacob Goldstein was out buying a pizza at the time of the robbery.

Beastie took a hundred and ten dollars, two cartons of Marlboro Lights, and a package of Twinkies from the sobbing, cowering Dora Goldstein. Beastie loved every minute of the robbery. He felt good about the power he held over the young Jew girl. He liked the way he scared her half to death, the way he bitch-slapped her across the face for nothing and knocked her down on the floor, bloodying her nose. Man, he thought to himself, that felt *good*. He also liked the way he could take whatever he wanted, including her if he wanted to, the way . . . well . . . the way he owned the fucking world. Steve Beastie liked owning the fucking world.

Beastie held his revolver pointed at Dora's head as he backed out of the liquor store and into the box of cheese, tomato, and mushroom pizza Jacob Goldstein was carrying for himself and his sister. Beastie whirled around and pulled the trigger of the gun pointed at Jacob Goldstein's chest. The gun blew up in Beastie's hand, saving him a murder rap. Beastie dropped the gun and Jacob dropped the pizza box. That's when Jacob Goldstein beat the shit out of Steve Beastie. Gave Beastie three broken ribs, a dislocated shoulder, a broken nose, a damaged eye socket, and a lot of internal injuries, to say nothing of his charred right hand from the exploding gun.

Jacob Goldstein took back the hundred and ten dollars in cash, the two cartons of cigarettes, and the package of Twinkies Beastie had stolen from the family store. Then he took the rest of Beastie's money, his stolen credit cards, and his gold chains, which Jacob put around his neck. When the cops came, Beastie complained to them that the Jew cocksucker (he pointed a finger at Jacob Goldstein) stole his gold chains.

"What gold chains?" asked Jacob Goldstein.

"Yeah, what gold chains?" asked one of the cops, who happened to be Jacob's younger brother Nate.

It was during Steve Beastie's interrogation by the Brooklyn North robbery detectives that he got his nickname: Cleveland Steve Beastie from Chicago. One of their questions was: Where were you born? Beastie had no idea.

"It was either Cleveland or Chicago," he said. "I ain't sure which."

He tried to explain to the cops that his mother and father traveled back and forth between Cleveland and Chicago a lot. He had no idea why. In one of those cities between one of those trips, Steve was born. He wasn't sure if it was in Cleveland or in Chicago. And then when he was only a few weeks old, his parents died in an automobile accident driving between the two. Steve Beastie was in Chicago at the time of the accident. He had been dropped off with his mother's younger sister. The next morning when the sister heard about the accident, she immediately looked up Chicago orphanages, picked one out, and left little Steve on the doorstep.

"It never made any difference to me where I was born," he said, "and no one in the goddamn Chicago orphanage gave a rusty fuck either."

A short time after Cleveland Steve Beastie from Chicago began his incarceration at Rikers Island, his grandma lay down on her living room couch one night and died. When young Steve got out of jail and came home, there were a bunch of his grandmother's Social Security checks lying in a pile of mail by the front door's mail slot. In memory of his sweet granny, Beastie cashed every one of her checks and spent the money on clothes, a new Oakland Raiders baseball hat, and new gold chains.

Nineteen years later, when Beastie was almost thirty-eight, he was arrested for causing a horrendous fatality. While drunk, Beastie ran a traffic light turning right on Sixty-fourth Street and Second Avenue in Manhattan. His truck struck and killed a doctor walking east across Second Avenue. The dead man's name was Dr. Pincus Klingenstein. Dr. Klingenstein was a famous endocrinologist on his way to the Cornell Medical Center to visit his dying eighty-five-year-old mother. He was fifty-three years old when he died.

Cleveland Steve Beastie from Chicago was convicted of vehicular manslaughter while driving intoxicated and sentenced to ten years in prison without parole. He was sent to Attica State Penitentiary in Attica, New York.

Cleveland Steve Beastie from Chicago was glad of one thing.

At least he had killed a Jew.

It was evening.

The producer was sitting in his favorite armchair deep in thought. He had on the silk and satin printed smoking jacket that he always donned prior to his evening cigar. His legs were crossed carefully so as not to crush the creases in his slacks. His hair was slicked back with a gel he favored. His brows were knitted together with concern. He was relaxing. This was the time the producer allotted for contemplation: the time to read one of the rare books he may have recently purchased or attempt to put a dent in his growing pile of *New Yorker* and *Economist* magazines.

Tonight he wasn't doing that.

Tonight, and all week, all he could think about was the disgusting cripple. He should have forgotten about that despicable bum the moment they parted, but he didn't. He couldn't. Why he wouldn't stop thinking about the cripple was beyond his comprehension.

Or was it?

The producer knew exactly why for seven days and nights he was unable to get the grotesque, germ-infested beggar out of his mind. The reason: the slim possibility that the mangy, crippled piece of shit just might have a really good idea floating around that vile head of his, an idea that could make the producer a lot of money. And let's not forget the fame part, he mused. The more fame the bigger *The*

New York Times obituary. Maybe he'd even make *The Wall Street Journal*'s front page when he died. That would really be nice.

Wouldn't it just be my rotten luck if the damned cripple *did* have a great idea and I ignored him. Perhaps a telephone call would suffice. If he telephoned the miserable cur, he might be able to extract a hint of the cripple's program concept, confirm his assumption that anyone's ideas other than his own were unairable, and get this filthy monster off his back. Damn it all, it certainly was worth a phone call. The longer I procrastinate, he reasoned, the longer I'll be unable to relax.

The producer picked up the receiver of the telephone by his chair and immediately hung it up. Slammed it down hard. Forget about it, he decided. The whole situation's a major waste of my precious time.

A few minutes later the producer picked up the receiver again. This time he consulted the scrap of paper and dialed the cripple's number. The telephone rang and rang and rang. The producer remembered the cripple saying, "It takes me a while to get to the phone, so let it ring." Just as he was about to take the telephone away from his ear, he heard a phlegmy voice say, "Yeah?"

The producer told the old cripple his name.

"Well, hello!" said the cripple. "Didn't recognize your voice. But then why should I? It's not like we speak to each other every day, is it? I'd just about given up on you. So look, let's meet. I think for safety's sake we should meet here, at my place."

"For safety's sake? Why do you say that?"

The cripple could hear the worry in the producer's voice. "Just a precaution. Possibly a bit neurotic on my part. I just don't want anybody following me to your apartment with the tape in my hand. Don't want to get conked on the head and have my idea stolen from me at this late—"

"Listen," said the producer, "why don't you spend a minute or two telling me a little about—"

"Not on your life! You out of your mind? If you want to hear what I have to say you'll have to come to my place. It's a crummy room but it's better than nothing. I know once you hear me out and see what I have to show you, and we sign all the necessary papers that say we split the profits fifty-fifty, you'll run like a banshee with my idea. You were the most powerful television producer the industry's ever known. Still are, for that matter. Believe me, you'll see the beauty of this idea in a New York minute and what's more—"

"What's your address?"

"I'm in the West Village, 273 Bleecker Street. My room's over a guitar shop. Umanov Guitars. Push the buzzer. I'll let you in. My room's up a flight of stairs. In the back. Come here as soon as—"

The cripple began to cough.

The producer waited.

The old cripple stopped his hacking and said in a gravelly voice, "As soon as you can. So when can I expect you?"

"Tomorrow."

"What time?"

"Around noon."

"Great."

The line went dead.

Cripple quit while he was ahead, thought the producer. Hung up before I could change my mind.

The next day the producer walked along Bleecker Street in the Village until he came to number 273. The address was a guitar shop. Umanov Guitars. Just where the old cripple said it would be. The producer could see a window that was probably an apartment above the store. He didn't feel like going up to the cripple's room. Not just yet. He wasn't ready for the hacking, burbling, saliva-ridden, spastic profligate. He wondered if ever he would be.

Anyway, he was early.

The producer looked around to see if there was someplace he could go and waste some time. There was a John's Pizza across the street, which was next door to a high-end ice cream parlor, which was next door to the Pink Pussy Sex Shop. The television producer wasn't hungry for pizza, expensive ice cream, or edible panties, so he decided to browse in the guitar store.

"Can I help you?" asked a salesman wearing a porkpie hat and jeans that ended about three inches above his ankles.

"Expecting a flood?" wisecracked the producer.

"Pardon?" said the young salesman, a blank look on his face.

"Never mind. I'm going to look around," said the producer, "by myself."

"Look all you want. If you have any questions, just let me know. Just ask for Jimmy Joel," said the salesman.

The television producer grunted and moved off toward a banjo player sitting on a stool trying out a six-string. The song the banjo player was picking for his own pleasure was "Riding the Danville Pike," a bluegrass tune the producer recognized. The producer loved bluegrass music. People were always surprised when he said so.

The producer stood listening to the banjo player for a few minutes, tapping his right shoe. The banjo player was a heavyset bald guy with lots of red hair everywhere but on the top of his head. He had bushels of it growing over his ears and flowing down the back of his neck onto his shoulders. He had a big, bushy red mustache and beard that hid the lower half of his face and neck. He wore green overalls, a white T-shirt, and sandals.

The banjo player looked up at the producer and smiled.

The producer didn't return the banjo player's smile. He moved away instead. He passed a glass case filled with mandolins. The producer had played a mandolin in college. The sight of the mandolins brought back memories of his university days, the campus's Great Court surrounded by those beautiful old ivy-covered buildings. The lunchtime crowd of students gathered in the open air to listen and watch the producer's trio: Joe Bigatel on bass, Weskar Medal on guitar, the producer strumming his mandolin. The three of them singing in decent harmony. God, that was fun, recalled the producer. Maybe the happiest days of my life. He wondered for a moment whether he could still play a mandolin or remember the chords of the old songs they used to sing.

"Can I show you a mandolin?" asked the salesman who was still waiting for the flood.

The producer looked at the salesman, said nothing, and walked out of the store.

The door to the rooms above the guitar store was to the left of the store's entrance. It was old and had big scratches and the paint was peeling. A brand-new letter slot had been recently added. The polished bronze looked out of place in its decrepit surroundings. To the door's right was a line of dirty worn buttons and little slots. Names written or typed onto old pieces of paper had been pushed into the slots. One, lettered in pencil and almost illegible, was the cripple's.

The producer pushed that button.

In 1985, when Theresa Mendavey was a kid, she was arrested at Disneyland.

Theresa's father, Hector Mendavey, had just arrived at the amusement park with Theresa and some of her friends for Theresa's twelfth birthday celebration. Theresa's arrest took place during the girls' first ride.

Hector had been looking forward to a respite from the Obnoxious Seven, his name for Theresa and her six friends. It would be Hector Mendavey's first moment of peace and quiet since they all had left their home in Manderville Canyon. Manderville Canyon was basically an enclave of expensive homes near Beverly Hills, California.

It had been a long, loud, hectic ride from Manderville. Hector had driven only a few miles before the girls—all seven of them—complained of extreme hunger, which was strange since they had all just finished breakfast. So Hector Mendavey took the girls to a Denny's. It hadn't been more than six minutes since they left Denny's when the Obnoxious Seven had to go to the bathroom *ensemble*. So Hector had to stop again. The first time at a scuzzy gas station. The girls refused to use the gas station's toilet. *"Gross,"* the ensemble chorused. So Hector took the girls to a Wendy's, bought a cup of coffee, and sat at the counter drinking it while the Obnoxious Seven did their peeing.

Now, with the girls off on some kind of miniature train ride, Hector Mendavey could finally enjoy reading his *New York Times* financial section in peace on an empty bench in the shade of an E ride. The quiet interlude was shattered almost immediately when he heard his name repeated over and over again on the park's loudspeakers:

MR. HECTOR MENDAVEY
PLEASE COME TO THE ADMINISTRATION BUILDING.

MR. HECTOR MENDAVEY
PLEASE COME TO THE ADMINISTRATION BUILDING.

Hector Mendavey was shocked. Then panic-stricken. Though it was Hector's first time at Disneyland, he hadn't heard any other parents paged during his brief stay there. Something very terrible must have happened to his daughter Theresa. Something terrible was *always* happening to his daughter Theresa, he reflected irritably, which wasn't true at all.

By the time Hector Mendavey found the Administration Building he was verging on a major coronary. He was also sweating like a pig. Theresa's father was given a curt greeting and then led down to the bowels of the building where the jail was located. The jail looked like a jail. Even the prison matrons looked like prison matrons: large and bulky and manly in their black suits, white shirts, black ties, and butch haircuts. Everything in Disneyland looked like what it was supposed to look like.

"I'm Hector Mendavey. Is my daughter Theresa okay?"

"Yes," answered the matron.

"Is she well? Is she in one piece?"

"Yes."

Thank God, thought Hector. If something bad had happened to Theresa, Edna would have given him a tin ear for weeks.

"At least you folks down here in the basement don't say 'Golly' or 'Gee whiz' all the time like all the other idiot employees at this park," said Theresa's father, trying to make nice-nice. "Okay, I give up, where is she?"

"She's in a cell, Mr. Mendavey."

"And what the hell has she done, pray tell, that has caused you to incarcerate the child?"

"Your daughter and a friend jumped out of one two-seater train car and into another."

"That's it?"

"Your daughter broke the rules."

"And that's why you locked my daughter up in your goddamn gulag?"

"There's no call for that kind of tone, sir."

"Is there some goddamn bail to pay or something, matron?"

"No. Just leave the park ASAP."

Though Hector's Rolls-Royce was packed with Theresa's best friends, it didn't stop Hector from berating his daughter the entire ride back to Los Angeles. Mr. Mendavey never stopped yelling until the car was safely parked in his garage. Then and only then did Hector Mendavey turn to his daughter and ask, "Why?"

"Why what?"

"Why did you get out of one train car and run and get into another one? What was the point?"

"To get away with it," answered Theresa Mendavey.

When Theresa was sixteen, she blossomed into a very pretty young lady. She was short and petite with beautiful brunette hair that fell to her shoulders. She had alabaster skin, full lips, and sparkling blue eyes. And she was sexy. Very sexy. Theresa reminded adults, particularly males, of the actress Sue Lyon from the original *Lolita* movie.

And Theresa Mendavey was brilliant to boot. She skipped two grades at the academically tough Harvard-Westlake School in Sherman Oaks, California. Her attendance rate was always one of the lowest at the esteemed prep school, yet she continued to bring home straight A's on every report card.

"Not that my parents give a damn," complained Theresa to her friends.

Theresa Mendavey did well in school because she had a photographic memory. She could read a page of any book, magazine, or newspaper and remember every single word.

Theresa's Mother, Edna Mendavey, was a bony woman with tight little curls on the top of her head and tight lips covering small dish teeth. When she smiled she showed lots of upper gum. Edna had little time for her daughter mainly because she needed so much time for herself. She was involved in more society charities than she could sensibly handle plus her weekly dermatological appointments for Botox shots and the occasional face-lift or tummy tuck. There were also her trips to the pharmacies for prescription drug refills so she could continue to enjoy her daily highs, tempered now and then by the need to come down a bit.

When Edna Mendavey was on uppers—which, like most Beverly Hills matrons, was every afternoon—she had a tendency to play demolition derby while parallel parking her Rolls-Royce in Beverly Hills. The Mendaveys had matching Rolls-Royces: hers white, his black. Over the years, Edna Mendavey did incredible damage to her own Rolls's grille and trunk. But the devastation Edna wreaked on other automobiles was awesome. The extent of the maiming and mangling depended upon the automobile's make. For instance, a BMW stood up to Edna's bashing fairly well. A Honda or Toyota, on the other hand, usually had its grille or trunk in an extreme concave state when Theresa's mother had finished parking. The damage was frequently irreparable.

And finally let us not forget Edna Mendavey's trips to Paris to see what the couturiers were showing and to England for her antique auctions. The net result: Edna Mendavey wasn't home very much. And when she was she had very little time for anything that might be important to her daughter Theresa.

Theresa's father wasn't much better at staying home. Hector Mendavey was a very busy man. He was building his already large conglomerate into a mammoth conglomerate. He spent a good deal of time attending stockholders' meetings in various cities and at dog and pony shows to raise millions of dollars his companies didn't need. He traveled to other parts of the world to chair meetings or partake in an occasional hostile takeover or two. He also took monthly trips to Vail to ski and Las Vegas to gamble. Consequently, Hector Mendavey was almost never home, which resulted in his having less time than his wife (if that were possible) for their daughter Theresa.

On the extremely rare occasions when Mr. Mendavey decided to spend an evening at the mansion in Manderville Canyon, suffice it to say the last object he expected to see parked in his driveway when he returned from his office was a Triumph Bonneville motorcycle. And the last person he anticipated seeing comfortably ensconced in his favorite armchair was the Triumph Bonneville's owner.

Theresa Mendavey's new boyfriend, Rex Redmond, was seventeen. He had tattoos on his arms, earrings dangling from his earlobes, and a Triumph Bonneville. The motorcycle was a gift from Rex's older brother Dave after Dave put it down on Pacific Coast

Highway. Rex Redmond, a mechanic at heart, had worked on the Bonneville day and night for weeks, mending and painting it until it looked brand-new.

If Theresa's father had taken the time to be civil and chat with his young daughter's new boyfriend Rex Redmond, Mr. Mendavey would have found the lad to be a rather intelligent and gentle young man. But Theresa's father had neither the time nor the inclination. Instead, Mr. Mendavey lashed out at the biker on sight, screaming profanities and demeaning accusations that deeply tarnished Mr. Redmond's character and good name. Mendavey concluded his tirade by shouting, "You are never to step foot in this house again. *Is that clear?*"

Frightened, Redmond was speechless.

"Is that *clear*?" repeated Mr. Mendavey.

"Yes, sir, that's clear," mumbled Redmond.

It wasn't clear to Theresa Mendavey, though. Nor was she the least bit frightened of Hector. She chased after her father and caught him halfway up the grand stairway. Theresa grabbed his belt, stopped him in his tracks, turned him around, and spoke her mind. She told her father he didn't have the right to speak that way to Rex Redmond. She said it was her house as well as Hector's, that Rex was *her* guest and Redmond would stay as long as she wanted him to and sit wherever he wanted to.

"And," she yelled, "as far as being a good father's concerned, you suck the big banana."

"How can you say that, Theresa? I took you to Disneyland, didn't I?"

"You took me *once,* four years ago."

"But I took you, didn't I?"

It was ten minutes after her discussion with Hector on the grand stairway that Theresa Mendavey and Rex Redmond rode off into the sunset, three weeks before she would have graduated high school.

The old cripple was sitting on the edge of his bed, thinking about what Bette Davis had said.

She had said, "Old age isn't a place for sissies."

"And she was right," the cripple said aloud. He stretched out on his cot, his hands behind his head, staring at his cracked ceiling and thinking about the world-famous hotsie-totsie television producer. The man was such a *putz*. Why was it that the guy you've been wanting to meet so badly and for so long ended up being a *putz*? It reminded the cripple of the joke where the wife says to her husband: If they held a contest for the biggest *putz* in the world, you would come in second. The husband says: Why second? Why not first? His wife answers: Because you're such a *putz*.

Rotten luck to get *that* producer, he mused. But then luck hasn't been my strong suit lately, has it? *Lately*? Try the last twenty-five years. Had a lot of luck for a while, though. Luck walked right beside me all through the sixties and seventies. And timing did too. Timing is just as important as luck. Luck's a figment of your imagination. Timing's real. Add courage and preparation. Luck, timing, courage, and preparation. The big four. I had them all. But then I made some bad decisions. Wasn't thinking. Got careless. Never had anyone to help me figure things out. Nobody with my interests at heart. Just advisers with their own interests at heart. Bastards is what those advisers were. And now I'm too old to start again, even with all my friggin' knowledge.

Too old.

What, he wondered, was so great about the Golden Years? Getting old was so wonderful? So much fun? Getting old was depressing, is what it was. The Golden Years meant it was time for arthritis. Time for loss of memory, sight, and hearing. Time to catch new diseases. It was the age when a minor head cold could turn to pneumonia and kill you. And if that didn't, your trip to the hospital would for sure. (Or as they say in California's San Fernando Valley, *fer sher.*) Growing old meant watching the nice members of your family and best friends die, while the rotten ones kept right on living. Growing old meant giving up all your wonderful bad habits: smoking, drinking, eating crap. Growing old meant nothing worked anymore (hips, knees, pecker) and nothing was allowed. No more masturbating (prostate). No more double scotches on the rocks (liver). No more cigarettes (cancer). No more glasses of cold milk with two Mallomars (cholesterol). No more grilled Nathan's hot dogs on fresh buns with mustard and a bag of fries (carcinogens). No more calves' liver, chicken gizzards, and calves' brains (a quick though tasty death). No more Cohiba cigars while taking a hot bath (heart attack). No more picking fights with strangers (you get beat up).

And what's so golden about waking up every morning knowing life is finite and wondering if today's the day you *don't* dodge the bullet. If today you'll take it in the heart and die. And then there's *how* you die. Will you keel over from a stroke while crossing Fifth Avenue and Fifty-seventh Street? Or will it be a long and painful death? And speaking of keeling over, is there an afterlife? Is there a heaven where everybody walks on little puffy clouds? Of course there isn't. What a crock. So if it's a crock, what *is* there?

The Golden Years, ha!

The shit years is what they are, if you ask me.

Boy, do they ever grow short. Funny how the older you get the faster time flies. You live to be a hundred, but it feels like you've been around for a little over a minute and a half. Who cares? Death gets you in the end no matter what.

Right?

Right.

Even Frank Sinatra wasn't powerful enough to beat death. And he had it all. Except a way not to die. I mean if Frank Sinatra couldn't beat it, who could? And he was a Catholic! He had the whole damn Vatican behind him! And he *still* died!

Listen, if you don't have someone to love at eighty-one, where are you going to find her? In an old-age home? In a geriatric hospital ward? In a mortuary? So go out and find yourself a young girl. Okay? And what would I do with her? How can you be anything but dejected and depressed when you wake up in the morning and there's no loving wife snuggled up against you? That is, *if* you wake up. What's that joke? Every morning when I wake up I stretch, and if I don't touch wood I'm still alive. It would be funnier if it wasn't so true. And another thing that's true is that the older a man gets, the more like himself he becomes.

Where did I read that? Shit, I forget.

The old cripple moved off the bed and stood up. He fetched his crutch and turned to face an imaginary auditorium filled to the rafters with people.

"Ladies and gentlemen, the way I see it, everyone falls into basically three tiers. The First Tier are those lucky people who die pain free and quietly at home at ripe old ages. These First Tier people have lived errorless, blameless, happy lives. At age ninety-five they spend their final hour lying in their own beds, under clean sheets, pain free, looking up at loving wives or husbands they've been married to for more than sixty years. All their grown children, some holding grandchildren and great-grandchildren, are standing around the deathbed looking on with misty eyes and warm, friendly faces. These lucky old First Tierers doze off and that's it. No pain. No strain. Gwan.

"Some First Tier people have collected treasure chests filled with honors and awards. Some have Oscars on their mantels, their handprints frozen forever in cement somewhere along Hollywood Boulevard. Some have not. To those who haven't any awards, keep in mind Gray's 'Elegy Written in a Country Church Yard': 'The paths of glory lead but to the grave.' The truth is, First Tier people have accomplished something far far better than any Emmy, Pulitzer, or Nobel prize. Their accomplishment is simply being in the First Tier. And these people are few and far between. Maybe seven all told in the entire United States. I'm not one of those First Tier people, that's for damn sure."

The cripple took a sip of imaginary water from a chimerical glass that was resting on a nonexistent podium.

"Now let me tell you about the Second Tier people. The Second Tier people are those with two plastic hips who can still play golf and carry their own golf bags, who haven't known terrible tragedy, who are still married to their first husband or wife, and whose kids never went to jail or became druggies. Maybe some of their kids will even come to the funeral. My guess is there are less than a million Second Tierers in the United States of America. I'm not one of those, either.

"And then, ladies and gentlemen, there's the Third Tier. Third Tierers consist of human beings who have nuts and bolts embedded everywhere in their pain-wracked bodies, and if they don't, they should have. Their bones ache all night long, no matter what position they get themselves into. They've all had one major operation (at least) and more than one life-threatening disease, not counting the one that's at present roaming around their soon-to-be-forgotten remains. The people in the Third Tier have seen several tragedies in their lifetime, are rarely lucky in love, and if they're still married to their second or third wife they've both forgotten when they stopped liking each other and when their hatred and indifference began. These people will slowly meet their maker in some hospital bed with only an apathetic nurse by their bedside. Maybe the ex-wife or ex-husband, but that's unlikely. The nurse will be waiting impatiently to pull the sheet over the Third Tier corpse's face so she can get to the local bar and meet some tattooed bohunk who will mess up her head as sure as she's a woman. If they're not in the hospital, then Third Tier folks will collapse on the floor of their apartment. They'll try desperately to crawl to the last thing they will ever see, the telephone they will never reach. Third Tier people will lose their balance putting on their boxer shorts or Big Whites in the bathroom, crack their skulls on the marble floor, and lie there looking at the ceiling until it disappears from view.

"I'm in the Third Tier, my friends. I'll end up having a series of strokes in a wheelchair in New York City on the corner of Sixty-third and Lexington Avenue like a lot of Third Tierers do. I will have been sunning myself and then suddenly I'll be spazzing around in my damn wheelchair and there's my fat-assed nurse whose name is Ysabel or Beatriz or something like that, who's wearing a white starched uniform that was given to her by the employment agency strictly for show, being that she's about as much a nurse as I am a rock star. I won't be able to afford to hire Ynes or Concertina but I will anyway because I'll be dead before I have to pay her agency.

"So there I am spazzing out on the sidewalk and Carlotta or Damaris, whatever the hell her name is, isn't paying any attention to me. She won't even notice when I fall out of my wheelchair and flop around on the pavement like a hooked mackerel. Carlotta or Damaris or whatever the hell her name is won't notice because the sight of me revolts her. She'll purposely be looking elsewhere.

"So there I am having these disgusting convulsions on the filthy, trash-filled pavement and Cantaloupe isn't paying attention. It wouldn't matter if she was, since the fat-assed nurse doesn't know the difference between a seizure and a salami sandwich. Anyway, this woman, who's supposed to be my nurse, who's supposed to be keeping an eye on me, who's supposed to wipe the snot from my nose and clean out the corners of my eyes, who's supposed to be rubbing off the drool from my chin so I don't look like the old damn fool I am, who's supposed to be getting rid of the dried spit that's lying on my cheek and the gross booger that's been dangling from my right nostril for the past twenty minutes, Cantaloupe won't be doing any of those things. She won't be paying the slightest bit of attention to me, not even when I'm lying there twitching my ass off in the gutter that I've bounced into on the corner of Sixty-third and Lexington Avenue. My alleged nurse Esmeralda or Restituta, or whatever the hell her name is, doesn't care. My big-ass beauty in the white uniform doesn't give two shits that I'm doing the Saint Vitus' dance up and down Sixty-third Street. Why? Because my nurse Begonia or Fantasia or something will be messing around with some hip-hopping dude named Snoop Kitty Ditty or Twelve Dollar 'N Six Cent who just walked up to her and made nice-nice. She'll be playing teasie-weasie with him, not the slightest bit concerned that I'm jerking around in the street like someone being electrocuted. Nor will she care that taxis are swerving this way and that trying not to run over me or that a line of New Yorkers are stepping over my half-dead butt so they can make the traffic light.

"So there I am almost a corpse lying on the filthy pavement when *finally* my alleged nurse in the white uniform turns around and sees me. I'm about to croak. My glazed eyes have glazed over. My rancid tongue hangs out of my gaping mouth like an exhausted hound dog. And what will Pocahontas's final words to me be before I slide into the big black chasm? The decisive and irrefutable sentence I shall carry with me to the bottomless pit? To the worms and grubs who will reduce my once dapper bod to a pile of moldy bones?

"It will be this: 'Shit, man! Why'd you go and do *that* for?'"

The cripple returned to his bed and considered the producer, who was due any minute. The odd thing is, he reflected, I've always wished that hotshot load of crap would cross my path. Something told me he was the one, the only person who would get my program idea done. Well, my prayers have come true, mused the cripple. At least some of them. The mean-spirited, conniving prick should be here soon.

And then the buzzer sounded.

The producer pulled the downstairs door open and walked up a staircase that was concave in the middle of each step from years of wear. Halfway up the stairs the producer heard a cheerful voice holler from above, "Is that who I think it is?"

The cripple had peered over the second-floor banister, smiling and waving the producer up.

The producer reached the top of the stairs, turned left, and trailed behind the old cripple, who was limping toward the rear of the hallway. As he walked, the producer could smell cooking, disinfectant, urine, and body odor in the hallway, none of it to his liking.

The old cripple's apartment door was open. The producer followed the cripple into the stale, stinking room. Except for patches of peeling paint, there was nothing on the room's walls. A cotlike bed oddly positioned in the center of the room had a dirty, lumpy quilt lying across it.

God only knows what's hidden under that quilt, thought the producer.

Two small pillows with gray cases were pushed up against the metal headboard, one in front of the other. On top of the bed a book was open and turned over. From where the book was broken it appeared to be about half read. The book was *The Moonstone* by Wilkie Collins. Some newspapers were piled up on the floor.

There wasn't a rug, just a small rectangular knitted mat with rows of tassels on both ends that was placed on one side of the bed. The mat looked Mexican. A little table leaned against one wall. On the table was a big wind-up alarm clock and a clean triangular glass ashtray that had DOMINIC'S RESTAURANT in large green letters on its three sides. In a cheap frame was a picture of the cripple and a woman holding each other around the waist. The cripple appeared to be in his forties. He was standing without a crutch. He looked robust and in good health. The producer noted that the woman was much younger than the cripple and very pretty. Also on the table was a set of keys hooked onto a rabbit's foot key chain. It lay next to a drinking glass used to hold pencils. A dark brown bureau with six drawers and a matching mirror on top leaned crookedly against the other wall. The mirror had a small crack in the upper right-hand corner.

Seven years' bad luck, thought the horrified producer to himself.

The cripple wasn't wearing the heavy woolen overcoat and seedy stained fedora he had on when the producer first saw him on Madison Avenue, and the producer noticed that he appeared much older and thinner now. He could almost pass for starving. His large head and broad shoulders seemed oddly misplaced on such an emaciated frame. He had a high forehead due to a receding hairline. What hair the cripple did have was gray. His face was gaunt with deep, sunken cheeks.

The cripple wore a pair of wire-rimmed spectacles stationed far down his nose. He still hadn't shaved. He was dressed in a baggy wool sweater. The cripple's neck seemed pencil thin surrounded by the sweater's stretched and ragged collar. Dirty, droopy jeans hung precariously low on his hips. Sweat socks and brown leather Birkenstocks rounded out his ensemble. The producer was sure the cripple's dirty sweat socks could walk away by themselves if they wanted to. And even though the cripple was inside his apartment, he had a woolen scarf wrapped around his neck.

"I get cold," said the cripple, noticing the producer's eyes. "I never used to get cold, but I do now. I never used to get a lot of things, but I do now. I never had gout. The big toe of my right foot. My back's a disaster area. My arthritic thumbs hurt all the time. I have a bad hip. I have other pains. I have no idea where they come from. I'm afraid to ask my doctors. I learned that at eighty-one, going on eighty-two, you don't ask doctors a thing. Besides, I don't want to know. When you get to be my age you don't want to know. You'll see. Have a seat." He waved his left arm, the one draped over the crutch, to one of the two chairs.

"I don't have much time," said the producer gruffly.

"What's a crime?" said the cripple.

"What?"

"You said something was a crime?" said the cripple.

"I didn't say . . . can we get on with—"

"Hey, I'll bet you don't remember who I was, do you," announced the cripple, ignoring his guest's apparent impatience. "You don't. I can tell. You're too young, I guess. What were you in the seventies and eighties? Five years old? Ten years old? You don't remember a thing about—"

"Your name sounded familiar."

"It sounded familiar, did it? Did you know I created and produced a bunch of hit TV game shows back in the sixties, seventies, and eighties? Or did I just say that? I just want you to understand I'm not some fly-by-night loon who doesn't know what he's talking about. Also, before you leave this room, I promise you'll be absolutely blown away by what you hear and see. That said, let's get on with it."

The cripple limped to the other empty chair, sat down next to the producer, and began his story.

The Empire Clothing Company was located on the third and fourth floors of the City Bank Building, a skyscraper that stood at the corner of Twentieth Street and Lexington Avenue in Manhattan. The cloth for the Empire Clothing Company's suits was made in woolen mills in Philadelphia and Newark. The bolts of material were shipped to the factory's third floor. The cutting of the patterns, stitching of the suits, and boxing and shipping of the finished product were done on that floor. That was where Billy and Luther something-or-other boxed the suits, on a long table by the shipping elevators.

The Empire Clothing Company's executive offices were on the fourth floor at the front, the showrooms at the fourth-floor rear. The company's head of sales was named Sonny Lieberman. The small Plexiglas cubicle that Sonny called his office wasn't much bigger than a medium-size walk-in closet. The only good thing you could say about the cubicle, if one deigned to say anything about a cubicle, was its proximity to the Empire Clothing Company's owner, Max Lieberman. Sonny's claim to fame, at least around the Empire Clothing Company, was being the boss's son.

Max Lieberman, the owner of the Empire Clothing Company, was a short, squat, rather displeasing man with blotchy skin, thick eyelids, and a red, bulbous nose. Max added insult to injury by wearing his suit pants almost under his armpits. Max had inherited the business from his father, Abe, a tough immigrant with a full head of hair parted in the middle and always slicked down with a greasy, sweet-smelling balm he bought somewhere in the South. Abe Lieberman, when he was alive, had given off a lasting offensive impression like an unpleasant odor. The man adored himself, which was a good thing because nobody else did. He was quite short, had a Hitler-like mustache, a long nose, mean eyes, and pencil-thin lips. His temper had been known up and down the East Coast and he was quick to anger, two traits his son Max would inherit. All in all, Abe Lieberman was your average mustachioed tyrant with a slit-eyed stare that could peel paint.

A week after Abe Lieberman arrived in New York from Prague, he was pushing a pushcart around the Lower East Side of Manhattan hawking used men's clothes. The pushcart led to a small store. The small store grew to a chain of eighty-six retail establishments located from New England to Florida. Abe Lieberman spent every day of the week visiting those stores. Abe never had an office. He worked out of an old leather briefcase. He lived a parsimonious, almost miserly life and died a millionaire many times over. Abe Lieberman succumbed on a train that was taking him back to New York from one of his retail outlets in Nashville, Tennessee. He was ninety when he collapsed, suffering a massive heart attack on his way to the dining car.

For the last twenty-plus years, Empire Clothing had grown big enough to go public and land on the New York Stock Exchange. Max Lieberman had a gigantic office on the southeast corner of the building's fourth floor. The office overlooked both Lexington Avenue and Twentieth Street and was referred to by employees as "Little Madison Square Garden." His son's cubicle was called the "Garden's broom closet" or the broom closet for short, as in: "Sonny wants to see you in the broom closet."

About a week after Billy Constable became an employee of the Empire Clothing Company, Luther something-or-other whispered in Billy's ear, "That's one of the bosses standin' over there. The tall one. The one standin' with them other dudes. That's Sonny Lieberman, the big boss's son."

Sonny was thirty years old and neither handsome nor ugly, with a stringy, marathon runner's body and a receding hairline. Sonny leaned toward Brooks Brothers clothes. Having graduated from Andover Preparatory School and Yale University, you could see why.

The next time Billy saw Sonny was three hours later on the street.

Outside the City Bank Building's entrance on Twentieth Street off Lexington Avenue, Billy watched Sonny open his new umbrella purchased that very day at Brooks Brothers during his lunch hour, then watched him walk briskly away. Billy found himself walking just as briskly in the same direction. Not far from the City Bank Building Sonny turned and stared at the skinny guy with the familiar face suddenly walking beside him.

"Haven't I seen you before?" asked Sonny.

"I think so, sir," said Billy, tugging down his wet red Western Kentucky University baseball hat, pulling up the collar of his coat, and sticking his hands in his pockets.

"What'd you say? Speak up."

"I said I think so, sir."

"Think what?"

"I think you saw me before, sir."

"I thought so. What do you do?" he asked the chinless boy with the bad posture.

"I work in the shipping department, sir," mumbled Billy. "I box suits, sir."

"What? Speak up."

"I said I work in the shipping department. I box suits, sir."

"Do what?"

"Box suits."

"What's your name?"

"Billy Constable, sir."

"I *have* seen you before."

"Yes, sir, you have, sir," answered Billy, still speaking up. "I saw you today. You were with some other gentlemen."

"They weren't gentlemen. They were buyers," said Sonny Lieberman, laughing lustily at his little joke.

Billy Constable was confused.

"Those guys you saw me with own a chain of retail stores in western Pennsylvania," explained Sonny Lieberman. "Cities like Pittsburgh, Altoona, Johnstown, and State College. Lots of coal and steel miners in that part of the country. Perfect customers for Empire Clothing. They love our suits," he said enthusiastically. "Our suits last forever. Buy one and you can keep it for life. Did you know you can drive a good-size nail through one of our pant legs or the suit coat, pull it out, and there won't be a hole? The cloth just closes up. Did you know that? Try it sometime. And did you know that all our suits come with two pair of pants? Anyway, those guys you saw me with, they're big customers of ours. Hey, do you like my new Yale umbrella? Blue and white. My school colors. Where'd you say you were going?"

"I didn't say, sir. I'm going to the subway station, sir."

"Me too. I catch the 4 train. How about you?"

"I catch the 5 train, sir," muttered Billy, liking how he was sirring his boss. Showed manners, a habit Billy was trying to adopt.

"What? You catch what?"

"I catch the 5 train, sir," he said louder. And then not able to stop himself, Billy said, "I'll bet you my 5 train comes in before your 4 does."

"How much?" snapped Sonny Lieberman.

Sonny's swift reply was instant proof he was a betting man. What Billy didn't know was that Sonny Lieberman was the worst kind of betting man. One who loved to win but absolutely hated to lose.

"Twenty bucks?" suggested Billy.

"You're on!" said Sonny. And so a fateful bet began.

Billy Constable noticed that the moment he mentioned the subway bet and Sonny Lieberman said, "You're on," Sonny picked up his pace. Billy picked up his pace too, matching Sonny stride for stride, or trying to. But Sonny Lieberman was taller than Billy and took longer steps. Billy had to walk faster to keep up. He was forced to take two or three steps to every one of Sonny's. It was like a Doberman and a Yorkie trotting down the street. When the two crossed Twenty-second Street heading for Twenty-third Street and the subway station, Sonny Lieberman folded his new umbrella and started to run.

So did Billy.

As the two entered the subway station entrance, Sonny Lieberman took the steps two at a time heading down to the turnstiles.

Billy switched to two steps at a time.

Sonny's subway card was already in his hand.

So was Billy's.

There they were, Sonny Lieberman and Billy Constable, subway cards at the ready, running down, down, down the long dark stairwell, the two men racing to the platform. At roughly the stair's halfway mark, Sonny began to pull ahead of Billy. You could see that athletic Sonny was focused, a picture of perfect coordination. His left arm sliding down the railing for balance, his right hand—the one holding the new umbrella—swinging like a pendulum by his side, his long legs in a high-step gallop, his chin jutting forward like the bow of a racing yacht.

Billy was just as focused. His chin would have been jutting forward too if he had one. But no matter how fast Billy Constable took the steps, Sonny Lieberman took them faster. Billy's mind and body were churning just as furiously as Sonny's, but it didn't seem to matter. Lieberman's lead grew and grew. If one could have frozen that moment in time—the two men in midstride, the tall one ahead of the shorter one—and told the shorter man to think about what he had inspired, the shorter one might very well have realized several things:

1. Never bet against your boss.

2. Never make impulsive bets.

3. Forget about numbers 1 and 2. Gambling was Billy's nature and there was nothing he could do about it. Billy Constable was just like the scorpion who couldn't control his nature, either. After the scorpion talked the turtle into giving him a ride across the river on the turtle's back, the scorpion stung the turtle in midriver. The turtle said, "Why did you just sting me? Now we will both drown and die."

"I can't help it," answered the scorpion. "It's my nature."

Sonny Lieberman was the first to reach the turnstiles. He had to swipe his subway card through before he could make a dash for the subway. When Billy arrived at the turnstile, Sonny Lieberman was still fumbling with his card, cursing his being all thumbs. Billy didn't fumble. In fact, he didn't even bother with the card or the swipe or anything. He just hurdled the turnstile, a maneuver that was both illegal and smart.

But alas, Sonny Lieberman's 4 train was already at the subway platform. In fact, it had been there for a minute or so and now was on the verge of departing. Sonny Lieberman knew he had to catch that 4 train or he would lose the bet. Billy Constable's 5 train was automatically next into the station.

Sonny Lieberman finally passed through the turnstile and ran as fast as he could down the platform as if his mortal life depended upon his getting into the last car of that 4 train.

Billy watched him go. There wasn't anything else he could do.

Sonny arrived at the last car as the doors began to close.

And then Sonny Lieberman did something Billy Constable would always refer to as "real smart."

"Back in 1980," the cripple told the producer, "when I was [he made quotes in the air with two fingers of each hand] the Game Show King of Television, I was producing a program called *Treasure Hunt*. The show had twenty-five huge boxes onstage, one of which contained a check for twenty-five thousand dollars. Three contestants answered a series of questions worth twenty-five points apiece. The contestant with the highest score got to pick one of the twenty-five boxes. After the winning contestant pointed to the box she wanted, a showgirl would fetch the box and bring it to the program's host. The host would open the box, all the while messing with the contestant, teasing her, trying to make her think she'd won the twenty-five thousand dollars, hoping maybe she'd faint or something. It was all part of the fun," said the old cripple, "part of the program's charm. The host's name was Jeff Edwards. He was good at teasing the women contestants. Once he—"

"What's this got to do with—"

"Please," said the cripple, holding up his hands, palms forward, as if pushing a door open, "don't interrupt. Let me tell this my way. The faster I tell you my story, the faster you'll understand what a great TV program idea I have here." The cripple paused a moment, took a deep breath, and said, "Sometimes I admit we carried teasing the woman too far. Sometimes Jeff would have the woman, it was always a woman, we only used women contestants on *Treasure Hunt*, sometimes Jeff would have the woman thinking she won something really big when all she won was a toaster. I admit, we'd drive those women bonkers. She'd be standing there hyperventilating, you know, screaming or gasping or putting her hands to her cheeks and jumping . . . jumping all over the stage until she heard what she *really* won. Then she'd spiral back to reality, often very disappointed but"—the cripple took a deep breath—"but she would always be left with something worthwhile. You know, a nice prize of some kind. Usually. Anyway, Mike Wallace accused me of tampering with the emotions of my contestants on *60 Minutes*. He said I put my contestants through an emotional roller coaster for my own enjoyment. He was wrong. Wallace didn't—"

"Please!" interrupted the frustrated producer. "Just stick to the story, will you?"

The old cripple chuckled to himself at the rest of the anecdote he would never finish. Then he began to cough. He hacked away for a minute or two, mumbling *"excuse me"* now and then until he stopped choking. The producer would later refer to the cripple's coughing, when he recounted the story to his lawyer, as "the old scumbag's infernal barking."

When the cripple had finally got his spasms under control, he took a filthy handkerchief from his pants pocket, wiped his mouth, then put the dirty handkerchief back where it came from.

"One day," said the cripple, slightly breathless, "we had this nice lady from Canoga Park on the show. Canoga Park is a suburb of Los Angeles."

"I know where Canoga Park is," said the producer.

"Good for you. Anyway, this lady from Canoga Park wore a little white blouse with flowers on it and orange Bermuda shorts. One bra strap hung down over her right shoulder, I think it was. I'll never forget what she was wearing or that bra strap as long as I live, which, as you can probably guess, isn't going to be that much longer." The old cripple gave a few cackles. "That's why we have to get this project up and running *soon*. Anyway," he said, "this lady with the flowered blouse, bra strap, and Bermuda shorts won her round and got a chance to pick a box. Which she did. Our model brought the box to the host, who put it on the podium. Jeff lifted the box's lid and looked inside, you know, going through the old routine, trying to surprise the woman into thinking she just won the twenty-five big ones. He didn't surprise her at all. Not that woman. So Jeff continued the drill. He pulled a card from the box and told the contestant she might not have won the twenty-five thousand dollars, but she did win herself . . . *a ham sandwich on whole wheat bread!*

"The woman contestant moaned with disappointment. She couldn't have cared less about a ham sandwich. She thought that was it, had a really angry look on her face, and started to walk away with her sandwich when Edwards called her back again and said, 'There's something else in the box, Martha,' or whatever the hell her name was. The contestant came running back all excited and watched Edwards pull out another card. This time he said, 'Yes sireeee, Martha, you *did* win something else. You won . . . well . . . you can put that sandwich guess where? Can't guess? The answer is . . . *into your very own, brand-new picnic basket!'*

"The model brought out the picnic basket. The lady was maybe even more angry than before, getting tired of being the butt of a boring joke, and started to walk away again. Then Edwards hollered, 'Hey, don't go away mad, Martha, there's something else in here.' The woman ran back a third time and watched Jeff Edwards pull yet another card from the box. Then Jeff said to the woman, 'This card says that you can put that picnic basket with the ham sandwich inside it . . . guess where? Can't guess. Well, Martha, you can put the ham sandwich and the picnic basket . . . into the trunk of your very own . . . *brand-new Ford Mustang convertible!!'*

"The woman went down face-first like a tree. I mean like a tree. She ended up flat out on the floor, her face mushed into filthy camera cables and sticky candy wrappers. The surprise of the new convertible killed her dead."

The old cripple had the producer's undivided attention.

And then the old cripple started coughing again. Goddamn it, he thought, what a time to start this.

Stifling his cough as best he could but barely able to regain his composure, the cripple continued talking because he had to. He knew the producer's attention was finally focused on him and his idea. Fighting to regain his breath, he went on. "Like I said," he gasped, "when the lady contestant . . . was told she had just won . . . a brand-new Mustang convertible . . . she went down like a tree." The cripple paused to try to breathe normally, gave up, and continued. "I was standing . . . right behind our director . . . John Dorsey . . . and heard him . . . frantically yell to his cameramen . . . 'Pan up . . . pan up, guys!' through the intercom . . . Get your cameras . . . the hell outta there! We don't want to show . . . a . . . a . . . dead woman on our program!'

"'*Keep those cameras . . . right where they are . . . John!*' . . . I yelled back on the intercom. 'Don't you move a thing . . . Just keep those cameras . . . glued to that corpse.'

"Nice, churchgoing John Dorsey . . . turned in his swivel seat, looked up at me . . . and said, 'The poor woman's a corpse . . . and she's lying . . . on top of trash . . . and dirty camera cables!'

"And I said, 'I don't give a damn . . . if she's lying on dog turds . . . Don't move those cameras!'"

The old geezer paused to take a breath.

"I was sure the contestant was dead," he continued, breathing better. "She didn't move a muscle. A tail of the blouse she was wearing had pulled itself out of her Bermuda shorts and her bra strap had fallen farther down her right shoulder. I stood there in the control room dazed, wondering if it was a good thing or a bad thing to have a dead contestant on my television show. Would we get a lot of press? Would we be on the evening news? Would our show be talked about? Would it help *Treasure Hunt*'s ratings? All these questions were running through my mind a mile a minute, and all the while the contestant was still lying there on the studio floor, dead."

The old cripple sat slumped in his straight-backed chair, exhausted. The producer wondered if he would be able to go on.

"And then," continued the cripple, "it all fell into place. Just like that! I suddenly was convinced, I knew without a doubt the woman's death was the best thing that could happen to the program. And while I fought to control my emotions, you know . . . tried not to look exceptionally happy, tried to look sad . . . the damn woman opened one eye. Then the other!"

Another coughing spasm took over. The cripple hacked his head off, coughed up spittle several times into his handkerchief, wiped his brow with his arm, and took some more deep breaths.

"Was she okay?" asked the producer.

"Yes, she was fine," muttered the cripple, still discouraged after all those years. "She only fainted. That was the bad news."

"What was the good news?"

"It's when I thought of *The Death Game*."

II

Time evaporated as it is wont to do.

Time evaporated as it is wont to do.

So did Theresa Mendavey's romance with biker Rex Redmond. Of course, Theresa never expected her fling with Rex to last. They really had nothing in common. She went with him to spite her father. Anyway, shortly after Theresa Mendavey's romance with Rex Redmond ended, she disappeared off the face of the earth.

Just like that!

One morning, a little after the noon hour in 1990, Theresa Mendavey's mother woke up in her pitch-black bedroom (electrified blackout curtains) and realized she hadn't heard hide nor hair from her sixteen-, no . . . *seventeen*-year-old daughter in maybe six months. That bothered Edna greatly, to a certain extent. The sudden awareness of a missing daughter caused her to toss and turn, which was irritating. Being unable to sleep when she wanted to was one of Edna's major annoyances, of which there were many. Eventually Edna was forced to do something about the nonsense of feeling guilty about her daughter before she lost any more sleep. So she got out of bed, pulled down her nightie, which had gathered up under her armpits, and walked in her bent-over, half-asleep position to the bathroom. Safely there, she turned on a light, which was pure torture, and opened the medicine chest. She sneaked a look at her face, filled with sleep wrinkles and devoid of makeup, and wasn't pleased. She opened the mirrored cabinet and squinted at the shelves jammed with prescription drugs until she found the 10-milligram Valium container. Edna took one from its small plastic container, broke it in half, changed her mind and swallowed both pieces with some water, returned to bed, and slept like the proverbial log.

More months rolled by without any sighting of or word from Theresa.

Then early one Sunday morning, Theresa appeared in the lobby of an apartment building at Ninetieth and Park Avenue in Manhattan, where her aunt Evie Walton lived. Evie Walton was the married sister of Theresa's father, Hector Mendavey.

"Let's get one thing straight," Theresa would say whenever Evie Walton's name was mentioned, "my aunt Evie is nothing like my brainless idiot of a father."

Evie Walton was a pleasingly plump woman in her late forties. She had beautiful prematurely gray hair and was extremely intelligent, quite attractive, and extraordinarily affectionate.

Evie was married to Hicks Walton. Big roly-poly Hicks was in his early fifties, with his white hair parted in the middle. Hicks was a corporate CEO and just as nice and affectionate as his wife. Evie and Hicks Walton were far and away Theresa's favorite relatives.

"What can I do for you, young lady?" asked Aunt Evie after the two hugged for what seemed like forever and kissed each other's cheeks about fifty times.

"Don't really know," answered Theresa.

"Hungry?"

"Ravenous!!"

When they had finished pancakes with hot syrup and butter, a rasher of bacon, and a pot of coffee, and while the two were still seated at the breakfast table in the kitchen, Evie Walton explained an idea of hers to her niece. She said, "Theresa, honey, I knew I would see you eventually and I had this idea I thought might be good for you. How would you like to go back to school?"

"No fucking way!" said her niece.

Aunt Evie slapped the kitchen table hard with the open palm of her right hand. The *thwack* scared the hell out of Theresa. Made her jump an inch or so off her chair.

"You listen to me, young lady," growled Evie Walton. "When we talk to each other, you watch your language, mind your manners, hear me out, do *not* interrupt, and most important you behave like a lady. Do you understand that, Miss Wisenheimer?"

"Yes," answered Theresa.

Theresa Mendavey listened attentively while her aunt Evie told her about a writing class offered at Sarah Lawrence College to female high school dropouts. Aunt Evie had heard about the course from a friend whose daughter had applied. Evie Walton looked into the situation for her niece. She explained the following to Theresa. "If after your first full term you have passing grades, which you'll surely have, you will be admitted into the general student population as a sophomore and you can get your college degree in liberal arts. If you want to do this, we don't have to let your parents know right away. There's no need to have your father or mother poking around, interfering with this opportunity to get yourself a college education, which they will certainly do. How long have you been away from home now?"

"A long time."

"Have you heard from either my brother or your mother since you've been gone?"

"Nope."

"Figures. The only time they'll bother to get involved is if you ask them for money. Best to keep them out of it for now. So . . . your uncle Hicks will happily pay your tuition. After you get started you can surprise your parents and tell them what you're doing whenever you want to. I'm pretty sure they'll be delighted to hear you've graduated college since they last heard from you."

"I'm not so sure about that. They don't give two hoots what I do. Or even if I'm still alive."

"Now now, Theresa, that's not completely true."

"Pretty close."

"Well, maybe. Anyway, what do you think? What a feather in your cap this would be. A real ego builder to pump up that gigantic ego you already have. So? Talk to me."

Theresa Mendavey agreed to give her beloved aunt Evie Walton's suggestion a whirl. She moved into their apartment's spare bedroom (temporarily) and sent a letter off to Sarah Lawrence that afternoon requesting application forms. During the next few weeks Theresa was subjected to a vigorous battery of pre-entrance writing requirements. She passed the entrance requirements quickly and with flying colors.

After her first term, Theresa Mendavey received all A's on her first report card. An editorial of Theresa's ran in the Sarah Lawrence student newspaper, a rare occurrence for a first-year student. On probation, no less.

And then one day, close to the end of her first year, Theresa Mendavey walked off the Sarah Lawrence campus with a middle-aged, good-looking English professor named Curtis Bok and never returned.

Neither did the professor.

Attica prison had neither a shortage of library books concerning the Islamic religion nor Muslim enthusiasts spreading the word. Cleveland Steve Beastie from Chicago was a natural prospect. The dozens of self-styled ayatollahs working out in the Attica prison gym or passing time outdoors in the exercise yard never let Cleveland Steve from Chicago out of their sight. It took less than six months inside for Beastie to convert to Islam, but then, Steve Beastie didn't know what he was converting *from*.

Anyway, Cleveland Steve Beastie from Chicago became a Muslim. And not just an ordinary Muslim. A fanatic Muslim. The first thing he did was change his name. He got rid of the hated moniker and became Rasheed Jamal. The next thing he did was build himself up. Rasheed Jamal—a large man to begin with—became even larger. Every part of him grew in size. Jamal never missed an opportunity to go to the gym and work on buffing up his body. He was slowly metamorphosing into something very scary looking. Using a combination of steroids and weights, Jamal turned himself into an absurdly muscular giant. He began to appear if not better looking, then at least loftier, more reverential, more imposing. His nappy hair had become prematurely gray and the gap between his two upper front teeth, though more pronounced than before, seemed to suit him. The space gave the convict a pleasant look when he wanted to appear pleasant. And finally, Rasheed Jamal personally ordained himself an imam. An imam is a respected Islamic scholar, a direct descendant of Muhammad, and a man who leads the prayers in a Shi'i mosque. No one in the entire prison population complained. No one dared to.

The Imam Rasheed Jamal was a student not only of Islam but

also of every illegal activity from bank robbery to big-time dope peddling to murder. His professors were his fellow Attica inmates. He was a quick learner and became if not a hardened criminal, then certainly a cunning and dangerous one. He served his ten years in Attica carefully avoiding any major incidents.

Bobby "Ears" Leventhal was born in South Philadelphia on Fourth and Shunk streets. (Is there a more revolting street name than Shunk?) Bobby's father was a bookie. His mother an ex–heroin addict. His older brother Noah ran away from home when he was seventeen and was never seen or heard from again. Relatives could only guess where he was and what horrors he would cause. They were all secretly pleased he was gone. Bobby's fourteen-year-old sister Rachel had a face full of zits and was already an easy lay. But it was Bobby, the youngest of the Leventhal children, who was considered the one most likely to become the biggest *shandeh* of all.

Bobby Leventhal got his nickname Ears in high school. Aside from having ears that were two sizes too big for his head, Bobby Leventhal was able to manipulate the lobe or the outer cartilage or something of his left ear so that it made a loud clacking sound. The clack Leventhal's ear produced was not unlike the *click-clack* of those store-bought metal things that look like frogs, the things little kids click endlessly with their thumbs and forefingers, annoying the hell out of adults. Young Bobby was someone who, no matter how hard he tried not to, always got on your nerves. Big-time.

One afternoon, during an excruciatingly boring high school English class taught by a strict disciplinarian named Miss Nellie Hiss, Bobby Leventhal clicked his earlobe, or whatever the hell he clicked, several times. That day Bobby's ear made the *click-clack* sound louder than usual. Miss Nellie, which she preferred rather than Miss Hiss, asked who had brought the heinous frog clicker into class. Practically everyone pointed a finger to the back of the room where Leventhal sat. He was summoned to Miss Nellie's desk.

"Give me that heinous clicker right now, Robert," demanded the English teacher.

"I ain't got a clicker," replied sixteen-year-old Leventhal.

"Don't you ever use the word 'ain't' again in my classroom, Robert, do you hear? This is an English class. Speak English, for God's sake. And give me that clicker immediately or it's off to the principal's office with you."

"I ain't . . . I don't have a clicker, Miss Nellie," he repeated. "It's my ear."

"Do not lie, Robert. Do not compound the felony you've already committed with lies," said Miss Nellie, who came from a family of New York cops. "Give me the clicker and you will be sent to the principal's office for only one felony: simple disobedience. If you don't give me the clicker I will send you to the principal for three felonies: disobedience, lying, and ungentlemanly deportment. Now give me the clicker."

"I don't have a clicker, Miss Nellie. I swear it's my ear. Here, let me show you."

That's when the first of life's many calamities struck Bobby Ears Leventhal. While the rest of the class tittered, Bobby stood in front of Miss Nellie, two hands wriggling the hell out of his left ear for a full two minutes, trying to make it click. It didn't. In fact, his ear would never click again for the rest of Bobby Leventhal's entire life. Ears was sent to the principal's office.

Five years later, when Bobby Leventhal was twenty-one, he was arrested for attempting to rob the Hampton Inn in Clearwater, Florida. Bobby received a six-month suspended sentence. Ears hightailed it to New York. Soon he was robbing motels again. He managed to hit a motel in all five of New York City's boroughs, a feat he was proud of. Eventually, Leventhal spread out and successfully hit a dozen more in the tristate area.

It wasn't long before Bobby Ears Leventhal began doing all the stupid things dumb crooks do. He was seen flashing a thick wad of money around the local bars, driving a new bright orange Pontiac Bonneville convertible, sporting flashy clothes and gold chains, living the high life. It was only a matter of time before Bobby was nailed again. The obvious occurred on an April evening in 1995. Leventhal was twenty-six years old when he was collared. Being deathly afraid of violence, Bobby confessed to everything in the small interrogation room surrounded by several angry large detectives. When asked by his disappointed public defender why he rolled over without a fight, the still frightened Bobby Leventhal answered, "I never lie."

Leventhal was sentenced to seven to nine years in Attica prison in upstate New York.

In 1996, when Vera Bundle was sixty-one, she decided to take a spur-of-the-moment vacation trip to New York City. The forecast called for snow in the East, but Vera Bundle didn't care. She was in a slightly desperate mood to have fun. She rationalized that she needed a good time to get out of her doldrums. The travel agency's "Winter Surprise" to Manhattan sounded like the perfect remedy for her blues. The brochure promised "five days of rollicking good fun." It was also perfect timing for economy fares to New York City, being that it was the dead of winter.

"Just what the doctor ordered," she said to Esther Wigton, more to bolster her own spirits than anything else. "It's going to be a fun trip."

"You're nuts," argued Esther. "No one goes to New York in February for fun. No one goes there in February for *anything*."

"Oh, pshaw," replied Vera. "What do you know? You're still bug-headed over that young eye doctor in Wheeling."

"It's bug-eyed, Vera."

Vera packed an old suitcase that was her husband Norville's back when he was a traveling salesman for Guy Macy's Worldwide Plastics company in East Steubenville. Worldwide Plastics wasn't really worldwide at all. The company didn't even cover all of Ohio. Anyway, if the old battered suitcase was good enough for Norville, thought Vera, it's good enough for me.

Besides, Vera needed only one suitcase. She was just going for five days. All she was taking were two nighties, three sets of underwear, one dress, a skirt and blouse, a pair of slacks, two white nylon slips, several pairs of stockings, and a cardigan sweater. Vera didn't need to pack expensive high-heeled shoes. In the first place she wasn't intending to go anywhere fancy and in the second place she didn't *have* any expensive high-heeled shoes. "My walking shoes with the thick crepe soles will do just fine," she muttered to herself.

At the last minute Vera Bundle threw in a scarf and Norville's old black woolen sailor's watch cap with the red pom-pom on top. Norville had sewn the pom-pom on himself. Said he wanted a wool watch cap that was different from all the others. Vera figured it would be cold in New York City. It was cold here in Steubenville, so it must be cold there. It *was* February, for heaven's sake, and if it was freezing in New York she'd just pull the wool watch cap down over her ears to keep them warm.

The flight to New York City was uneventful and uncomfortable. For one thing, Vera's seat was in the last row of the economy section. She was unable to push her seat back if she wanted to relax due to the partition behind the last row, *her* row. Another major annoyance was Vera's misfortune to be sitting between two overweight traveling salesmen. The thugs allowed her hardly any legroom at all. Finally, the food was abominable. A packaged tuna fish sandwich on stale whole wheat bread and a small can of warm tomato juice. The brochure said a luncheon meal would be served on board.

"Is a tuna fish sandwich on stale whole wheat bread any kind of meal?" she asked the men sitting on either side of her.

First one, then the other. Both men examined Vera's face, then quickly returned to their magazines without saying a word.

"Hell, no," Vera answered herself.

Vera Bundle vowed she would write a letter to the airline complaining about the food as soon as she returned home. *And* the partition behind her that prevented her from sitting back like everybody else.

She told the two men exactly what she was going to do.

They couldn't have cared less.

And the two fat thugs sitting next to me, she would add in her letter. I'll write the airline about them too. Yuck on them. Of course the airline won't be able to do anything about who sits next to me. Next time I'll simply ask for an aisle seat. If there ever is a next time. At least that would limit the number of potential thugs to one.

A broken-down van in desperate need of a fresh paint job shuttled the "Winter Surprise" tour members from Kennedy Airport into Manhattan. Vera sat on a seat by herself in the rear of the van. She didn't feel like joining in the forced hilarity going on up front. It was mostly the men doing the carrying on there. The wives were peeing their pants with laughter in support of their raucous, red-faced husbands.

The Baldwin Hotel was located on the corner of West Thirty-third Street and Eighth Avenue. It was not one of Manhattan's higher-quality hotels. Nor was it one of the city's better neighborhoods. But since this was Vera's first trip to Manhattan, she didn't know any better. But then, Vera didn't intend to stay in her room very much. She was going to do some heavy sightseeing. She had her guidebook. She had her maps. She was all set. Though it was late afternoon and cold and miserable outside, Vera Bundle wouldn't be deterred. Besides, what else would she do with herself? Sit in her drab hotel room and stare at the four walls? The possibility caused Vera to start having serious second thoughts about the so-called Winter Surprise she had paid good money to be part of.

Now stop that, Vera, she said to herself, and went down to the lobby.

"So what's going on in the city this week?" Vera asked the concierge at the front desk, an elderly black man named Elwood Figgus. That's what the pin on his suit coat said.

"Not much," Elwood answered with a smile, scratching his curly gray hair. "It's February," he said, "and not much happens in February 'cept it snows. An' it gets cold. Real cold. That's about all it do in February. Matter fact they be spectin' a big snowstorm in the next hour."

"Who said so?" interrupted Vera.

"The radio do," said Elwood. "Radio's been givin' all these snow eee-lerts. They say they be spectin' lots a snow t'night. I'd stay in yo room if I was yo. For t'night least. Sorry to say this, ma'am, but February ain't a good time to come to New York to be sightseein'. These be the dog days a winter."

"I think the term 'dog days' refers to summer," corrected Vera Bundle, flashing her brittle teacher's smile, a smile that wasn't meant to be pleasant. "How would I get to Central Park?" she asked.

"Yo still wants to go out?" said Elwood with a good deal of surprise.

"Of course I do."

The old concierge looked at his wristwatch, an old Swatch on a loose and tarnished cheap metal band. "At this hour?"

"Yes, at this hour," answered Vera, a tad testy.

"Okay, then the best directions I can gives yo," said Elwood Figgus, "is go out the front door, walk up to the corner and grab yoself a cab. Axe the driver to drop yo off at Fifty-ninth and Sixth Avenue. The park's right there. Can't miss it."

"I'd rather walk," said Vera Bundle.

"I don't advise no walk," suggested Elwood Figgus.

"Thank you for your advice, Mr. Figgus," said Vera Bundle, becoming more annoyed by the minute, "but please give me—"

"Please call me Elwood."

"Elwood . . . *please* give me the directions."

"Okay," said Elwood Figgus, shrugging his shoulders. "Go out the door an' take a leff and when yo gets to the corner which be Eighth Avenue, take another leff and start walkin'. When yo gets up around Fifty-ninth Street, axe someone where Central Park is."

"Thank you . . . Elwood," said Vera Bundle.

Vera tied her scarf around her neck, buttoned her coat over the scarf, pulled Norville's woolen watch cap out of her coat pocket, and tugged it down over her ears. "Good thing, Elwood, I brought my husband's wool cap, don't you think?" asked Vera in the form of a peace offering.

"Sure is," answered Elwood cheerfully, leaning on his elbows.

With her handbag swinging from the crook of her arm, Vera Bundle went out the hotel's entrance and made a left. At Eighth Avenue she made another left and started walking. At the very next corner, while waiting for the light to change, she was bumped rather severely by a rude young tough carrying some dry cleaning over his arm. The collision almost knocked Vera down. The young tough needed a shave and wore a black watch cap pulled down over his forehead and ears. Instead of apologizing, the hoodlum glared at her and, shifting the dry cleaning he was carrying over his arm, walked away.

Somewhere in the fifties, Vera Bundle stopped another young man and asked where Central Park might be. This young man was tall and thin with a sweet face. He told Vera the best thing for her would be to cross Eighth Avenue and go in that direction—he pointed east—until she hit Sixth Avenue. "Then take a left and walk until you see the park. But I think instead of goin' to the park you should be goin' home, if you don't mind me sayin' so, ma'am."

"Oh, pshaw," was Vera's reply.

"Then maybe you ought to be closin' your pocketbook, ma'am. I wouldn't walk around the city with your pocketbook open like that. Lots of bad guys might get to pokin' around in there when you ain't lookin', tryin' to find your wallet."

Vera Bundle was shocked at the sight of her open handbag. She always kept it closed. "Funny thing is," she said to the tall boy with the sweet face, "I don't remember opening it. My goodness."

"You probably opened it to get somethin' and just forgot to close it."

"Well, I appreciate your telling me, young man. What is your name?"

"Jimmy Joel Jenks, ma'am. What's yours?"

"Mrs. Vera Bundle. Are you a New Yorker, Mr. Jenks?"

"No, ma'am. I'm from Knoxville."

"I'm from out of town too. I'm from Steubenville."

"Don't know where that is."

"Steubenville's in Ohio. Well, thank you for the directions, Mr. Jenks."

"No problem. Take care, Vera," said Jimmy Joel, and walked away.

Vera reached Sixth Avenue and Fifty-ninth Street at five fifteen. It was dark and beginning to snow. The temperature was falling almost as fast as Vera's spirits. She couldn't help but wonder what had prompted her to take this godforsaken trip to New York in the first place. Vera hated to admit it, but Esther Wigton was right. God, was she ever. Vera wished she was back in her armchair under the Tiffany lamp right now, sipping a cup of tea laced with scotch and perusing a volume of the *Encyclopaedia Britannica*.

The snow started coming down in thick sheets. The wind was picking up too, blowing so hard the snowflakes stung Vera's face and made her squint.

"You okay, lady?" asked a New York City policeman.

"Yes, I am, thank you," replied Vera politely, though she really wasn't. She was freezing cold and worried. She hadn't seen an available taxi in a while and she became slightly panicky wondering how she would get back to her hotel. Her shoes were sopping wet from the new snowdrifts and street puddles. Her stockings were soaked and her toes were numb. So were her fingers. Vera had forgotten to bring gloves from Steubenville. She would have to buy a pair.

"I would get to wherever you're going as soon as you can," suggested the policeman. "This storm is going to hit hard and fast. It'll be much worse than this, lady, and soon. The streets are going to be a mess in about ten, fifteen minutes."

"Thank you, officer. I'll get to where I'm going right away."

The patrolman saluted Vera Bundle and walked away.

As he disappeared around a corner, Vera felt lonelier and more apprehensive than before. At least the policeman was company.

Now even he was gone.

It had been almost two years since Theresa Mendavey walked off the Sarah Lawrence campus with English professor Curtis Bok, when she reappeared at her mother's newly constructed mansion in the flats of Beverly Hills. Theresa's parents were divorced by then. With part of the divorce settlement, Theresa's mother bought an old home, tore it down, and built a bigger, better one. Well, a bigger one. Theresa's father stayed on the original estate in Manderville Canyon.

Edna Mendavey's mansion had ten bedrooms and fourteen bathrooms. It was constructed to look like Tara, from *Gone with the Wind.* The mansion had six white pillars in the front. The four-car garage was built to resemble a barn with two huge wooden barn doors that swung open (electronically). Inside the garage were four parking places, one each for Edna's Rolls, Edna's Mercedes, Edna's Jaguar convertible, and one spare parking place for a guest's automobile. Being that there were two apple trees on the property, Edna Mendavey named her mansion the Love Apple Plantation. According to Edna, it was a saucy play on words, apples being a sly name for a man's balls.

Edna Mendavey thought that was funny.

Edna would.

The Love Apple Plantation was an architectural abomination. It was the most abominable of all the architectural abominations in the flats of Beverly Hills, a municipality in which countless architectural abominations existed.

One of Edna's maids, a Colombian woman named Maria Elephantes, was the first to see Theresa Mendavey roll up her mother's driveway. Theresa was on the back of a Harley-Davidson motorcycle, her arms wrapped around an enormous black man. The enormous man wore a stocking on his head, a black leather vest with BLACK OUTLAWS OF BAKERSFIELD, CALIFORNIA in big red letters circling a black shield with the orange HARLEY-DAVIDSON in the middle. He had on black leather chaps over a pair of black jeans. He wore laced-up black boots. The boots had orange flames painted on both sides. The man's head under the stocking was bald as a billiard ball. His arms were huge. They resembled a champion weight lifter's. Both arms sported major tattoos. The tattoo on his right arm featured the American flag, flames, and dragons. The other arm had a replica of the Statue of Liberty with the name Bernice tattooed over it. The tattoos ran from the top of the powerful Negro's shoulders to his mammoth wrists.

Theresa was in some sort of black leather outfit that had studs all over the place. The studs ran down the length of both sleeves, across her shoulders, and down the jacket's sides. The studs went around the fly of her black jeans and up the pant's ass crack. Different kinds of silver chains hung hither and yon from both her jacket and jeans, including a long silver key chain that started on a belt loop, made a big semicircle that almost touched the ground, and ended in one of Theresa's rear jean pockets. The two lovers walked from the Harley to the front door with their arms wrapped around each other's waists.

Edna's maid watched the pair approach through a dining room window. They were coming to the front door! She turned and ran upstairs in a great panic to fetch her mistress. She spoke to Edna Mendavey in a blubbering Spanish as if Edna were a Colombian Scarlett O'Hara and Zapata's army were marching to the Love Apple Plantation's front door intent on pillage and rape. With her maid screeching Spanish psalms behind her, Edna Mendavey scurried down the stairs. The nonstop blubbering behind her was making Edna Mendavey a nervous wreck.

"Shut *up*, Maria."

"¿Por qué? Yo no entiendo."

Edna Mendavey was torn between answering the doorbell, calling the police, or going back upstairs and hiding under her bed. But who was she hiding from? She never could understand anything her spic maid said. Edna peeked through the front door's peephole and became weak in the knees, wobbling back a few steps. Maria Elephantes steadied her.

What am I worried about? pondered Edna. My daughter wouldn't let anything happen to me. Or would she?

"Theresa has her arm around the gorilla's waist!" Edna Mendavey whispered loudly to Maria Elephantes.

"¿Por qué? Yo no entiendo."

"Shut up and open the goddamn door," ordered Edna Mendavey.

"¿Por qué? Yo no en—"

Edna opened the door.

When Theresa Mendavey saw the expression on her mother's face, Theresa smiled. Her mother's terrified look made the long trip worthwhile.

The enormous Negro smiled too.

Later, while Andrew Jackson Brown—for that was the enormous black man's name—was sitting in the living room draining a can of Coors Light, the heels of his black leather boots resting on an expensive and extremely fragile Louis Quatorze coffee table, Mrs. Mendavey led her daughter into the kitchen and whispered, "How could you *do* this to us?"

"To who?"

"To us. To your father and me."

"Do *what*?"

"You know what." Theresa's mother motioned with her head toward the living room.

"You mean you and Father would rather I didn't bring a nigger back to your houses so you both could be spared meeting the man I'm going to marry?"

"Going to *what*?" yelled Mrs. Mendavey. "Going to *what*?"

"Listen, Mother, you and Father never cared about anything, including each other. Why in the world would you two all of a sudden give two shits about me? If you did, Mother, it would be the first time you cared about anything other than yourself in your entire fucking life."

"*Language,* Theresa, *please.* And that's not true," huffed Edna Mendavey, adding, "You did say marry, didn't you?"

"Of course it's true. And yes, I did say marry."

"Oh, God, how could you *do* this to me? How could you marry a destitute colored man? I mean"—Mrs. Mendavey lowered her voice—"I mean I don't mind a colored man. Really, I don't. But couldn't you have chosen a colored doctor or a colored lawyer? No. You had to pick a . . . a . . . colored *motorcycle rider*!"

Mrs. Mendavey heaved a monumental sigh.

"It's too late for sighs, Mother," said Theresa, and walked away.

As her daughter disappeared over the horizon holding on to Andrew Jackson Brown atop his huge black Harley, Edna Mendavey stood crying into her kitchen sink.

Why, she asked herself, was her only daughter always on the back of a *shvartzer*'s motorcycle, this one being the biggest, blackest *shvartzer* she'd ever seen in her entire life? And on the biggest, blackest motorcycle she'd ever seen in her entire life. Of course her daughter could go out with a colored man if she absolutely had to. She had explained all that to Theresa not a half hour ago. But pick a light-skinned, gentlemanly, *rich* colored man. They do exist, Theresa, she had said. Go out with someone like that, she had said. Or did she? Did she mention the part about the light-skinned colored man? She didn't think so.

And . . . and . . . but that, that *nigger*! God forgive me, but there was no other word for a man that black. And Theresa holding on to him tight like she was when they rode off, her nose in his neck, *smelling* him. My God! I think I'm getting queasy just thinking about it.

When Edna Mendavey got herself together, she telephoned her ex-husband and sobbed, "Hector, you'll never guess."

"I'll never guess *what*?" snapped Hector Mendavey. He wasn't in the mood to hear Edna's whiny voice or play her little guessing games.

"She came to my house a little while ago with a *huge* nigger about nine feet tall and blacker than—"

"Who came, Edna? Who came to the house? Stop playing your goddamned guessing games for a minute. And stop your goddamned whining."

"Your daughter. Theresa. That's who came. Who do you think, Hector? Who do you think comes to this house with black men week after week, Hector?"

"She doesn't come week after week."

"I mean pitch-black. This time the black man was bigger and blacker than any black man I've ever seen in my entire life. They were holding hands like . . . like . . . like *lovebirds*!"

"See," said Hector Mendavey, "didn't I always say she was a bad kid? From birth she was a bad kid. Jesus Christ, how many kids get arrested in Disneyland?"

"Come on, Hector, running from one train car to another train car doesn't seem like the crime of the century."

"Yeah, well . . ."

"God damn it!" shouted Edna Mendavey into the telephone, suddenly furious, watching her next-door neighbor's huge curly black standard poodle take *another* dump on her lawn! On her property, for God's sake! The second shit that morning. And this one larger than the first! And only an hour apart! I mean, how many craps does a normal dog make in one morning and why the hell didn't the fucking poodle crap in his own yard? Edna yelled her frustration out the closed window, "God *damn* it, you black bastard!"

"Easy, Edna," said Hector. "Just simmer down and talk to me."

"I'm going to poison that black son of a bitch."

"How you gonna find him?"

"What do you mean how am I going to find him? He's right next door!"

"He's living next door! In the house next door to you?"

"*Yes!* I can see him right now."

"I don't know if you should kill him."

"No? Well, he's crapped twice on my lawn, Hector. Twice in the last ten minutes!"

"He did? Twice? How do you know?"

"I *saw* him, Hector!"

"You *did*? You actually saw him crap on your lawn?"

"Yes, I did."

"Still, I wouldn't kill him. Not for just doing *that*."

"You wouldn't? What a dolt you are, Hector. Well, I would."

There was a moment of silence.

"So what are we going to do?" asked Edna Mendavey.

"About what?"

"About Theresa's *new* nigger boyfriend."

"Wasn't that who we were just talking about? Theresa's boyfriend? I thought you just told me you were gonna kill him."

"I'm so confused," whined Edna.

"*You're* confused? Listen, Edna, I've got a foursome waiting for me at the club."

"I guess you're right, Hector."

"About what, Edna?"

A fit of coughing engulfed the cripple again.

The producer watched and waited while the sickly old man alternately coughed and spit into his handkerchief for at least two minutes. During the attack, the cripple's face was all purple and his eyes teared. During most of this time, the producer found himself not knowing what to do or where to look. He thought it was all terribly annoying and wondered how long he would be able to last in the ancient creep's apartment.

When the cripple finally finished his seizure of sorts, he wiped his brow with his arm and took some deep breaths. The old man was exhausted. "As I said," he continued, practically panting, "the woman's fainting on *Treasure Hunt* was the genesis of *The Death Game*."

The cripple explained how he had gone home from the studio the night the contestant fainted feeling terribly disappointed. The cripple couldn't put his finger on the cause of his discontent. The show they taped that evening was good. Better than good. Extremely entertaining. And the poor lady had only fainted and not died and that was good, he supposed. Still, he couldn't seem to shake his discouragement until he figured out what he was so discouraged about. It was the woman's recovery that put him in such a funk, wasn't it? Of course it was. His serious letdown came, he realized, the moment the woman opened first one eye and then the other. The fact that she did *not* die was the cause of his despair.

"That night I thought of *The Death Game*," said the cripple. "Why not? It was the natural progression of things. If I felt so disappointed that the fainting woman only fainted, then why not create a show where the possibility existed that a contestant could die? A weekly, prime-time television program whereby a contestant would either win a lot of money or be executed! On camera! On coast-to-coast television. Like I said, it would have to be a lot of money to lure anyone to the program to make that kind of personal gamble, wouldn't it?"

"Why would you even think of such an idea?" asked the producer.

"For one thing, nobody else had. And for another: Why not? Times change. Laws of the land change. Hell, I knew that. And when they did change, I would be ready. The problem turned out to be the times didn't change fast enough. Listen, when I was in the industry I was famous for pushing the envelope, and a television program that featured an execution would certainly be pushing the envelope, wouldn't it? It would be innovative . . . no . . . the idea would be past innovative. It would be revolutionary. Scandalous. It would be the most talked about television program in the world. Don't you agree?"

The cripple didn't wait for the producer to reply. "I became completely obsessed with my idea," he said, "so obsessed that I overlooked some extremely important points. Mainly the legality of what I had in mind. Remember, this was back in the early eighties. Two presidents ago. No, three presidents ago. Something like that. I'm bad at math. Anyway, euthanasia wasn't legal then. Funny when you think about it. Back then suicide wasn't a crime, but *assisted* suicide was! Someone could take their own life and that was okay. But if some person *helped* the poor soul take his or her life, *that* was a crime! Anyway, it was stupid of me to think of such a show during those years, right? Of course it was. But oddly enough *you* stand to benefit from my stupidity."

"Me?"

"Yes, you."

"How?"

"By producing the program now that it's legal. Sharing in the credit and the profits with me fifty-fifty. The profits will be tremendous. I would suggest you act as soon as possible before someone else thinks of this idea, which is sure to happen *and* which will deprive us of everything." The old cripple smiled.

The producer said nothing.

"You see," remarked the cripple, "I was ahead of my time. I was always ahead of my time, which, as far as I'm concerned, is as bad as being behind the times. Neither works. Neither is anything to be proud of. The thing to be is *on time,* right on the money, as they say. That's what counts."

"Yes, yes. Get on with it."

"Anyway," said the cripple, "other than the sick and dying, hardly anyone would do *The Death Game.* Not for the amount of money I could offer. And I really couldn't blame them. Back then it was a dilemma. I couldn't go anywhere for a loan. I couldn't go to a bank or a network because the idea wasn't legal. But today it wouldn't be hard to raise that amount of money."

The producer asked the cripple how much money he thought a show like *The Death Game* would have to give away today to make gambling on your life worthwhile. "I'm talking about a healthy person," he said. "Not someone terminally ill."

The cripple noted with satisfaction that the producer was asking questions. He's interested, he said to himself. "How much? Fifty million dollars, perhaps."

"Fifty mill . . . You think some healthy person would gamble their life for a paltry fifty million dollars?"

"In a New York minute. There will always be prospective contestants, desperate people willing to gamble their lives for that much money. Daredevils, supreme egotists, publicity freaks, people with desperate situa—"

"And you think the networks will put up that kind of money for this idea?"

"In a heartbeat. Big-money budgets are easier to get these days than small budgets. And not every *Death Game* will have a hundred-million-dollar winner. On some shows the program won't have to pay out a thing. Every time a contestant misses the final question and is executed, the show will save fifty million dollars. The more contestants you kill, the more money you save. See? So in the end the program will amortize itself out to being downright economical. Am I right or am I right?"

The producer said grudgingly, "I suppose so."

"Say you have to go? That's the door there," said the cripple, pointing to the bathroom.

"I didn't say anything about having to go."

"I thought you just said you had to go."

"I said *I suppose so.* You deaf too?"

"As a matter of fact I am. Should be wearing my hearing aids, but they're too much trouble. Anyway, back in the eighties, when I finally got around to making a pilot show of *The Death Game,* I had to use all the money I had in the bank. I withdrew every penny and sold every possession of mine and it still wasn't enough to get good contestants. I had gathered together a kitty worth roughly seven and a half million dollars! Over five hundred thousand dollars of that went for my production expenses. I thought seven million dollars was a lot of money to give away, particularly in the eighties. But it wasn't enough. The only contestants I could get willing to risk their lives for seven million dollars were the terminally ill."

"Okay, you've covered all that. How did your program work?"

The cripple explained the show's rules.

The famous television producer stood and paced back and forth in the small space allotted to him in the dirty little room. Again the astute cripple was aware of the producer's strong interest in what was being discussed. Why else would he be pacing back and forth?

The producer said, "I know this has nothing to do with the laws of the land today, but I find it hard to believe that back then your lawyers didn't inform you you were doing something very illegal. That they didn't point out to you the moment you tried to air your pilot program you would be immediately engulfed in massive legal problems. Not only legal problems, but criminal problems as well. You spent seven, no . . . seven and a half million dollars on a project knowing full well what you were doing was against the law. You did this, when, in the eighties? Except for a few states, euthanasia wasn't legal in the eighties. What you were doing was committing murder! You spent seven and a half million dollars of your own money to commit murder! Is that correct?"

"Yes, that's correct."

"Then tell me this. Why didn't your lawyers, who knew as well as you that you were about to commit murder, why didn't they prevent you from making the pilot? Why didn't they stop you from your destructive course of action?"

"They tried to stop me. God knows they tried, but I refused to listen to them."

"Why? Why did you refuse?"

"As I said, I was obsessed."

"So what you're telling me is that making your illegal pilot was worth going broke over. It was worth spending every last cent you had to commit a murder? Wait! And possibly going to jail for!"

The cripple sighed sadly. "In those days I wasn't very rational. In those days an idea was more important to me than money. I wasn't the first person who obsessed over an idea to the point of self-destruction. And I daresay I won't be the last. General Billy Mitchell—"

"Stupid," said the producer.

"Worse. Insane . . . to a certain extent."

"What do you mean 'to a certain extent'?"

When DP Brady was ordained a priest, he requested and was assigned his old grammar school's parish, St. Matthias, and began his priesthood there. He lived in the rectory of St. Matt's and did what a priest does in a local parish: took confessions, married some folks, baptized others, and buried the dead. It is said a priest takes care of the family from the cradle to the grave. Father Brady performed those duties with grace and enthusiasm. His parishioners quickly grew to love the young priest. So did his boss and mentor, Father William Deuber. Father Deuber, the pastor of St. Matt's, was a former football star at the University of Pennsylvania and an Episcopalian turned Catholic during the Korean War. Why he did what he did, switch religions like that, Father Deuber never explained.

Father Deuber and Father Brady became good friends.

Father Deuber, a once stocky and muscular halfback, had aged appreciably. The fringe around his head had turned a silver gray and a serious paunch was growing larger and larger, bulging over his belt. The old warhorse—who had been running the St. Matthias parish for more years than he liked to admit—had become more and more persnickety as he grew older. He scolded and sometimes punished his young assistant pastors as if they were kids and he were their daddy. Father Deuber was called "the old prick" by the newer priests, but always behind his back.

The monsignor was different with Father Brady, who reminded Father Billy Deuber a lot of himself when he was the young priest's age. He considered Brady a clergyman of exceptional calling: fiercely loyal to the church, a strict disciplinarian, and at one with his flock. There were, of course, those parishioners at St. Matthias who didn't share Father Deuber's opinion of Father Daniel Patrick Brady. Most of the younger members thought Father Brady too prissy and old-fashioned, too caught up in old clergy precepts, too tied to all of the Vatican's dated and out-of-style laws, *too* strict. But those malcontents were in the minority, for churches in those days were not filled with the young.

Along with maturing into a learned priest, Father Brady had matured into a fine-looking young man. For one thing, he had grown. He stood well over six feet with broad shoulders, a husky body, wavy blond hair, clear and penetrating blue eyes, a great smile, and a handsome face. Some of the teenage girls in Father Brady's parish considered the priest a "hottie."

Father Brady's mother, Emma Brady, passed away while he was an assistant pastor at St. Matthias. She had never been a healthy woman. Once she was buried, Flynn Brady flourished. So did his appliance business. Flynn began working sixteen-hour days, something he'd always wanted to do but couldn't because of marital duties. He also drank more, another habit he had been prohibited from indulging in while his wife was alive. Emma Brady had nagged her husband into not taking that extra drink by saying over and over again, "God will cause you to drop dead when you least expect it." And Flynn Brady was a superstitious man.

As a result of Flynn Brady's sixteen-hour days, the net worth of his appliance business soared (along with his blood pressure). Now more than ever Flynn Brady wanted his son, *needed* his son to join him at work. The load was getting to be too much for Flynn Brady. So was the stress. But Flynn Brady was innately afraid of strangers. He had a phobia about trusting them and consequently never hired anyone he didn't know.

The day finally came when the old Irishman knew the dream of his son coming into the business he had founded was dead as a doornail. That was the day Father Deuber told him (proudly) that Cardinal Michael Ruffing, head of the Catholic Archdiocese of Philadelphia, had his eye on Flynn's son *and* Father Deuber's assistant. Word had it the cardinal was going to transfer the assistant pastor to the church of His Eminence.

Within a month of hearing the news, Flynn Brady's son was transferred from run-down St. Matt's to the Cathedral of St. Peter and St. Paul located at 222 North Seventeenth Street, in Philadelphia. The cathedral was a dramatic green-domed building surrounded by trees in center-city Philadelphia. The rust-colored, ornate brownstone structure belied a simple interior made up of a main aisle, pews on either side of the aisle, and a pulpit front and center. The cardinal's office was there, but His Eminence lived elsewhere. The cardinal's residence was a palatial mansion, courtesy of the Vatican, on the corner of Cardinal Road and City Line Avenue. The office and cathedral were known to Philadelphia priests as "The Twos."

Father DP Brady was summoned to "The Twos" and made secretary to the cardinal, a rather awesome promotion for such a young priest.There were many things Cardinal Ruffing liked about Father Brady. The cardinal had found out from several of his sources that Father Brady was devout, that he had "a lust for the clergy," the church's way of calling the priest ambitious (but not "pushy"); and the young priest's reputation for strictly adhering to Catholic dogma, which, the cardinal was told, Father Brady did without seeming dictatorial, was a plus.

In truth, Father Daniel Patrick Brady had become obsessed with Catholicism. His religion colored his moods. On several occasions the priest would verge on losing his temper—and sometimes did—

when the subjects Father Brady heard in his confessional concerned infidelity, divorce, or childbirth out of wedlock. Of these three sins, Father Brady was violently unsympathetic toward unwed mothers.

Father Brady's attributes, even his occasional loss of composure, were admired by Cardinal Michael Ruffing. Soon Father Brady became the cardinal's favorite priest. The cardinal admired Father Brady so much that he sacrificed having him work in the office adjacent to his and sent Father Brady to Rome to study Scriptures, canon law, and moral theology.

The word was out. Father Daniel Patrick Brady was a Golden Boy, on the Catholic Church's fast track.

When Bobby Leventhal entered Attica to serve his sentence, he had matured appreciably since high school. He'd gone from a chubby, nerdy little kid to a chubby, nerdy little man.

In popular prison vernacular, big-eared Bobby Leventhal was "juicy."

The first day in Attica, while Bobby was being processed, one prisoner said to another, "Man, that little fat white honky's got hisself some bugger-grips, don't he? An' you know what *theys* good for, don't ya? Good for blow jobs is what theys good for. You know . . . somethin' to grab on to."

"Yeah, somethin' to grab on to," said the prisoner's buddy, sniggering.

Two hours after entering Attica, Bobby Ears Leventhal was incarcerated in a seven-by-ten-foot jail cell. The cell had two bunk beds, a chair and table, a toilet, one lightbulb in the ceiling that was never turned off, and a cell mate: the huge, muscular, black, anti-Semitic Muslim named Rasheed Jamal. Jamal hated a lot of things, but he hated Jews most of all. It was a grievous mistake of the prison authorities to put the Jew Leventhal in a cell with the vicious anti-Semite Jamal, but they put the harmless Leventhal into his cell anyway.

When Bobby Leventhal met Rasheed Jamal for the first time, he attempted to be light and friendly, but Bobby's actions didn't come across that way. They never did, never have. His nervous laughter and nerdy personality gave him a pushy rather than a funny quality. He was the old button pusher. Just like he was in high school. Poor Bobby's personality got on everybody's nerves since grammar school.

"So what do I call you, big guy?" he asked, giggling nervously. "Do I call you Your Holiness or Your Highness? Prime Minister? How 'bout Mr. President? Or just plain Rasheed? So what is it?"

It didn't take a rocket scientist to know the imam would look down on Bobby Ears Leventhal with disdain. Even if Leventhal weren't a button pusher. Jamal despised the Jew on sight. And to be disliked intensely by the imam could cause a basically gentle, plump, and cowardly man like Leventhal infinite sleepless nights.

"So what *do* I call a hotshot Muslim priest?" continued Bobby, hoping to ingratiate himself but doing exactly the opposite. "That's what I heard you were. Some biggity-big Islamic wonder boy. You gotta help me here, buddy. I never had the pleasure of meeting a full-fledged holy man before. I never even met a rabbi, and I'm Jewish. You're sorta like a rabbi, aren't you?" Bobby giggled and picked his nose. "I mean, we're gonna be in here together for years, hotshot, so what are you comfortable with? Me, I'm Bobby and—"

"You don't call me *anything*, motherfucker, you hear? In fact, don't even *look* at me."

Bobby Leventhal was suddenly frightened. "So where am I supposed to look, big guy?" he asked the imam, a quaver in his voice.

"Didn't I just tell you, you dumb white Jew shit, not to ever *talk* to me? So why are you talking to me? Look anywhere as long as it's not at me, you stupid white trash Jew motherfucker."

"Hey, hold on there," said Leventhal bravely.

"Hey fucking *what,* kike?"

The tall, muscular, and very angry Jamal took one step forward and stood chest to chest with the little porker. Well, not exactly chest to chest. The top of Bobby's head came to the imam's breastbone.

"Just shut the fuck up, kike, and look somewhere else, you hear?"

"Yeah, I hear," said Bobby, who might have been trembling.

It wasn't long after that discussion that all hell broke loose for Bobby Leventhal. Rasheed Jamal played right into the hands of the Jew-hating warden by throwing Bobby to the prison population with the following instructions: Just make sure the Jew spends more time in the infirmary than in my cell.

Bobby Ears Leventhal was trashed.

As instructed by the imam, a large number of inmates of Attica got rid of their frustrations by beating the crap out of Bobby Leventhal. Most of the punishment was barbarous, cruel, and disfiguring. Leventhal suffered multiple kicks to his mouth until he lost almost all his teeth. The only ones left were a few molars in the back, which was the object of those kicks. Then the Muslims and blacks and Hispanics and hard-core Aryan Nation toughs and stupid whites could use Leventhal's mouth for cocksucking without any of his teeth in the way. And his nice fat ass for butt-fucking.

And his big ears for holding on to.

Bobby Leventhal ended up a half-dead mess. His nose didn't have any cartilage left. It lay flat against his face. His mouth was a sunken hole, puckered inward like an old man's. He was blind in one eye and deaf in one ear. The blind eye's lid drooped. He limped badly and slept poorly. He was in constant pain and, as ordered by the imam, spent most of his time in the prison's infirmary.

One afternoon, during the start of Bobby's second year in Attica, he sliced open his wrists with the sharp and jagged lid of a Campbell's soup can. He found the empty can while working in the prison kitchen. Bobby was rushed to a hospital in the city of Attica. Eventually the warden announced that the fat Jew had died. This news made a great many of the inmates sad. They wouldn't have the toothless motherfucker's mouth to suck their cocks anymore. Or his plump ass to butt-fuck.

Or his big ears to hold on to.

Sixty-one-year-old Vera Bundle was last seen standing on the corner of Fifty-ninth Street and Sixth Avenue thinking she might cry. That nice colored man at the hotel, Mr. Figgus, told Vera not to go out, but she wouldn't listen to him. I should have, she told herself. Vera Bundle even forgot what the purpose of her walk was. Just to spite that nice colored man, most likely. Stupid, stupid, stupid, she thought. Anyway, what's the big deal? We get snowstorms in Steubenville.

She *ordered* herself to get a grip. But then a particularly vicious gust of wind almost blew her over. It also blew away any hope of getting a grip. Shaking her head, Vera muttered to herself aloud, "I think you better get moving."

But where to? she asked herself.

Back to the hotel, that's where, she answered herself.

So the elderly tourist pulled her head into her shoulders as far as it would go, pointed her nose into the blustery wind, and began walking (hopefully) toward Eighth Avenue. But she was all mixed up and didn't get very far. The icy cold, the wind, and the snow were becoming too much for her to handle. And apparently for other people too. The pedestrians had thinned out. There was almost no one walking anywhere on the sidewalks. Just the occasional automobile or taxi went by.

What I could use is a strong cup of tea, thought Vera. Or better yet, a cup of tea with a double shot of scotch in it. Why not? I'm on vacation, aren't I? On second thought, the hell with the tea. A good stiff drink is what I need. A good stiff drink would be good for what ails me. I'll have that drink as soon as I get back to my hotel. But then Vera quickly changed her mind. Why wait? she decided. The change of heart was helped immeasurably by the simple fact that she was standing in front of a place called the Essex House Hotel & Bar.

"Hotel and bar. How fortuitous," she said to herself, perking up a smidge. "Absolutely fortuitous."

Vera turned and walked through the revolving doors and entered the hotel's lobby. Almost immediately Vera Bundle went from being lonely and bummed out to feeling almost happy. For one thing, the lobby of the Essex House was warm. For another, people were bustling about doing things. Vera didn't feel alone anymore. She took off her coat, stuffed her scarf into one sleeve and the wool hat into a coat pocket, threw the coat over her arm, and looked around for the bar. She noticed the entrance to what looked like a restaurant or bar to her left. The place was called Journeys.

Strange name for a bar, thought Vera.

She wondered if it was proper for a woman her age to go unescorted into a bar in New York City. The hell with it, she concluded, and crossed the lobby and walked into the restaurant-bar called Journeys. The place was almost empty. Vera made herself comfortable at a small table for two. Across the aisle from Vera at another table for two sat a man by himself looking at his clasped hands. He glanced up at her.

She smiled.

He smiled.

The man looked much younger than Vera, maybe in his forties. She guessed there was probably a good twenty-year age difference between the two of them. Maybe more. The man was well dressed in a suit and tie. He was quite good-looking. His hair was parted in the center. Hair parted in the center was old-fashioned, but Vera liked it. A lot. Based on looks and dress, Vera marked the man sitting across from her as a gentleman.

When the waitress arrived to ask Vera Bundle what she wanted, Vera surprised herself and asked for a daiquiri. A daiquiri, she mused when the waitress had gone away, my my. Vera Bundle had drunk a daiquiri only one other time in her life, the evening of the day she turned twenty-one. It was the drink she ordered at the bar of the Elvira Hotel in Steubenville on that historic night.

The restaurant's windows were behind Vera. She turned and looked out onto Fifty-ninth Street. The storm was hitting the city hard. The tops of the trees across the street were already wearing little white hats. The waist-high wall that bordered Central Park had maybe three or four inches of snow on top if it. Vera sighed. How was she ever going to get back to her hotel? She hadn't seen one single taxi go by outside. I should have listened to Mr. Figgus and stayed in my room. He warned me. I should have listened. Better yet, she thought downheartedly, I should have listened to Esther Wigton and stayed in Steubenville. Vera was pushing herself deeper and deeper into a new and more depressing mood.

The daiquiri arrived.

Vera took a sip, then twirled the stem of the glass a few times. As she did, Vera stole several glances at the lone man sitting across from her. She noticed he was constantly checking his wristwatch, maybe half a dozen times since she'd been sneaking looks. The man was obviously agitated and upset. Probably stood up by a good-looking young lady. See, said Vera Bundle to herself, you're not the only depressed person in this city. She snickered and twirled her daiquiri stem twice. I'll bet there's a couple of million screwed-up people living here. At least. Well, doggone it, I'm not going to be one of them. I'm on vacation. I'm going to damn well enjoy myself even if it kills me. Vera Bundle took a sip of her drink. A big sip.

Time passed.

Vera Bundle was halfway through her second daiquiri. The man across the aisle from her continued to look at his wristwatch over and over again. He has a problem, decided Vera Bundle, and gulped down the last of her second daiquiri, which added appreciably to Vera's buzz and her need to strike up a conversation with the gentleman sitting across from her. "You have a problem, don't you?" she asked—perhaps a little too motherly—the man across the way.

He nodded.

Maybe motherly was good. "Can I help?"

The man shook his head.

"Excuse me for asking, but what happened?"

He shook his head again and said, "I'd rather not say." Then the man looked away from Vera.

He obviously doesn't want to talk about it, at least not to me, thought Vera Bundle. She sighed and decided New Yorkers weren't very sociable. Vera returned to twirling her empty daiquiri glass.

A few more minutes passed.

Maybe in a little bit the handsome man will change his mind and talk to me, hoped Vera.

More time went by.

The handsome man apparently wasn't going to change his mind.

Oh, well.

Vera signaled the waitress she wanted to leave. The waitress, sitting on a bar stool talking to the bartender, saw Vera's waving arm and headed her way. When she arrived at Vera's table, she smiled a worn-out smile and said, "Another daiquiri?"

"Goodness no!" answered Vera a little too loudly. "Another daiquiri and I'll be on my Jeanie Keister and you'll be having to pick me up. Jeanie Keister's a friend of mine. Don't know when I started saying that, calling my keister my Jeanie Keister. And it won't be so easy picking me up if I do fall on my Jeanie Keister being as how I've been putting on some weight lately. I'll just have the check, please."

The waitress returned with the check. She placed it on Vera's table and left. Vera moved her pocketbook onto her lap and opened it.

"Oh my God!" she shrieked.

Linus Major IV had the good fortune to be born into an extremely wealthy dynasty and the misfortune to be born with a lisp. Some folks liked to say Linus was born with a silver spoon in his mouth and that's what caused his lisp. Linus IV's lisp made him sound exactly like a youngster who spoke without his front teeth. Little Linus pronounced an *s* or a *z* like the *th* in "third" or "thick," giving his speech a sibilant rhythm, childish and halting.

This handicap may have been the root cause of Linus Major IV's reckless approach to life. As a kid, Linus made up for his "sissy" lisp by being a daredevil. He slid down hills other kids wouldn't go near on his sled. He was the first boy his age to swing himself out and over the Mohican River (on a dare) from a rope that hung from a thick tree branch so that he could drop into the water and swim back to shore. Linus was also the culprit who (on a dare) rang Mr. O'Brien's doorbell. Mr. Colin O'Brien was the red-faced, potbellied, tyrannical junior high school principal. When he opened the door, Linus, standing in the shadows of the principal's front porch, heaved a quart of milk in a glass bottle into the principal's living room. After Linus heard the bottle shatter, he rode off into the night on his bicycle.

Linus Major IV was the son of world-renowned sportsman Linus Major Jr., who was the son of industrialist Linus Major Sr., the founder of Major Iron & Steel, Major Aeronautics, Major Lackawanna & Tijuana Railroad—better known as the Wanna-Wanna Railroad—and about thirty other Major companies in the United States and around the world.

Linus Major IV was neither a corporate giant like his grandfather nor a polo-playing, skeet-shooting, mountain-climbing, deep-sea-fishing, croquet Hall of Famer like his father. Nor a ne'er-do-well layabout like his older brother Linus Major III, nicknamed Trey. Our Linus graduated from Yale, as did his younger sister Sally, his older brother Trey, his father, and his grandfather. But other than a strange predilection for archaeology and dinosaur bones, which he kept up for no apparent reason, and his daredevil stunts, Linus didn't do much. Among members of Linus Major IV's family and friends, he was known as Linus Minor.

Over the years, the lisp that Linus had as a child disappeared, which helped the young man face the world a bit more assured about things in general. Unfortunately, Linus continued his daredevil ways, perhaps more aggressively than ever, for reasons known only to him. And though he never made a name for himself in family affairs, his propensity for daring helped him establish new entries in *The Guinness Book of World Records.*

In 2000, when Linus was nineteen years old, he ate more hot dogs than anyone else at Coney Island—forty-nine in an hour—earning him his first *Guinness* record. In 2001, Linus bungee-jumped the longest vertical drop ever recorded, stepping off some forgettable bridge over some godforsaken gorge in Crested Butte, Colorado, for his second *Guinness* record. In 2002, Linus dropped the greatest distance in free-fall parachuting in the history of the sport. Linus scared even his most sniveling detractors by keeping his parachute closed longer than any other parachutist in the nation's history up to that time. The jump earned him his third *Guinness* record. In 2003, Linus piloted a lighter-than-air balloon from the Boston Commons to the fairground adjacent to the San Diego Zoo, entering *The Guinness Book of World Records* for the fourth time. And in the year 2008, at the age of twenty-seven, Linus flew around the world in fewer than seventy hours for his fifth and final *Guinness* record.

Time magazine said this about Linus: "His resolute attitude, giving peril the back of his hand, is what separates Linus from all the other Majors." *Finally* Linus was bathed in recognition from an independent source that wasn't bragging about another member of his family.

How gratifying.

But not for long.

Unfortunately, shortly after that interview was recorded but before the magazine went to press, Linus's father was arrested for embezzling the sizable sum of nine hundred and ninety million dollars from several of the family's companies. When the news of Linus Major Jr.'s crime hit the newsstands, all hell broke loose. The Major family was ridiculed by the president of the United States, taken to task by both houses of Congress, and crucified by the press.

The *New York Post*'s front page screamed:

MAJOR GREEDOLA!!

Linus Major Jr.'s defense? A pathetic statement issued from corporate headquarters, to wit: "I don't crunch the numbers. Someone else does that."

Time magazine decided to dump Linus's interview. Instead they ran a cover story on his father's fall from grace. Once again our Linus was nudged out of the national spotlight by a member of his once distinguished family.

During the ensuing years, members of the Major family fell into heavy debt and major disrepute. Linus Major Jr. was sent to Lompoc, a gentlemen's jail, for seven months and owed the government (and stockholders) barrels of money. His wife, Lucy Major, checked into the Betty Ford Center for addiction to prescription drugs. She was at Betty Ford longer than her husband was in prison. Daughter Sally checked into Betty Ford on general principles. Older son Trey Major checked out of the United States for parts unknown, leaving a trail of warrants and bad debts. Our man, Linus Major IV, checked into Cedars-Sinai in Los Angeles for injuries suffered from a daredevil bet. He was attempting to drive his Yamaha 500cc motorcycle over three parked yellow cabs, and failed.

The Major family was in tatters—mentally, physically, and financially.

When Linus was twenty-eight, he was released from Cedars-Sinai. He had recovered from his injuries but was left with neither a functional family nor a lucrative trust fund. Using the last of his financial resources, ten thousand dollars in cash strapped in a money belt around his waist, Linus hitchhiked to New York to find employment.

His résumé wasn't impressive. What few openings there were didn't seem to require someone specializing in hot dog consumption, or jumping into gorges from some forgettable Colorado bridge with a rope tied around his legs, or trying to hurdle three taxicabs on a motorcycle and getting only halfway across.

As the weeks rolled by, young Linus found himself running out of cash and spirit. He didn't have any friends in Manhattan. Or in the entire state of New York, for that matter. And he was tired of staying in a flophouse in the East Village. Linus was just about busted. And then, just when our man was battling the onset of what might have become a catastrophic depression, he answered a Help Wanted ad for a position at the Museum of Natural History on Central Park West.

Linus Major IV, nervous as all get-out, waited for his job interview sitting on a wooden bench in a dreary hall by a museum vice president's office door. The interview went exceedingly well, helped a great deal by young Linus's long-held penchant for archaeology and dinosaurs.

Linus got the job.

Unfortunately, the position did not necessitate the use of Linus's meager archaeological background. He was to be a maintenance man. No matter, Linus was thrilled. The mere fact that he was working, and working *near* dinosaurs, was just fine by him.

The imam's prison time was up on Monday, February 11, 2005. He would be paroled two days shy of his forty-eighth birthday. On the morning Jamal was paroled, he took a train from Ossining, New York, to Manhattan. He arrived at Grand Central Station on Forty-second Street at noon. He walked out the Lexington Avenue side of the station and walked north until he saw Bloomingdale's Department Store. The store's flag was snapping in a cold, strong breeze. Next to it were the flags of the United States, Israel, Germany, Italy, and New York State. The imam wondered why the Israeli flag was flying up there with its big Jew star for everyone to see.

That bothered him.

Across from Bloomingdale's, on the southwest corner of Fifty-ninth Street and Lexington Avenue, was a crummy redbrick building, squashed between two tall modern office towers. The old building's door and ancient window frames needed sanding and paint. The dilapidated structure housed a branch of the state's Probation Department. Rasheed Jamal pulled off one of his old work gloves with his teeth (he had been wearing the same pair when he was arrested) and took a crumpled piece of paper from his pants pocket. It had "140 East 59th Street" written on it. It was the address of the dilapidated building. The imam opened the building's old door and walked in. He took the rickety stairs one flight up to the probation officer's floor. There was only one door on the first landing. Printed on its dirty window was:

BRANCH OFFICE
STATE OF NEW YORK
CORRECTIONS DEPARTMENT
Lester Bodkin — Probation Officer

The imam pushed open the door and stepped into a small waiting room. The door to the main office was opened a crack. A voice from behind the door ordered the imam to "get the hell in here."

Lester Bodkin's office smelled like a dirty clothes hamper.

The imam's PO was an obviously out-of-shape, bald, pudgy, prissy-looking man named Lester Bodkin, aka Bodkin the Turd. Bodkin was half the size of Rasheed Jamal, maybe less than half, and had a drinker's red, puffy face. The probation officer's protruding potbelly hung over his belt and strained the buttons of his shirt. This merciless little man wore rimless eyeglasses and a bow tie. Bodkin resembled a moon-faced Himmler. His three-day-old shirt was stained from some past meal. Bodkin had very short legs. He leaned on the front tips of his shoes when he sat up straight in his desk chair but wouldn't lower the chair. That would force him to look up to most of his ex-cons.

All parole officers are generally assholes, but this mean little despot was one of the worst. He was a psychotic stickler for details and rules. Bodkin sent more paroled cons back to prison than any other PO in New York State.

Bodkin said, "Sit down." It was an order, not a request.

The imam sat down.

None of Rasheed Jamal's old clothes fit him anymore. He was too muscular. The neck of his shirt was choking him. When he sat down, the waist of his pants was so tight Jamal could hardly breathe. Jamal tried to make himself comfortable in the hard wooden chair. The chair didn't even have arms. None of that helped the imam's increasingly foul mood.

The PO's fidgety hands squared a pile of papers on his desk over and over again. Eventually he looked up and said, "Steven Beastie, also known as Cleveland Steve Beastie from Chicago, right?"

"I prefer to be addressed as Imam Rasheed Jamal now."

"Oh, ya would, would ya? Now ain't that sweet." Bodkin squared the same pile of papers again and said, "By the way, you're one black dude, you know that?"

"You got a problem with that?"

"Anyone in this room with problems got to be you," said a pissed-off Bodkin, jabbing his finger at Jamal. The PO had taken immediate umbrage at the parolee's tone of voice and had a fierce dislike for the big nigger. Bodkin smiled a venomous smile at Jamal, then turned his squinty eyes behind his rimless glasses to the papers in front of him. It was the pile he was continually squaring. Bodkin was searching for something. "Where is it? Ah, here it is. Beastie. Steven Beastie, right?"

"I prefer—"

"Why is it all you niggers come outta prison immediately got to change your name to Muhammad this or Allah that? Huh? Anyway, *Beastie,* as I said, if anyone in this office has a problem, it's you, my friend."

I ain't your motherfuckin' friend, the imam almost said.

"Let me explain the rules to you, *friend,*" said Lester Bodkin, proficient in the most perverse ways to infuriate any living creature. His instincts seemed to be working especially well on the con sitting in front of him. The probation officer leaned back in his chair so he could place his shoes up on his desk and into the face of the imam. The chair squeaked when he did this. The soles of the PO's shoes were filthy.

"Let me be the first to inform you, *Beastie,* of what you can and cannot do. We'll go down the list one at a time. I'll tell you this. There ain't much you *can* do." Bodkin giggled. His giggle was high-pitched, like a girl's giggle. Bodkin continued. "You can't own a firearm or any other dangerous device. Let's see, are you a convicted drug felon?"

Bodkin pushed forward in his squeaking chair so that he was sitting up straight. He examined Beastie's sheet again and saw that the con wasn't a druggie and didn't have to submit to regular drug testing. Bodkin pushed his chair back, put his feet up again, clasped his fat fingers together over his fat potbelly, and said, "Don't make me repeat myself, Beastie. I asked you a question. You have any drug convictions?"

"Paper there says I don't, right?"

"I didn't ask the paper, I asked you. We're not getting off to a good start here, are we, Beastie? I ask the questions, you don't. You give the answers, I don't. Got that?"

"Yes, I understand," answered Jamal.

"Good," said Lester Bodkin. "Okay, where was I? Oh, yeah. You can't use any drugs of any kind. Let's see, you can't leave the state of New York without my permission. You will notify me of any change of address immediately if not sooner. You will *always* keep me informed as to your whereabouts. You will notify me immediately of any arrests *including* traffic tickets. You understand so far, Beastie?"

"Yes."

"Ever been married, Beastie?"

"No."

"I can understand that. What woman would want a piece of shit like you?"

"None so far," replied the smiling imam.

Lester Bodkin chewed on that answer for a moment to see if he could detect any wise-guy attitude in it, including Beastie's shit-eating grin. Bodkin decided there wasn't any wise-guy attitude in what the coal-black son of a bitch jiggy had just said and that maybe he shouldn't push this big buck too far. The guy could kill him faster than you could say jack shit. He'd known it to happen too. The man was one big nigger.

"You need a job and fast," said Bodkin to the imam. "You keep me abreast of all your job interviews. I'll expect you to be employed within two weeks. If you're not, I'll have to decide whether or not to send you back. Understand that? And finally," he said, "you have to tell me the truth at all times. If I catch you lyin' to me you'll go back to the can faster than you can say Jackie Robinson. All you niggers know who Jackie Robinson was, don't you?" said a smirking Lester Bodkin.

"Yes, I know who Jackie Robinson was," answered Jamal Rasheed.

"Oh, my God!" Vera Bundle shrieked again.

"What on earth is the matter?" asked the man at the table across the aisle from Vera, sitting up with a jolt. "You're white as a ghost."

"My wallet's gone! It's not in my pocketbook. It's gone! My wallet's *gone*!" Vera was on the verge of tears.

"Are you sure?" asked the man, moving to Vera's table. He pulled out the the chair opposite Vera and sat down. "Dump everything out of your pocketbook onto the table here." The man moved her empty daiquiri glass to the side, along with the small silver stand holding a card that explained the cover charge and minimum. "Make absolutely sure."

As though in a trance, Vera obeyed the man. She took her purse from her lap and emptied all its belongings onto the table. "See," she said, "it's not there." Tears began sliding down Vera Bundle's cheeks. This was a catastrophe. All of Vera's identification was in that wallet: Her metro bus card. Her Sears & Roebuck charge card. Her library card. A blank check. Her American Express card, which she intended to charge most of the expenses of this trip to, and receipts not only from today but from three days prior to her leaving. There were also some supermarket food stamps and coupons and even her lottery ticket, which she probably hadn't won. But you never know. Maybe she had won a small prize. Most important, there were three hundred dollars in hard-saved cash in her wallet. "Oh, Lord," she moaned aloud, "what am I to do?"

The man sitting across from Vera said, "Try and be calm. Think. Where could you have left it? Where were you before you came here?"

"I wasn't anywhere," she answered, wiping tears away with one hand, putting her possessions back into her purse with the other. "I came straight to this place from my hotel."

"*That's it!* That's where you left your wallet. In your hotel room," said the man with as much certainty and cheer as he could muster.

"I know I didn't leave it in the room. I remember checking my pocketbook to make sure my wallet was in it before I left the hotel. Oh dear, oh dear, oh dear," wailed Vera Bundle.

"Are you a tourist?" asked the man.

"Yes. I'm from Steubenville. Steubenville's in Ohio."

"Yes, I know."

"I just got here this afternoon."

"I see." The man thought for a moment and said, "Where is your hotel?"

"It's the Baldwin. It's on Thirty-third Street and Eighth Avenue."

"That's not the best neighborhood. Did you walk uptown from there?"

"Yes."

"Do you remember being bumped or jarred on your way here?"

"Bumped or jarred?"

"I'm only asking because I had my wallet picked out of my pocket not too long ago after I was bumped on the street. Were you bumped coming up here tonight?"

"Yes," said Vera, "as a matter of fact I was. I do remember being bumped. I was bumped by a mean boy while I waited for a traffic light to change. He almost knocked me down."

"It's an old trick of pickpockets. They'll distract you by bumping into you and at the same time they'll open your purse and take out your wallet, or if you're a man, slip your wallet out of your pants pocket. Sometimes they carry an overcoat over one arm and they'll slide whatever they take out of your purse into the hand hidden under the overcoat, or whatever it is they're carrying."

"Dry cleaning. The boy had been carrying dry cleaning," recalled Vera, and remembered her open purse when she met the other lad. The nice one.

"Sounds like you had your wallet lifted, poor thing," said the man.

Now Vera was sure her wallet was gone. Irrevocably gone. "My God," she wailed, "all my identification. My receipts from this trip. My . . ."

Vera Bundle sat against the back of her seat and wept.

The man patted the top of Vera's clasped hands but said nothing.

The waitress came over and spoke to Vera. "What happened, dearie?"

"Had her wallet stolen," said the man.

"Oh, my," said the waitress, frowning, obviously distressed, her chin resting in the palm of her right hand, her left hand propping up her right elbow.

"What am I going to do?" moaned Vera, rocking from side to side, putting her hands to the sides of her face. "I can't get back to my hotel. I can't pay for a cab. With all that snow out there, there isn't even a cab to pay for. I won't be able to pay my hotel bill. Oh, my God, what am I going to do?"

"Ma'am," said the waitress, "maybe I can ask if they have a room here for you."

"What'll I use for money?" snapped Vera, surprisingly cross. "Don't you understand? *I've had my wallet stolen!"*

The waitress shrugged. "Only trying to help," she said, and walked away.

"May I ask your name?" said the man.

"Vera Bundle," she answered, distracted, sorry she yelled at the waitress.

The man withdrew a black alligator billfold from the inside pocket of his suit coat. He slid out some money and handed the bills to Vera. "Please, Vera, take this."

Thunderstruck, Vera said, "I can't . . . *you* can't . . . you can't do this. I can't take your money. I can't. I don't even know who you are or where you live. I wouldn't be able to . . . to pay you back."

As Vera spoke, she looked at the money in her hand. It was all hundred-dollar bills! Six of them! The man had given her six hundred dollars!

"If you need more, tell me," said the man, writing his name and address with a gold ballpoint Cross pen on a piece of paper he had taken from a matching black alligator pocket secretary. "You'll pay me back. I'm not worried. Here's my address."

"Oh dear," was all Vera could say. She read the man's name

engraved at the top of the piece of paper. JOHN J. SUGHRUE. She also noticed that the kind man lived in a town called Greenwich, in Connecticut.

"Listen," said the man named Sughrue, "it looks like it's going to be a disappointing night for me too, so the least I can do to make *me* feel better is make *you* feel better."

"What a sweet thing to say," said Vera. "Why is it going to be a disappointing night for you?"

"Oh, it's a long story, Vera. Let's let it go at that. Anyway, you take this money. You have my name and address on the paper I gave you. Repay me whenever you can. You can go to your hotel now and I'll go to mine." Sughrue paid both their checks and the two stood. The man named Sughrue helped Vera into her coat and put on his. The two wrapped themselves in their scarves, pushed down their hats, and walked out of the bar and onto the pavement outside. Vera was still bitterly disappointed at the loss of her wallet. All that cash she had squirreled away for months and months was now gone forever. On the other hand, she was thrilled with her new attachment to the handsome young man named John J. Sughrue.

The weather outside was frightful. The storm had become much worse. It was now an honest-to-God blizzard, one with enough force to surprise Sughrue, a hardened New Yorker. There wasn't a vehicle or a human being anywhere to be seen on the street or pavement. Just Vera Bundle and John J. Sughrue under the Essex House Hotel marquee.

Rasheed Jamal left Probation Officer Lester Bodkin's office, took the flight of stairs down to the street, and stepped out into the Manhattan sunshine.

I got things to do, he told himself.

There were crowds of people walking back and forth on Fifty-ninth Street and a lot of traffic on the street. There was construction too, guys working under tents in the middle of the street. Con Edison was the name of the company on the workmen's truck. From where the imam was standing, if you walked a straight line across the street, you ran smack into a branch of the Chase bank. And not far away from the bank was a subway entrance.

The imam walked that straight line from the door of the PO's building, across the street, and into the Chase bank. He robbed it just as he was taught to do by his prison associates.

No gun.

Just nerves.

When Jamal arrived at the teller's window, he pulled a note out of his jacket pocket he had printed in big black letters before he left jail. It read:

> *I'M DESPERATE.*
> *I've got nine sticks of dynamite*
> *strapped around my waist. I will*
> *kill you AND me unless you hand*
> *over all the cash you have.*

The terrified bank teller passed wrapped packages of money to Jamal. He stuffed the money into a large leather carry-all. It was the same carry-all he had used when he was arrested for manslaughter ten years ago.

Jamal literally ran to the subway entrance on the corner not fifty feet away from the bank. He stepped onto the first train out of the Fifty-ninth Street station and left the vicinity. The imam surfaced in Forest Hills on Continental Avenue. He took a taxi to the nearest automobile showroom and bought the cheapest used car he could find with his stolen money. The sleazy used car salesman said nothing about the suspicious cash that came out of the cheap old carry-all.

The imam drove back into the city and parked across the street from the dilapidated brick building where his parole officer worked. He walked up the rickety stairs and stepped into the man's office. He turned the key in the back of the front door and locked it. Then Jamal walked to the PO's door and pushed it open. Lester Bodkin had his feet up on the radiator. He was looking out the window, cleaning his fingernails with a toothpick, listening to news on WINS radio. His back was to the imam.

When Bodkin heard footsteps on his squeaking office floor, he whirled around and faced Rasheed Jamal. The sight of the big ex-con made Bodkin sit bolt upright, a terrified expression on his face.

"You ever hear of knockin'?" he asked in a high, squeaky voice filled with fear. "Whattaya want?"

Rasheed Jamal said nothing. He just walked toward the probation officer.

"Forget to tell me somethin'?" asked Lester Bodkin, his voice breaking. "Is that it?"

As Bodkin spoke to Jamal, he tried to slowly slide open his desk drawer and find his revolver. Jamal, without saying a word, walked up to the desk and slammed the drawer shut on Bodkin's hand, making the PO scream. Jamal took the gun out of the drawer and jammed it in the small of his back under his windbreaker. Then he walked around Bodkin's old wooden desk chair and grabbed his probation officer's neck with his big gloved hands from behind and began choking the life out of him. Bodkin, still seated, his back to Jamal, took hold of the imam's wrists with both hands but couldn't budge them. Bodkin kicked his feet furiously, smacking the toes of his dirty brown leather shoes against the underside of the desk. He kicked so hard he smashed the wooden drawer to pieces. One of his shoes came off in the melee and lay on its side under the desk. The imam continued to squeeze Bodkin's neck. Bodkin made rasping, gurgling sounds. His eyes bulged out of their sockets. Drool dribbled out of his mouth. Then Bodkin's fingers loosened on the imam's hands, his arms fell to his sides, and he stopped making gurgling sounds. The imam kept tightening his fingers around the victim's neck until he was absolutely certain Bodkin the Turd was dead.

When Rasheed Jamal finished killing Lester Bodkin, he looked through Bodkin's desk until he found the file folder with his name on it. Jamal stuffed the folder into his carry-all.

The imam Rasheed Jamal left the dead parole officer's office, locked his front door with the door key, walked down the stairs, and crossed the street to his parked car. There was a traffic ticket under his windshield wiper. The imam removed the ticket, opened the door of his car, threw the ticket onto the passenger seat, and drove to Tulsa, Oklahoma, robbing banks as he went. On the way to Tulsa, Jamal tossed Bodkin's office key out his car window. In a motel room near Vinita, Oklahoma, he burned the traffic ticket.

With the money from the banks he robbed, Rasheed Jamal purchased a small, vacant, broken-down old church on the outskirts of Tulsa. That's where Jamal began his career as a minister of the Muslim faith. Sunday services were minuscule to start but slowly built in size and exuberance. The money Imam Jamal collected during those services helped finance a growing drug trade in the cities close to Tulsa, like Broken Arrow, Stillwater, Bartlesville, Ponca City, Guthrie, and Shawnee. The imam ventured as far southeast as Pocola, Poteau, and Fanshawe.

Soon Jamal moved to a bigger, more impressive church in Tulsa. Though he never touched the stuff, his drug business grew to cartel proportions. But the good imam wasn't satisfied with the success he nurtured in the great Southwest.

He wanted more. So he moved again, this time to Miami Beach, Florida, a thriving drug market and the part of the United States with the largest-growing Muslim population.

Rasheed Jamal became a zillionaire.

"Yes," said the cripple, "my lawyers tried valiantly to stop me from doing *The Death Game* pilot. Of course they tried to stop me. But I ignored them."

"I find that hard to believe. I find it incomprehensible that none of your lawyers prohibited you from committing murder, that they weren't insistent. Didn't lay their jobs on the line if they had to."

"Well, for one thing, all the contestants on my pilot were, as I explained before, terminally ill. They couldn't have cared less if they died. In fact, most of them preferred it. If I'm not mistaken, *all* of them would have had someone help them take their own lives if they could, but they couldn't. In those days assisted suicide wasn't legal. Also the families, either secretly or not so secretly, would have preferred their poor family member to pass on. The sooner the better. Then they'd all get some relief from their personal agonies and financial stress. Though they would never admit it, I guarantee you the family members wanted a respite from those burdens. I made that happen for one of those poor souls," said the cripple. "I was actually doing the contestant and his family a favor. And as far as my lawyers putting their jobs on the line was concerned, they wouldn't have given that idea any thought at all. They were all being paid too much money to put their jobs on the line."

"So what happened? How did you get away with never being arrested for doing what you did?"

"How did I get away with it? I never showed *The Death Game* to anyone. I buried the show. That's how I got away with it."

"What about a studio audience?"

"I didn't have a studio audience. I used laugh and applause tracks."

"How did you do financially?"

"Financially? Financially the project obviously sent me directly to the poorhouse without stopping at Go. I've never recovered financially. Not even mentally, for that matter. Not really. I think the entire experience did something to my head, made me become physically sick."

"You mean *committing murder* did something to your head? I certainly should think—"

"No. *Going broke* did something to my head. *That's* what did something to my head."

"You committed the perfect crime," said the producer, somewhat impressed.

"Yes, I committed the perfect crime. So what?"

There was silence in the shabby room.

"You will be the first outsider to see the videotape," said the cripple.

"You trust me?" asked the producer, the makings of a sneer on his face.

"Not as far as I can throw you," answered the cripple, "but what are my options?"

"Someone else," suggested the producer.

"No one else," said the cripple. "I'm stuck with you because you'll make it happen."

"I still can't believe none of your lawyers stopped you from committing murder."

"Well, believe it. When I was the game show king of television, nobody, I mean nobody, prohibited me from doing anything I wanted to do. I wouldn't let them. I had an ego bigger than . . . bigger than yours!" The cripple snickered to himself for a moment. Which led to a coughing attack. And that to multiple instances of spitting into the cripple's dirty handkerchief. When the cripple was finally in control of himself again, he looked white faced and wretched.

"Well, get on with it," ordered the producer. He had just about enough of the cripple, his coughing and spitting and malodorous room. He wanted out of there, and the sooner the better.

"I sense you want to leave," said the cripple.

"I am intrigued, I must say, and—"

"Would you rather go . . . or stay . . . and see a videotape of *The Death Game*?"

In the year 2010, Retta Mae Wagons was seventeen, black, and a whore. And extremely pretty. She was tall and slim with great tits and an equally splendid ass. Sometimes she wore her hair in cornrows and sometimes she didn't. When she didn't, the girl's brown hair was unnaturally soft. She had a wonderful smile, big white teeth, big brown eyes, and eyelashes that went on for miles. She was a beauty.

Retta Mae had been a hooker for almost a year. She knew all the tricks of the trade and was good at what she did. She knew she was good too. The johns considered her one of the best. Retta Mae Wagons got top dollar on the Upper East Side, which was where her pimp, Dannyboy Marley, placed her. Another thing Retta Mae Wagons was, was smart. If she'd gone to college, she could've been anything she wanted to be and been good at it.

The girl knew all those things.

The year before Retta Mae Wagons became a whore, she lived with her mother and eleven brothers and sisters in a project at Ninety-third Street off York Avenue in Manhattan. As a child she loved school and got straight A's. She even skipped the ninth grade.

"It's a rotten shame this child cannot apply for college," Retta Mae's high school principal told her mother. "It's just a dirty rotten shame. Your daughter's brilliant. And she *loves* to study."

"What would I use for money to send the girl to college?" said Retta Mae's distressed mother.

"There are ways to do it," said the principal.

"Not when you're as poor as us and black as us," said Retta Mae's mother. "Besides, I need Retta Mae to go out an' get herself a job. We got a lot of mouths to feed in our family."

The principal said, "It just breaks my heart."

"It breaks my heart too," was all Mrs. Wagons could reply.

And it did. Literally. The next morning Retta Mae Wagons's mother dropped dead where she worked, behind her counter in a Woolworth's Five & Ten Cent Store on 125th Street and Third Avenue. During the autopsy at Bellevue Hospital, the doctors found nothing wrong with the woman. It's hard to diagnose a broken heart.

After her mother's death, a mean and embittered Retta Mae Wagons dropped out of school and joined an angry gang of toughs. The gang roamed the Lower East Side mugging tourists and yuppies. Retta Mae was particularly rough on those they robbed, pistol-whipping and punching people unnecessarily. More than once she was pulled off a victim by one of the gang.

"Why'd you do that? Why'd you pull her off that woman?" asked a gangbanger who went by the initials BMF.

"She woulda kilt her," explained another one called Big Stick. "That Retta Mae got a lotta mad in her."

"So? Next time, let her do what she wants to do," said BMF, whose initials stood for Bad Mother Fucker. "If the nigger wants to kill, let her."

The gang did well and generally played it smart until the night BMF, high on meth and some other shit, murdered a tourist from Germany. The hood shot the lady three times in her face. The crime made the front pages of all the New York papers. Retta Mae Wagons and the three thugs she hung with were rounded up within hours and booked. The four had their pictures in the *New York Post,* one underneath the other. It was shortly after her *Post* newspaper picture that good things started to happen for Retta Mae Wagons.

Retta Mae could credit her lucky break to the pimp named Dannyboy Marley, a sporty Jamaican with a penchant for white-on-white dress shirts and black-and-white wingtip shoes. He saw Retta Mae's picture in the newspaper and fell head over heels in love. In Dannyboy's own words, "I see dat newspaper picture of Retta Mae Wagons an' I say to myself dat's de prettiest woman I ever see in my life. I wonder if dat woman's as pretty as dat picture."

Dannyboy Marley decided he'd have to see for himself if Retta Mae Wagons was as beautiful and sexy as he imagined. And how old she *really* looked. That was important too. The newspaper didn't mention her age. Only that she was a minor.

Dannyboy Marley followed the course of the gang's trial in the tabloids. Bad Mother Fucker was sent away for life. Big Stick and the other eighteen-year-old member of the gang, Oney Davis, went to jail for a couple of years. Seventeen-year-old Retta Mae Wagons was released for lack of evidence, no prior record, and being a minor.

Dannyboy Marley was lingering on the courthouse steps when Retta Mae Wagons walked into the sunshine. When their eyes met, Dannyboy's heart skipped four or five beats and did a flip-flop or two.

"What are you looking at, nigger?" asked Retta Mae.

"I'm lookin' at you," said Dannyboy, dressed to the teeth in his best black pin-striped suit, white-on-white silk shirt, black tie, and brand-new shiny black-and-white wingtip shoes. He wanted to look good for this Retta Mae girl. "I tink dat you're de prettiest girl I ever seen."

"I ever saw or I've ever seen. Speak the King's English, nigger," snapped Retta Mae.

Dapper Dannyboy Marley was a goner. "My heart flew de coop back when Retta Mae asked me what was I lookin' at," he would tell his friends. "And den when she told me to speak de King's Engleesh, well, man, dat did it! *Dat* was de cherry on de sundae."

Dannyboy Marley's goose was cooked!

In a matter of weeks, Retta Mae Wagons was ensconced in a relatively luxurious one-bedroom apartment on a corner of Madison and Ninety-first Street, opposite the Jackson Hole Restaurant. They made the best pancakes in New York City at the Jackson Hole Restaurant.

As part of her new job, Retta Mae was told to commit to memory a set of rules laid down by her new pimp, Dannyboy Marley. "In de first place," he said, "you gonna meet de john down in de lobby. You never meet him at de apartment's front door. I'm gonna give de john a card wit a code word on it dat only you and me knows."

"You and I *know*. Like what kind of code word?"

"Like New York Mets or Count Basie or somethin', unnerstan'?"

"Okay."

There were other rules and regulations Dannyboy Marley stated. Stuff about condoms, Retta Mae's personal hygiene requirements, and making the john show his dick. "'Cause if he don't want to, den he be vice or somethin' like dat, unnerstan'? An' remember dat I'll be checkin' up on you to see if you be stickin' by de rules, unnerstan'?"

"I understand. And can't you say *un-der-stand* and not unnerstan'? You really going to check on me, Dannyboy?"

"You can bet on it," he answered. "I be checkin' johns to see if you be stickin' to de rules. If you're makin' 'em show dey dicks and cleanin' yourself an' shit like dat. If you don't be stickin' to de rules, I fire you. I tink it break my heart to do dat, Retta Mae, but I will do dat. Bidness is bidness, Retta Mae. If dere's one ting dat's more important to me over affairs a de heart, it's affairs a de bidness."

Retta Mae Wagons was an instant hit.

The johns loved her. She was the most requested girl in Dannyboy Marley's stable. This pleased the pimp and also made him insanely jealous. A strange combination if ever there was one.

When Retta Mae Wagons wasn't hooking, she was reading.

Retta Mae was a voracious reader. The employees of the New York Society Library on Seventy-ninth Street between Madison and Park avenues couldn't recall a member quite like Retta Mae Wagons. The young girl read *everything*. And quickly. At least she said she did, and the librarians believed her. All the employees of the New York Society Library played games guessing what Retta Mae Wagons did for a living because she was so pretty and so eager to learn.

They never came close.

Dannyboy Marley doubled then tripled Retta Mae's fee. Nineteen-year-old Retta Mae Wagons was pulling down an average of ten thousand dollars a week. Half of that was hers, more money than she ever dreamed she'd earn. Some of the money went to helping her brothers and sisters. The rest she put in a new savings account she started to help poor black kids from her old neighborhood go to college. There wasn't enough money to help both her family and bright but disadvantaged high school kids, not yet, but that was her goal. To set up the Retta Mae Wagons Scholarship Fund for Underprivileged Kids. Give some smart dirt-poor teenagers like she used to be the chance she never had to go to college. She was getting there. Retta Mae was taking baby steps, but she was getting there.

And then the thing happened that all pimps and some whores dread the most. The event that for some strange, unexplained reason often screwed up plans, destroyed wishes, occasionally lives. Frequently forever. Young, beautiful, bright Retta Mae Wagons made the mistake of falling in love with a john.

His name was Rasheed Jamal.

In the beginning of the year 2011, Linus Major was a full-fledged member of the janitorial staff at New York City's Museum of Natural History. He felt quite good about that. He looked rather spiffy too, dressed as he was in his blue long-sleeved shirt with the white word MAINTENANCE above his left pocket and the white L. MAJOR above his right pocket. He wore museum-issued blue work pants and was given a stick broom, which he happily pushed up and down the museum's long marble corridors. He also emptied the garbage receptacles into large green Hefty bags.

Linus loved his job.

When he wasn't sweeping he was studying the dinosaur exhibits one after the other, memorizing all the pertinent facts. And the exhibits were endlessly fascinating, or so it seemed. After all, New York City's Museum of Natural History was one of the finest dinosaur museums in the whole world. Linus spent whatever spare time he could muster studying the *Tyrannosaurus rex*—aka the "Tyrant King"—and the huge *Hypselosaurus priscus,* the tallest and longest dinosaur ever. He never tired of walking through the museum's corridors mesmerized by the agile, bipedal hunters, the *Herrerasaurus* and the *Eoraptor* found in Argentina and the flying *Peteinosaurus,* the reptile with the elongated fourth finger. What a place to study a subject that interested you, he joyfully reflected over and over again.

Linus also loved the constant flow of small children running lawless and rampant through the museum's halls, screaming excitedly as they dashed about in their little jeans and colorful sweatshirts, tripping over strollers occupied by their wee sisters and brothers. Linus loved the kids and the kids loved him. When they saw Linus they would run to him and give him hugs around his legs.

"It's funny to be surrounded by so much death and necrobiosis in the museum, yet there's so much life," Linus told his new friend, young Jimmy Joel Jenks, the latest addition to the museum's janitorial staff.

"Necro what?" asked Jimmy Joel.

"Necrobiosis. The degeneration of body cells, leaving you with a skeleton or a reconstructed body," explained Linus.

"Gotcha," replied Jimmy Joel pleasantly.

Linus thought Jimmy Joel Jenks was a really nice guy, though a tad dense.

"And," Linus remarked to old-time maintenance man Artie Flowers, "these amazing animals, reptiles, whatever you want to call them, are just that—*amazing*!"

"You get used to them, Linus," replied Artie, uninterested in much of what life had to offer except beer and the New York Mets baseball team.

Slowly but surely Linus Major became a happy man.

Or putting it another way, a happier man.

Or putting it still another way, about as happy a man as he could ever remember being.

"And we actually get paid to do this," Linus said to Artie and Jimmy Joel one morning in the locker room when they were all getting dressed for work. "Who said, 'The best job in the world is the job you can't believe you're getting paid to do'?"

"Somebody said it," remarked Jimmy Joel Jenks, attempting to appear learned.

"Work is work," said Artie Flowers. "I'd rather be home with a beer watchin' the Mets."

"Hey," said the cripple to the producer, remembering an important point, "CNN's already televised an execution! The one in Texas where they gave a black guy a lethal injection. Had the poor bastard wiggling in pain right there on coast-to-coast TV. Damn if it wasn't downright gripping the way the guy twisted and turned, trying to scream but for some reason not able to. Didn't matter that he couldn't scream. The wiggling and twisting made for great drama. That guy was being executed right in your living room. While you ate your veal cutlet on your nice coffee table. Bet that dude's screaming and wiggling stopped plenty of forks in midair around the country. Did you see it? No? I'll bet you were the only one who didn't. Did you happen to read about the size of the television audience? It was huge! And what did it cost CNN? Nothing. Not a damn cent. Just the cost of plugging a TV camera into an outlet at the prison. And one other thing. Can you imagine how much CNN jacked up the price of their minute spots surrounding the electrocution? They must have made a fortune on that event. I never saw so many commercials on CNN before, did you? It was awesome, wasn't it? Oh, that's right, you missed it."

The producer humphed and said, "Didn't you just promise to show me *The Death Game*?"

"That electrocution in Texas," said the cripple, ignoring the producer's question, "was reality television at its best. At its very best. And at its timeliest. You know the old game show axiom: the biggest audience for the least amount of money. The execution in Texas hit that nail right on the head. Let me tell you, someone's going to think of my idea sooner or later. Especially now that CNN executed a guy on coast-to-coast TV. I'll bet you know that too, don't you? If you didn't, you do now."

The producer said, "*The Death Game*. I want to see the vi—"

"Look," said the cripple, "our dear new president declared euthanasia legal. Said we owned our bodies, that we could do whatever we wanted with them. Not only was the president right but he also opened the floodgates for shows like mine. It's just a shame the guy wasn't elected twenty-five years ago." The cripple sighed. "Oh, well. Like I said, someone's going to think of this idea any day now. Tell you the truth, I'm surprised you haven't thought of it yourself. Okay, so what's the bottom line?" asked the cripple. "The bottom line is today *The Death Game*'s a more brilliant idea than ever before," answered the cripple. "As I see it, since the late nineties, three things have changed in the game show business. At least in my opinion three things have changed. The first change is game and reality programs on network and cable television have gotten more and more expensive. The second change is the networks are running out of ideas. All their programs are starting to look the same. The third change is game shows have become meaner. Almost hateful."

The producer said, "Killing someone on coast-to-coast TV isn't hateful?"

"It's quite hateful," said the cripple. "*The Death Game* will be the most expensive, most unusual, most hateful program *ever*!"

Silence filled the shabby room.

The old man's mind had wandered. It tended to do that. The cripple shook his head and thought to himself: Old age. In a blink of an eye I'm going to be dead. Time is going by so fast I don't even get time to enjoy it. Still, there must be one redeeming factor about getting old. Something better than always thinking about being dead. But what is it?

"When can I see the videotape?" asked the producer.

"There isn't one," mumbled the old cripple.

"There isn't one?!"

"There isn't one redeeming factor about getting old," replied the cripple calmly.

Jesus Christ, what an idiot! thought the producer.

"How did you lose all your money?" he asked.

"What's so funny?"

"I didn't say anything was funny," said the producer.

"Then what *did* you say?"

"I said how did you lose all your money?"

The cripple sighed. "That's another thing. My hearing. It's getting wor—"

"How. Did. You. Lose. All. Your. Money?" asked the enraged producer.

"One of the contestants did me in. Her name was Caroline Sedaka. She was dying of ALS, Lou Gehrig's disease. She had three or four years to live. Caroline Sedaka played in the championship round against Jonathan Denko, a quadriplegic. Sedaka gave the correct answer to a really tough question. Denko missed it. That set up Sedaka for the final question, the one worth the money or the coffin. That's when disaster struck."

"What do you mean?"

"She got the final question right! Can you believe that!? She got it *right*! And it was a tough question. I was counting on her missing the question. But that bitch answered it, and by answering the big question correctly, she fucking bankrupted me."

"Bankrupted you? How did she bankrupt you?"

"I had to pay her off, and I did. She said her family would be well-off now. She said that's why she agreed to do the show. That was her gamble. Makes sense, I guess. Anyway, seven million dollars is what I paid her. Seven damn million dollars! The production costs were a little higher than I estimated, so I sold my house, my cars, and my Patek Philippe wristwatch collection. They were all auctioned off at Sotheby's. I loved those watches. Hated selling the watches most of all. Didn't I tell you all this before? I forget. If I did tell you—"

"Go on."

"If I didn't pay Sedaka the seven million, she was going straight to a telephone and call her lawyer. And the newspapers. She had me dead to rights. If she did what she threatened to do, *then* I would have gone to jail. You see, I had signed papers agreeing to pay the winning contestant seven million dollars. How else would I get someone to risk their life on a TV pilot? I found out the hard way that even terminals want to get paid a lot of money to risk their lives. They prefer cash over the casket. True, most terminals want to die, but—"

"You keep repeating and repeating yourself," snapped the producer. "Get to the damn point. How did you lose your money?"

"I had no idea Caroline Sedaka was going to go for the money. I made a big mistake and paid for it."

"*What* big mistake?"

"Not making the last question, the final question, the one worth all the money, unanswerable. I should have used the question about the Great Wall of China. There isn't any correct answer to the Great Wall of China question. Not using that question was my big mistake. No, more like my *tragic* mistake."

The cripple started coughing again. His face turned crimson. He pressed his chest with his fists. He wanted to stop coughing in the worst way.

And finally he did.

"Anyway," he said, "we paid Caroline Sedaka her seven million dollars and then asked her, as a favor to me, would she agree to do the next-to-last question again—and miss it this time—so we could tape the execution we needed to have on our pilot. She agreed. She had her money, what the hell did she care? And that's what we did."

The old cripple smiled as he relived the exciting execution. He was preparing enthusiastically to describe the gory details but was quickly deflated when the producer said, "How did you provide for the executed contestant's family?"

"How did I provide? I promised the contestants, whoever was executed, I would take care of all of his or her beneficiaries."

"*How*? How would you take care of them?"

"Financially. I took care of them financially. It wasn't that expen—" The cripple started coughing. It was such a violent attack he had to sit down on the side of his bed.

The producer inhaled angrily.

He exhaled the same way.

The producer's mood didn't help the cripple's coughing attack. Under pressure to stop, the cripple only coughed more. His spasms were quite phlegmy, causing the producer to squinch up his face with scorn and disgust.

Eventually the cripple recovered his composure and continued. "As I was saying, it wasn't the biggest expense in the world, not like the grand prize for answering the big question. I would give the executed contestant's beneficiaries a flat twenty-five thousand dollars to be split up among them, something like that. Remember, the contestants were mostly elderly. None of them had a hell of a lot of money to start with or a lot of relatives still living."

"Go on. Finish your story."

"I went back to the studio to retape the correct ending, the ending where a contestant is executed. I had to. The pilot would have been a useless sales tool without an execution. I picked up with Denko and Sedaka in the championship round. Denko beat Sedaka, as planned. Our host asked Denko the big question, the one about the Wall of China. Denko didn't know the answer because, as I said, there isn't any. The host said he was sorry, that Denko would have to be executed. Denko wanted to die, maybe worse than any of the others. The guy had been paralyzed from the neck down since he was twenty-six. He was forty-nine back at the time of the pilot. Poor bastard had a diving accident. Dove off a cliff in Baja. Didn't know the tide was out as far as it was. Smashed into a rock, headfirst. Broke his neck. Everyone told him how lucky he was to be alive. Denko didn't think so. Anyway, Denko was thrilled when he realized he was going to be executed. He even looked it. I wasn't sure I liked his joyful expression. Not at that point in the show. I'm going to have to remember to tell the losers to look horrified when they hear they're going to be executed."

"If the contestants aren't, as you say, terminals, I don't think they will be too happy to be executed."

"Yes . . . well . . . maybe . . . maybe you're right." The cripple started coughing, but mercifully, for the producer's sake, it was only a short spasm. He wiped his mouth with his dirty handkerchief and continued. The cripple appeared to be very tired. "Okay, so Jonathan Denko missed the big question and we killed him. You know the rest. End of story."

"Wait a minute!" yelled the producer. "Hold on. Give me details. How did you kill the losing contestant, that Denko fellow? What did you do? I think you said you used poison. What kind of poison?"

"I used potassium cyanide in a glass of Madeira," answered the suddenly exhausted cripple. "I decided to offer the loser a choice of either sherry, port, or Madeira. Regarding the poison, I asked my doctor which was the quickest and best one to use on a human being. Of course my doctor didn't have a clue what I wanted to do with the poison. He thought I needed the information for a book I was writing. The doctor said potassium cyanide was one of the fastest-acting poisons known to science. I asked how long it would take before the person ingesting it died. The doctor said anywhere from three to fifteen minutes depending on the person's physical constitution. He said the poison was relatively painless and tasteless. I had them put the potassium cyanide in Jonathan Denko's glass of Madeira. I figured if his death took more than five minutes, I'd edit it down. We placed Denko in a hospital chair, the kind that you can adjust into various positions, so that we could make Denko as comfortable as possible. The poisoned Madeira was on a table by the chair's side. It smelled like bitter almonds. I couldn't get it out of my nose for weeks.

"We put a straw in the glass. Denko couldn't use his hands. He was a quadriplegic. Did I mention that? I think I did. My memory's getting worse right along with my hearing. Anyway, Denko sipped the Madeira through a bent straw. I had a video camera trained on Denko sitting in the hospital chair. Toward the end, Denko wiggled and winced quite a bit but never shouted or screamed in pain. The doctor did say the poison was painless. I think the poison could have been a little more painful. I think I would have liked it better if Denko did scream a little. He just died quietly. Too quietly for my taste. But his skin turned bluish. *That's* something to see on TV. I may change the poison when I do it again. Like I said, something more painful, though I must say, painful or not, Denko's death was a fascinating thing to watch."

"How long did it take?"

"From the first swallow? I'd say maybe . . . maybe six minutes. The length of time was fine. Six minutes is a long time on television, but it was worth it. I'll tell you this, it was absolutely hypnotizing to watch Denko die. He sat for a moment just smiling. Then you could see his face twitch ever so slightly. Then the twitching increased and Denko suddenly became quite spastic. You'll see it all on the video."

"For God's sake, when can I see the damn video?"

"How about now."

Sitting there beside the cripple about to watch *The Death Game* had the producer's heart racing and his palms sweaty. The producer found it hard to believe that a chance meeting on the street with this miserable piece of shit had progressed to this, to his actually watching the cripple's bizarre creation. He also couldn't get over the fact that he was so tense and nervous.

The show began with the usual hyperbole regarding what the viewers were about to see. "The game show to end all game shows," ranted the high-pitched, melodramatic voice of the show's announcer. Then the announcer introduced the four contestants as cheerfully as possible. The four were sitting behind a dated console with old-fashioned running lights that spelled out *The Death Game*. The ancient and sickly quartet of contestants, two men and two women, waved happily. One of the two men sat behind the console, stone-faced. The other, also behind the console but sitting in a wheelchair, winked at the camera.

The winker was Jonathan Denko.

The host was introduced. He appeared to be a clean-cut, wavy-haired blond named Dusty Rhodes. Rhodes fairly skipped out to center stage, bowing modestly to exuberant recorded applause. He spoke as if the television program was already on the air. He said, "Welcome to *The Death Game,* America's most watched television show." Overstatements, lies, and exaggerations drooled from the man's mouth. Eventually he explained the same rules the cripple had already outlined to the producer. Then Rhodes clapped his hands merrily and shouted, "Okay, let's get started."

The first round was won by the winker in the wheelchair, Jonathan Denko.

The second round by a woman named Caroline Sedaka.

Denko and Sedaka were asked the important elimination questions of the championship round.

Caroline Sedaka didn't know the answer to her question. Jonathan Denko knew the answer to his. Denko was declared the finalist! The audience sound track blared wild applause.

A black slot indicating a commercial came and went within ten seconds.

When the show returned to the TV screen, Denko was in a hospital chair at center stage. Host Dusty Rhodes said something cheerily stupid and out of place like, "This is the moment we've all been waiting for!" Rhodes proceeded to move the table with the glass of poisoned Madeira closer to Denko and placed the straw in his mouth. Denko sucked the contents out of the glass into his body through the straw. The program's host disappeared from view as the camera crawled closer and closer toward the face of Jonathan Denko.

Denko twitched and winced and . . .

III

Early one morning the executive vice president of expeditions . . .

Early one morning the executive vice president of expeditions was wandering the halls as he sometimes did before the Museum of Natural History opened to the public. The veep enjoyed the quiet prior to the hustle and bustle of his workday. While walking the halls he was somewhat startled to find another employee, a maintenance man, leaning on his broom and sipping a cup of Starbucks coffee, staring in wonder at the *Brontosaurus.*

Dr. Gregory Bukinberg, a man who himself had risen from the maintenance department to become one of the museum's leaders, watched with interest as the enthralled janitor moved from one exhibit to another. The last exhibit in the aisle, the huge *Deinocheirus* discovered in the sixties by members of a Polish-Mongolian-American expedition, seemed to fascinate the maintenance man the most.

"Amazing, those long arms, are they not?" remarked Dr. Bukinberg, walking up to the maintenance man.

Linus Major, his mind miles away, jumped with surprise, then quickly pulled himself to attention. Linus recognized Dr. Bukinberg immediately and was terribly distraught to be caught with a cup of coffee in his hand. It was against museum rules to have food of any kind in the museum. Especially while on the job. He'd intended to throw the coffee away a few minutes ago, long before the museum opened, but his interest in the *Deinocheirus* had made him lose track of time.

"We can both get rid of our cups when we finish our coffee," said the noted archaeologist in a quiet, clear voice, producing his cup from behind his back with a smile.

It was instant affection, at least as far as Linus was concerned.

Both men returned their attention to the extremely large arms of the *Deinocheirus.*

"These were the only bones found on that Polish-Mongolian expedition," explained Dr. Bukinberg, a long, narrow man in a blue and white seersucker suit complete with matching vest and an extra-large green foulard bow tie with red polka dots wrapped around his skinny neck. Bukinberg was in the process of going bald. What hair he had was cut close to the sides of his head. Dr. Bukinberg wore rimless octagonal spectacles, which he used for reading. When he wasn't reading, the glasses were held around his neck by a thin chain. The glasses rested on his chest that morning.

"I know they were the only bones found, sir," said Linus Major. "I read a book on that expedition."

"I wrote that book."

"My gosh!"

"I was on the expedition. It was my first."

"First book?" asked Linus.

"No. First expedition."

"What an honor!"

"Yes, it was."

"I guess you all must have been flabbergasted by your team's discovery. I can only imagine how high the *Deinocheirus* stood if its front two arms were that large, sir," said Linus Major, standing rigid, his broom handle by his side.

Dr. Bukinberg was tempted to say, "At ease, soldier," but didn't. The maintenance man might think his superior was making fun of him. Instead Dr. Bukinberg said, "I think those mammals stood thirty-five to fifty feet high. Quite large."

"Quite," agreed Linus.

"Major, is it?" asked Dr. Bukinberg, his eyes darting down to Linus's right shirt pocket, then back up again.

"Yes, sir. Linus Major."

"Well, Linus, you and I appear to appreciate the early-morning quiet."

"I always like to arrive before my shift starts, Dr. Bukinberg. I come early to familiarize myself with our museum's various exhibits. They never cease to amaze me." Linus particularly enjoyed saying "our" museum. "And always get rid of my coffee way before the museum—"

"It's hard to realize," remarked Dr. Bukinberg, "that nothing in our museum is a figment of one's imagination."

"True," said Linus Major, thinking to himself, that is true.

Dr. Gregory Bukinberg would continue to keep his eye on his protégé, Linus Major. Eventually Dr. Bukinberg would singlehandedly prod the museum's board of directors into promoting Linus to a job worthy of his interest, diligence, and intelligence.

"I am grooming you for paleontological greatness," Dr. Bukinberg told Linus on the day of his promotion to the Bone Department.

Linus, grinning from ear to ear, said, "I appreciate your confidence in me, Dr. Bukinberg. I won't let you down."

Linus Major was finally going to make a name for himself in something other than the *Guinness Book of World Records*. He was going to become someone his disgraced family would be proud of. He just knew it.

And Linus was right.

At the beginning of 2012, when Linus Major became the Museum of Natural History's director of bones, the position—silly as it sounded—was an extremely important one.

Arthur Durch was a thirty-seven-year-old practicing sex therapist.

He wasn't always a sex therapist. Before becoming a sex therapist, Arthur Durch was a junkie. Durch started ingesting drugs when he dropped out of high school. That was back in 1992, when Arthur turned eighteen. He joined the army that year, was sent to the Middle East but missed any fighting in the first Gulf War by about six months. Three years later and a dishonorable discharge to his credit for molesting a Lebanese woman, Durch left the army and continued his determined effort to kill himself with drugs.

Not long after his discharge he served time in the Petersburg Correctional Complex (medium security) in Petersburg, Virginia, for breaking and entering. Durch was caught inside an abortion clinic. He just wanted something to make him high, though he wasn't sure exactly what that might be. The clinic was in Richmond. When being fingerprinted there, Durch jokingly said, "I used to do drugs. I still do drugs. But I used to, too."

As fate would have it, on the day Arthur Durch was sentenced to prison, his mother was too. Upon hearing the news of her son's being sent to jail, Edna Durch suffered a severe and debilitating heart attack and was sentenced to life in bed. The heart attack occurred in her lawyer's office. She had gone there to strike her black sheep son Arthur from her will, but before she could, she had the attack. The jolt of her massive heart attack caused Mother Durch to slump across the family lawyer's desk, knocking various writing implements over and staining his expensive tooled leather-top desk with an overturned bottle of ink. According to the extremely superstitious lawyer, his expensive gold pens and pencils and desk were jinxed by the dead woman and unusable forever. He had them all replaced.

The bed Edna Durch was doomed to stay in was located in the master bedroom of her duplex penthouse apartment on the fiftieth floor of the Trump Grosvenor House. It was the only penthouse apartment at the very top of the building at Eighty-eighth Street and Fifth Avenue. The penthouse's master bedroom faced west. It overlooked most of Central Park and at night the twinkling lights of the West Side.

Older son Colin Durch immediately vowed to take care of his invalid and supremely wealthy mother, which he did with the perseverance and dedication of Florence Nightingale, less the altruistic motives of that beloved lady. Colin and his bespectacled dumb-as-shit wife, Donna, were not as intensely focused on Mother Durch as on the sickly woman's will. With ne'er-do-well brother Arthur already excommunicated, Colin was sure he was now heir apparent and the odds-on favorite to receive Mother Durch's vast fortune. The avaricious pair considered it just a matter of time, and a short amount of it at that, before they might become an extraordinarily wealthy couple.

They sold their own dilapidated, cockroach-infested apartment and moved into the luxurious duplex penthouse of Colin's dying mother. Colin even sacrificed his run-down, quasi-bankrupt law practice so that he could spend more time looking after his failing mother's affairs. Daughter-in-law Donna went along with the plan if not joyfully, then resolutely. The thought of being able to buy as many pairs of Christian Louboutin shoes as she wanted for the rest of her life gave her the needed resolve. She *loved* Louboutin's red soles.

Meanwhile life continued on a downhill slant for Arthur Durch, even after his parole from the Petersburg Correctional Complex. The late nineties were a sad litany of terminated jobs and miscellaneous disappointments for the ex-con. Things didn't seem to get better for Durch until that historic evening in 2006 when Arthur met his soul mate.

The event took place at Durch's first Alcoholics Anonymous gathering in a Korean church on Sixty-second Street between Lexington and Third avenues in Manhattan. Arthur was never going to give up drinking. He went to the meeting to meet girls.

When it was time for Durch to speak, he came to the podium wearing overalls and a straw cowboy hat and said, "Hi! I'm Arthur."

Everyone said, "Hi, Arthur!"

Then he said, "I used to do drugs. I still do drugs. But I used to, too."

The only sound anyone heard at the end of Arthur's sentence was a girlish giggle coming from somewhere in the back of the room.

Arthur explained to the crowd of ex- and present alcoholics that he had just told them a joke.

Silence.

Arthur wondered if alcohol killed sense-of-humor cells in the brain.

After the meeting, a skinny, flat-chested, flat-assed, sticks-for-legs recovering alcoholic woman walked up to Arthur and said, "I thought the drug joke was really funny."

"Was that you laughing in the back of the room?"

"Yes."

"Jesus," said Arthur, "I think I'm falling in love with you. What's your name?"

"Evelyn Lounge."

So there was our hero Billy Constable, standing on a subway platform watching Sonny Lieberman race to his about-to-depart 4 subway train. A twenty-dollar bet was in the offing to whichever one exited the station first. And then just when everything appeared lost for Sonny Lieberman (his 4 train's doors were closing just as he got there), he did something that according to Billy Constable was "real smart."

But it didn't turn out to be "real smart" after all.

The subway doors closed anyway and the subway departed the station without Sonny Lieberman.

But with his umbrella.

Talk about dejection.

Watching that kid Billy what's-his-name step onto his 5 train and ride off into the sunset, the sunset in this particular situation being a dark and scuzzy subway tunnel, was bad enough to sore loser Sonny Lieberman. Double that despair when he lost his spanking-new Brooks Brothers blue and white umbrella, the one with the Yale University colors. There it went sticking out of the closed subway doors like someone's arm. Triple the despair when Sonny lost his temper, kicked a soda pop machine, and jammed the big toe of his right foot.

A trifecta of bad luck.

Billy Constable stared out of his subway window unaware of his boss's toe jam. But he did know about the umbrella. He saw it disappear into the tunnel. Not only that, but it finally dawned on Billy that he had just beaten his boss—his new *boss*!—for twenty dollars. When he told the story to his buddy Jimmy Joel Jenks, JJ said, "Not smart."

The next morning Billy dreaded going to work.

On his walk to Dunkin' Donuts to pick up a cruller and a coffee with milk and two sugars, he debated whether to go to work at all or just look for another job.

He decided to face the music. Jobs, he remembered, were hard to find.

Billy's apprehension turned to downright fear during his subway ride. It metamorphosed into a sweaty panic while he was walking to the office building on Twentieth Street. The panic changed to a vise-like clutch in his chest when he strolled into the building's lobby.

As soon as Billy Constable's elevator doors opened on the third floor, there was Sonny Lieberman waiting for him, arms crossed over his chest, a ferocious look on his face. Or maybe it was just his normal face.

"Billy, follow me," growled Sonny.

Billy was embarrassed by Sonny's order, issued like that in front of the other company employees on the elevator. You didn't have to be a genius to know the skinny kid from Kentucky named Constable was in a whole lot of trouble.

Billy shuffled off the elevator wearing his hooded sweatshirt over a stretched-out sweater, baggy jeans, and dirty sneakers. He followed behind the tall, well-dressed boss's son all decked out in his cashmere sport coat, yellow open-necked sport shirt with the blue vertical stripes, solid brown slacks, brown alligator belt, and brown wingtip Florsheim shoes. Billy noticed that Mr. Lieberman was limping. He hadn't been limping last night.

Lieberman led Constable to the broom closet, stepping aside so Billy could walk in. Sonny followed Billy into the small space and shut the door. Billy sat on one side of Sonny's desk. Sonny took a seat opposite Billy and began fumbling with the various things in front of him: pencils, pads of paper, interoffice memos. How complicated was it to say, "You're fired"?

When Sonny Lieberman finally attempted to speak, he started, then stopped, cleared his throat, and started again. "Billy," he said in a low voice so he wouldn't be heard through the thin walls, "well, first of all, here's your twenty dollars." Sonny Lieberman opened his top desk drawer and produced a twenty-dollar bill that he had obviously placed there before Billy arrived.

"Thank you, sir," said Billy Constable, smiling feebly. He took the bill and started to stuff it into his jeans pocket, then, thinking better of it, placed the bill on Sonny's desk instead. "I was only fooling about the bet, Mr. Lieberman. Honest, I was."

"Nonsense. It was an honorable bet and I lost. And now that the twenty's yours I think I'm entitled to give you a bit of advice."

"Certainly, sir," said Billy Constable, quite sure the cow pucky was about to hit the fan.

"First of all," said an extremely serious Sonny Lieberman, speaking in a voice that was almost a whisper, "in the future I don't advise betting against your boss. He may not be as nice a guy as me. You may lose more than a twenty-dollar bill."

"You're right, Mr. Lieberman, sir. That was really stupid of me."

Sonny smiled a sickly smile.

Billy matched him.

"I'm a great judge of character and talent," said Sonny Lieberman (which he wasn't; he was perhaps one of the worst judges of character and talent that ever lived), "if I do say so myself. I can see in you, Billy, trust, honesty, drive, ambition, initiative, perseverance, stick-to-it-tiveness . . . and uh . . . what else? Let's see . . . sportsmanship. Ah yes, sportsmanship . . . and . . . and the desire to take a chance."

"You do?" said Billy, sort of amazed.

"Yes, I do. Consequently I want you to leave Empire Clothing and come to work for me in my new business."

"You *do*?"

Arthur Durch fell head over heels in love with Evelyn Lounge, the girl who laughed at his joke at the AA meeting.

Three days later, Arthur asked for Evelyn's hand in marriage.

She said, "Listen, Arthur, it's true that at this point in my miserable life I'm desperate. Shit, I'd marry a snake with a harelip, but . . . but . . ."

"But! But what?" asked Arthur. "Why not me, for Christ sake?"

"You didn't let me finish."

"So finish."

"I'm confused."

"That's it!? That's finishing?"

"Uh-huh."

"Jesus, Evelyn, I mean, I tell you . . . I admit to you I've fallen head over heels in love with you, and it doesn't even dent you. Let's face it . . . I mean, let's face it, Evelyn, you're not God's gift to men, you know."

"I know."

"I mean I love you like crazy, I really do. I know myself pretty well, Evelyn, and I can tell you with mucho assurance, I love you. BUT . . ."

"But?"

"But you're not very attractive, Evelyn, and you're not very bright."

"I know these things, Arthur. That's why I'm constantly selling myself short."

"With good reason, Evelyn, and . . . and . . ."

"And what?"

"Well . . . I didn't want to bring this up . . ."

"Go ahead. Bring it up."

"You have a funny smell."

"That's because I work as a dental assistant, Arthur. I mix Dr. Kalman's batters."

"Who the hell is Dr. Kalman?" asked Arthur, feeling his first pangs of jealousy.

"Dr. Morris Kalman. He's a dentist, Arthur. I take all his upper and lower impressions. Consequently, I constantly smell of alginate mixed with hydrophilic and vinyl polysiloxane. It's what I put in the batter to make the molds."

"Whatever it is, Evelyn, it's quite pungent."

"It's what?"

"It smells bad."

"Yeah. Most men find the smell a turnoff."

"Oddly enough, I don't," said Arthur. "I like it. Your impression stink smells like sweet summer breezes to me."

"You're sweet, Arthur."

"Alas, love doth oft blind the eye and dull what other senses one might possess."

"Who said that, Arthur?"

"Me."

"Oh, Arthur."

Arthur Durch and Evelyn Lounge courted for another week but never had sex. At the end of the week, Evelyn said she wanted to wait another week.

"Wait for what?" asked Arthur.

"I just want to wait," she whined.

"For what?"

"Until we're married," she whined.

"So let's get married. I keep asking you to marry me and you—"

"You want to marry me just to . . . to . . ."

"So what, Evelyn?"

"I want to wait," she whined.

"God, Evelyn, you whine *constantly.* I don't want to wait."

"Why, Arthur? Why marry so soon? We just met, practically."

"I'm horny."

"What's that mean?"

"You know what that means."

"I *don't* know what it means, Arthur. I really don't."

"It means I want to fuck you, is what it means."

"Oh, God," said Evelyn Lounge.

"What 'Oh, God'? What are you talking about, Evelyn? Sex is such a bad thing that the mere mention of the word 'fuck' and you start oh, God-ing all over the place? I want to fuck you, Evelyn."

"Oh, God, Arthur."

"There you go again."

They were married on the third weekend of their whirlwind courtship.

The sex was awful.

The problem was Evelyn. She didn't like having sex. At least not with Arthur.

"You're perpetually in heat, Arthur."

"You mean I'm hot to trot," said Arthur, snickering.

"I mean you always want to do it and I don't think it's funny."

Arthur had turned off quite a few women in his day. But then maybe Evelyn found sex with any male repugnant. Maybe it was having intercourse that disgusted Evelyn. Maybe she just didn't like being made love to, period. That wasn't an inconceivable speculation. And then one late afternoon when Arthur and Evelyn had finished "a little matinee humpty-dumpty," as Arthur liked to call it, an unusually bold and supine Evelyn Lounge Durch told her husband, "You know something, Arthur, you can't do it worth a damn."

"Do what?"

"IT!"

Arthur took immediate umbrage. "How the hell would *you* know, Evelyn?"

"You're a sexual loser, Arthur."

"I repeat, how would *you* know?"

"You're a cold fish, a dickless wonder, Arthur," baited a suddenly perky Evelyn Lounge Durch.

"Okay, what's going on, Evelyn?"

"You're one step up from a eunuch, Arthur."

"You don't even know what a eunuch is."

"Yes, I do."

"No you don't, you stupid bitch."

The stupid bitch part was the provocation she was looking for. She wiggled out from under her husband, scrambled off the couch and stood up, straightened her clothes and, with her hands on her hips, said, "Stupid bitch, huh?"

Evelyn stomped out of the apartment.

Arthur yelled, "Don't let the door hit you in the ass."

Evelyn Lounge Durch didn't hear him. She was already on the elevator. She returned for her clothes a week later when Arthur wasn't home.

Billy Constable was stunned.

"Yes, that's right, I want you to come and work for me," repeated Sonny Lieberman. "I'm starting a sports promotion company. I'm going to be the next Tex Rickard in this town. Do you know who Tex Rickard was?"

"No, sir."

"Tex Rickard was a fight promoter who worked primarily here in New York City. Rickard was a genius. He was also a tricky son of a bitch. Like for instance, Rickard used the race card to promote the sellout Johnson-Jeffries fight."

Billy told Mr. Lieberman he didn't know what the race card meant.

"White against black. That's what it means. Black Johnson and white Jeffries. The fight drew a really big crowd. Everybody wanted to see the white guy beat the shit out of the black guy. You Southerners know about that stuff, right?"

Billy had no idea what Mr. Lieberman was talking about, but he nodded anyway.

"Rickard had an even bigger sellout crowd using out-and-out flag-waving patriotism as the draw for the Dempsey-Carpentier boxing match."

"What year was that?" interrupted Billy.

"A long time ago," answered Sonny, quickly, because he didn't know. "Anyway, Dempsey was American. Carpentier was French. The Dempsey-Carpentier fight was the first million-dollar gate in boxing history."

Billy Constable smiled from ear to ear to show his appreciation for Mr. Rickard's incredible career.

"Rickard was brilliant. He really was," sighed Sonny Lieberman, stars twinkling in his eyes. "Rickard made being a fight promoter prestigious."

Billy wanted to stop Mr. Lieberman and ask what "prestigious" meant but decided to quit while he was ahead.

"It isn't prestigious anymore," continued Sonny Lieberman. "Most fight promoters, no, make that *all* fight promoters these days are thugs. I'm going to be the next clean-cut Ivy League Tex Rickard–type fight promoter. I'm going to make boxing prestigious again."

"What will I do, Mr. Lieberman?"

"You will be my assistant."

Billy Constable was stunned again.

"You'll get a raise and your own office, and your own secretary. Or . . . maybe you'll share a secretary with someone I may bring in."

Billy mumbled, "Thank you, sir. Who may you bring in?"

"A white-bread guy. We need a white-bread guy around the office. A Dick Clark type. Me, I'm a Jew, and you're a hillbilly, no offense intended. So a white-bread publicity and promotion executive may be just what the doctor ordered. You know, a nice Christian face to offset you and me."

Sonny smiled at Billy.

Billy smiled at Sonny, even though he still hadn't the faintest idea what a white-bread guy was.

"So," asked Billy, "are you going to hire Dick Clark?"

"No. Someone who *looks* sorta like him. I have someone in mind."

"Great!" said Billy Constable with enthusiasm, trying to get in the spirit of things.

"That will be all for now, Billy. I have to tell my father I'm leaving the company. Onward and upward."

"Why the limp?" asked Sonny's father.

"I tripped."

"Serves you right, you clumsy fool. Whattaya want?"

"I'm leaving the company."

"Leaving the company!" thundered a red-faced Max Lieberman, sitting behind his mammoth desk in his mammoth office. *"To be what?"*

"A fight promoter, Pop."

"A what?"

"A fight promoter. I'm going to promote fights."

"Get the fuck outta my office before I crack your goddamn head open."

Those were the last words Sonny's father would ever say to him for the rest of either of their lives.

The following week, Sonny departed the Empire Clothing Company for good and always, with skinny Billy Constable in tow. The two worked out of Sonny's place in the Century Apartments at 25 Central Park West. Sonny had an imitation bronze plaque made for the apartment door that read:

INTERNATIONAL BOXING PROMOTIONS
SONNY LIEBERMAN—PRESIDENT
BILLY CONSTABLE—ASSISTANT

Unfortunately, a week after the plaque was up, it had to come down. The apartment house board of directors wouldn't allow names of businesses on residential doors. Sonny Lieberman ranted and raved about that. He threatened to sue the apartment house's board of directors, swore he would deduct the cost of the plaque from his next month's rent. But to no avail. The plaque came down and Sonny paid the same rent he always paid.

"A minor defeat," said Sonny Lieberman to Billy Constable. "Onward and upward."

"Onward and upward" seemed to be Sonny Lieberman's favorite expression.

Sonny Lieberman was funding his company from his considerable savings account. But the savings account wasn't considerable enough to put up the necessary collateral to accomplish Sonny's boyhood dream: promoting a world heavyweight championship fight, like Tex Rickard did.

So Sonny went to his bank to get a loan. The bank turned him down. Sonny then proceeded to visit the treasurer of the local Teamsters' union to see if he could get a loan from him. Most of the truck drivers who drove around New York's garment district were Teamsters. A lot of the Teamsters were Sonny's friends. They drove the trucks that carted Empire Clothing Company's suits. The man Sonny approached for a loan was a friend named Dino Galhardi.

"I like ya, Sonny," said Dino Galhardi. "I always have and I'd like to help ya. But I don't do that sorta thing. I don't make loans. Not from our union's treasury. Most of our money's all tied up in pension funds, but even if it wasn't, promoting boxing matches doesn't sound like a good business proposition to me. Sounds more like a risk. But I'll tell ya what I'll do. I'll put ya in touch with someone who might be interested in investing in your boxing idea."

So Dino Galhardi set up a meeting for Sonny with Giuseppe "The Chop" Sanseli. Legend had it Sanseli used a meat cleaver on several unfortunate business associates' fingers when they crossed him on his way to the top of the Staten Island Mafia family he controlled. If Sonny Lieberman had been a wise man he would have stayed miles away from Giuseppe "The Chop" Sanseli. But Sonny Lieberman wasn't a wise man, so he went to Staten Island and explained his idea to Giuseppe Sanseli.

"I'm not gonna give you a loan, Lieberman," said The Chop, sitting behind his restaurant table and a cloud of cigar smoke.

"You're not?"

"No, I'm not. I'm gonna *give* you the money."

"You are?"

"There's a but involved."

"There is?"

"Yeah, there is. The but is, you gotta give me somethin' in return."

"I do?"

"Yeah, you do. You're gonna make me your silent partner."

"I am?"

"We're gonna split everythin' down the middle."

"We are?"

"Fifty-fifty."

"Fifty-fifty?"

"Yeah, Sonny. If you want the money to promote your heavyweight champions fight, you are."

And that would be the only mistake enterprising Sonny Lieberman would ever make as a neophyte boxing promoter—taking money from Giuseppe "The Chop" Sanseli.

But it was a big one.

After Evelyn left him, Arthur Durch remained unemployed. Unfortunately, Arthur lost his only source of income when Evelyn walked out. That precipitated another significant change in Arthur's life. He moved from a passable apartment in TriBeCa to a seedy one in Bensonhurst.

And then one day, while watching the Sex Channel on television, Arthur Durch began to wonder if he had taken the wrong tack with his ex-wife. Perhaps he should have helped Evelyn instead of insulting her. This was surprisingly astute thinking for a world-class numbskull. His unusually intelligent musings led Arthur to what he would always consider a "masterpiece of thinking." He would become a sex therapist. Unlicensed, for sure, but a sex therapist nonetheless. He would help women who hated sex learn to fuck like rabbits. So he wasn't licensed, so what? Who would point an accusatory finger?

Arthur visited his local Barnes & Noble store and purchased the following books on his American Express credit card: *The Joy of Sex* by Alex Comfort, *The New Joy of Sex: A Gourmet Guide to Lovemaking for the Nineties* by Alex Comfort, *Erotic Surrender: The Sensual Joys of Female Submission* by Claudia Varrin, *How to Have Magnificent Sex: Improve Your Relationship and Start to Have the Best Sex of Your Life* by Lana Holstein, M.D., *Kosher Sex: A Recipe for Passion and Intimacy* by Shmuley Boteach, and *Orgasms for Two* by Betty Dodson.

Several weeks after he'd bought the books, Arthur's mother died in Manhattan. She had lived ten years longer than the doctors predicted.

"I didn't think the old bitch would ever go," moaned Donna Durch to anyone who would listen. "God, what a pain in the ass. And speaking of asses, all that bedpan changing and emptying. And pumping all those medicines down her wizened throat. All those sleepless nights when the old bitch woke with another infantile demand. I swear I felt like smacking the old crone right across her face more than once. And most important, all that precious time irrevocably gone. Maybe the best one hundred and thirty months of our lives down the toilet with the rest of her shit."

Donna Durch was obviously miffed.

The only saving grace about Edna Durch's death watch as far as Colin and Donna were concerned was the monumental collection of fabulous jewels, the real estate, and the incredible amount of money Mother Durch was about to leave them for their selfless sacrifice. It was Mother Durch's will, and only her will, that had carried Colin and Donna through the ordeal.

Arthur Durch didn't bother to attend the reading of his mother's will. (What for?)

But Colin and Donna did, along with other members of the Durch family hoping for a bone or two.

Colin and Donna arrived at the Durch family attorney's office dressed a tad too spiffy for a reading of a will. Colin had on a black-and-red checkered sport coat, gray slacks, and an open-neck yellow sport shirt. He was also wearing his most expensive and flamboyant toupee, the blond number with the long sideburns pasted in place. The toupee made the asshole look like a gay gunslinger.

Wife Donna-the-numbskull wore a very expensive and very low-cut bright red dress, which hid her fried-egg breasts. She was about to tell the gathering it was a happy frock for a happy occasion but stopped herself just in time. Donna also wore her traditional Coke-bottle eyeglasses and perpetual frown. Colin and Donna's spirits were as joyful as the clothes they wore. An antidote, perhaps one could say, to the family attorney's depressingly dark office.

When everyone was seated, a dour old lawyer named Biggs, who breathed through his mouth, opened the matriarch's last will and testament and read its contents aloud. The text amounted to one simple sentence: "Edna Durch has left her entire estate—her cash, her real estate, her jewelry—to her son and firstborn, Arthur Durch."

What followed was the most pregnant of pauses.

Then Colin Durch whispered, "To who?"

"To your brother Arthur," answered the lawyer.

Donna Durch whispered, "To *who?*"

"To your brother-in-law Arthur," answered the lawyer.

"Arthur?" screamed Donna. *"Arthur Durch? My brother-in-law Arthur Durch? Edna Durch left every single thing to my fucking brother-in-law? She left everything to that worthless no-good cocksucking son of hers! Please tell me I'm deaf. Tell me I heard wrong."*

"I believe you heard correctly, Mrs. Durch," said the lawyer calmly. "Your brother-in-law Arthur will inherit every cent of your mother-in-law's vast fortune."

"Every cent?" whispered Colin.

"Every cent," said the lawyer.

"Every cent?" whispered Donna.

"Every cent," said the lawyer.

Donna Durch dropped dead.

Billy Constable telephoned Jimmy Joel Jenks and asked Jimmy Joel whether he could meet him at Billy's office after work. Billy waited for Jimmy Joel Jenks outside on the pavement by the Century Apartments' canopied entrance. When Jimmy Joel arrived, they hugged and slapped each other's backs. Then they took an elevator to the seventeenth floor. Billy led the way to Sonny's office/home. They walked into the apartment, and there on the inside of the front door was a large bronze plaque that read:

INTERNATIONAL BOXING PROMOTIONS
SONNY LIEBERMAN—PRESIDENT
BILLY CONSTABLE—ASSISTANT

"Wow," said Jimmy Joel, wide-eyed.

"It used to be on the other side of the door but the apartment people made my boss take it down."

"Wow," repeated Jimmy Joel.

"If only my family could see this," said Billy.

"Take a picture."

"Don't have a camera."

"I'll loan you mine. I got me a cheap Kodak. Takes good pictures, though."

"Don't matter," said Billy, shrugging his shoulders. "My folks don't care much what I do. Don't know why I even brought it up."

Billy showed Jimmy Joel around the office. He told Jimmy Joel that his boss Sonny Lieberman had hired two new secretaries and a publicity man named Wayne Whitmore. "Wayne used to do publicity for the Military Academy at West Point," said Billy. "My boss thought it was real important to have a white-bread guy like Wayne workin' for his company."

"Whataya mean a white-bread guy?" asked Jimmy Joel.

"You know, havin' a good Christian face walkin' around here."

"What's wrong with your face? You're a good Christian."

"Sonny thinks I'm a hillbilly."

"You *are* a hillbilly," said Jimmy Joel, "but you're a good Christian too."

A week later Sonny Lieberman added three more employees. One of the three was a young secretary named Billie Berry.

Billie Berry was thin, excitable, a tad bucktoothed, and borderline pretty. She wore her hair short, flapper style, and spoke with a slight Southern accent. (The accent was fake.) She thought she had a sexy smile (in truth it was faintly cruel) and great legs. She was convinced she was a movie star waiting to be discovered and acted accordingly.

The rest of the office pegged Billie for a former bartender.

Except Billy Constable. He fell head over heels in love with Billy Berry.

Billy, too smitten to detect the fake accent, thought she was the prettiest girl walking. To him, Billie Berry was a Southern belle right out of the ol' y'all mint julep South. (South Manayunk, Pennsylvania, is where Billie Berry was really from.) Billy's heart skipped a beat or two every time Billie Berry walked into his cubicle.

"Wanna get somethin' to eat after work tonight?" Billy Constable would constantly ask Billie Berry the minute she stepped up to his desk with a new interoffice memorandum.

"Not with you, Billy Constable. You're not rich enough to take me out," Billie Berry would answer.

Billie Berry had come to New York City from outside Philly to find a rich husband. And by God a rich husband was what she was going to find. Not a damn hayseed like Billy Constable. I mean, come on, she was the cat's meow. A real heartbreaker. A family buster-upper. A *si-reen,* as she was secretly fond of calling herself while staring endlessly at her naked bony body in her bedroom's full-length mirror.

The brazenly conceited Billie Berry never gave heartsick Billy Constable the time of day. She ignored all the notes he sent her signed Billie & Billy inside the outline of a heart. Billy drew his heart outlines with a red pencil. One night, after everyone had gone, Billy Constable found a collection of his red-outlined hearts with their names inside torn to shreds in Billie's wastebasket. He was devastated.

A month after Billie Berry joined the company, Sonny Lieberman gathered his employees together in his office so that he could make an announcement. "Our company, International Boxing Promotions, has acquired the rights to the next heavyweight championship fight!" he said.

His employees let out whoops of joy.

"The fight will take place September the fourteenth of this year, a little less than two months away. It will be the biggest sporting event of 2012."

More whoops and lots of clapping.

"At last," he said, "my lifelong dream is going to come true."

More whoops and clapping.

"We're going to use out-and-out flag-waving patriotism as the draw for this fight," Sonny told his troops.

Everyone applauded again. A few yelled, "Way to go, Mr. Lieberman." Things like that.

"The American champion," continued Sonny, "is going to fight a

Swede who happens to be the heavyweight champion of Europe for the heavyweight championship of the world. We're going to make this fight America versus Europe."

"And the rest of the world," yelled someone.

"Yes," said Sonny, smiling victoriously and pointing a finger at the beatified employee, "and the rest of the world. It's going to be the best thing that's happened to the fight game since Dempsey fought Carpentier. Onward and upward!"

Everyone cheered.

Some yelled, "Onward and upward."

"Maybe I'll marry Sonny Lieberman," mean Billie Berry, the self-styled vampette, told a perpetually shattered Billy Constable.

The Swedish heavyweight champion was described as "big as a house and strong as an ox" in the sports pages of the New York *Daily News*. What the *News* didn't say was that the Swede was also a world-class playboy and cocksman who was absolutely incapable of keeping his fly zipped up.

The other information the newspapers failed to mention was that most of the money Sonny Lieberman needed to buy the rights to the fight—and it was a considerable amount of additional money—came from his new "silent" partner, Giuseppe "The Chop" Sanseli.

Donna Durch's Coke-bottle eyeglasses lay on the end of her nose, her stare fixed on some imaginary spot on the ceiling. Some spit had dribbled down the side of her lifeless mouth. She sat dead in the family lawyer's armchair, a thick, important-looking maroon affair the lawyer had waited six months to get.

"God Almighty," moaned the very superstitious and very depressed lawyer, "how many more Durch heart attacks do I have to go through in my office? First the mother jinxes my gold desk set and desk and now the daughter-in-law throws a kibosh on my brand-new armchair."

While EMS attendants loaded Donna's corpse into their ambulance, her husband, Colin Durch, stood on his tiptoes among the semicircle of gawkers, trying to see what was going on with his dead wife. While standing there, Colin fully realized the awful truth of everything that had just transpired, suffered a paralyzing stroke, and fell to the pavement.

The EMS attendants slid his paralyzed body into the ambulance next to his dead wife.

When Arthur Durch heard the news of his brother's stroke and his sister-in-law's death, he was shocked beyond belief. Not by the two catastrophes but rather by the *cause* of their catastrophes: the attorney's announcement that his mother had left all her riches to *him.* That's what shocked Arthur Durch. As soon as his stupefied state wore off, Arthur began hopping and jumping about his seedy Bensonhurst apartment, whooping and yelping like a crazy fool. It was as if Arthur had just won the lottery. As a matter of fact, it was better than winning the lottery. Arthur didn't have to pay half to get the whole pot quickly.

Arthur Durch spent a moment wondering why his mother would do such a thing. As soon as that moment passed, he canceled the battery of doctors constantly by Colin's side and had his severely paralyzed brother moved out of the Trump Grosvenor House and into a crummy hospice in the Hell's Kitchen section of New York City. Colin Durch died within a month from lack of proper care.

Three days after Mother Durch's funeral, a crew of workers finished fumigating the dead woman's duplex apartment and Arthur moved in. A week after that, he opened his sex therapy practice to the public.

And guess who was his first patient?

The snowstorm of '96 was a record breaker.

The most snow ever.

The strongest winds ever.

The blizzard's wind was so loud, John J. Sughrue had to put his mouth next to Vera Bundle's ear to say, "I forget. What hotel did you say you were in?"

She shouted back, "I'm at the Baldwin, Mr. Sughrue." Vera pronounced his name Sh-GA-ru. She made it sound Oriental.

"My name is pronounced Sh-GREW," he said. "It's an old Irish name. Where did you say the Baldwin was?"

"It's on Eighth Avenue and Thirty-third Street."

"You'll never get down there," said Sughrue. He had to speak so close to Vera's ear that she could smell his after-shave cologne. It smelled good. "Not in this snowstorm. Come with me. I'm staying at the Sherry-Netherland hotel. When I heard the storm warnings on the radio I took a room at the Sherry for tonight. The Sherry-Netherland is just a few blocks down the street. We can walk. They know me there. I'm pretty sure I'll be able to get you a room. Don't worry. I'll pay for it. You'll pay me back."

Vera Bundle could hardly keep her eyes off of John J. Sughrue's face. He was so tall and handsome. She and her new acquaintance bucked the stiff wintry gusts and swirling snowflakes as they trudged several blocks east to the Sherry-Netherland hotel.

Inside, the hotel's lobby was warm and comfy, just like the Essex House lobby. Vera shook the snow off her coat and hat and watched Sughrue check for messages, then walk over to the manager's desk and speak with the man sitting there. Eventually Sughrue returned and told Vera he had gotten her a room. It was just for the night, he said.

Vera Bundle was ever so thankful.

Sughrue took Vera to the drugstore off the lobby to buy her a toothbrush and some toothpaste. Embarrassed and blushing, Vera told Sughrue that she needed something to sleep in. "I'm sure they don't sell nightgowns in this drugstore," she said, "but I can't sleep in the . . . in the . . ."

"Please don't worry about it, Vera. We'll get something here."

They did. Sughrue bought Vera Bundle an extra-large T-shirt that had I ♥ NEW YORK printed on it.

Then the two boarded the elevator. Vera's room was on the fourteenth floor, Sughrue's just down the hall. When the elevator arrived at their destination, they both stepped out. Sughrue helped Vera find her room and opened her door for her with the room key. He gave Vera the key, told her in what direction his room was in case she needed anything, said good night, and walked away.

Vera quickly slipped into the extra-large T-shirt with I ♥ NEW YORK printed on it. It was long enough to end just above her knees. Vera looked for a robe but couldn't find one. Oh, well, she thought,

John's room was just down the hall. And he *did* invite me to come, didn't he? He said in case I need anything, and that's as nice a way of saying come to my room as a gentleman can say it. I'll just have to do the inevitable for both of us, won't I?

Vera opened her room door. She looked left and right down the hallway and noticed it was clear. Excited and flushed, Vera scurried to John Sughrue's door, took a deep breath, and knocked.

Hard.

During the months of July and August 2012, Billy Constable was assigned the responsibility of running the heavyweight boxing champion of Europe's training camp at Grossinger's Resort Hotel in the Catskill Mountains.

This meant the postponement and possible ruination of Billy's chances to win the attentions of Billie Berry. He was getting nowhere, but now getting nowhere would be a sure thing. She would most certainly have a boyfriend by the time he came back to the city. So Billy Constable departed for Grossinger's with a broken heart made more so by Billie Berry's indifferent facial expression when she waved good-bye that Friday at five o'clock. Billy wouldn't be in the office the next week, or for weeks after that, and she knew it.

"I'm leaving tomorrow for a month or so. Wanna grab a quick good-bye beer with me?" he had pleaded earlier in the afternoon.

"No," she replied curtly, and disappeared down the hall.

"She didn't even say, 'No *thank you*,'" Billy told Jimmy Joel Jenks. "I think she was glad to see me go."

The two were splitting a hamburger and a beer after work at P. J. Clarke's on Third Avenue at Fifty-fifth Street. Billy was setting out for the Catskills early the next morning. The two friends stood at the bar eating their half a burger and splitting a bottle of beer.

"My romance is over, JJ," moaned Billy.

"I don't think it ever really started," replied Jimmy Joel Jenks.

"You know what she told me this afternoon? She said, 'I hope you find a cute girlfriend up there.'"

"Billy, you're just too dumb to know she's doin' you a favor."

"I am one sick puppy dog."

"Like my grandma says, 'You'll get over it.'"

So young Billy Constable, from the green hills of Kentucky, rode a bus up to the green hills of New York's Catskill Mountains.

Once the lad stepped foot onto Grossinger's resort property, he suffered immediate culture shock. He was amazed at how fat all the guests were and how the couples romped around in their matching blue, green, and magenta sweat suits like overweight gazelles. He was mesmerized by the number of people playing Simon Says for hours and hours. He suffered the resort's bullying waiters who forced him to eat three and four portions of strangely delicious dishes that had weird names like kugel, flanken, latkes, kasha, kishke, derma, gefilte fish, kasha varnishka, halvah, mamaliga, lox, sable, challah, knishes, tsimmis, rugelach, babka, and forshpice.

Billy asked a waiter what forshpice was.

The waiter said, "I don't know, just eat it."

The crotchety waiters ignored Billy's pleas and supplications that he was full and couldn't eat another morsel. They turned deaf ears to his entreaties and all but physically pushed helpings of marble, sponge, and chocolate cake down his throat. And always when he was bloated beyond his wildest imagination, the waiters compelled the poor boy to drink two or three egg creams before leaving the dining room.

Billy wondered why the waiters were trying to kill him. He had done nothing to them.

Billy watched in awe as the breakfast and lunch crowds departed the dining room, walked only as far as the thickly padded beach chairs a short distance away on the huge patio, and flopped into them as if they had just run a marathon when all they had done was eat. They lay there *grepsing* (belching) horrible bursts of unpleasant-smelling air. They sounded like the walruses they resembled. Then, after a few hours, Billy watched in awe as the herd got up from their beach chairs and waddled like incredibly plump penguins back to the dining room for another meal.

At night Billy followed the guests into Grossinger's hyperkinetic nightclub. He stared dumbfounded at the attire of the nighttime crowd. Everyone dressed to the nines in satins, sequins, cashmere, and silk. The fat, balding married men suavely checking out the unmarried women while picking food out from between their teeth with the fingernail of their little finger. The seedy, self-adoring, would-be lotharios; the hot-to-trot, long-in-the-tooth secretaries; and steamy divorcées seething with general unhappiness and desperation, jealous of what the other women looked like and the makeup they used. Some married couples brazenly gloating over having captured a revolting mate against all odds. Two loud Latin bands took turns playing so that there was never a moment of quiet or a time the dancers could rest.

Everyone dancing the rumba, mambo, and cha-cha-cha with the facial expressions of brain surgeons, concentrating on their steps as if performing a life-or-death operation. Everyone sweating as though they had just stepped out of a shower, their shirts and dresses plastered to their backs. Everyone's lips moving as they counted time—ONE, two, three, four, ONE, two, three, four—doing the traditional box step with all the verve and panache they could muster, praying to God they wouldn't lose the count.

And who was always on the dance floor mamboing with a different partner every fifteen or twenty minutes? Who had to be pushed out of the nightclub by his exhausted trainers long after closing time? Who was always the last one seen disappearing into the rising sun with at least two or three boxing groupies in tow?

The European heavyweight champion of the world.

The Swede.

After making sure Vera Bundle was safely in her room, John J. Sughrue went to his suite.

He shook out his hat and overcoat and hung them on hooks by the door. He walked into the suite's living room, sat down in an armchair, and thought about his disappointing wait at the Essex House bar. Sughrue was crushed. The beautiful woman he had met earlier on the plane had led him on and most likely never intended to come to the Essex House at all.

Their paths crossed on the red-eye flight from Los Angeles to New York. The beautiful woman had a handsome man friend, a swarthy, good-looking foreigner, possibly in his late forties or early fifties. Sughrue assumed the man friend was a foreigner. He wore his topcoat over his shoulders. Isn't that what foreigners did, wore their topcoats over their shoulders? The man friend even walked the beautiful woman onto the plane and to her seat. She had the first-class seat by the window. Sughrue had the aisle seat next to her. Sughrue stood to let the beautiful woman pass by. She had wonderfully soft blond hair that smelled freshly shampooed, and when she smiled and said thank you to Sughrue, he was besotted.

Not long after the plane took off, the beautiful woman and Sughrue began talking to each other. They talked all through the night, intimately and suggestively. Sughrue didn't see a wedding ring on the beautiful woman's beautiful hand. He himself had been widowed for five years and realized that he had fallen head over heels in love. It was the first time he had experienced the sensation since Susan died. The woman beside him on the airliner did have a man friend, but then wasn't everything fair in love and war? Sughrue asked the woman if she would meet him at five that evening at Journeys, the bar in the Essex House Hotel on Central Park South. She said she would.

It was during his disappointing reenactment of events that Sughrue heard the violent pounding on the door of his suite.

BAM! BAM! BAM! BAM! BAM! BAM! BAM!

Startled and concerned, Sughrue walked briskly across the room.

BAM! BAM! BAM! BAM! BAM! BAM! BAM!

The violent pounding continued until Sughrue arrived at the door and pulled it open with a jerk.

There in the hallway stood Vera Bundle in her I ♥ NEW YORK T-shirt, moaning, "I love you, John. I love you. I'm so lonely. Please let me stay. Please let me feel the warmth of a man's body beside me again. Please, John. I beg you. Let me stay with you. Please."

Sughrue panicked.

"Vera!" he said, terrified. "Go back to your room. Immediately!"

"I can't, John. I can't." Vera Bundle began to sob loudly.

Several nearby hotel room doors opened. Various heads peeked out to see what the fuss was about. The guests were dumbfounded when they saw an elderly woman down the hall dressed in nothing but a T-shirt. She was crying and moaning to the man standing in the room's doorway.

"Vera, I'm going to call hotel security if you don't leave."

"Please don't do that, John. Please, please let me sleep with you tonight. Please, John."

"Vera," he hissed, "get the hell out of here."

John J. Sughrue slammed his room door in Vera Bundle's face.

The john Retta Mae Wagons fell in love with—Rasheed Jamal—was the owner and director of a Muslim mosque in Miami Beach, Florida. He also had a syndicated network of television programs that originated from his mosque's pulpit and was a leader of the Shi'i community in South Florida. The two would never have met if the good imam hadn't decided to go to Manhattan for a weekend of fun and relaxation.

Jamal called his friend and onetime inmate at Attica, pimp Dannyboy Marley, a week before he came to the city. Jamal wanted Marley to pick out his best hooker. The imam knew he could trust Marley. The ex-con from Jamaica would keep it all hush-hush.

The pimp procured Retta Mae Wagons for the imam.

Dannyboy explained to Retta Mae, "When it comes to Rasheed, you can forget most a de rules like makin' him show his dick. Shit like dat. He'll still have a whatchacallit . . . a password. Just forget about most a de rest. Unnerstan'?"

Retta Mae nodded yes.

"I'll describe the imam to you. He's a big mudafucker. I mean real big. Lots of muscles. The dude's got nappy gray hair, a split between his two front teeth you could run a truck through, an' he dresses smart. If the john fits dat description, do whatever he says."

"How do you know what he looks like?" asked Retta Mae.

"I seen him before."

"*Saw* him before, you dumb shit."

Retta Mae laughed.

So did Dannyboy.

They liked each other.

Later that evening, someone knocked *dump-ditty-dump-dump, dump-dump* on Retta Mae's apartment door. When Retta Mae opened it and saw the powerhouse brute with the gapped front teeth standing in front of her, she fell in love. As far as she could remember, it was her first crush. "Just one look," she was fond of singing over that first weekend, "that's all it took."

Same with the imam. "I went down for the count," he'd say to his friends. "Despite our thirty-year age difference, it was love at first sight."

At the end of the weekend, when Rasheed Jamal asked Retta Mae Wagons to come back to Miami Beach with him, she didn't think twice. Of course Dannyboy Marley had a shit fit and rightly so. He was losing the biggest moneymaker in his stable.

"I tink you should tink 'bout it, honey."

"There's nothing to *tink* about, Dannyboy. I know what I'm doing."

"I don't tink so."

On the Sunday Retta Mae and Rasheed were scheduled to leave New York for Miami, Marley's friend and partner, Fat Herbie Cheskis, told Dannyboy to stop Retta Mae from going. Fat Herbie Cheskis had partnerships with several pimps on the Upper East Side along with owning a chain of pawnshops and strip joints.

Fat Herbie said, "I'm upset about the potential loss of income."

"Dere ain't no potential 'bout it, Fat Herbie."

"So do something."

"Do what zactly, Fat Herbie? Cross de imam? No fuckin' way."

So off to sunny Miami Beach went Retta Mae Wagons and her imam on his private jetliner, a slick battleship gray affair that was so plush inside it made you want to live there. On the way down to Miami Beach, when the imam wasn't skimming through his religious and business magazines or flirting and grab-assing one or the other of the two cute stewardesses who worked for him (which Retta Mae did *not* like) and Retta Mae wasn't reading *L'Assommoir* by Balzac, they would make love. The imam told Retta Mae he felt like a damn high school kid with a crush. Retta Mae said she was the happiest she'd ever been in her entire life.

Retta Mae was amazed at the size of the imam's Muslim empire, which the imam showed her in his Rolls-Royce on the way to his home. The mosque was huge. It took up an entire city block. It had a tall minaret that seemed to go up forever beside the golden-domed *masjid* and an ornate iron fence ten feet high that went from corner to corner around the block.

Jamal's house was even bigger.

The large and imposing mansion, a four-story Mediterranean villa, was eighteen thousand square feet. The home featured a large circular tower and Romanesque arches. It was situated on ten acres in between the inland waterway and the Atlantic Ocean. Jamal's palatial estate had an Olympic-size indoor-outdoor heated swimming pool under an arched pavilion. The home had eleven-foot ceilings, stone and marble floors, and seven fireplaces. There was a separate bungalow for watching movies and extrawide-screen television, a Jacuzzi large enough for ten people, a fully stocked wine cellar, a steam room and spa area, and a magnificent airy kitchen. On the palm-tree-studded grounds was a small one-story building that housed Rasheed Jamal's office, complete with liquor, beer, and coffee bar, a bathroom with matching marble bathtubs, and a luxury billiards room. There was a guesthouse with two guest suites that most people would give their right arm to call home.

Shortly after the blissful couple arrived at the mansion, Retta Mae said, "Rasheed, tell me something. Where the hell did you get the bread to put together—"

WHACK! WHACK!

Jamal bitch-slapped Retta Mae across her face, hard—one side, then the other—with his open hand. The whacks knocked Retta Mae down to the floor. When she looked up, Jamal seemed to tower over her. He just went up and up forever.

"Don't you ever question me about my personal, financial, or business affairs again, girl, hear?" growled the good imam. "Never again."

It was several days before Billy Constable could catch up with Sven Svenson, the Swedish heavyweight boxing champion of Europe, and introduce himself. For a while Sven slept when Billy was up, and vice versa. When the two finally did meet, the first words the heavyweight boxing champ of Europe said to Billy were, "I am heavyweight boxing champ of Europe."

"I know."

"I'm going to be champ with the world you can make sure."

"I hope so," Billy said, being diplomatic. This was a new twist in Billy's life. Being diplomatic. Billy wanted to add, "I don't think you're going about it the right way," but didn't. It wasn't diplomatic.

"This," said the heavyweight champion of Europe, making a muscle with his right arm and pointing to it with his left index finger, "is tunder of Tor."

"Is what?"

"Is tunder of Tor."

"What he's trying to say is he's strong, and he is," said the Swede's English-speaking younger brother, who was at least seventy-five pounds lighter and three inches shorter than the heavyweight champion of Europe. "The god Thor is the Norse god of thunder, which means war and strength and things like that."

Billy Constable really liked the heavyweight champion of Europe's brother. The brother's name was Roddy, which was an anglicized twist on the Scandinavian word *rod,* meaning "red." Roddy Svenson's hair was red.

"There are not many Swedes with red hair," he told Billy.

"My lucky . . . my lucky . . . ," said the heavyweight boxing champion of Europe, looking at his brother for help.

"Charm," said Roddy. "I am my brother's lucky charm."

"Yeah?" said Billy, thinking, he's going to need more than his little brother if he keeps dicking around with the girls like he's doing all day and all night.

"I am killing Negro," said the heavyweight champion of Europe. "Bet money. Bet lots of money on me killing Negro."

In your dreams, thought Billy Constable, to himself, of course. It wouldn't have been diplomatic otherwise.

The old cripple was shocked.

When the producer had finished watching *The Death Game* he walked out of the apartment without saying a single solitary word. Nothing.

It was a catastrophe. The cripple lay down on his bed and stared at the ceiling. He remembered feeling this bummed only twice before in his entire life. The miserable feeling of gazing sadly at the ceiling while lying almost comatose on a bed. The first time was when he was supine for weeks on a cheap cot in his twenty-five-dollar-a-month office in the Writers & Artists Building on Little Santa Monica in Beverly Hills. It was right after ABC-TV passed on *The Dating Game* in 1965. That was bad, but not a catastrophe. The network changed its mind and put the program on television a month later. But when the movie of the cripple's book *Confessions of a Dangerous Mind* tanked, *that* was definitely a catastrophe. It was probably the biggest disappointment of his life. The cripple remembered that disaster as if it were yesterday.

I stayed in bed in my penthouse for a month over that one, he told himself, recalling that dismal time in his life. A once-in-a-lifetime opportunity and the film fucking tanked. It was history in less than a month. And it had big stars. Julia Roberts. Drew Barrymore. George Clooney.

Gone in a month, if that.

Why did it disappear so fast?

But then I know why, don't I?

Stop! he told himself. Stop thinking about it. How many years ago was it? Ten. Still not enough time has gone by. If I let myself think about the *Confessions* fiasco it'll make me totally miserable, and I'm feeling miserable enough as it is.

And now my life has come full circle, he mused, and I'm back on a cheap cot staring at a ceiling again because a jerk-off producer leaves my room without saying a word after he finishes watching my pilot. What a loop-de-loop life *I've* led, thought the old cripple. A bunch of memories is what I have left. Just a bunch of mem—

The telephone down the hall began ringing.

The cripple limped out of his room as fast as he could. He picked up the receiver on the ninth ring.

It was the producer!

"Well, hello!" said the cripple cheerfully. "I'd all but—"

"Come to my apartment tonight. I'll send my driver. He'll pick you up in front of your door at eight o'clock sharp."

Chubby Billy Constable had gained fifteen pounds during his stay at Grossinger's. He was beginning to enjoy the resort and forget about Billie Berry. The cause of Billie Berry's sudden demise was the appearance of a cute, plump, sexy little redhead named Rosie Feinstein.

Rosie came from a highly respected German-Jewish family. Her grandparents and great-grandparents used to live in sumptuous apartments on Riverside Drive in Manhattan. A large number of German Jews used to live in sumptuous apartments there, but not anymore.

Now the Feinstein family lived in the West Village. Rosie's father, Myron Feinstein, was a noted psychiatrist. Rosie's mother, Sylvia Perchick Feinstein, was also a noted psychiatrist. Both were driven with ambition from early childhood to become noted psychiatrists. The doctors Feinstein shared a suite of offices in a brownstone at Charles and West Fourth streets, catty-corner from a restaurant called Mary's Fish Camp. The brownstone was also their home.

Rosie's younger brother Milton was a sophomore at Harvard. The skinny four-eyed boy was driven too, destined to attend medical school and become a noted psychiatrist. Rosie Feinstein wasn't driven. She hadn't any intentions of becoming a noted anything. Nor did she have high expectations or the need to win awards or recognition. All she wanted to do was live.

Rosie Feinstein tried but couldn't stay in college for the life of her. She had been asked to leave three Ivy League universities. Not for doing anything wrong, mind you, or for poor scholarship (her grades were surprisingly good). Rosie was asked to leave for lack of interest. Which in turn resulted in poor attendance. Which in turn prompted various deans to point Rosie Feinstein toward the open road.

The only drive Rosie appeared to have was the ability to drive her goal-driven parents crazy.

"If a member of this family doesn't want to go to college and then medical school to be a doctor or psychiatrist," explained Rosie's frustrated mother to her daughter, "then . . . then . . ." Rosie's mother could never finish the sentence.

"What's to become of her?" Rosie's father asked the synagogue's rabbi every weekend at services.

"God only knows," was the rabbi's astute reply.

Rosie Feinstein never attended Saturday morning services at the synagogue just across the street. She preferred to visit the zoo, or stroll in Central Park, or wander around the Met, or MOMA, or the Museum of Natural History. On weekdays you could often find Rosie sitting on a wall at Lincoln Center watching the agile, slender-as-swans female and male ballet dancers walk by. She admired their beauty and their bony bodies. Rosie Feinstein could never have been a ballet dancer. She was too short and stubby. She was barely five feet tall, with thick curly hair on top of a deliciously compact, robust figure. Any man who liked a deliciously compact, robust figure—a figure that sported breasts bulging out of their bra and an ass that a Cossack would love to grab onto—then Rosie Feinstein was his girl. Quite a few males considered Rosie Feinstein sexy as hell.

Billy Constable was one of those males.

Billy was at a loss as to why he felt the way he did about Rosie Feinstein. Probably because Rosie Feinstein the New Yorker was a whole new wonderful world to Billy Constable the Kentuckian. Rosie was a major reason Billy began loving Grossinger's.

Rosie Feinstein loved Grossinger's too. Always had. She went as often as she could scrounge up the money, summer or winter, it didn't matter. What Rosie craved was the food, playing Simon Says, and the ease with which she could indulge her *soupçon* of nymphomania.

Rosie detested fixed.

She preferred mixed.

"It's not that she's a nymphomaniac," said a girlfriend who didn't sound a hundred percent sure. "It's that Rosie believes variety is the spice of life."

Rosie Feinstein had a predilection for the offbeat, and Grossinger's had a plentiful supply of idiosyncratic males. A drummer here. A horny borscht belt comic there. A cloak and suiter with his greased-up hair and pinkie ring everywhere. And the gentile hillbilly from Bowling Green, Kentucky.

If there was one thing Rosie Feinstein loved it was *shtupping* the hillbilly. Billy Constable liked it too once he found out what *shtupping* meant. He reckoned he was semiretarded in the *shtupping* department, which he was, due to his lack of practice, but Rosie Feinstein was happy to give the well-endowed hillbilly an intensive crash course. She'd say, "Come on, Kentucky, let's *shtup*," or, "Remember, Kentucky, practice makes perfect," just about every other hour of the day. At least that's how it felt to Billy. Not that Billy minded. It's just that his endurance didn't match Rosie's, nor did he have the time. He *did* have another job.

"Jesus," Billy told Jimmy Joel Jenks on the telephone, "if you figure in foreplay—"

"What?"

"Foreplay. It's what you do first. If you figure in foreplay, the *shtuppin'* part—"

"The what? Stoopin'? What the hell's stoopin', Billy?"

"*Shtuppin'*, JJ. That's Jew for screwin'."

"Is Rosie a Jew?"

"Yeah. Anyway, if you figure in foreplay an' *shtuppin'* an' post-whatever-you-call-it snugglin', Rosie Feinstein is more time-consumin' than overseein' the trainin' camp."

Billy Constable began to commiserate with the heavyweight boxing champion of Europe, who was sparring and jogging less and less every day. Keeping Rosie Feinstein happy didn't come close to the champ's great numbers of young women he was servicing. But Billy did begin to wonder if it was a good or bad thing that Rosie Feinstein took such a liking to him.

Between the pushy waiters and Rosie's sexual appetite, Billy Constable wondered if he'd ever get away from the Catskill Mountains alive.

The producer's Lincoln Continental arrived in front of Umanov's Guitar Store at exactly eight P.M. The driver stepped out, walked around the car, and opened the rear door.

The cripple thanked the driver.

The driver didn't say, "You're welcome."

The driver was a stout white man wearing a black chauffeur's hat with a shiny brim, white shirt, black tie, and black suit. The cripple managed to get his useless body into the limo's backseat. The driver didn't help. He preferred to stay as far away from the cripple as he could. As if the cripple were a carrier of some horrible European disease.

The limousine drove to 1 Beacon Court, a luxury high-rise on the Upper East Side of New York. The Beacon Court doorman helped the cripple out of the limousine. The driver remained seated behind the wheel.

The elevator rose seventy-two floors in less than thirty seconds.

A butler dressed in black tie and tails greeted the cripple at the front door of the producer's apartment and led him down the long main hallway filled with paintings on the walls and sculptures on marble pedestals. At the end of the hallway was the apartment's living room with floor-to-ceiling panoramic windows that overlooked the world. The producer was standing with his back to one of those windows, watching the cripple approach. All the lights of New York City twinkled behind the producer.

The producer was wearing a green and yellow foulard smoking jacket over a white dress shirt open at the neck and a crimson ascot tucked into his shirt. Black slacks and black Gucci loafers minus socks completed the outfit. The producer's arms were folded across his chest. He acknowledged the cripple's presence by one nod of his head.

A second man was sitting in front of and to the side of the producer. The man was staring at the city's lights. The back of the man's large head and the back of his equally large leather armchair faced the cripple. The man in the armchair didn't stand to greet the old cripple. As far as the stranger was concerned, the cripple didn't exist.

The cripple limped to the middle of the living room and turned so he could see who the hell the man in the armchair was. "If the mountain won't come to Muhammad, Muhammad will come to the mountain. Let me introduce myself. I'm—"

"This is my lawyer, Sigmond Levy," said the producer.

The lawyer named Sigmond Levy remained seated. Glancing at the cripple, he mumbled, "Good evening." He wore an expression of someone repulsed by the intrusion of a despicable stranger.

One thing was quickly apparent and that was no amount of tailoring, no matter what the cost, would ever prevent the fat, burly stranger from looking anything but sloppy. Sigmond Levy had a large, red, round face; thick, wet lips almost covered by a long curved nose; and several chins under his jaw. His bushy hair was tight and curly. But the feature that frightened the old cripple the most were the lawyer's eyes. They were malevolent and froglike, with dark pouches under them. The grossly obese lawyer was constantly changing his position in the leather armchair. He seemed to be perpetually uncomfortable.

The cripple had worn his best clothes for the occasion. He wore a cardigan sweater over a black T-shirt and a pair of old, stained jeans. The sweater was the only one the cripple owned without holes.

"Now that you have *finally* arrived," said the producer to the cripple as if the cripple were late, "let us have dinner."

Was he late? wondered the cripple. He didn't think so. He was waiting for the limousine to arrive outside in front of the Umanov Guitar Store before eight. The car arrived at exactly eight o'clock. So what was the sly dig about? To put me on the defensive, guessed the cripple. And it succeeded, didn't it? he mused.

The producer led the procession to the dining room, followed by the lawyer and then the cripple limping as fast as he could on his crutch, trying to keep up. In the dining room the butler was standing behind the chair at the head of the table. The butler pulled the chair from the table, allowed the producer to sit down, then he and the producer pushed the chair close to the table.

The producer said, "Thank you, Bunter."

The lawyer sat in a chair to the producer's immediate right. The butler also helped Sigmond Levy into his chair. The butler told the cripple, "This way, please," and led him down to the other end of the long dining room table, miles from the producer and his lawyer. The butler pointed to the cripple's place as if the cripple were a fox terrier that knew how to get up on a chair. Then the butler named Bunter left the room.

"You serious about this Rosie girl?" asked Jimmy Joel Jenks.

"Think so," said Billy Constable thoughtfully. "I must be 'cause I met her *mishpokhe*."

"Her what?"

"Her *mishpokhe*."

"What's a *mishpokhe*?" asked Jimmy Joel Jenks.

"That's Jew for Rosie's parents. Rosie's mother and father."

First Jimmy Joel said, "Oh." Then he said, "Why don't Jewish people just say mother and father?"

"Dunno."

Grossinger's set up a boxing ring.

It was erected in a spare recreation building to sharpen the Swede's boxing skills. Its real purpose was for entertaining the guests.

The fun-loving but exhausted Swede knew that one of these days he needed to start getting in shape for the heavyweight championship fight coming up the following month at Yankee Stadium. His trainer/manager, Rolf Aberg, insisted the Swede work hard for at least three hours a day fighting a string of sparring partners, one after the other. The problem the squat, tough, cunning Aberg had was getting the Swede into the ring. The only way Aberg could entice his boxer out of bed in the morning was to promise him sparring partners half his height and weight. Consequently, the Swede happily battered one miniature fighter senseless after another. That went on for weeks, until most of the sparring partners were either seriously injured or quit. Toward the end of August, the Swede was down to drunks and derelicts, who were no more than human punching bags for the heavyweight boxing champion of Europe.

The Swede's sparring bouts became such bloodbaths that Grossinger's guests stopped coming. It ruined their appetites for lunch and/or dinner. Billy Constable stopped coming, too, the afternoon he saw the heavyweight boxing champion of Europe give a grotesque beating to his younger brother, the lighter and shorter Roddy Svenson. When the heavyweight boxing champion of Europe was finished, Roddy's face was a mess of saliva, snot, and blood. The heavyweight champ of Europe was supposed to be tough. Didn't the New York *Daily News* say the Swede was "as big as a house and strong as an ox"? If that was the case, wondered Billy Constable, why was Rolf Aberg allowing the heavyweight champ of Europe to fight such puny sparring partners? Why was his trainer letting the heavyweight champ of Europe beat up on his little brother Roddy? And why was Aberg allowing the heavyweight champ of Europe to sleep with so many groupies?

And then one night in the middle of a *shtup,* Billy figured it all out.

"He's here for the money, Rosie honey," said Billy, suddenly jumping out of bed and pacing back and forth.

"What?" asked Rosie Feinstein, miffed at the hillbilly's sudden damn coitus interruptus.

"He's here for the loser's purse, period," said Billy, quite pleased with himself. "That's why he don't give a shit, Rosie. Because he's only here for the money!"

The cripple was immediately anxious.

He didn't care that the butler hadn't helped him into his chair. He was more concerned with the fact that he was seated so far away. The cripple didn't have his hearing aids with him. He wasn't used to taking them and had left them behind in his apartment. It would be very difficult for him to hear what transpired seated like he was in New Jersey.

"May I move to the chair on your left?" the cripple asked the producer. "I can't hear very well."

The producer appeared extremely annoyed by the cripple's request. "My lawyer and I will speak up," he replied.

"Sneak up? Sneak up on who?" asked the cripple.

"*Speak up.* We will both *speak up,*" said the producer, very irritated.

"See what I mean?" said the cripple.

The two at the other end of the table didn't see.

The cripple sat down in his assigned seat.

A middle-aged woman dressed in a black uniform with a frilly white collar and a white apron brought in three lobster cocktails. When she placed the lobster cocktail in front of the producer, he said, "Thank you, Millie."

Sigmond Levy never looked at the cripple. In fact, he never looked up. His eyes were riveted on his lobster cocktail. The cripple recognized Levy's wristwatch. He wore an expensive Patek Philippe gold perpetual. The cripple once owned the same watch but had to sell it. The old cripple really liked that watch.

"I want to do *The Death Game,*" said the producer, breaking the silence.

As it grew closer to the big fight, Billy Constable began receiving telephone calls asking who he thought was going to win. Billy, puffed up by this new attention, was happy to give his "expert" opinion to one and all.

One day Billy Constable received a phone call from someone who simply said, "Who's this?"

"Billy Constable."

"Whataya do?"

"I run the heavyweight champion of Europe's trainin' camp."

"Then you're the guy I wanna talk to. So, whodaya like?"

"Who's this?" asked Billy.

There was a long pause, then the voice said, "I'm calling for Mr. Giuseppe Sanseli."

"And who am I speakin' to?" asked Billy, all friendly-like but still curious.

"Never mind who ya speakin' to, putzo. Just tell me, whodaya like?"

"Who do I like?" asked Billy, legitimately confused.

"Whodaya think is gonna win da fight, you moron."

"Oh. Who do I think is gonna win?"

"Ya a fuckin' parrot or somethin'? Yeah, putzo, whodoya think is gonna win?"

"Well," said Billy, once again pleased to be considered a knowledgeable boxing authority by whoever was calling, "if it was my money I'd put every cent on the American."

"Ya think the nigger's gonna win this fight?"

"Let me tell you, Mr. . . . who'd you say you were?"

"I didn't. Why would ya put your money on da nigger, putzo?"

"Well," said Billy, his eyes squinting with seriousness, shifting the telephone receiver to his other ear, "for one thing, I read that the

American is trainin' like crazy down at Pompton Lakes, New Jersey. I can tell you this, Mr. . . . sir, the Swede ain't trainin' like crazy. He's doin' everything *'cept* trainin' like crazy. I think he's up here at Grossinger's for the . . . for the . . ."

"For da pussy?" asked the man on the telephone.

"No. For the money. Least that's what I think. It's my . . . you know . . . my honest opinion. I've been studyin' up on fighters who fought in championship fights and none of them spent their time dancin' and sparrin' with drunks and derelicts . . . an' . . . an' . . ."

"Fuckin'."

"Yeah, and *that*."

"So I was right, putzo, da guy's up there for da pussy."

"That and the money. You tell Mr. Sanseli this is comin' from the horse's mouth."

"So you're not a parrot. You're a horse. So tell me, Mr. Horse's Mouth, is 'at what the foreigner's doin'? Dancin' and fuckin' all the time?"

"That's what he's doin'."

"Lucky foreigner." There was a pause and then the phoner said, "The boss is gonna put a lot of money on this fight."

"Well, tell Mr. Sanseli to put all his money on the American. Tell him Billy Constable sez so. That's me. I'm Billy Constable. Like I said, I'm the director of this here trainin' camp."

"Da boss don't like to bet on niggers."

"Tell him to bet on this one."

"Ya said ya would bet on da nigger?"

"Yeah," answered Billy Constable, "I'd bet on him. If I had some serious money."

"What'd ya say your name was?"

"I told you. It's Billy Constable."

"I thought ya said ya was the horse's mouth. Ya that too?"

"Yeah, that's me."

"Okay, Horse's Mouth, thanks."

"You're welcome."

"An' Horse's Mouth."

"Yeah?"

"Ya better be right."

Later that same night Rosie Feinstein and Billy Constable were in bed in Rosie's room at Grossinger's Resort Hotel in the Catskill Mountains. Billy Constable was in the middle of telling Rosie about his telephone conversation with the guy who called Billy Horse's Mouth.

Rosie had her mouth full so she couldn't reply.

"It was kinda scary," Billy said.

Rosie made a throaty sound signifying interest.

"But then I got to thinkin', if I'm right, which I know I am, I mean if the nigger's suppose to be really trainin' like they say he is an' the Swede ain't trainin' at all, I mean the Swede's doin' nothin' but dancin' until two or three every mornin' and God knows what he's doin' with the girls he takes back to his room every night after he leaves the nightclub . . ."

Rosie's head popped up. She said, "I know what he's doing." And then she went back to work.

" . . . and he's boxin' sparrin' partners that are half his size an' half dead, I mean he was beatin' the crap outta his brother the other day. Jesus, Rosie, you don't beat the crap outta your own brother."

Rosie made another throaty sound. This time signifying amazement. Or agreement. Or something.

"I mean, after talkin' with that there business associate who telephoned yesterday, and explainin' to him the ins and outs of the comin' fight, I talked myself into wantin' to bet on the nigger too."

Rosie's head popped up again. This time she was cross. She said, "I absolutely *hate* that word and you've said it twice just now. Cut it out!"

"What word?"

"Nigger. It's a Southern thing and I personally detest the sound of it. Stop saying it."

"It ain't a Southern thing, Rosie, it's—"

"Just stop saying it."

"Okay, okay I'll stop sayin' it. Anyway, if ever there was a sure thing, this gotta be it. The nigger's gonna . . . I mean the American's gonna win this fight walkin' away. It won't even be close, Rosie. The American's gonna *kill* the Swede."

"You're absolutely certain?" asked Rosie Feinstein, having stopped for a bit.

"Absolutely certain."

"If you're absolutely certain . . . I'll lend you twenty dollars so you can bet."

"That's not what I'm talkin' about, Rosie, honey."

"So what *are* you talking about?"

"I'm talkin' about bettin' twenty *thousand* dollars. Maybe a hundred thousand dollars. That's what I'm talkin' about."

"Goodness," said Rosie Feinstein in a small voice.

"The only problem is . . ."

"Is what?"

" . . . is where am I gonna get that kinda money?"

Ten days later Billy Constable found the box.

"What? Please speak louder," begged the cripple at the producer's dinner table.

"I said I want to do *The Death Game.*"

The cripple breathed a sigh of relief. "Great. I knew you would. Only you coulda said something at my place. You know, told me—"

"I will want to change several aspects of the program, including its name, the qualifications for your contestants, and the way you eliminate them from the competition."

"Well, I think—"

"I am not the least bit interested in what you think," stated the producer, "and I shall continue without interruption, *if I may.*"

The cripple was clearly shaken. He glared down the long table at the producer, trying to control the anger simmering in his chest. Lousy for the blood pressure, he thought to himself. And this is the last place I want to drop dead, on this bastard's dinner table. Still, nobody speaks to me like that.

"I will call the program *The Big Question,*" continued the producer. "I will pick contestants that are experts in their field. There will be other changes I won't bother to mention here."

"I'll think about what you just said," said the old cripple bravely. "I'll want a list of the other changes you have in mind that you haven't men—"

"You don't seem to understand," snapped the producer. "I am not the least bit interested in your approval and you will not receive any such list."

Sigmond Levy cleared his throat. The producer and the cripple turned their heads in the direction of his phlegm. Levy said, "My client"—the lawyer nodded in the producer's direction—"will own the show. He will receive an executive producer credit and a created by credit. You will not receive any credits. You will not be permitted to come to any of the show's tapings. You will get a royalty, period."

"Wait a minute. I don't—"

"As he mentioned before," interrupted Levy, "my client is not the least bit interested in what you think. And as my client mentioned, he loathes to be interrupted. If you are not happy with the situation, then I suggest you find another backer for your program."

"There's a damn good chance I will," said the cripple.

There was silence in the room.

"Keep in mind," continued Sigmond Levy, never taking his eyes off his lobster cocktail, talking with chewed chunks of lobster in his mouth, "a substantial royalty is nothing to cavalierly pass up. Having just finished investigating your personal and financial resources"—Levy swallowed—"we have discovered that your debt is rather substantial and your living conditions somewhat barbaric."

"And exactly what will this substantial royalty be?" asked the cripple.

"One-tenth of the package price," replied Sigmond Levy, turning to look at the cripple.

"*One-tenth!*" shouted the cripple.

The lawyer returned to his lobster cocktail.

"Yes, one-tenth," said the producer.

"That's not sharing the project fifty-fifty in any way, shape, or form. I thought we were—"

"I don't recall fifty-fifty ever being mentioned," interrupted the producer. "In any case, that is our offer. Take it or leave it. We think it's quite generous. For doing nothing."

"Think about it," suggested the producer's lawyer, chewing.

"I'll think about it, all right. Just keep in mind what my old friend Sugar Ray Robinson once told me. Sugar Ray said, 'Fifty percent of something is better than a hundred percent of nothing.' If I pass on your ridiculous offer, your ninety percent of the package price won't be worth a red cent. Don't worry, gentlemen, you'll definitely hear from me. Probably as soon as I get home. This is very disappointing but, what the hell, I've been disappointed before. I'll see myself out." The cripple stood, threw his napkin down on the table, grabbed his crutch, and started limping out of the dining room. He hadn't touched his lobster cocktail.

Before leaving the room, the cripple turned and faced the two men.

"You know something?" he said. "I'm finished thinking about it. I'd rather not do the show than let you two pricks make a lousy dime on the project. As far as I'm concerned you can take your offer, divide it in half, and stick it up both your asses."

The old cripple opened the dining room door and slammed it closed behind him. Then opened it and stepped back into the dining room. Looking directly at the producer, he said, "And if you and the fat fuck lawyer of yours try to steal my idea, I'll sue your asses from here to hell and back." Once again the cripple slammed the door behind him.

The producer and his lawyer looked at each other . . .

. . . and continued eating their lobster cocktails.

The serving maid came into the producer's dining room and began collecting the lobster cocktail goblets and plates. The producer waited until the maid had gone, then got up out of his chair and began pacing back and forth alongside the dining room table opposite his lawyer.

"You never saw anything as mesmerizing as the execution on *The Death Game,* Sig. The sheer excitement of watching someone slowly die was mind-blowing. And even when the cripple was forced to use terminally ill contestants, and even though the person being executed *wanted* to die, it was *still* incredible to watch. Imagine if the person didn't want to die! My God, how great would that be? It was enthralling, Sig. Knowing that agony and extinction were on the way for the contestant and . . . and . . . the fact that you were actually going to see an execution take place! *See someone die in front of your eyes!* The old coot said it was . . . what was the word he used . . . hypnotic, that was it, hypnotic . . . and he was right. It was. It was absolutely hypnotic. Then, when the first signs of the poison set in . . . the twisting and turning . . . the facial tics . . . the eyes widening, the mouth grimacing, the fingers starting to claw at the arms of the chair . . . and . . . and . . ."

"Easy. Easy. Calm down," said the producer's lawyer. "You're getting yourself all—"

"I didn't say a word when I left the creep's apartment. I didn't want to let him know how excited I was. I'm going to do that program, Sig. I *must* do that program. I must be the one to bring that idea to television, and nobody, I mean nobody's going to stand in my way, especially a little piece of *scheise* like that old cripple. If I have to have the idiot killed, I'll have him killed."

"If you must, you must," said the lawyer named Sigmond Levy, sucking out a chewy piece of lobster caught between two teeth.

The maid returned with the main course.

One afternoon, someone knocked on Arthur Durch's office door, opened it, and walked in.

"Evelyn Lounge! What are you doing here?" said Arthur.

"Evelyn Lounge *Durch,*" corrected Evelyn.

My God, thought Arthur to himself, it's so good to see her. Her ratty hair. The dirty wisps across her forehead. The sunlight on her face. Her bloodshot eyes. Her flat chest. Her sticks for legs. God, she's beautiful. God, I love her. "God, you're beautiful, Evelyn. God, I love you," he said, the words just popping out of his mouth.

"Beauty's in the eyes of the beholder," replied Evelyn Lounge.

"What's that supposed to mean?"

"I don't know. It's just . . . it sounded like something I should say."

"Okay. Whatever. So why are you here?"

"I need therapy, Arthur."

"What kind of therapy?"

"Your kind, Arthur. Sex therapy. That's what you are, a sex therapist, aren't you?"

"Yes, I am."

"Well?"

"Why do you think you need sex therapy, Evelyn?"

"Because I'm nurturing other boyfriends and I—"

"Nurturing?"

"Yes, nurturing . . . I am nurturing a group of new boyfriends—"

"A *group*?"

"Yes, more than one. Would you let me finish a sentence, please. And I would like to . . . to . . . to . . ."

"*Fuck*? Is that what you would like to do? *Fuck* your new group of boyfriends? The new group of boyfriends you're nurturing?" asked Arthur Durch with considerable anger.

"Yes, that's what I would—"

"You want to *fuck* your nurtured bunch of new boyfriends. Is that right?"

"Yes, Arthur. You just said that and yes, that is right, but God, that is *such* an awful word. I hate that word, Arthur."

"What word, Evelyn?"

"You know what word, Arthur."

"Say it, Evelyn."

"No. I will not say it."

"Come on, say it."

"Why?"

"To get rid of your inhibition about . . . about . . ."

"About what?"

"About saying the word 'fuck.' About the *act*!"

"*What* act?"

"*Fucking*. The act of fucking."

"No. I won't say that awful word."

"For me, Evelyn?"

"No. Not even for you."

"Say it, Evelyn. I'm not kidding now. Just say the word 'fuck.' Say it out loud."

"*No!*"

"Come on, Evelyn. Say it. Don't be such a pain in the ass."

"Go fuck yourself, Arthur."

"There! *You said it!* You said it, Evelyn! You said 'fuck' out loud. A breakthrough, Evelyn! A fucking breakthrough!"

"Seriously, Arthur?"

"Yes, seriously, Evelyn. You've made an important breakthrough. Marry me, Evelyn."

"We *are* married, for God's sake."

"Good. Then come back to me."

"Do you know one good reason why I should?"

"I can give you three good reasons."

"Just three?"

"For starters."

"What are they?"

"I love you, Evelyn. I am crazy about you, Evelyn. And I adore you, Evelyn. That's three."

"You really feel that way about me, Arthur?"

"Cross my heart."

"Awww," said Evelyn Lounge Durch, and climbed onto Arthur Durch's lap.

On a hot muggy afternoon in July 2012, somewhere off the New Jersey Turnpike, the producer and a man named Morris Rothberg were talking to each other through the open windows of their automobiles, parked alongside each other. The cars were idling on a barren road in a barren industrial marshland near Elizabeth, New Jersey. The turnpike rose over railroad tracks in the distance, far, far away.

"Morris, I need you to do me a favor."

"Like what?"

"I want you to dispose of someone."

"When?"

"Soon."

"Okay. Sure."

"What's the ticket these days, Morris?"

Morris Rothberg was nicknamed "Moe the Hook." He was reputed to have hung several adversaries by their necks on meat hooks in an ice locker down in the meat-packing district of New York City. Absolutely no one called Morris Rothberg "Moe the Hook." It was Mr. Rothberg to everyone, with the exception of a few friends who called him Morris.

"A hundred grand, fifty grand up front," said Rothberg.

"The price has gone up appreciably, Morris."

"You asked, I told."

"I didn't come prepared to pay that much up front."

"Call me when you have it."

Morris Rothberg's window slid up. When the black-tinted window reached the top, the automobile drove away.

Father Daniel Patrick Brady had never been outside of Philadelphia. Consequently, Rome was truly a magical city to the wide-eyed priest.

He particularly enjoyed the outdoor marketplaces, especially the ones on the Campo dei Fiori. And there were the colors. Always the colors. The Vespas in yellow, green, and bright red; the colorful flags and balloons everywhere in the city; the red strawberries, green melons, blueberries, and oranges in the markets; the brightly colored canned goods on shelves in the open mobile stores; the horse-drawn blue chariots with their fire engine red wheels; the donkeys festooned with ribbons and bows that pull the tourist carts; and the yellow Fiats, the white-robed nuns, the golden arches, and the pale green statues.

There were the bridges along the Tiber River at sunset. The Piazza di Spagna, the Trevi Fountain where Father Brady threw a coin, and the magnificent Sistine Chapel and its most famous mural, *The Creation of Adam.*

Father Brady was simply overwhelmed.

The priest went to school in a small room within the Museo d'Arte on the Piazza Santa Marta. He slept in a dormitory across the street above the Papal Guards. His teachers were uniformly humorless and strict, and taught in either Italian or Latin, languages Father Brady spoke fluently.

Father Brady loved his daily routine. Waking and going to Mass at dawn. Then to school, where he relished learning the form and arrangement of public worship as set down by the Catholic Church in the Scriptures. He savored the study of canon law and the sacrament. But what he delighted in most was the subject of moral theology: mastering consciously and properly informed choices as described in the traditions of the church and the application of the teachings of Jesus Christ to modern everyday situations. When writing to friends at home, Father Brady would repeatedly say his intellectual pursuit at the Vatican was, as far as he was concerned, heaven here on earth.

It was during Father Brady's first months in Rome that the priest's father, Flynn Brady, died of a massive heart attack. The coronary took place in the family row house on Stoneway Lane. Flynn had just finished his third shot of whiskey when the attack occurred. The shot glass fell out of his hand and rolled under his armchair.

Not many family or friends attended Flynn Brady's funeral, mainly because Flynn Brady didn't have many family or friends who cared that much about him. Just a few employees from his appliance company and a brother from Detroit. In Rome, Father Daniel Patrick Brady said a prayer for him in the church of Santa Maria in Traspontina on the Via d. Conciliazione in Vatican City.

After Father Brady prayed in the church of Santa Maria in Traspontina for his father's soul, he went to the Spanish Steps to try to recall the nicer attributes and traits of Flynn Brady. The priest's favorite place in all of Rome was the Spanish Steps. Father Brady spent as much time there as he could. He found the steps a good place to relax and think. The hundred-and-eighty-degree view of the city from the top of the steps constantly amazed him. The way the buildings of Rome were bathed in seemingly perpetual sunlight. Their amazing ocher and terra-cotta colors practically blinding him. It was all a living miracle. Father Brady could never describe the view of Rome from the Spanish Steps to his satisfaction.

It was while Father Brady ate his lunch on the Spanish Steps that he met the woman.

On the other side of the steps from Father Brady were two young ladies taking the afternoon sun and finishing slices of pizza. The priest kept sneaking glances their way between bites of his salad. Once he brought his plastic fork to his mouth only to find there was nothing on it. He watched both ladies put their hands to their mouths to hide giggles when the priest poked his lip with the fork's empty tines. This was somewhat new, this checking women out, and something the priest noticed he had been doing more and more of late. He kept sneaking peeks nonetheless.

The women looked somewhat alike. They both wore strappy black dresses, black sandals, and sunglasses. One wore her hair down, one wore hers up. The one with her hair up had thinnish lips, the other's lips were fuller. The one with the full lips got up, came down a step, crossed over, and sat beside the priest.

"You're a hottie," she said in Italian. Her voice was raspy. A smoker, most likely.

"So I've been told," Father Brady replied in Italian.

"I shouldn't wonder. I think you're the best-looking priest I've ever seen."

"Thank you."

"Do you live in Rome?"

"No. I just go to school here."

"At the Vatican?"

"Yes."

"Hmmm," said the woman.

Neither one said anything for several moments.

"What is your name, Father?"

"Brady. Daniel Patrick Brady. My friends call me DP."

"May I take you to dinner tonight, Father Brady?" she asked, her raspy voice adding to her sex appeal. "I have never taken a priest to dinner in my entire life."

Father Brady didn't know what to say. He tried to think of an appropriate answer from what he learned in his moral theology class, but his mind was fogged by the smells and beauty of the woman sitting beside him. *"Aiuto!"* said the priest. Help!

"Fermate!" Stop! said the woman, holding up her hand like someone directing traffic. She took a ballpoint pen from her handbag and an old, crumpled piece of paper. She wrote an address on the piece of paper and gave it to Father Brady. "This is a good restaurant. Simple. Not fancy. The clergy is poor. I will pay. Also, if you come, that is good. If you don't, it is not so good for me, but at least I will enjoy a good meal and a good book, which I will bring to the restaurant as a safeguard in case we do not see each other again. *Ciao, padre.*"

Her name was Rosa Gambino. She was thirty-six years old and a high-priced call girl. So was her girlfriend, Maria Rigarda. When

Rosa Gambino spotted Father Daniel Patrick Brady sneaking peeks at her, she bet Maria Rigarda one thousand lire she could sleep with the priest. "I've always wanted to sleep with a priest," she said that sunny afternoon as they walked down the Spanish Steps.

IV

Across the street from the Umanov Guitar Store . . .

Across the street from the Umanov Guitar Store in the West Village, a dirty gray van worked its way into a parking place. Dark blue letters across both sides of the van read **Edward Antoian & Sons Oriental Rug Gallery.** Three men with the company name stitched on the backs of their blue jumpsuits stepped out of the van's front seat and onto the street. They walked to the back of the van, opened its two doors, and pulled out a long Persian rug tied by rope at both ends and in the middle. The three men hoisted the rug onto their shoulders—one man at each end and one in the middle—and carried it across the street. They stopped at the black door with the bronze letter slot that led to the rooms above the guitar store. The man in the middle released the rug, opened the door, and pushed the button of the name that matched the one written on the piece of paper he held in his hand.

After a while the door buzzed open.

The three men lugged the long rug into the dark hallway and began to walk up the stairs. The old cripple suddenly appeared, standing on the floor above them. He leaned over the rail and shouted, "Hold it! Where the hell do you guys think you're going with that rug? I didn't order any rug."

"This is a present," said one of the three men.

"From who?"

"Wait just a second, please," said the speaker politely. With his free hand the man pulled a piece of paper from a back pocket, unfolded it, and read the note aloud: " 'This beautiful Persian rug is a gift from your partner in *The Death Game*. I want to make amends for my rude behavior at dinner last week.' "

"The prick had second thoughts, did he? Can't say as I blame him," said the cripple from over the banister to the delivery men below.

"I'm sorry, what did you say, sir?" said the man.

"Nothing. So what the hell am I going to do with a friggin' rug, for Christ sake?"

"We have strict instructions to make sure we put it down on your apartment floor," said the speaker, "or we get our heads handed to us."

"That rug isn't going to fit in my place. It's too big."

"We'll make it fit, sir. Don't you worry about that."

The cripple thought for a moment. For one thing, he didn't have a rug. A rug would be nice under his bare feet. For another thing, the rug must be worth something. He could always sell it.

"Okay," said the cripple, "bring it up."

The guy who did the talking took his place under the middle of the rolled-up rug once again, and the three men continued walking up the flight of stairs with their burden. The cripple stood by the open door of his apartment. The three men, all very large and wearing work gloves, walked in. The cripple followed them inside and shut the door. The man who had spoken stepped forward and whacked the cripple across the side of his head at the temple with a blackjack. The eighty-two-year-old cripple crumpled to the floor.

One of the men untied the ropes that bound the rug and spread it across the floor, pushing the furniture out of the way as he did. The men picked up the unconscious cripple, rolled the rug back with the old man inside, and tied the rug in the same three places. They replaced the furniture in its original position, then hefted the rug onto their shoulders and walked out of the apartment. The last man closed the door behind him.

At the foot of the stairs an old biddy made way for the three men and said, "Didn't know that grumpy old codger had such a nice rug in his apartment. That must have cost him a pretty penny. Having it cleaned, is he?"

None of the men answered her. They just continued walking out of the building and crossed the street. One of the men opened the van's rear doors with a free hand and all three pushed the rug inside. The speaker locked the back doors, and the three climbed into the van's front seat. Each one lit a cigarette. After a few minutes the van pulled away from the curb into traffic and slowly disappeared.

Forty minutes later, the dirty gray van with **Edward Antoian & Sons Oriental Rug Gallery** on its sides drove down the same barren road past the spot where Morris Rothberg and the producer had their business discussion several days before. At a certain distance from the beginning of the road, the van turned left and went exactly two-tenths of a mile and stopped. The driver climbed out of the van and walked to a freshly dug grave six feet long, four feet wide, and eight feet deep. The driver returned to the van and joined his two partners by the rear doors. The three men carried the rug with the old cripple in it and tossed the rug and body into the hole.

The driver returned to the rear of the van and pulled out three long-handled shovels. After the hole was filled, the men lugged sections of pregrown grass from the rear of the van back to the grave. They rolled out the small blocks of grass over the fresh dirt. The three collected twigs and bits of garbage in the area nearby and sprinkled the debris onto the blocks of grass around the grave. The three men walked back and forth across the area several times, pushing and kicking the dirt with their boots. When they finished, the three got into the van and lit cigarettes.

After a while the van drove away from the marshland.

It was the middle of August 2012. Training camp was over. The big fight was just weeks away and Billy Constable had arrived back in New York City.

The first morning in the office, Billy spent about twenty minutes searching for an old pair of his sneakers in a conference room closet. He remembered throwing the pair into the back of that closet months ago, or thought he did. Billy wanted to go running in Central Park during his lunch break. The problem of finding his sneakers in that closet was that everyone in the office threw things into it. The closet was the company catchall.

Billy couldn't find his sneakers.

But he did find a box.

The box was buried under a lot of old flyers and pamphlets, snow boots, file folders, boxes of typing paper, manila envelopes, outdated electronic equipment, stuff like that. When he saw what was buried inside, Billy was dumbfounded.

"Why?" asked Jimmy Joel Jenks. The two friends were having a beer that evening at P. J. Clarke's. "Why were you dumbfounded?"

Billy looked to his left and right before answering, then said, "The box was filled with stacks and stacks of red, white, and blue hundred-and-fifty-dollar ringside seats to the fight. I mean *stacks* of 'em."

"For the big fight at Yankee Stadium you're workin' on?"

"Yeah."

"Holy mackerel!" said Jimmy Joel Jenks. He wiped some beer foam off his upper lip with his shirtsleeve and said excitedly, "When's the fight takin' place?"

"I've told you a hundert times. The first Friday after Labor Day," said Billy. "September the fourteenth."

"That's not too far away," said Jimmy Joel.

"I *know,*" said Billy.

The two boys were standing at the restaurant's bar.

After sucking on their beers for a minute or so, Billy said, "I'm kinda stoked about findin' them tickets."

"Yeah, and kinda scart too, I'll bet," said Jimmy Joel Jenks.

"Yeah, kinda."

"Scart as a long-tailed cat in a room fulla rockin' chairs, I'll bet."

"Maybe not that scart," said a serious Billy Constable, squinting up his eyes at Jimmy Joel.

The boys were quiet again.

"Actually, you know somethin, JJ? Findin' them tickets is the answer to my prayers. It's as if God Almighty knew of my problems."

"What problems?"

"My problems with the bent noses."

"With the who?"

"The bent noses." Billy Constable pushed his nose to one side with his forefinger. "That's what they call them Eye-talian mob guys. Bent noses."

"Why?"

"I don't know. I think it's 'cause most of their noses are broke. From fightin', I guess. Anyways, my problem is bein' over my head in gamblin' debts. With them guys. You don't go gettin' into money problems with them guys. That's one thing you don't do."

"Why?"

"'Cause they beat the shit outta you if they catch you. Or worse."

"Or worse?"

"Yeah, or worse."

"You owe them nose guys money now?"

"Yeah, sorta."

"How much?"

"Eight hundert," said Billy.

"Dollars?"

"Yeah, dollars."

"Wow!"

The boys were quiet again. They stared at their beers.

"I pray a lot," said Billy Constable.

"I'll bet you do," said Jimmy Joel.

"More than before."

"Because of them bent nose guys?"

"Yeah."

"You in a little trouble or a lotta trouble?"

"A lotta trouble."

"And prayin' pays off?" asked JJ.

"Yeah, I'm sure."

"You're sure of what?"

"I'm sure prayin' pays off. Look what He did for me."

"He who?" asked Jimmy Joel, bewildered.

"God. Who do you think, JJ? He . . . God . . . dropped a shitload of valuable fight tickets right outta heaven into my lap."

"I thought you found them tickets in a closet."

"Aw, come on, JJ, you know what I mean."

"Yeah, I know what you mean. That was a joke, sorta. Why are the tickets so valuable?" asked Jimmy Joel, wiping more beer foam from his upper lip with his shirtsleeve.

"Because I can sell them ringside tickets for at least three times what they cost, that's why. That box's the answer to my prayers."

"You sure?"

"'Bout what?" asked Billy.

"'Bout them tickets bein' the answer to your prayers."

"I ain't worried, if that's what you mean."

"You said you were."

"When'd I say that? I never said I was worried. I said I was scart, not worried."

"Maybe you ought to be worried too."

"Maybe you ought to shut up."

Of course, if Billy Constable had thought about it, and considered why the box was buried like it was under all that stuff and placed as far back in the closet as it was, Billy might have been worried too.

Very worried.

Theresa Mendavey traveled to San Francisco, took up with a crowd of hippies, met friends named Sunshine, Harmony, Tiger, Plump One, Moonbeam, Aquarius, and Angel Dust. She did some new drugs, slept with some weird guys and a few weird girls, woke up a couple of months later on a putrid, stained-from-God-knows-what futon on a dreary Saturday morning in 1997. She was twenty-four years old. She had just awakened from a sound sleep totally bummed. What am I doing here in this flophouse in the Haight? she wondered. And why am I lying next to this damn fool, skinny, no-good, drugged-up jerk? I'm here because I'm rebelling, right? But exactly who am I rebelling against? My mother? My father? Are they a worthwhile cause? Are those two losing one ounce of sleep over me?

"I THINK NOT!" she yelled aloud.

"What?!" asked Kip Dynamite, shooting up to a sitting position next to her. He had been sound asleep and was now all bleary-eyed and very halitocular. "You say something?"

Kip Dynamite, whose real name was Allan Gorchick, was a twenty-year-old dropout from Stanford University. Kip had been a brilliant premed student for about five minutes. He was also hypochondriacal and confused, a kid who couldn't take the pressure and dropped out of Stanford to major in hallucinatory products.

"I refused to allow the force per unit my studies exacted on my expendable brainpower to interfere with making up for all the sex I missed not being around in the sixties," Kip Dynamite would pontificate. He often said stupid things like that, more often than required. Dynamite was a tall, undernourished-looking slob with bloodshot eyes, a red, runny nose, and a horsey face. Kip wasn't fully awake at the time of Theresa Mendavey's outburst. He had gotten himself really blitzed the night before at a family bar mitzvah.

"Good-bye, Kip," said Theresa.

"What? *Wait!*" said Kip Dynamite. "What are you doing?"

"I'm leaving you," explained Theresa Mendavey, stuffing her shoulder pack with the few possessions she had. "I'm finished wasting my precious youth with the likes of you, Gorchick."

"My name's Dynamite," whined the junkie, "and I'm your boyfriend."

"Were. Past tense," said Theresa Mendavey, wondering how she ever allowed someone like Allan Gorchick to become her boyfriend.

Theresa Mendavey's slide into serious decadence had begun picking up steam when she'd ridden off into the sunset sitting on the back of Andrew Jackson Brown's "big ol' hog." Andrew's mighty Harley took Theresa Mendavey from her home and family, leaving Theresa's mother sobbing at her kitchen sink.

Anyway, Andrew Jackson Brown got on Theresa Mendavey's nerves almost as fast as the standard poodle had her mother's. The constant Harley this and Harley that. And all his stupid buddies with their imbecilic macho T-shirts and asinine conversations. Jesus Christ Almighty. What a bunch of lowlife, blowhard dickheads. Theresa couldn't wait to get away from Andrew Jackson Brown, Andrew's motorcycles, Andrew's gang, and Andrew's LA.

"So what are you going to do?" asked Kip, ripe with really bad body odor.

"I'm going back to school," said Theresa.

"Good for you," he said with a big smile. Kip Dynamite may have been a foul-smelling loon bird, but he was nice. "What do you want to be, T?"

"A brain surgeon."

Home from Italy, Father Brady appeared somewhat distracted. He tended to forget things, lose track of conversations. His mind wandered.

"Still in a tizzy from all the wonders of the Eternal City, I suppose," said the cardinal.

"Yes, Your Eminence," replied Father Brady.

The cardinal must have been correct. The wonders of Rome obviously had caused Father Brady's confusion, as the priest, over time, seemed less and less unhinged. After a few months, Father Brady became his former conscientious self and the cardinal breathed a sigh of relief.

And then one evening, more than a year after he had returned to Philadelphia, Father Brady was hearing confessions. A woman, speaking in Italian, said, "Father, I have fornicated with a priest."

"Dóve?" Where? asked Brady, his heart suddenly pounding in his chest. He knew that raspy voice.

"In Rome," replied the woman.

"In Rome!" repeated Father Brady.

"Yes, in Rome," said the woman. "I have had your child, Father. She is a beautiful little girl. She is sitting on my lap."

The priest covered his face with his hands. "I thought you were on birth control," he whispered angrily.

"I thought so too."

Later that evening, Rosa Gambino sat on a motel room bed holding her baby in her lap. The baby was cooing and drooling. The bed's mattress squeaked every time Rosa, or the baby, moved. Father Brady sat as far away from the pair as he could get, on an uncomfortable chair in a far corner of the room. They spoke in Italian.

"Why did you come here, Rosa?" he asked.

"Why did I come to Philadelphia?" The question seemed to startle her.

"Well?"

"I came here to find you."

"Why?"

"Because I love you."

"But what good would your coming here do? What did you think you would accomplish? Do you want money?"

"I want *you*."

"In what way do you want me? Do you want me to leave the priesthood and marry you?"

"Yes! I want you to return to Rome and marry me and take care of us. I want you to stop being a priest and find a job in Rome. I will also find a job. Not doing what I used to do, but something else. I will work in a department store. Or a beauty shop. I'm sure I can find a job. I'm sure you can too. And then we can live like other people do. Like a family."

"And where will I work?" asked Father Brady. "In a beauty shop too?" The priest made a strange sound that might have been a laugh.

"You will find a job," she said. "I will too. We will be together. The three of us. Look at your daughter. She is beautiful, no?"

"Yes, she is beautiful."

For the first time, Rosa Gambino smiled.

"I don't know the first thing about babies."

"You'll learn," said Rosa Gambino. "Do you want to hold your daughter?"

"I'll drop her."

"No, you won't."

"They cry all night."

"You'll get used to it."

"You have to burp them. I don't know how to do that."

"I'll show you."

"I don't know why we're even discussing this. Do you want money?" the priest asked, returning to his priestly demeanor. "I don't have much but I can get—"

"I don't want *money.* I want *you*. I love you." Rosa lifted a full breast from her blouse and let the baby suckle. "Do you love me?" she asked.

"I'm very . . . fond of you."

"Fond of me?" she said, looking up at the priest. "Fond of me?"

"Yes. I am very fond of you," said Father Brady, trying to sound enthusiastic, "and . . . and—"

"Well, I'm *not* fond of you," said Rosa Gambino. "I *love* you. But if you don't love me, if you are only *fond* of me, and if you do not intend to come back with your daughter and me to Italy, then . . ."

"Then what?" said the priest in a cold voice.

"Then I *do* want money. Lots of money."

"You want lots of money? Ha! From a *priest*? That's . . . that's . . . And where do you expect me to get lots of—"

"You miserable, self-righteous prick," hissed Rosa Gambino from behind clenched teeth. "You don't think it's unforgivable to fuck a woman and make her pregnant, just that it's unforgivable the woman you fucked came to confront you. You are a priest completely unconcerned about being virtuous in the eyes of God. You are only concerned with being virtuous in the eyes of the people around you." Rosa Gambino took a deep breath and said, "All right, then, I want money and I want it soon."

"But how in God's name am I going to—"

"You figure it out, Golden Boy," she said. "Isn't that what you told me you were? The Golden Boy of the Catholic Church. Well, Mr. Golden Boy, you either come back to Rome with your child and me, or . . . or . . ."

"Or what?"

"Or I will go to the cardinal and tell him I am the unwed mother of your daughter."

"You wouldn't dare do that."

"Oh, wouldn't I? Think of something quickly, Father. I do not have the resources to stay long in your country. Maybe a month at the most."

Three days later, Father Brady walked out of the Cathedral of St. Peter and St. Paul, ran across the huge traffic circle, passed the Franklin Institute, and headed up Nineteenth Street. He crossed Walnut Street and entered Rittenhouse Square. It was a small park, two blocks long and two blocks wide. It was six o'clock in the morning. Only a few joggers were exercising at that hour. Father Brady walked into the park, chose a bench, and sat down. Often on his breaks, Father Brady would go to Rittenhouse Square, find an empty bench, and read. Today he needed to talk to himself.

"How does a private person like myself," he said aloud, "become something so demeaning as a game show contestant? How can I expose myself to such ridicule? I have to, that's why. I need the money. Is the money so important? Of course it's important. I will be able to give Rosa and the baby millions of dollars, enough money to live in comfort for the rest of their lives and still have hundreds of millions of dollars to give to the church. The church can do more good with those millions than I could ever do in a hundred lifetimes. And if I should die? Then so be it. It's God's will."

The priest sighed.

"Perhaps when all is said and done, I will have absolved myself of my sins. Nonsense. You will never be able to absolve your sins in the eyes of God.

"But perhaps I will in *my* eyes."

In the doctors' lounge of New York–Presbyterian Hospital, the discussion concerning *The Big Question* continued.

"*The Big Question* is that new television reality game show that everybody's talking about," said the anesthesiologist to Dr. Mendavey. "It debuts in a month or so."

"So what's so . . . I mean, why is everybody talking about it?" asked Dr. Theresa Mendavey.

Dr. Mendavey, the soon to be head of neurosurgery at New York–Presbyterian Hospital, and her operating team were on a coffee break between operations in the doctors' lounge. Theresa stood leaning against a cabinet, sipping a cup of hot black coffee, thinking. Myth had it that Dr. Mendavey could think of ten different subjects at the same time. Even when she spoke she was also thinking. At that moment in time, along with the new television show *The Big Question,* Dr. Mendavey was thinking about the the female construction worker with the nail accidentally shot into her skull that had pierced her brain and whom she would be operating on next, yet another life-or-death situation.

Dr. Theresa Mendavey was thirty-nine years old. She had evolved from a beautiful teenager into a beautiful woman. From a druggie dropout to graduating with honors from Stanford University and Johns Hopkins Medical School. Theresa had never been married. Her friends said she never would be. They said the woman was extremely content with her life as it was and hadn't any desire to change it.

Working with Dr. Mendavey came with an extremely dark side. The doctor was an arrogant, tough leader who neither brooked mistakes nor tolerated stupidity. Any occasion for either and more often than not the culprit was thrown not only off her team but often out of the hospital as well. Such was the deep-seated ill will a coworker might incur from Mendavey. And she was a sometimes vicious, Captain Queeg–like taskmaster. She berated underlings in front of others and tended to shout at them when angry. Her favorite expression was, "You're not listening." The phrase was melodically spoken, starting low and ending high (YOU'RE **NOT** LISTENING!). Dr. Mendavey would not have a man on her team and operated only on female patients. Exacting and dictatorial, Dr. Mendavey was one of the very best brain surgeons in Manhattan, and her associates knew it. There was rarely an opening on her operating team. The odd thing about Dr. Theresa Mendavey was this: Even though most of her colleagues couldn't stand her, they were all proud to work beside her. It was a feather in a woman's cap and an excellent career move to be connected with the doctor.

One afternoon ten years before, Theresa's mother, Edna Mendavey, lay down on the bed in a guest room of the Love Apple Mansion and died from an overdose of barbiturates. No one was sure whether it was a suicide or an accident. Theresa's father, Hector Mendavey, became a billionaire in 2009. While celebrating the event in Las Vegas, Hector suffered a fatal heart attack playing craps and fell onto the table, his head landing in a pile of his one-hundred-dollar chips.

Theresa Mendavey lived alone in a four-story town house on Sutton Place in Manhattan. The rear of the town house faced the East River. She preferred to take care of her graystone town house herself. "Doing housework relaxes me," she often said. The brain surgeon also owned a dark blue Bentley four-door sedan with red leather interior she rarely drove and a house in East Hampton on the beach she seldom found time to use.

"You haven't heard *anyone* talking about *The Big Question*?" asked the stunned anesthesiologist. "I can't believe how bumpkinly you are."

"Bumpkinly? I love the vocabulary you create," said the chief brain surgeon. "So, Anne, what's *The Big Question* about?"

"I really can't believe you haven't heard about it," persisted the anesthesiologist.

"YOU'RE NOT LISTENING, Doctor. I *said* I haven't heard about it."

"I'll bet you'll watch it when it comes on," said the anesthesiologist. "The premise is fascinating."

"What's so fascinating about it?"

"It's a quiz show," explained the anesthesiologist.

"They're the most boring shows on earth," said the brain surgeon.

"Not this one. If a contestant answers the big question correctly," explained the anesthesiologist, "the contestant wins one hundred million dollars!"

"*A hundred million dollars!* That's an awful lot of money," said Dr. Mendavey. "And what happens if the contestant misses the big question?" she asked, taking a gulp of coffee.

"The contestant's executed!" said a nurse.

"*What!*" blurted the neurosurgeon, coming very close to choking.

"Yes, executed. Right in front of your eyes!"

"You've got to be kidding."

"I'm not kidding."

"How?" asked Dr. Mendavey.

"Poison, I think," replied the nurse.

"Yes, poison," said a nurse-in-training, pleased to be part of the conversation.

"Executed on television. I don't believe it."

"Believe it!" said several members of the team in unison. Then they giggled.

There was quiet in the lounge as all of the Mendavey team thought their own thoughts.

Dr. Mendavey was the first to speak. "A hundred million dollars, huh?"

"Yes," said someone.

"What kind of questions do they ask the contestants?" asked the brain surgeon.

"They ask questions based on the contestant's expertise," said the assistant anesthesiologist.

"And if you don't have an expertise?" asked Dr. Mendavey.

"I think they have a category called general knowledge," replied the assisting neurosurgeon.

"But you *do* have an expertise, Doctor. The brain."

"That's right, I do. In fact, I daresay there's not a question they could ask me about the brain I couldn't answer."

"You're not thinking of trying out for the show, are you?" asked the anesthesiologist.

"As a matter of fact, I am," replied the brain surgeon.

"Why?"

"I'm *really* smart."

"What about the death factor?" asked the anesthesiologist.

"It's a non sequitur," said Dr. Mendavey.

What an ego, thought an attending nurse to herself.

When the team was finished with their break and were walking down the corridor that led to the operating room, Dr. Mendavey asked her chief nurse, "Tell me about this afternoon's patients. Tell me about the construction worker with the nail in her skull."

"She's alert and feeling no pain. In fact, she's pretty sharp."

"Good."

"What's the plan?" asked the chief nurse.

"It's a relatively easy plan. We'll drill around the nail, pull out the piece of skull, pound the nail out of the piece, and put the hunk of skull back in her head. What else?"

"It's bad," said the chief nurse.

"How bad?"

"She was struck by an out-of-control cab that jumped a curb near Saks at Fiftieth and Fifth Avenue, Doctor. The accident caused an epidural hematoma. The hematoma is located between the left outer covering of the brain and the skull. She's suffered several seizures already. On the plus side, the patient is young and strong. She appears to be in basically good health with good pressure and a good pulse. I have all the X-rays and scans up on the reflector in the OR."

"Do you know the patient's name and what she does for a living?" asked Dr. Mendavey.

"I don't know her occupation," answered the chief nurse, "but her name is Billie Berry."

Father DP Brady telephoned the offices of *The Big Question* to request information about being a prospective contestant.

The jolly person on the other end, a girl with a very young, very high, very loud voice, asked the priest if he lived in New York City. When Father Brady told her he did not, that he lived in Philadelphia, she explained to the priest that if he could come to New York and visit *The Big Question*'s offices, it would make his becoming a contestant that much easier. "I'm lettin' you in on a little secret, okay?" yelled the girl into the phone.

"What's that?"

"Like it'll help you a lot more to come yourself, okay?" she said.

"Okay. Do I have to bring anything?"

"Golly no! Just yourself, okay? Oh, and one other thing. What do you do?"

"I'm a priest."

"No shit! You are? We've never had a priest try out for the show before, okay? We've had a black cat . . . sorry . . . a nun, sir, okay? But she screwed up and we're not using her. You're the first priest, okay?"

"Okay."

The priest made an appointment for early Friday afternoon, September 14.

When the date arrived, the priest took an Amtrak train to New York City and a cab to the address he was given. *The Big Question*'s offices were on the third floor of a building on Forty-fifth Street between Eighth and Ninth avenues. It was just starting to rain as DP entered the building. He took an elevator to the top floor. The door of the elevator opened onto a large loft that had been partitioned into various cubicles, some large, some small. But first was an immense reception area. There were posters of past game and reality shows tacked onto the walls. At least two dozen old public school chairs with the large right arm for writing were lined up in rows. A dowdy woman in her late seventies was seated in one of them. She gave Father Brady a pallid smile when he walked in.

The priest smiled back, wondering if all the contestants on *The Big Question* would be elderly or terminally ill.

DP walked up to the receptionist, who looked fourteen or fifteen, tops. She boomed, "Hi!"

Father Brady looked behind him to see who she was shouting at. Realizing it was him, he said, "Hello."

"You're applying to be a contestant for *The Big Question,* right?" she yelled.

"Right."

"Great!" she boomed.

The girl handed the priest a clipboard and ballpoint pen. "Please take a seat, any seat you want, and fill out the contestant form attached to the clipboard. Also, please read the rules of the game that are explained on the last piece of paper. Hurry back, now!"

The young girl with the exuberant voice was wearing jeans and a man's blue button-down oxford shirt with the sleeves rolled up. The buttoned buttons started about four down from the top. The young girl was showing a great deal of cleavage. The priest hurriedly took the clipboard and ballpoint pen and found a seat. He was about to begin filling out his questionnaire when he sensed he was being watched. The priest looked up and saw the dowdy woman sitting in a chair against the far wall he noticed when he first entered the room. She was looking his way, still smiling her pallid smile.

When their eyes met she asked, "From out of town, Father?"

"Yes. I'm from Philadelphia."

"I'm from Steubenville. That's in Ohio. This is my second trip to New York. I had several bad experiences on my last trip. I was caught in a terrible snowstorm, I had my wallet stolen, and I met a very rude man who went to great lengths to embarrass me in the hallway of the Sherry-Netherland hotel. I sure didn't think I'd ever come back to this place. Tell you the truth, I had plenty of second thoughts about trying out for this show. I've never been lucky in New York. If these TV people hadn't offered to fly me, I wouldn't have come. That's what they did, they paid for my plane ticket. Both ways. I told them about myself over the phone. I explained how I had lived long enough without my Norville. Norville was my dear husband. He died a long time ago. Too long a time. I told the person on the telephone I truly wanted to see my Norville again, but if I won the millions of dollars I certainly would have plenty of uses for the money. I would spend the money on dozens of good causes. Like I said, I told the TV people if they didn't fly me here from Steubenville I wouldn't come. I told them where I wanted to sit on the plane. On the aisle. I told them if I couldn't sit on the aisle I couldn't come. I had a bad experience when I flew to New York the time before. I was sitting between these two—"

Father Brady interrupted and said, "I better get to this form."

Without waiting for a reply, he turned away from the woman and began filling out the questionnaire. The form asked the following questions: (Name) Daniel Patrick Brady, (Occupation) priest, (Age) almost 45, (Address) Cathedral of St. Peter and St. Paul, 222 North Seventeenth Street, (City) Philadelphia, (State) Pennsylvania, (Zip) 19004, (Likes and dislikes) the priest skipped this, (Family members) none, (Pets) none, (The one subject you consider yourself to be an expert in is?) Catholicism, (Names, number of beneficiaries, and their relationship to the contestant) none.

During the time Father Brady was filling out his questionnaire, a tall, skinny young man wearing too-short jeans walked into the waiting room holding his own clipboard. He yelled out, *"Mrs. Vera Bundle!"* as if there were a large, noisy crowd and he was compelled to make himself heard. DP Brady wondered if all young people in New York made it a habit of speaking loudly.

"I'm Vera Bundle," answered the only woman in the room.

"My name's Jimmy Joel Jenks," said the young man. "Welcome to *The Big Question*. Would you please follow me?"

"Haven't we met before?" asked Vera Bundle, looking at the man in an odd way.

"I don't think so."

The woman disappeared on the other side of the waiting room door behind the boy named Jimmy Joel Jenks.

Friday night, September 14, 2012, was the night of the heavyweight championship fight.

That afternoon, Billy Constable was talking to Gil Rogin, a writer for *Sports Illustrated* magazine. The two were standing not far from the boxing ring, centered where second base would normally be on the Yankees' playing field. That was when Billy saw the raindrop land on the shoulder of Gil Rogin's blue-and-white-striped seersucker sport coat.

Rain meant postponing the outdoor event, which translated into a potentially huge loss of income. Promoter Sonny Lieberman picked a Friday night for the simple reason that Fridays were paydays and fight fans would have cash in their pockets. By Saturday night a lot of those paychecks would have evaporated in the city's barrooms. That's why the spreading gray spot on Gil Rogin's shoulder caused Billy to gasp.

"What's the matter, Billy?" Gil asked, concerned. "You're white as a sheet."

"Rain," moaned Billy Constable, pointing to the splotch on Gil Rogin's shoulder.

And rain it did.

It came down in buckets.

Later that afternoon, Billy Constable was sitting in the Yankee dugout with the team's groundskeeper, Carl Canzona Sr.

Sonny Lieberman called Billy every hour on the hour and asked, "Any chance?"

"Any chance, Carl?" Billy would automatically ask the elderly groundskeeper.

Carl Canzona Sr. was a nice guy but a bit of a grump. He had been with the Yankee organization for forty-six years. Every time Billy asked Canzona what the conditions were, Carl would mumble some curse words, heave his hefty, disheveled body up off the dugout bench, walk out into the rain holding his suit coat over his head to keep himself dry, push the toe of his shoe into the soggy turf along the first base line, then shake his head no.

"No," Billy would tell Sonny Lieberman on the telephone.

"If it's still no at four I'm going to have to postpone until tomorrow night," said Sonny Lieberman. "Onward and upward."

"What'd he say?" asked Canzona, walking back into the dugout.

"He said onward and upward."

"Brilliant," said Canzona.

"Mr. Daniel Patrick Brady?"

When Father Brady said "Yes," Jimmy Joel Jenks walked over to him and repeated his speech: "My name is Jimmy Joel Jenks. Welcome to *The Big Question*. Would you please follow me?"

The priest told the man named Jenks that he would prefer being addressed as Father Brady, not mister.

"Sorry about that," said Jimmy Joel, blushing.

Father Brady stood and followed Jenks through the waiting room door, down a hall, and into a cubicle. There seemed to be a lot of activity on that side of the waiting room door. Telephones were ringing nonstop, young people were speed-walking back and forth, most of them carrying Styrofoam cups of coffee. Everyone had pencils behind their ears and carried clipboards with bunches of paper attached to them.

Inside a cubicle the young man offered Father Brady a bridge chair and took another for himself. He sat down opposite the priest on the other side of a small wooden table.

"Has it started to rain outside?" asked Jimmy Joel cheerfully.

"Yes, it has."

"How you feelin' today, Father Brady?"

"Fine."

"Good. Trouble findin' this place?"

"No."

"Good. Like I said, my name is Jimmy Joel Jenks and welcome to *The Big Question.* So you're interested in bein' a contestant on the show?"

"That's obviously why I'm here."

"Okay, fine. You know the basic premise of *The Big Question*?"

"You either win a hundred million dollars or you die," answered the priest.

"I guess you wouldn't have a problem with winnin' a hundred million dollars, would you?" The young man laughed. "Who would? But how 'bout the dyin' part? You're a young man."

"I'm not planning on dying," said the priest.

"Yeah?" commented Jimmy Joel.

Yeah, thought Father Brady.

The young man named Jenks seemed to be waiting for Father Brady to continue talking about why he wasn't counting on dying. When nothing was forthcoming, Jimmy Joel Jenks said, "Have you ever had a terminal disease?"

"No."

"Do you take drugs of any kind?"

"No."

"You left out fillin' in your likes and dislikes."

"Couldn't think of any."

"I need a few. One or two of each. I catch hell if I don't get them. It's for the script. It's what the writers—"

"Tomato soup."

"Pardon?"

"I dislike tomato soup. I also dislike broccoli rabe and cilantro."

"How do you spell that?"

The priest spelled broccoli rabe and cilantro.

"I like blue and a Mercedes convertible," he added.

"You like a blue Mercedes what?"

"No. I like the color blue and a Mercedes automobile."

"Yeah. Okay. Thank you."

"You say here"—Jimmy Joel held up the priest's form and pointed to what he was talking about with his finger—"you say you're an expert on Cath . . . Cath . . ."

"Catholicism. That's right."

Jimmy Joel Jenks checked DP's form again, then said, "Would that stuff be the subject you'd be an expert on?"

"I suppose it would," said Father Brady with a smile. The priest understood the boy was trying to sound important and make his job more respectable than it was.

"You know how the game works?" asked Jimmy Joel Jenks, glancing at his notes. "How you answer questions on what you're an expert on? You get a point for every question you get right. And if you're the first guy or girl—course you're not a girl." Jenks snorted a laugh. "Sorry. Anyway, if you're the *contestant* with the highest score after three questions, then you go on to play the winner of the other round on the show. Each program is two rounds."

Father Brady nodded.

"Then if you win that championship round against the winner of round two . . . the other way around . . . I mean . . . you can be in round two instead of round one, and . . . Jesus, I think I'm makin' it worse for you."

"I think you're making it worse for yourself. I understand how the game works. I read the rules on the paper that was given to me when I filled out my forms. There are two rounds of three contestants each. We're each given a number of questions to answer. If I win my round, I play the winner of the other round. We're asked another bunch of questions. The winner of that round, what you call the championship round, goes on to try and answer the big question."

"Perfect," said Jimmy Joel Jenks with a big smile, exhaling a long sigh of relief.

"Glad to be of help, son," said Father DP Brady.

"Fine. I see here," said Jimmy Joel Jenks, holding up Brady's questionnaire and pointing to the part he had in mind so DP could see what he was about to discuss, "you have no what we call beneyfishyaries. Is that correct? See, they get twenty-five thousand dollars if you get kilt. So it is correct that you don't have no what we call beneyfishyaries, right?"

"That's correct."

"Okay. That's fine, Father. Can you please keep the month of October open? 'Specially the beginning part. That's when we would be doin' our first shows, if you're selected to participate on one of our first shows, that is. Got that?"

"Yes, I've got that."

Jimmy Joel checked the form. "Thank you, Father Brady."

Outside it was raining buckets. The priest opened his umbrella and walked to the street to hail a taxi. At the same time a troubled Billy Constable sat in the Yankee Stadium dugout with the grumpy head groundskeeper, Carl Canzona Sr. It was four o'clock. Billy would have to tell Sonny Lieberman to postpone the big fight. The field was a holy mess. While Billy Constable dialed Sonny Lieberman, Carl Canzona Sr. was already ordering his crew to put tarpaulins on the field.

Father Brady was heading back to Pennsylvania Station in a taxi.

Saturday night, the stars were shining in the Bronx.

It was clear as a bell.

The crowd streaming into Yankee Stadium was big. Not as big as Friday's might have been, but big enough. At every entrance to the stadium, a New York Yankees employee stood taking tickets. Behind him stood a Sonny Lieberman employee checking the New York Yankees employee. And behind the Sonny Lieberman employee stood a Giuseppe Sanseli employee checking the Sonny Lieberman employee who was checking the New York Yankees employee.

Billy Constable, Jimmy Joel Jenks, and Rosie Feinstein had ringside seats, courtesy of Sonny Lieberman. As a matter of fact, all of Sonny's employees were sitting at ringside. All except Billie Berry.

Throughout the preliminaries, Billy Constable was a nervous wreck. Jimmy Joel and Rosie were unable to do a thing about it.

"I think he's bet too much on the fight," Rosie told Jimmy Joel. "He's so out of it he didn't even say anything about poor Billie Berry."

"Yeah, you're right 'bout that. He really *is* nervous. How much did he bet, Rosie?"

"A hundred and ninety thousand dollars."

"Mother of God," said Jimmy Joel Jenks. "Where'd he get it?"

"Don't know."

"Who'd he bet it on?"

"The American," said Rosie Feinstein.

When the Swede entered the ring, he pranced around in a circle, making a muscle with his right arm and pointing to the muscle with the index finger of his left hand. And while he circled the ring the Swede was mouthing the words, "Tunder of Tor. Tunder of Tor." It was unclear whether anyone in the stadium had the faintest idea what he was saying.

In the first round, the Swede came out of his corner, looked hard at the American, and threw a punch that almost took the American's head off and sent him straight to the canvas. He lay there for what seemed like forever, flat on his back, arms and legs akimbo. The crowd was on their feet. Most of the audience thought the fight was over. But the American righted himself so that one knee was on the canvas and took an eight count. With the referee pushing his fingers into the American's face, shouting the count as he did, "One . . . two . . . three . . . ," the American stayed on that one knee, trying desperately to shake the cobwebs out of his head.

A total of fourteen seconds of the first round had gone by.

Billy Constable became nauseous and dizzy. He thought he might faint.

The American was hurt but not badly hurt. He stood up and spent the remainder of the round trying to get his legs to stop wobbling and hiding from the big Swede. Then, just as the round was about to end, the Swede knocked him down again. This time the bell saved the American.

The Swede dropped the American four more times in the second round and three times in the third. All the American's trainer, Jake Munza, could do was shout at his boxer to get up. Munza yelled so loudly and so often his voice became nothing more than a pitiful squeak. The veins on both sides of his neck resembled taut cables.

Between the end of the third round and the beginning of the fourth, the American's trainer got on his knees and begged his fighter to do this and that. Pleaded with him. Practically broke down in tears trying to make the American understand what he wanted him to do. When the bell rang and just before the American stood to go out for the fourth round, Munza hugged him and kissed his forehead.

In the fourth round, the American took a hard uppercut and went down again. The Swede appeared to be just what his advance billing had said he was: big as a house and strong as an ox. Jake Munza cursed God and his fighter. He used the Lord's name in vain over and over again. He shouted obscenities. His face turned beet red. He spit when he shrieked. When the American went down hard for the second time in the fourth round, Munza screamed in frustration, "Get up, you lazy fucking nigger, you black bastard! Get the fuck up!"

The American got up.

Jake Munza said nothing to his fighter between the fourth and fifth rounds.

In the fifth round, the Swede knocked the American down two more times. The last time the American champion just stayed on his hands and knees, shaking his head, trying to clear his eyes and nose of blood and his brain of God knows what. While the American was on his hands and knees, his teary-eyed trainer threw a white towel into the center of the ring.

The fight was over.

The Swede had won the heavyweight boxing championship of the world.

Billy Constable vomited between his legs.

"When I first got the call from the kidnappers," said Arthur Durch, "and they told me they had my wife, my first reaction was to say, 'Keep her.'"

He burst forth with a nervous giggle.

"That's a natural reaction," said the stone-faced detective. "If it were my wife I'd a had the—"

"That's *not* a natural reaction," said a suddenly furious Durch. "I was joking, for Christ sake. I love my wife. I really do. I adore her. Always have. The first time I saw her it was love at first sight. When we got back together for the second time it was still love at first sight. I didn't think we'd last a week the second time and it's lasted . . . it's lasted . . . how many years has it lasted? My friggin' mind's a blank. I can't even remember how long we've been married."

"Yeah. Okay," said the detective. "So what else did the kidnapper say?"

"Ah . . . let's see. What else did the . . . what did you say your names are?"

"Murphy. Lieutenant Mike Murphy." Murphy turned and pointed to the second detective, the one standing behind him. "And this is my partner, Sergeant Liam Lynch."

"Your partner doesn't talk much, does he?"

"He's a man of few words. But when he speaks, it's profound. So what else did the kidnapper say?"

"You see, my wife and I were married before. To each other. This is the second time around. For both of us. We split up after the first time. Then we got back together again."

"Yeah. Right. Mr. Durch, let's see if we can concentrate on the—"

"My wife had problems with . . . you know, with . . ."

"With what?"

"With making love," said Durch.

"That was a problem?"

"Yes, a *big* problem. But see, I'm a practicing sex therapist."

"A sex what?"

"Therapist. I straighten out people's sex problems. I even straightened my wife right out. Sexually, that is. She still has a few annoying personal habits, but now she fucks like a mink."

"I see," said the detective named Murphy, wriggling in his seat. He was a white guy with a nice smile when he wanted to smile. He had crew-cut brown hair, wore a gray suit and tie, and had a double chin. At that moment he was in decent shape, but he wouldn't be for long. You could see exactly how he was going to look when he was seventy-five years old. "Can we get back to the kinda—"

"It was the cherry on the sundae," said Durch.

"The what?"

"The cherry on the sundae. It made our union perfect. A textbook case that sex therapists live for. Straightening out an unhappy marriage. And the unhappy marriage I straightened out in this case was *my own*! How 'bout them apples?"

"Yeah, right," said Detective Murphy. "So, Mr. Durch, what else did the kidnapper say? Did he make any demands? I assume the kidnapper was a he."

"It was a he and he did make demands. He demanded five million dollars in small bills. Untraceable. I think that's what he said. 'Make sure they're untraceable.' Yes, that's exactly what he said. He gave me forty-eight hours to put the money together."

"Then what?"

"Then he said he'd call me in two days with further instructions."

"Two days from now?"

"Yes, two days from now. That's when he said he'd call with further instructions."

"Did the kidnapper say what he'd do to your wife if you didn't pay the ransom?"

"He said he'd kill her."

"He actually said that?" asked the heretofore mute Detective Lynch, a cop straight out of central casting. He was fat, slovenly, out of shape, shirt sneaking out over his belt, always perspiring, and getting balder by the day.

"Yes, he said he'd kill her."

"Could you tell us more about the kidnapper?" asked Detective Lynch.

"More what?"

"Like maybe what he looked like. If there was more than one, stuff like—"

"What he *looked* like? If there was more than one? Aren't they stupid questions, Detective? He was on the *phone,* dum-dum. I never saw him. How the hell am I going to tell you what he looked like if I never saw him?"

"From his voice," said Detective Lynch, unfazed by Durch's tirade. "Sometimes, not often, but occasionally you can get an idea what the guy looks like from the way he sounds. If he's a heavy, big guy with a strong, loud voice or a small guy with a squeaky, thin voice. And if there's more than one involved. Like maybe hearing someone in the background who accidentally says something. Sometimes you can tell if the kidnapper sounds young or old. Or smart or stupid, or—"

"It was just a *voice,* Detective. It wasn't a videophone or something like—"

"Why did the kidnappers pick your wife?" asked Detective Murphy, changing the subject. "What I'm trying to say is, how did they know you could afford such a large sum of money?"

"My mother, Edna Durch, was one of the richest women in New York. When she died, it made all the newspapers. Even the wire services. I was the sole beneficiary in her will. That also made all the newspapers and wire services."

"I see. So what did you say when the kidnapper demanded five million dollars?"

"At first I didn't know what to say."

"Did you say anything at all, anything that might be helpful to us?" asked Detective Lynch.

"No." Durch didn't like Detective Lynch.

"Nothing?"

"Nothing."

"You mean you didn't say anything for the rest of the time you were on the phone?" asked Detective Murphy, annoyed.

"I said a few more things," Durch said petulantly.

"We're here to help you, Mr. Durch," said Lieutenant Murphy. "We want to get you your wife back unharmed. So if you can just cooperate a little and tell us—"

"Well, I said . . . let me see . . . I said . . ."

"What did you tell the kidnapper after he demanded the five million dollars?" asked Detective Murphy.

"I told him for one thing I didn't have five million dollars. I told him I did have that much at one time. Way more than that. But I don't have it anymore. We spent it on expensive homes in East Hampton; South Beach, Florida; and Umbria in Italy. We bought a yacht and had it anchored in Saint Tropez. We got fancy cars. A Rolls for my wife and a Bentley for me. Evie bought out most of the stores in Manhattan. You'd be surprised how fast you can spend a lot of money."

"What did the kidnapper say when you told him you didn't have the money?" asked Detective Murphy.

"He said he didn't believe me. He said sell one of the houses. I told him it takes time to sell a house. He called me an asshole and changed the ransom to ten million dollars and said he'd give me a week to get it together."

"Did they let you talk to your wife?" asked Detective Murphy.

"Yes. They put her on the phone. She never said a word. She just cried. All she did was cry. Even the kidnapper asked me if there was any way to shut her up. He asked if she cried all the time at home."

"Can you describe your wife, please?" asked Detective Lynch.

"Plain, five foot five, unattractive, whiny voice, brown stringy hair, brown eyes, shows a lot of upper gum when she laughs. Even when she smiles. Skinny, no figure to speak of. Flat as a breadboard. No ass. Not the pick of the litter. But sweet. And humps like a mink. Since I treated her, that is. I worry about that."

"About what?" asked Detective Murphy.

"About her humping. Since I straightened her out she can't get enough. I mean, you've never seen such a turnaround. I'm worried that maybe she'll get horny and want to hump one of the kidnappers. Or *all* of them if there's more than one."

"Yeah," said Detective Lynch, "it could be a—"

"So how do we catch these guys?" asked Arthur Durch. "How do I get my sweet wife back? I love her so much. You know how much?

More than there are stars in the sky. You know who said that? 'I love my wife more than there are stars in the sky'?"

"No," said Detective Murphy.

"Neither do I. Somebody did 'cause I've heard it before. I miss my wife terribly. She listens to all my new poems and tells me what she thinks of them. I wrote a new poem last night she hasn't even heard. Wanna hear it? It goes like this:

Hamlet Hamlet,
You make a great omelet.

"What do you think? No comment, huh? My wife would have had a comment. See why I miss her? Listen, you guys, if I had twenty million dollars or forty million dollars, it wouldn't matter. I'd give it all to the kidnapper to get my wife back, I really would. I'd go back and live in Bensonhurst if I could just get her back. And you know what I'll do if I don't get her back?"

"What?" said the detectives.

"I'll kill myself, that's what I'll do. I swear I will. You don't believe me, do you? You don't think I love Evie enough to really kill myself, do you? Well, I do. And I will. I'll kill myself. I'll take a shitload of drugs and kill myself."

"Easy, Mr. Durch. Easy," said Detective Murphy.

"Life won't be worth living for me," said Durch, crying now. "I swear it won't. So tell me, fellas, what should I do?"

"You could always try out for *The Big Question,*" said Detective Lynch.

Durch stopped crying. "What's *The Big Question*?"

The day after the championship fight, Sonny Lieberman telephoned his staff to be at his office at exactly five o'clock. When Sonny's employees arrived, many of them were in bad moods. Most of them had been working very hard the last few weeks of the promotion and were looking forward to having Sunday off. Once everyone was there, a white-faced Sonny asked the gathering whether anyone had seen a box of ringside tickets.

No one answered.

"There were a thousand ringside tickets worth a hundred and fifty dollars each in that box," said Sonny, trying, but failing, to keep the anger out of his voice. "That's a hundred and fifty *thousand* dollars' worth of tickets. They could have been scalped for three or four times that much last week. If that box was taken before the fight, then that's the same as taking a box full of cash. Same as holding up a bank, if you get my drift. Now, I'm not saying anyone *took* it. I'm just asking if anyone *saw* it. Saw the box of tickets. Anybody see the box of tickets I'm talking about?"

Quiet.

Even though the air-conditioning was blasting in his office, Sonny Lieberman was sweating profusely. He kept clenching and unclenching his fists. There were large wet stains around his armpits.

"Did anyone see the box of tickets *after* the fight?"

Sonny was visibly angry.

"The theft of that box of tickets is a felony!" he shouted. And then, calming down, quickly added, "If no one seems to know anything about them, I'm going to have to call the police."

There was silence in the room.

Billy wondered whether he might vomit again. He did everything in his power not to.

"So nobody knows anything about the box of tickets?"

Quiet.

"Oh, well. Onward and upward."

Sonny Lieberman walked out of the room.

"Sonny knows somethin'," said Billy Constable to Jimmy Joel Jenks later at dinner. The two were eating McDonald's around the corner on Broadway, near Sonny's Upper West Side apartment office.

"What's Sonny know?"

"Sonny knows the box a tickets was in the back a the closet. I bet he stole 'em from Sanseli or somethin' so he could scalp 'em himself."

"That's a grade-A stupid thing to do, you ask me. Steal somethin' from Sanseli." Jimmy Joel wiped ketchup from his mouth with a paper napkin.

"And then when Sonny went to get them to scalp the tickets, they were gone."

"Where'd they go?"

"Damn it, Jimmy Joel, *I took 'em.* You *know* I took 'em. Damn it, boy, pay attention."

"Jesus, Billy, you took Sonny's box of tickets *which he took from Sanseli!*"

"Yeah."

"Grade-A stupid, if you ask me."

"What is?"

"Takin' that box a tickets. You're dumber than Sonny."

"Thanks a lot."

"But Sonny doesn't know you took 'em, does he?" asked Jimmy Joel.

"No, he doesn't know. He can't figure out what happened to them tickets. Only problem is, they ain't worth nothin' now."

"How come?"

"'Cause the fight's *over.* Jesus, JJ, use your head."

"Yeah," said Jimmy Joel, "the fight's over."

"Now the problem Sonny has is that they weren't his tickets in the first place. If they were Sanseli's tickets, then The Chop's gonna be mad as shit and blame Sonny. Jesus, Jimmy Joel, maybe I'll get away with this."

"Yeah. That's great. Now you'll only owe your bookie a hundert and ninety thousand dollars."

"Plus the eight hundert dollars I owed him before the fight," said Billy Constable sadly.

"I forgot about that," said Jimmy Joel.

"Well, it's a lot better than owin' *both* guys a hundert and ninety thousand dollars, ain't it?"

"I'm lost," said Jimmy Joel.

"I owe the bookie a hundert and ninety thousand dollars plus eight hundert dollars now," explained Billy patiently, "for a total of"—Billy did the addition with his finger on top of the restaurant table—"a hundert an' ninety thousand eight hundert dollars. If Sanseli finds out about the box of ringside tickets and pins it on me, I'll owe *him* a hundert and ninety thousand dollars too. If I add that to what I owe the bookie, I'll keel over from a heart attack."

"Me too," said Jimmy Joel Jenks.

The two boys sat quietly for a minute.

"What if Sonny can't explain?" asked Jimmy Joel. "Or what if The Chop doesn't believe—"

"Damn it, JJ, why do ya keep makin' things worse than they already are? It ain't my problem if Sonny can't explain anythin'."

"You're right, it ain't," said Jimmy Joel Jenks, thinking to himself, thank the good Lord I ain't in poor Billy's shoes.

Billy Constable walked back to the office wondering how in the hell he got himself into such a mess. As he approached the entrance to the apartment building, he saw Sonny Lieberman being escorted by two tough-looking guys to a gray van parked around the corner on West Sixty-second Street. One of the tough guys pushed the door open. Billy watched as Sonny was shoved inside, watched him forced into a seat on the left side of the van against the side that didn't have a door. One of the tough guys sat between Sonny and the door. A driver and another man were sitting up front. Two other men were sitting on the seat behind Sonny Lieberman. Billy recognized one of the men sitting in the back. The one Billy recognized was Giuseppe "The Chop" Sanseli.

The tough guy who had accompanied Sonny to the truck slammed the door shut and smacked the window, signaling to the driver to go. The man on the pavement walked west on Sixty second Street. He turned right on Broadway and got lost in a crowd of pedestrians.

Billy Constable never saw Sonny Lieberman again.

Nobody ever did.

Before one week was out, Retta Mae Wagons understood that she had made a terrible mistake. Though she never questioned Jamal about anything again, he slapped Retta Mae around "on general principles," he liked to say. It didn't make a lot of sense to Retta Mae, but then she wasn't living with a sensible man. She figured the imam just got his kicks that way. Got his blood going. Got *something* going, she guessed. The fucker sure wasn't any Fourth of July in bed.

Retta Mae Wagons wasn't yet twenty years old. She was still beautiful and brilliant, and knew it. Retta Mae constantly caught men looking at her. Men had been checking Retta Mae out since she was sixteen. Only now, even a man *glancing* at her could become a horrible nightmare. The imam was jealous and didn't need much of an excuse to give Retta Mae Wagons a beating, though his punches never left a mark on her. The imam seemed to know exactly where to hit.

"It's an art I learned in prison," he once told her, smiling.

But though the beatings were bad, they never stopped Retta Mae Wagons from piecing together the answer to her original question. All she had to do was observe and listen to the gossip, innuendo, and remarks from the imam's drunken friends and sycophants. Even Rasheed Jamal's bragging helped her figure it out. In time, Retta Mae Wagons was able to connect all the pieces, much the same as doing one of her easier crossword puzzles, about the Imam Rasheed Jamal, aka Cleveland Steve Beastie from Chicago. And all that detective work made her more fearful than ever.

It certainly didn't set her free.

And then one evening, at the dinner table of Rasheed Jamal's Florida mansion, Retta Mae Wagons said, "I want to go up to New York City."

"What for?" asked the imam.

"I want to try out for that new TV program *The Big Question*."

"That's the one where you can win a hundred million dollars, isn't it?"

"Yes, it is."

"What would you do with all that money?"

"I'd figure something out."

"You think you're smart enough to win a hundred million dollars?"

"Yes."

"Buy yourself a lot of fancy dresses, couldn't you? A lot more fancy dresses like the ones you have packed in all three of your closets."

"I could do that," said Retta Mae Wagons, "but I wouldn't. No, Rasheed, if I won a hundred million bucks I'd set up the Retta Mae Wagons Fund."

"What kind of fund?"

"Money for kids who can't afford to go to college."

"That's really nice, Retta Mae," said the imam, his sport shirt unbuttoned to his belt, allowing the hair on his chest to breathe. "You're willing to risk your life for some poor nigger kids?"

"In a minute. And they don't have to be black. The kids can be anything. At least my life would have some meaning, Mr. Imam. It sure as shit doesn't have any meaning now."

"Well, that's mighty public-spirited of you," said the imam, his words dripping with sarcasm. "A young girl like you willing to risk her life for such an altruistic cause? Very commendable, Retta Mae."

The sun was setting in Miami Beach. It sent a warm orange glow over the imam's dinner table. A white trawler chugged by the mansion on the inland waterway. All was right with the world of Rasheed Jamal.

"So can I take the plane?" asked Retta Mae.

"Only if I go too," said the imam. "You know the rule. You don't go anywhere on my plane alone."

"Afraid I'll run off with your damn pilot?" baited Retta Mae.

The imam said nothing. But his expression changed. He turned his head toward the inland waterway and watched the trawler's wake disappear through his dining room window.

"We're enjoying a nice calm dinner," he said quietly. "Don't tempt me into ruining it all by having to hit you, sister."

"Any excuse, right, Imam?"

Silence.

God, she hated the man. There was no way of getting out from under him. If she ran away, his goons would find her and kill her. Could she kill him first? Probably, and if she did she'd gladly go to prison. It would be a better life than this one. That's for sure. Only she'd never get to prison. Rasheed's lieutenants would bury her *and* the imam in the Everglades before the cops even heard about it, then carve up his empire. But then, maybe if she got to New York alone she could disappear in the city and . . .

"Think I'll come to New York with you," said Jamal, smiling. "Think I'll try out for that TV program too."

"You have your congregation to milk, Rasheed."

"I'll let Imam Deekins take this Friday's television hour."

They were quiet. Retta Mae tried to think of what to do next. She asked Rasheed Jamal what his field of expertise would be on *The Big Question.*

"Islam. And yours?"

"General knowledge," she said quickly. "I'm smart, Rasheed. My high school principal told my mother I had the IQ of a genius. I could have gone to college if I had the money."

"Then you should be a shoo-in to get on the program, right?"

"That's right."

"I'll bet I get on and you don't," said the imam.

"For how much?"

"If I get on and you don't, you marry me."

"And," asked Retta Mae, "if I get on and *you* don't?"

"I marry *you.*" The imam laughed a hearty laugh.

"What if you lose, Rasheed? You ready to die?"

"Are you?"

"Yes," answered Retta Mae.

"Honestly?"

"Yes, honestly."

"How come, honey?"

"I'm tired of living."

"That tired?"

"Yes, that tired."

Quiet settled again over the dining room table.

It was late September 2012.

A little over a week had passed since the big heavyweight championship fight. And now Billy Constable was in the same dirty gray van with the one sliding door, sitting in the same seat he had seen Sonny sitting in. There were two thugs up front. A third thug, sitting next to Billy, was squashing Billy's left shoulder up against the side of the van. The thug was huge and ugly and wore a leather porkpie hat. His job was to keep Billy away from the sliding door. Sanseli was sitting behind Billy, talking into Billy's right ear. Someone was sitting to the right of Sanseli, but Billy didn't know who it was because he had been told not to turn around.

"So I was listenin' to this Markowitz guy on the radio," said

Giuseppe Sanseli. "That's his name, somethin' Markowitz, right? Anyway, this Markowitz guy is gettin' blown by some broad while he's doin' his radio show!"

Sanseli laughed.

All of the Sanseli thugs in the van laughed.

"An' you could hear the girl givin' this Markowitz the blow job. You could hear her makin' all these slobberin' noises. It was real funny."

Sanseli laughed.

All of the Sanseli thugs in the van laughed.

"So I hear ya was peddlin' ringside tickets around Yankee Stadium, country boy."

All the Sanseli thugs in the van stopped laughing.

"Ya was doin' that a week before the big fight, weren't ya? Am I right, country boy, because if I am, it wasn't a smart thing to do, was it? So were ya peddlin' ringside tickets around the stadium or not?"

Billy Constable swallowed and whispered, "Yes, sir, I was." All Billy could do was whisper.

"What's that, country boy? What'd ya say?"

"Yes, sir, I was," said Billy as loud as he could.

Billy Constable could smell a sickening body odor. He wasn't sure if the stink was coming from the moron sitting next to him or Sanseli sitting behind him or from himself.

"See, country boy, I got people on my payroll all over the fuckin' place. I even own most of the cops walkin' the beat 'round Yankee Stadium. In fact, I own the precinct the stadium's in. Did ya know that, country boy?"

"No, sir, I didn't," whispered Billy, so scared he was barely able to get the words out of his mouth.

"I didn't fuckin' think so," said Sanseli.

"I got a lotta people on my payroll, country boy," said Sanseli. "I own most of the guys peddlin' shit around the stadium. I own the ticket takers, the concessions, and a shitload of other crap. As a matter of fact, there isn't much in the Bronx I don't own. Ya know what bothers me, country boy?"

"No, sir. I reckon I don't, sir," whispered Billy.

"What bothers me is that with all those dimwits on my payroll, why didn't I find out what you did sooner? That's what bothers me," said Giuseppe Sanseli. His voice was hoarse. Maybe he was catching something.

"I didn't think I was stealin' from you, sir. I thought I was stealin' from Mr. Lieberman."

"Those fuckin' tickets were *my* fuckin' tickets, not Sonny's. Ya was stealin' from *me,* country boy!"

"Yes, sir. But those tickets were in a box in a closet in one of the rooms in Sonny's office. Since Sonny owned them offices I thought he owned them tickets too. I didn't put them tickets in his office closet. If I didn't put them there, then he must a put them in there. I wouldn't steal nothin' from you, Mr. Sanseli. I may be a dumb country boy, but I ain't *that* stupid."

"I see what you're sayin', country boy, but the way I figure, ya was stealin' *my* ringside tickets. The way I figure, Sonny stole them from me, then ya stole them from me . . . an ya *sold* 'em!"

"I'm really sor—"

"Enough of the sorry shit!" The Chop spit on the floor of the truck. "So how much ya make from sellin' the duckets, country boy?"

"Close to a hundert an' ninety thousand dollars, Mr. Sanseli."

"That's not so good. You shoulda made a lot more. How come ya made only a hundred and ninety Gs?"

"The rain delay hurt, an' . . . an' . . . an' I guess I wasn't a very good hustler."

"That's still a lotta money, country boy."

"Yes, sir, it is," whispered Billy, "sir."

"That's money ya owe me, right?"

"Yes, sir. It is, sir. I guess."

"You guess?"

"No. I'm sure. It's your money, sir. I'm *sure* it's your money."

"So where is it, country boy?"

"I lost it, Mr. Sanseli."

"*Lost it?* Like in ya don't know where it is but if ya keep lookin' you're gonna find it? That kinda lost?"

"No, sir. Lost like in I lost the money bettin' on the American in the heavyweight championship fight. That kinda lost . . . sir."

"*That* kinda lost, huh?"

"Yes, sir."

"All of it, country boy, all hundred an' ninety Gs?"

"All of it, Mr. Sanseli."

"So now you're in twicet, right? Once ta me for a hundred an' ninety an' once ta da bookie for a hundred an' ninety."

"Yes, sir."

"This is very distressing news, country boy."

"I'll say it is."

"You supposed to be the horse's mouth. That's right, innit? You supposed to know what's goin' on, in that right, kid?" asked Sanseli.

"I think I . . . I mean about bein' the horse's mouth . . . I was just jok—"

"You don't know shit, kid!" screamed The Chop.

There was a momentary lull in the conversation.

Then Sanseli said, "I lost much more money than ya did bettin' on the nigger, country boy. Or should I call ya Horse's Mouth? An' who told me to bet on the nigger even though ya was told I never bet on niggers? Huh? Huh, Horse's Mouth? Who did I trust to tell me where my money should go? Huh? Who? Answer me, Horse's Mouth."

"Me, sir. I did, sir," whispered Billy. "I told you to bet on the American."

"What? I can't hear ya, country boy. You're whisperin'. What did ya say?"

"I said it was me, sir. I did, sir," Billy said as loud as he could. "I told you to bet on the Amer . . . on the nigger."

"I want ya to think about that, country boy."

"Yes, sir. I'm thinkin' about that right now."

"An' while you're thinkin', say hello to Mr. Rothberg here, sittin' next t'me. Mr. Rothberg here was the last person to see your friend, the Jew cocksucker, alive. No offense, Morris."

"None taken, Giuseppe."

"Hello, Mr. Rothberg," said Billy, looking straight ahead, suddenly very sick to his stomach.

The van started down a barren road in the marshlands of Elizabeth, New Jersey. Billy had never been in the middle of a marshland before, though he had a pretty good idea what happened on desolate marshland roads like this one. Particularly when you were with someone like Giuseppe "The Chop" Sanseli. Billy had read enough pulp fiction crime novels and seen enough movies to know that guys got riddled with bullets then dumped in marshlands just like the one he was riding through. He started to sweat, the kind of sweat that made him feel as though he had just stepped out of a shower.

"Ya did me dirty, country boy," said Sanseli. "I lost twicet now. Once on the skinny ya gave me and again on the duckets ya stole from me. Once ya cause me to lose, that's not enough? Huh? Whatsamatta, ya ain't satisfied unless you make me, Giuseppe Sanseli, lose twicet? Twicet, country boy!"

Billy sat staring at his clasped hands in his lap. He tried his best to control his sick stomach.

"Okay, so it happens," says Sanseli. "There are . . . whatta they call it in sports? Like . . . like . . ." Sanseli was snapping his fingers.

"Upsets," suggested Morris Rothberg.

"Yeah, upsets. That's what makes bettin' excitin'. Shit happens, right, country boy?"

"Yes, sir, Mr. Sanseli, shit happens."

"The point is, country boy, I don't remember givin' ya permission to bet *my* money on *dick*!" shouted Sanseli into Billy's left ear.

Billy winced.

Sanseli spit on the floor of the van. He was furious. "Stop the goddamn truck!" he yelled.

The truck stopped.

Billy's heart started pounding like crazy in his chest.

"So, country boy, whattaya think I should do with ya? Huh? What?"

Billy shook his head mournfully. He prayed to God he wouldn't vomit in Sanseli's van.

"I like ya, country boy," said Sanseli, calming down. "You're respectful an' I like that. An' you're honest. Ya didn't try to bullshit me. I like that too. An' then there's that mix-up, ya thinkin' the duckets were Lieberman's. I'll give ya points on that too. So I'll tell ya what I'm gonna do. I'm gonna give ya two weeks to get the hundred and ninety thou up. Two weeks, hear? And no vig. Unnerstan'? I'm givin' ya a break by not chargin' ya any vig. An the money goes to me first, not to that asshole bookie, unnerstan'? The bookie gets the *second* hundred and ninety Gs, unnerstan'? If I don't get that money in two weeks, I'm bringin' ya back here for good. It's somethin' I won't like t'do, but I gotta set an example. Nobody fucks with Sanseli. An' don't try an' run away. Believe me, country boy, I'll find ya. I'll send my boys to whatever state ya go to and drag ya back to this marsh. Unnerstan'? An' I'll tell ya this. You'll wish I never did find ya. Now *that's* somethin' ya can bet on, country boy. Let him out, Patty."

The thug sitting next to Billy Constable stood, banged his head on the van's roof, cursed, and then bent over so he wouldn't bang his head again and slid the van door open.

Outside the air was full of gnats. Billy thought he heard crickets or something. And there was that rotten smell. Also Billy was sure there were snakes. He hated snakes.

"Mr. Sanseli, sir."

"Yeah. What?"

"How am I supposed to get home?"

Giuseppe "The Chop" Sanseli did something he rarely did. He laughed out loud. "Be glad you're still alive, country boy."

The van's door slid shut with a bang

Retta Mae Wagons and Imam Rasheed Jamal flew to New York City on the imam's very own black and silver G4 luxury airliner. Retta Mae Wagons spent most of the trip from Miami Beach to New York City under the imam. The imam thought he was a stud. None of the sex was even close to being good.

Retta Mae Wagons loathed the trip from beginning to end. She thought about things, something she seemed to be doing more and more lately. And she had plenty of time to do it. It was close to two hours from Miami to New York. Retta Mae thought about how sad her life had become. She thought about all the times she put herself to sleep at night thinking of ways to escape Rasheed's clutches. But even if she did escape him, then what? She had gone over that possibility so many times she was tired of thinking about it.

As long as she was tethered to the damn imam, Retta Mae didn't care if she won or lost on *The Big Question*. The one hundred million dollars meant nothing to her. Life meant nothing to her. If Retta Mae got on that program she wouldn't care if she did well *or* badly. Who cared about living or dying? Who or what would she miss? With the exception, maybe, of Dannyboy Marley, she didn't like anyone and didn't know of anyone, other than maybe Dannyboy, who liked her. She never should have left Dannyboy Marley and the apartment he set up for her at Madison Avenue and Ninety-first Street.

Shoulda, woulda, coulda.

Retta Mae daydreamed she was back in her apartment on Madison Avenue and Ninety-first Street. She missed the laughs she and Dannyboy had together. Laughs that left them with aching sides and gasping for breath. Retta Mae couldn't remember the last time she ached from laughing. And the gang at Jackson Hole where she had her late breakfast and sometimes her lunch and dinner. Palamone and Bobby and Tony behind the counter, Tommy the owner and his son, Little Steve. And Big Steve, and the young kid, Georgie, who painted during his off-hours. He had given her a painting. She had hung it on a wall in her apartment. All nice people. All her friends.

Now she didn't have any friends.

Now she didn't even have a deli counter to sit at anymore and read the Page Six gossip in the *New York Post.* God, she missed the Page Six gossip. It was the simple pleasures she yearned for. Just the simple pleasures. Two things she had learned from her Rasheed Jamal nightmare. The first thing was that when you have a good thing, you never know how good it is while you have it. The second thing was fairly obvious, the knowledge that you can't go back. You can only go forward. There was nothing she could do about that, either.

"What are you thinking about?" asked the good imam, getting off her to have a cigarette.

"Nothing," answered Retta Mae Wagons.

Now here's the funny part.

The next day in New York City the two tried out for *The Big Question.* Retta Mae Wagons did well but not well enough to make the first program. She was designated as one of two standbys.

And Rasheed Jamal was chosen as one of the six contestants for the premiere show!

With a little more than two weeks before *The Big Question*'s first television program, Billy Constable went to their offices to see if he could be a contestant. Rosie Feinstein went along to keep Billy company and give him moral support.

"When JJ told me 'bout this show," Billy told Rosie in the show's crowded waiting room, "I knew it was a message from God. God was makin' the suggestion, not Jimmy Joel Jenks. Or maybe He was makin' the suggestion *through* JJ, know what I mean?"

"Sort of. What was the message God sent you?" asked the profoundly atheistic Rosie Feinstein.

"The message was, 'You gotta get picked.'"

"I think you've gotten yourself a little crazed, Billy."

"No, I haven't."

"And what if you don't get picked? Then what's God going to say?"

"That ain't gonna happen, Rosie. I'm gonna get picked to do the show. I know it. God's goin' to make it happen. You'll see. An' when I get picked, I'll win. It's a case of life or death for me, and God knows that. I asked JJ if he'd put in a good word for me at *The Big Question* office. He said he would, but he don't think it'll matter very much."

Of course Rosie Feinstein couldn't discuss her dark notions with Billy, but her feeling was that all this God talk was unadulterated bullshit. That Billy's chances of being selected for the program were slim to none, which was a good thing. Because if he *did* get selected as a contestant for the show it would be Billy's luck to go all the way, miss the big question, and get himself executed. The last thought gave Rosie Feinstein goose bumps.

"Don't worry, Billy, God's good word is better than JJ's help. You'll get picked," said Rosie encouragingly.

What Billy didn't tell Rosie was that it didn't make a hell of a lot of difference if he missed the big question. He was a dead man anyway.

"And," continued Billy, "when I do win I'm gonna ask you to marry me. You will, won't you? We'll have enough money to live on. Whattaya say, Rosie?"

"Jesus, Billy, what a time to propose."

Billy Constable filled out all the forms and answered all the interviewer's questions. He played a practice round in front of the producers with three other prospects. When Billy finished, everyone smiled and said he did very well, that they would contact him one way or the other the next day.

"Can't you tell me now?" he asked nervously.

"We have to talk it over," said some big deal named Elsa, "but I can tell you this, Billy. You did very well."

"One of the people from the show said I did very well," Billy told Rosie on the way to his place. Right after Billy returned from Grossinger's, Rosie had moved out of the nest and into his apartment. Billy said, "She was an older woman and her exact words were, 'You did very well.'"

At ten the next morning, Jimmy Joel called Billy to tell him that things were really looking up for him. "But I better get off the phone in case someone from the show wants to call you and give you the good word."

Billy never moved from the telephone table in Rosie's apartment for the rest of the morning, the entire afternoon, and into the evening. But no one else called from the TV program. Until seven that night.

It was the woman. Billy recognized her voice. It was the older lady who told him he did very well. She said her name was Elsa Metzger and that she had good news.

Billy felt incredible joy. He covered the phone for a moment with his hand and sang into Rosie's ear, "We're goin' to the chapel and we're gonna get marr-rried!" and then went back to the telephone.

"So what's the good news?" asked Billy, smiling.

"You're not on the show, Billy."

"I'm not on the show?" gulped Billy, feeling wobbly, his smile vanishing.

Rosie didn't know whether to feel good or bad.

"No . . . *but* . . . you've been chosen as one of our two standbys."

It was a beautiful, sunny late September morning.

The producer sat behind an enormous desk in an enormous office in the National Broadcasting Company's television center at 30 Rockefeller Plaza. He had gathered his production staff into his office to discuss the up-and-coming premiere episode of *The Big Question.*

The producer's personal secretary, Ms. Pickle, sat across the desk from him. Ms. Pickle, a wrinkly, tall, bone-thin spinster whose hair was falling out, had a personality just like her name. She was famous for her temper tantrums, being a tattletale, and having a mean and sour disposition. She wore outdated clothes, had a perpetually sneering mouth, and reminded everyone of their meanest grammar school teacher. Ms. Pickle had been with the producer for over twenty years. She hovered around him like a protective mother monkey. The two were a fearful combination.

A young production assistant named Tammy Teesdale stood beside the producer, her clipboard at the ready. Tammy was your typical television production assistant: pretty, competent, loyal, a good figure and sweet personality, but definitely not a rocket scientist or one whose name would ever be remembered by anyone she ever came in contact with.

Four very skinny, fashionably dressed gay men, the show's writers, were crammed onto one of the couches. The program's director, a nervous, bigoted homophobe named Donny Carruthers, was seated in an armchair opposite the couch. Until the meeting came to order he spent his time glaring at the writers.

A harried script girl with wild, unkempt hair and a new baby cleaved to one hip, named Marge Wreck, walked in and stood against a wall. The show's assistant director, a competent young woman named Jennifer Cobb, was also standing against a wall. The contestant coordinator, Elsa Metzger, staring at everyone from behind her huge tortoiseshell eyeglasses, was leaning against another wall. Members of the network's Standards and Practices Department (the censors), two tense, elderly bureaucrats named Albert Kligman and Herbert Siegel, were seated on a couch. The producer's lawyer, Sigmond Levy, sat with them. Levy was dressed expensively as usual but looked like he had just rolled out of bed. None of the writers on one couch or the three men on the other couch offered a seat to any of the three women standing against the walls.

The producer tapped his desk with the top of his gold Cross ballpoint pen and ordered everyone to be quiet. "First of all, Ms. Wreck, must the child be in this office?"

"Yes. My sitter is sick."

"Can't the child play elsewhere while this meeting is in progress?"

"No."

Marge Wreck was an excellent script girl, so the matter was dropped.

The producer sighed. He then said, "I want to discuss any problems we might have on our first show. Please keep in mind it is extremely important, I repeat, *extremely* important that we have an *execution* on our first program and *not* a boring cash payout. The first show's ending will determine the success or failure of *The Big Question*. If the payoff's an execution, *The Big Question* is a monster hit. If the payoff's a boring cash payout, we're a failure. So I repeat, we *must* have an execution on our premiere show."

"Legally," said Kligman, one of the network censors.

"Legally, of course," added the producer, tossing a repugnant look at the obsequious Kligman. "With that in mind," continued the producer, "I want to replace Theresa Mendavey."

"Why?" asked Elsa Metzger, who was in charge of contestants. "Why replace Dr. Mendavey. She's terrific. She's young and pretty and smart . . ."

"She's too smart," said the producer.

"What's so bad about *that*?" asked the director, Donny Carruthers, who tended to process things slowly.

The producer gave Carruthers a withering stare. "I just finished explaining, Donny, that what we need on our first program is an execution, and Mendavey is too smart. She will win the money."

"You *cannot* replace Dr. Mendavey," said Sigmond Levy.

"Why not?" asked the producer, shocked at being countermanded by anyone, including his lawyer. "Why can't I replace whomever I want to replace, Sig?" he whined.

"Replacing the doctor has become a problem."

"A *problem*? What kind of problem?"

"A big problem," said Levy.

"What kind of big problem, Sig?" said the obviously nervous producer.

"Clear the room," ordered Sigmond Levy.

"Everybody out!" shouted the producer. "That means *everybody.* Now!"

Kligman and Siegel, the executives from the network's Standards and Practices Department, looked at each other. The expressions on their faces showed confusion and worry. They would be declared wimps and (more important) derelict in their duties if they allowed themselves to be ordered out of a production meeting. The alternative would be butting heads with not only the producer but his lawyer too. Both men were known to become violent if challenged. The two network executives stood up and walked out of the room.

Sigmond Levy, still on the couch, crossed one leg over the other. Pale white skin showed above the black sock of the top leg. Levy lifted his thick, froglike eyelids a bit and focused on the producer. He said, "Mendavey's already informed us she must be a contestant. She's figured out that you might consider replacing her because, as you just said, she'll win. Rather astute of her, I must say."

"I'm not the least bit interested in how astute the bitch is," said the producer, working himself into a snit. "I'm only interes—"

"As I was saying," continued Levy, annoyed by the producer's interruption, "Mendavey has figured out that a cash winner is *not* what you want. She is quite certain she will answer any question regarding the brain the show has to offer, any question that has a legitimate answer. And, I might add, she will challenge the show on any answer she gives that the show says is incorrect. She is quite certain she will answer anything you toss at her *and* she is aware she's running at cross-purposes with you. You want an execution. Dr. Mendavey is smart. She's put two and two together. Mendavey knows that an execution will mean huge ratings and a surefire hit for you, whereas a big money payoff won't mean shit. In other words, she knows everything you know. You don't have to be a brain surgeon to figure out what's going on around here, and Dr. Mendavey *is* a brain surgeon."

The producer remained silent while Sigmond Levy paused to relight his cigar with his gold Dunhill cigar lighter. When the cigar's end was in flames and a halo of thick gray smoke circled the lawyer's head, he continued.

"Your contestant, the good Dr. Mendavey, is an extremely intelligent, highly motivated, egocentric young lady driven to prove and re-prove herself. And possibly impress her parents . . . if they're still alive. All she cares about is accomplishment. Accomplishment upon accomplishment upon accomplishment. I sound like a psychiatrist and I am obviously not, but this conceited, self-centered woman is a classic case of someone with a tremendous ego who considers him- or herself . . . how shall I say it . . . godlike. Completely above the fray. I've seen dozens of them in court. That's why I speak with authority. Also, she knows as well as you do that you're running out of time. Mendavey will hold up your taping any way she can think of. The good doctor knows she can hang you and your show out to dry, and believe me," said the producer's lawyer, Sigmond Levy, "she will. Dr. Mendavey also knows it's horrible publicity for the show and for the network if you try to get rid of her so you can execute a contestant you know will fail. It's the kind of publicity you absolutely do not need or want, and Dr. Mendavey knows that as well as you do. The good doctor will take fifty million dollars to leave . . ."

"Oh, she will, will she."

" . . . *and* she promises to leave quietly. Mum's the word as far as she's concerned. Or use her. Those are your two choices when it comes to the good Dr. Mendavey."

"Has she spoken to a lawyer, Sig?"

"Not that I'm aware of."

"So all of this, so far, has been between you and the good doctor?"

"That is correct."

There was silence in the big office while the producer thought. His arms were crossed over his chest and he was staring at the ceiling. "Tell me this, Sig. Why would such a bright woman with such a brilliant future ahead of her want to try out for *The Big Question*? What I mean is—"

"I know exactly what you mean," said the lawyer Sigmond Levy. "You want to know why Dr. Mendavey would take a chance on being executed. The answer to your question in my opinion is this. The possibility of her being executed has never entered her mind. As far as she's concerned, her dying is a total non sequitur. Remember, she's a brain surgeon, and all brain surgeons think they're God."

"Well, she's not and—"

"*And* . . . she knows she'll win. One way or the other. Mr. Producer, I'm afraid the good doctor's got you by the balls."

"The fuck she does."

Two days after the production meeting, the following conversation took place in a marshland off the New Jersey Turnpike.

"Morris."

"What now?"

The two men spoke to each other through the open windows of their automobiles.

"I need another favor."

"When?"

"This week."

"That's short notice. It'll cost ya."

"Just do it."

"Give me the details."

The producer handed a white envelope to Morris Rothberg. The envelope was held out between two fingers of an expensive black pigskin glove. Rothberg took the envelope between two fingers of an expensive brown pigskin glove. And then Rothberg's black-tinted window slid up. When it reached the top, the automobile drove away.

One evening a week later, a gray van with **Edward Antoian & Sons Oriental Rug Gallery** on its sides was parked at the corner of Sutton Place and Fifty-sixth Street. Three men sat in the van's front seat, smoking. One of the men pointed to a woman walking along Sutton Place. The driver, using a small flashlight, compared the woman to a photograph he held in his hand. It was the same woman. Dr. Mendavey opened the door of her graystone, walked inside, and closed the door behind her.

The men waited a little while longer.

Inside, Theresa had just finished making herself a perfect martini when she heard her front doorbell.

"Now who the hell—"

When she looked through the door's peephole she saw three men holding a rug on their shoulders. She chained her door and opened it a crack.

"Yes?"

"For Dr. Theresa Mendavey," said the man nearest the door.

"I didn't order a rug."

"It's a present, ma'am," he said.

"A present! Who from?"

"Let's see, ma'am." Still holding the rug on his shoulder with one hand and using his free hand to dig, the man pulled a crumpled piece of paper from a pocket of his overalls. He read the note aloud: " 'This beautiful Persian rug is a gift from the producer of *The Big Question* for being selected to be on the program's premier show.' "

"Isn't this a strange time to be delivering anything?"

"We've been running very late today," said the man, crumpling up the note and pushing it into an overall pocket, "and we were told we absolutely had to get this—"

"And who the hell gives a damn rug as a present?"

"I'm sorry, ma'am, I really can't answer that question."

"So the bastard changed his mind and wants to make peace."

"Ma'am?"

"What am I going to do with a damn rug?"

"If I don't deliver it to you, he'll fire us sure as I'm standin' here. He's a mean man, that producer is. We can just bring the rug in tonight and put it where you want it tomor—"

"Oh, for God's sake."

Theresa closed the door, removed the chain, and opened it. "Just leave it here in the hall."

It was ten in the morning on Wednesday, October 3, 2012.

The first show would air live at eight that evening.

The producer was nervous and jumpy. He had been like that the last few days. "Let's go down the list one last time and let's make it fast," he said to his staff gathered once again in his office.

The four young and extremely skinny question writers were crammed together once again on one couch. Others on the staff—

Cobb, Carruthers, Wreck, Metzger, the network censors Kligman and Siegel—were seated or standing about the room. The production assistant named Tammy Teesdale was at her usual place, standing beside the producer. As usual, she had her clipboard at the ready. Her new skirt was so short it barely covered her ass. When the PA reached above her head for anything, her panties showed.

Ms. Pickle was seated in her usual place, in front of the producer's desk, frumpy and repellent as ever, her face wrinkled up in anger. It wasn't hard to determine the cause of Ms. Pickle's ire. It was the PA's postage stamp skirt. Everyone knew that's what was bothering Pickle, including Tammy the PA.

"Read the list, Tammy," snapped the producer, exchanging knowing glances with Ms. Pickle. "Who's first?"

"Vera Bundle," said the PA cheerfully, completely unaware of anything as subtle as a knowing glance.

"I like her," said the producer. "I want her to go as far as she can go. She's a lovable old biddy who people will hate to see executed." Turning to the quartet of question writers on the couch, he said, "Make her questions easy until you get to the big one, then make that one hard as hell. Make it the China question. As a matter of fact, make the big question the China question, period."

"The China question is fine for Vera Bundle," said a writer. "Her subject is geography. But what about all the other contestants who get to the big question? None of their categories are geography. How are we supposed to work the China question in—"

"You having a problem with your hearing? I said, *use the China question as the last question*. You figure the other shit out. That's what you get paid to do. Who's next?"

"No, wait!" said Siegel the censor. "The rules state that the contestant's final question shall be a question in the same category as the —"

"Just figure it out, goddamn it. I want to move on. *Next!*"

Ms. Pickle wrote in her notebook: Writers to make the China question the final question *for everybody.*

"Next is Father Daniel Patrick Brady," said Tammy.

"Give him tough questions," the producer told the writers. "Nobody likes priests. Ms. Pickle, tell Metzger to avoid priests and black cats. Next."

"Black cats?" asked Ms. Pickle.

"Nuns. *Next!*"

Ms. Pickle wrote in her notebook: Metzger, avoid priests and cats.

"Next is Arthur Durch," said Tammy the production assistant.

"He repulses me," said the producer. "Make his questions hard. Get rid of him as quickly as possible. Next."

"Retta Mae Wagons."

"She's the substitute, isn't she? Get rid of her quickly too. Nobody cares if a black's executed. No offense, Kyle." One of the four writers on the long couch, Kyle Wells, was black.

"Next."

"Rasheed Jamal," chirped Tammy.

"Same with him," said the producer. "Not only is he black, but not one person in this country would give two hoots if he was executed. I think most people in this country would *want* the bastard executed. I certainly would. I get a bad vibe every time I lay eyes on him. I haven't the faintest idea why the black moron was selected. Why *was* he selected, Elsa? Didn't we have better choices?"

The woman in charge of contestants, Elsa Metzger, said, "The pool wasn't that big. Certainly not as many good selections as we had hoped for. It's a tough contestant to find. The contestant has to be in decent health, bright, and—"

"I know what the contestant has to be. You're not answering my question, Metzger."

Elsa Metzger was a very thin and nervous lady. She chain-smoked and wore huge horn-rimmed glasses. "I'm guessing," she said, "that after we're on the air our contestant numbers should go up and we'll have a better—"

"You're *guessing* our numbers will go up?" snorted the producer. "If they're not up you'll be out of a job. And Elsa, if you're still employed next week, cut down on the blacks."

Elsa Metzger dropped her head in shame.

"Get rid of that goddamn Jamal ASAP," the producer said to the question writers. "Hard questions, you hear? Go back and check out his questions again. If the ones you've written aren't hard, make them hard. And if they're already hard, make them harder."

Ms. Pickle wrote in her notebook: Give Metzger a hard time about blacks.

"Next."

"The last contestant of the first game is Linus Major," said the production assistant.

"I like him," said the producer, pepping up a bit. "He's a good one. Young, refreshing, ingratiating. People like him. They would be sorry to see him executed. Make his questions easy."

"Who would be your favorite in the first game?" asked a suck-up junior executive in the back of the room.

"Favorite?"

"To be executed."

"Vera Bundle," said the producer to the suck-up without hesitating.

Billy Constable had a dream.

It took place in the early hours of the morning while he was tossing and turning in bed unable to sleep. He dreamed he was back at the county fair in Bowling Green, Kentucky, and when the roulette wheel stopped spinning the little rubber arrow pointed to $100,000,000!! He was so excited he had to wake Rosie from a sound sleep and tell her.

"What's the matter, honey?"

"I had a dream, Rosie."

"Tell me about it, Martin Luther."

And that's what Billy did. He told Rosie Feinstein about his dream. Then he said, "My dream's telling me I'm gonna get on the damn program and *win*! My dream's a . . . whattya call it, Rosie . . . you know . . . a . . ."

"An epiphany? An omen?"

"Yeah! One a them. God's going to answer my prayers."

"Absolutely," said Rosie the atheist.

"I'm tellin' ya, Rosie, dear, I'm gonna get on the show and I ain't gonna lose!"

V

Showtime!

Showtime!

It was now eight in the evening and every seat in the large television studio was taken. Because of fire laws, standing wasn't allowed. Consequently, a big part of the overflow audience was turned away.

Three spotlights turned in three circles over the closed curtain. A drumroll was heard in the background. The program's announcer, Johnny Jacobs, was cued and—cupping his right ear with his right hand for no discernible reason other than announcers had been cupping their right ears with their right hands since the early days of radio—spoke his one line into a backstage microphone: "Ladies and gentlemen . . . it's time for *The Big Question*. . . . And now here's your host . . . *Rip . . . Puckett!*"

The curtain opened. Three spotlights came up to reveal a high-tech set. A shower of sparkling white fireworks was continuously shooting up in the air out of tubes embedded in the studio floor. In the center of everything were three large soundproof tubes that looked like something constructed by NASA. In the rear, center stage, was a huge sixty-second clock with one gigantic hand. The clock rose up and disappeared into the ceiling, revealing a large thirty-piece orchestra playing behind a filmy blue see-through curtain in the rear of the stage.

All three spotlights converged on the right side of the stage. *The Big Question* host, Rip Puckett, skipped merrily out from the side where the spotlights had gathered. The lights followed him to center stage and surrounded him. His wavy brown hair and sparkling white teeth gleamed in the glow of the bright lights. The orchestra played with gusto. The studio audience applauded and cheered as they had been instructed to do.

Rip Puckett was a tall man with a long face, a large pompadour, and a mouthful of enormous capped teeth. The teeth were brand-new and extremely white. They looked like rows of kitchen appliances. Rip Puckett had paid a fortune for his teeth. His dentist didn't want to make them so big but Puckett had insisted.

Rip Puckett, whose real name was Isadore Hershkowitz, had chosen to wear a shiny black tuxedo with an enormous collar, an orange dress shirt, and a huge fire engine red bow tie. Rip Puckett wanted to be noticed.

"Before . . ." started Rip Puckett over thunderous applause, then stopped. He waited a bit for the applause to subside, then began again. "Before the next hour is over, one of our six lucky contestants will have the chance to win *one . . . hundred . . . million . . . dollars . . ."*

The orchestra played "Hail, Hail, the Gang's All Here" while the audience cheered like crazy.

" . . . or be *executed!!"*

A morbid organ struck the funereal notes *Dum Dee Dum Dum,* and the audience booed just like they had been told to do.

"We'll be back," screamed Rip Puckett, "with our first contestant on *The Big Question* . . . right after these messages!"

The program paused to cut away to a commercial.

The studio lights went on and the audience warm-up guy ran onstage bubbling with good cheer, dutifully keeping the studio audience in good spirits. A makeup lady appeared beside the host and began dabbing Rip's face with Kleenex, blotting up incipient sweat from various parts of his face and neck, and showing him a mirror so he could appraise his hair. The musical conductor was excitedly making sure all his musicians were literally on the same page. Suddenly, the makeup lady and warm-up clown were gone, Rip Puckett was back on his mark, the cameramen and camerawomen were bent into their eyepieces focusing their cameras on Rip, music was playing, and—just like that—the program was back on the air.

"And now," said host Rip Puckett, taking a deep breath and reading from cue cards, "let's meet the three contestants chosen from thousands who will vie for big money . . . or . . . *eternity* . . . tonight on *The Big Question.* Here are our three contestants for tonight's first game. From Steubenville, Ohio, a woman who's not afraid to admit her age—she happens to be seventy-seven years young—a widow and former schoolteacher whose favorite pastime is reading her *Encyclopaedia Britannicas* and browsing through her *National Geographics*—Mrs. Vera Bundle!"

Vera Bundle walked to the center of the stage and joined host Puckett. Vera was wearing a cheerful flowered dress and a new hairdo that did absolutely nothing for her looks. The frizzy brown bangs that resembled dead weeds still lay across her forehead.

"So, Mrs. Bundle, what are you going to do with that hundred million dollars . . . *if* you should be the lucky winner?"

"Well, Rip, first of all I'm going to buy back my old house in Steubenville. Steubenville's in Ohio, Rip."

"I know," said host Rip Puckett.

"Then I'm going to make a big contribution to the public library, maybe add a Norville Bundle wing for reference books named after my late husband. Not the books, the wing. And then I'll go to places I've always wanted to see like Al Jizah, Timbuktu, and Kilima—"

"Ha ha ha ha," laughed Rip. "I'm sure you have more plans than we have time to go through, Mrs. Bundle. Ha ha ha ha. Here's hoping you win the big prize. And your subject tonight will be . . ."

"Geography, Rip."

"Great! Ha ha ha ha. Geography. Ha ha ha ha. Well, Mrs. Vera Bundle, why don't you let the Beautiful Monique lead you over to your soundproof capsule, the one on the far left. You get ready for the first round of *The Big Question* while I introduce our next contestant."

A beautiful, tall model came to center stage and pulled Vera by her elbow, more like jerked her toward one of the capsules.

"Good luck, Mrs. Vera Bundle!" yelled host Rip Puckett, showing his new capped teeth to the camera.

The studio audience applauded insanely.

Every reality, talk, and variety program on television has a green room.

The green room is basically a lounge where refreshments are served while the guests of the program, primarily those who will be performing and secondarily their family and friends, can enjoy refreshments while watching the show's progress on a television monitor. There are others who crowd into the green room. Guests of the production staff, agents, lawyers, press agents, hangers-on, and the like. Often the green room becomes quite crowded. It is hard for the show's ushers and security personnel who stand guard by the entrance to the green room to determine who should or shouldn't enter. Eventually they quit trying.

The green room on the night of *The Big Question*'s first show was full. Round two's contestants nervously watched the first half of the program. Friends and family of contestants were watching too. Father Brady, who was onstage, had come alone, but Arthur Durch, also onstage, invited Detectives Michael Murphy and Liam Lynch, who were delighted to come. Linus Major was sitting in the green room with his coworker and buddy Artie Flowers and his mentor Dr. Gregory Bukinberg. He had already hugged Jimmy Joel Jenks when Jimmy Joel walked into the green room with standby Billy Constable and Billy's girlfriend, Rosie Feinstein.

Retta Mae Wagons was a very surprised replacement for the "suddenly gone missing" Dr. Theresa Mendavey. The problem of why Dr. Mendavey didn't show was of no concern to Retta Mae Wagons. What did concern Retta Mae was her own couldn't-care-less attitude. Neither the doctor's disappearance nor the doctor's reappearance—if that should happen—nor her being the doctor's replacement moved Retta Mae one way or another. Normally she would have thought this was her extraordinarily lucky day. But sitting there in the green room, Retta Mae Wagons wondered if anything meant anything to her anymore, or if everything meant nothing. She should have been excited, but she wasn't. Isn't it odd, she mused, that I don't give a rat's ass if I'm on or off, win or lose, live or die?

"What are you thinking about, girl?" asked the imam.

"Nothing," said Retta Mae Wagons. She stood up and walked across the room to the refreshment table. She had to put some space between her and the insufferable imam.

"Coffee?" asked Linus Major.

"Please."

"Regular or decaf?"

"Regular. Please."

Linus poured Retta Mae a cup of coffee. "Scared?" he asked.

"Kinda."

"Me too."

"You too?" said Retta Mae Wagons, surprised. "Aren't you supposed to be a daredevil? That's what the newspapers have been calling you."

"Yeah, well . . ."

"Yeah, well what?"

"Not really. This entire experience has been somewhat life altering. At least as far as I'm concerned."

"In what way? And stop making those goo-goo eyes at me."

"I find you incredibly beautiful," said Linus Major.

"You're not so bad-looking yourself."

"And sweet," said Linus.

"Fine. So let's get back to how this experience has altered your life, huh, Linus?"

"What?"

"You were saying how this *Big Question* experience has altered your life. How has it altered your life?"

"It all has to do with missing the big question and . . . and . . . being executed. I mean I . . ."

"What? What do you mean?"

"I want to live, Retta Mae. I can't accept anymore the thought of being executed at the end of the program and my life being over. I mean . . . Jesus."

"You should have thought about that before you volunteered to be a contestant."

"But that was before I met you," said Linus Major, looking at the floor.

Billy Constable sat in a corner of the green room, fidgety and tense. He was just one skinny body of jangling nerve ends. He kept rubbing his palms together as if he were washing his hands. When he wasn't doing that he was scratching the backs of his ears, first one, then the other. He was constantly shaking his right foot.

His friends Jimmy Joel Jenks and Rosie Feinstein sat on either side of him. "Calm down, Billy," said Jimmy Joel.

"I can't. I gotta get on this program. I just gotta. I'm a dead man if I don't."

"Worrying yourself to death isn't going to help," said Rosie Feinstein.

"You could be a dead man if you get on the program too," said Jimmy Joel. "Ever think of that?"

"You know what really bugs me, Rosie?" said Billy. "What really bugs me is they picked that girl over there, the black one, an' not me. They already got one black guy, the big dude sittin' on the couch next to her. Ain't that enough blacks?"

"I don't like that kind of talk, Billy. I really don't," said Rosie Feinstein, turning away from Billy.

"Yeah, well . . . ," mumbled Billy.

"Imagine," said Jimmy Joel Jenks, "meetin' my ol' coworkin' buddy Linus Major here! I had no idea he was gonna be on the program."

"He sure was glad to see you, JJ," said Rosie Feinstein.

"You hear what I just told you two?" snapped Billy angrily.

"Yes, we heard you," said Rosie. "You've got to get on the program."

"But, Jesus, my buddy Linus *is* on the program," said a wide-eyed Jimmy Joel Jenks. "I had no idea they picked him too. He didn't even tell me he was goin' up to the office. He didn't say nothin' at all. An' we work together! His locker's right next to mine! Look at him. He don't look nervous or nothin'. I think that's kinda amazin'."

Billy couldn't care less about Jimmy Joel Jenk's goddamn stupid buddy being on the show. All he cared about was getting a crack at that hundred million dollars.

"I'm not gonna get on that damn show, am I, Rosie? Not really. Even with my damn omen an' prayin', an' my dream, an' God talkin' to me, even with all that, my chances are still pretty slim, ain't they? Slim to none is what they are, ain't they, Rosie? But what if I *do* get on the show but miss the big question? I'll miss winnin' all that money."

"And get yourself executed," said Rosie, her eyes watering up.

So what, thought Billy to himself. If I drink the damn poison I'll die an awful death or if Sanseli catches me I'll die an awful death. Any way I look at it I'm gonna die an awful death. An' if I don't get on that damn TV program, where in God's name will I come up with three hundert an' eighty thousand dollars to pay off all my gamblin' debts? Damn, I never should have stole them box seats.

"Don't forget about your dream, Billy, and your omen," said Rosie Feinstein cheerfully, trying everything she could think of to pep him up.

"Yeah," said Billy, thinking to himself, I should never have left Bowling Green is what I should never have done.

"I can't get over seein' Linus," said Jimmy Joel Jenks. "Wow!"

Billy wished he had never met JJ.

Very few people could sit still in the green room. They wandered about playing with the refreshments. They fingered the muffins, poured coffee from the urns into paper cups, took sips, then placed the nearly full cups on any available space they could find and walked away.

Among the unidentified guests loitering about the green room was a new arrival: a short, plump fellow in his fifties. He was dressed in a herringbone sport coat over a flowered sport shirt and tan slacks. The man had a patch over one eye, which he hid behind dark Ray-Ban sunglasses. The man wore his topcoat over his shoulders, European-style. One arm was bent at the elbow and pushed into his sport coat between two buttoned buttons, Napoleon-style. The other arm was jammed into his sport coat pocket. The short, squat man looked around the room, spotted the imam, and walked straight to him.

"Remember me?" asked the man in a very low voice hardly anyone else could hear.

Retta Mae Wagons, sitting beside Jamal, looked up from her magazine.

The imam checked the man out, then calmly answered, "No."

Retta Mae returned to her magazine.

"That's odd. I know you. I know you very well. I would never be able to forget that shit face of yours as long as I live. You *sure* you don't remember me?" asked the man.

Retta Mae Wagons looked up from her magazine again.

"I don't remember you," said Rasheed Jamal, without looking up.

"You're Cleveland Steve Beastie from Chicago, aren't you?"

"You have the wrong person, mister," said the imam.

"That's funny. Thought you were Cleveland Steve Beastie from Chicago," said the man. "Thought you were the ex-con two-time loser they sent up to Attica for involuntary vehicular manslaughter while driving under the influence. Could have sworn you changed your name to Rasheed Jamal before I got there. Even proclaimed yourself some kind of reverend or something. I thought for sure we shared a jail cell together. Cell Eight/Third Tier? You don't remember any a that?"

"No, I don't," snapped the imam, not looking up at the man.

Retta Mae Wagons went back to her magazine.

But stopped reading it.

"Come on, stop foolin' around, Beastie. I can understand your not recognizin' me, my face like it is. Or maybe it's been a long time. Is that why you don't recognize me? It's been too long a time, right? Or maybe you don't want to remember my name. Which is it, Beastie?"

Retta Mae Wagons continued holding her magazine to her face.

The Imam Rasheed Jamal made a halfhearted attempt to rise up off the couch.

The man's voice turned into a growl when he said, "I wouldn't do that, Cleveland Stevie."

The imam sat down.

"Damn," said the man, still in that stage whisper voice of his, "I coulda sworn you were the guy who ordered my teeth kicked out so I could suck off most of the Attica prison population with a smooth set of gums. Hold on to my big ears while they got themselves some smooth suckin'. What they call my ears, Cleveland Stevie? Bugger-grips. That was it. Bugger-grips. Ruined my face is what your prison friends did. Blinded my right eye. Gave me dizzy spells for life. Made me deaf in one ear. Naw, they didn't ruin my eye or my ear. Those convict buddies of yours ruined my *life* is what they did. An' you were the one who turned me over to the entire Attica prison population to do whatever they wanted to do to me, weren't you? You told them to keep me outta your jail cell, to keep me in the infirmary, didn't you, you fuckhead? You made me have to live with this face and those memories every day of my life since I had the miserable luck to be put in the same cell with you, you cocksucking bastard. Isn't that so? Still don't remember any a that, pissface?"

"No."

"You lie like a fuckin' rug."

"I'm telling you I haven't the faintest idea who you are. And if you don't lea—"

"You thought I died, didn't you? Mr. Reverend or whatever the fuck you are. But as any fool can plainly see, even a stoop like you, I didn't die, did I? Fooled everyone, including you, isn't that right? You see, Cleveland Stevie, the fact that I didn't die back in Attica some sixteen years ago worried that anti-Semitic psycho warden we had. He figured maybe he pushed it a little too far for his own good, having me beaten almost to death like I was, thanks to you. Wanted to keep the incident as quiet as possible. So he announced to the prison population that I was dead. Then in the middle of the night in 1996, the middle of the night so no one would know, the warden had me transferred from the Attica hospital to the Ohio State Penitentiary in Columbus. Our motherfuckin' warden told the Ohio motherfuckin' warden another prison might just straighten me out, seein' how I was a troublemaker. I was some troublemaker, wasn't I, Stevie. An' you really believed I died, didn't you, asshole? But you were wrong because *voilà,* here I am! Aren't you happy about that, Cleveland Stevie? If you are, you don't look it. I don't think you are."

The imam said nothing.

"Aw, come on, Stevie, you remember me. I'll bet you a Twinkie you do."

"How did you find me?" hissed the imam.

"See! I *told* you you knew who I was! You owe me a Twinkie! Now to make absolutely sure you're not just pulling my leg, what's my name?"

"I said how did you find me?"

"Saw your picture in the newspapers. All you contestants have been in every newspaper and magazine. I recognized you because you got a face that someone like me won't ever forget as long as I live."

"I'm not going to tell you again," said the imam. "Get the hell out of here before I have you thrown out. You leave quietly and I'll forget about the whole thing."

The stranger stood for a moment looking at the imam, smiling. He had a weird look in his eyes. "Ain't that sweet? You'll forget about the whole thing. I'm sure you will, big guy. The problem is . . . I ain't. Not in a million years. Now listen to me, Mr. fuckin' Cleveland Steve from bullshit Chicago, for the last time, tell me my fuckin' name. After all I went through, I don't want you ever forgettin' my name. Not until the day you die, you hear? Come on, say my name."

"I said get the hell out of here *now,*" hissed the imam, "or I'll have you at the bottom of the Hudson River before midnight."

"You better stop scaring me, Stevie Beastie, or I might do something you'll regret." The stranger smiled. Then said, "I ain't goin' nowhere until you say my name."

Retta Mae slowly inched herself as far away from Rasheed Jamal on the small couch as she could get.

The imam stared furiously at the disfigured face in front of him.

"Thought I was dead, didn't you, asshole?" said the disfigured face. "Thought I was a dead fish, didn't you? You know how long I've been waitin' for this moment? Know how many nights I put myself to sleep dreamin' of this moment? Huh, do you?"

Retta Mae studied the furious imam and the angry stranger and wondered whether she should do anything.

She decided not to.

The imam pushed forward on the couch. He looked up at the man and said, "Look, you little kike—"

"Easy, Cleveland Steve," whispered the man. "I'm holding a Glock 9 under this coat of mine. I've got a good grip on it with my finger on the trigger, okay? So don't make no sudden moves, okay? So here's what's goin' to happen. I'm gonna give you one more chance to get this right and prove to me you know who I am. Okay? But I can tell you this. Little Kike just ain't gonna cut it, Cleveland Stevie. I want you to speak my name out loud. Okay? So one more time. Who am I?"

"You're the Yid motherfucker who died in Attica, I thought. I'm sorry you didn't die, but I'll make sure of it as soon as I get out of this television studio," hissed the imam.

"Oh, I'm sorry, Stevie Beastie. Yid Motherfucker is *not* the correct answer. The correct answer is Robert Hirsch Leventhal. Bobby Leventhal would've worked too. I'm really sorry you missed the big question. You know the rules of the show, Beastie. You miss the big question, you get executed. Bye-bye, you nigger fuck."

The fat little man brought the gun he was carrying in his sport coat pocket out from under his topcoat, pressed the barrel against Rasheed Jamal's forehead, and pulled the trigger. The entire back of the imam's head smashed up against the wall behind him. Jamal fell backward into the couch. Then to make absolutely sure he was dead, Leventhal shot the imam nine more times in his face. When Bobby Leventhal finished with Rasheed Jamal, aka Cleveland Steve Beastie from Chicago, he was unrecognizable.

And it all happened just like that.

"It all happened just like that!" squealed Tammy, the production assistant.

She wasn't sure the producer heard her. He seemed to be staring off into space.

"It all happened just like—"

"I *heard* you. I'm thinking."

"Should we go on?" asked Tammy.

"Of course we go on," answered the producer. They were in the production office down the hall from the green room. "You can't buy this kind of publicity for a million bucks," said the producer, more to himself than to the PA. "It's absolutely fantastic. Now if we get an execution at the end of the show, we'll be home free. We'll have the biggest hit this country has ever seen."

"The green room's a mess," said Tammy. "I mean, there's gook all over the—"

"Have someone clean it up. Find another green room and move everybody into it for the time being. Take a dressing room away from someone."

"A dressing room's too small."

"Well, find a room that's big enough, for Christ sake."

"Retta Mae Wagons has blood all over her."

"Get her a new dress from wardrobe. Jesus Christ, whatever your name is, can't you figure anything out for yourself?"

"Two detectives were in the green room," added Tammy, sailing along as usual, unmindful of digs and insults. "Friends of Arthur Durch. They immediately arrested the killer. Who should we replace the dead man with?" she asked routinely, as if game show contestants were murdered every evening in the green room.

"What kind of question is that, for Christ sake? Isn't there just *one* standby?"

"Yes, sir."

"Who is it?"

"The hillbilly, sir."

"Billy Constable?"

"Yes, Billy Con—"

"Are there any other choices, dum-dum?"

"I don't think so."

"Then I guess we'll have to use Billy Constable, won't we, dum-dum?"

"Yes, sir. How hard do you want his questions to be?"

"I like Constable. He's a good kid. In fact, he might be a good one to execute. Tell the goddamn writers not to make Constable's questions too hard. I don't think he's very bright. Except the last question, of course. Make that one very hard. The writers know what to do."

The commercial break was over.

Neither Rip Puckett, the first game's contestants, nor the studio audience were aware of the shooting that took place in the green room.

"And now let's welcome the second of our three contestants for the first game!" shouted host Rip Puckett over the applause. "He's from Philadelphia, Pennsylvania, he's a hotshot in the Catholic Church. . . ." Here host Puckett decided to ad-lib a cute remark he had just thought of and said, "Who knows, he may be our next pope. Ladies and gentlemen . . . Father Daniel Patrick Brady!"

Father Brady walked across the stage to the master of ceremonies.

"Nice to have you on our first show, Father Brady."

"Nice to be here," answered the priest with a smile.

"Ha ha ha ha. You're all boned up on your specialty, I presume?"

"I am."

"And what might that be?"

"Catholicism."

"Catholicism. How about that! Happy-go-lucky subject if there ever was one. Catholicism. Well, great! Ha ha ha ha. Wonderful! Tell me, Father Brady, what are you going to do with all that money if you answer the big question correctly?"

"Give it to the Catholic Church."

"Ha ha ha ha. Give it right back to the church, right?! Ha ha ha ha. What splendid joke, Father. Ha ha ha ha."

"It's not a jo—"

"That's wonderful, Father! Now if you will allow our model Beautiful Monique to take you to your soundproof capsule . . . the one in the middle, Monique. He's all yours, Beautiful Monique. Just make sure you remember your celibacy vows, Father. Ha ha ha ha ha ha."

Before Beautiful Monique turned to lead the priest to his soundproof tube, she angrily whispered, "Goddamn it, you asshole, stop telling me where to take the fucking contestants. I know what the hell to do with the fucking contestants," loud enough to be heard from coast to coast on Rip Puckett's lapel microphone.

"Good luck, Father Daniel Patrick Brady," yelled Rip Puckett into a television camera, flashing once again his new capped teeth and ignoring Beautiful Monique.

After the shooting of Rasheed Jamal, the original green room was off-limits to everyone except the police. It had become a "crime scene" and had police guarding its entrance. The new green room was down the hall, farther away from the studio. Instead of ushers and pages, it now had police standing guard there. The producer was ecstatic: The shooting of Rasheed Jamal and now the police guarding the entrance to the new green room were all great publicity hooks. He could see tomorrow's newspaper headline:

**BIG QUESTION CONTESTANTS NEED
POLICE PROTECTION
EX-CON LOSES BEFORE THE GAME BEGINS**

"Contact our PR guy . . . what's his name . . . ?" the producer asked Ms. Pickle excitedly.

"Lupa," she answered. "Paul Lupa."

"Tell Lupa to get this blurb to Liz Smith." The producer pulled a scrap of paper from his sport coat pocket and read the following: "'Because of a shooting death in the *The Big Question*'s green room at the NBC Television Center in New York City, police were posted at the green room's entrance to protect those inside from jealous contestants who didn't make the cut.' Tell him to make the quote better, but those are the essentials. Got that?"

"Yes, sir," answered Ms. Pickle, taking the producer's quote down in shorthand in her notebook and adding: Tell Lupa to make Liz Smith better.

Life went on in the new green room. Linus Major, Retta Mae Wagons, and Billy Constable—Game Two's contestants—posed for publicity pictures. All of the show's contestants had become instant celebrities. While the digitals snapped away, Billy Constable turned to Retta Mae Wagons and said, "I guess we're lucky, you and me."

"Getting on the show like we did? Is that what you mean?"

"Yeah! Of *course* that's what I mean."

"Isn't it a little scary, though?" asked Retta Mae.

"Why do you say that?"

"I don't know. You feel lucky about getting on the show, and then you miss the last question and you're executed. So what's so lucky about that?"

"I ain't gonna miss the last question, Retta," said Billy Constable.

"Retta Mae," corrected Retta Mae.

"Retta Mae," said Billy, scowling.

"Yes, well, life's funny that way, Billy. I guess. I'm beginning to think there's some truth to that old saying, What goes around comes back around to bite your ass off. Is that the way the saying goes?"

"I agree with you, Retta Mae," chimed in Linus Major, all goo-goo eyes and stupid grin. "That slimy producer may use some kind of unanswerable question at the end of the show. It would be just like him to do—"

"I don't care. I just want to get to the last question," snapped Billy Constable. "There ain't nothin' about boxin' I don't know."

"But what if the big question isn't about boxing?" asked Retta Mae Wagons.

"It has to be. That's my dang category."

"The last question doesn't have to be related to your category. Not in the new rules they passed out," explained Linus Major.

"When they pass out new rules?" asked Billy.

"This morning," answered Retta Mae Wagons.

"And now let's meet our third and final contestant for Game One," said host Rip Puckett, obsequious as hell like most game show hosts usually are. "He's a sex therapist from Manhattan who says he's 'been around.' His specialty is . . . what else . . . sex! Now, *that* should be interesting. Ladies and gentlemen . . . Mr. Arthur Durch!"

Arthur Durch entered and walked across the stage to join Rip Puckett, cocky as all get-out.

"Welcome to *The Big Question*, Mr. Durch,"

"Call me Arthur."

"Okay . . . uh . . . Arthur," said Rip Puckett. "So tell us . . . Mr. . . . uh . . . Arthur, what is your—"

"May I say something to my wife? She couldn't be here tonight. I wondered if I could say something to her."

"Uh . . . sure . . . uh . . . go ahead, Mr. Durch."

"Call me Arthur."

"Arthur!" said the host, beginning to look horribly rattled.

Arthur Durch turned and looked at a television camera. "I'm really sorry you can't be here with me tonight, Evelyn dearest. I just want you to know I love you more than there are stars in the sky."

"What is your specialty, *Arthur*?"

"Pardon?"

"Your specialty. What is your specialty?"

"You already said it. Sex!"

"Oh, *God* . . . I mean, *goodness* . . . ha ha ha . . . I said it, didn't I? I said God. I mustn't, you know. It's taboo to say God on the air. Or is it? So Mr. Dur . . . so *Arthur,* what are you going to do with one hundred million dollars . . . if . . . if you answer The Big Question correctly."

"For me to know and you to find out," replied Arthur Durch, winking at the camera.

"Oh, ha ha ha ha ha ha. For me to know and you to find out! Clever, clever, clever. Okay, Mr. Durch . . . I know, I know. *Arthur.* Okay, Arthur, our model Beautiful Monique will take you to your soundproof capsule—the one on the far right. Let's have a big good-luck hand for . . . for . . . Arthur!

Durch received nothing resembling a "big good-luck hand." It was more like a smattering of applause. He wasn't a favorite.

"We'll be back to start the first round of *The Big Question,*" yelled host Rip Puckett over the cheering audience, "right after these messages."

"You've lost it, Puckett!" screamed the livid producer, showering spittle on the host's face the instant he stepped backstage. *"You've completely lost it!"*

"I . . . he . . . that guy Durch threw me for a loop with his badgering," said Rip Puckett, wiping his face dry with his handkerchief.

"*What* badgering?"

"He told me to call him by his first name. He rattled me. I think he was *trying* to rattle me."

"Well, he certainly succeeded. Call *everybody* by their first name, *idiot!*"

"Okay, okay," muttered the host. "I just wish you wouldn't call me an id—"

"And stop your goddamn laughing. It's getting on everybody's nerves."

"I'm trying to act jolly."

"Fuck jolly, do you hear?"

While the producer was ripping Puckett a new one, someone from the Nielsen Corporation, the company that had rated the nation's television and radio shows for decades, called the National Broadcasting Company. The Nielsen man spoke to the network's vice president of research and development.

"Right now," said the Nielsen man, "three out of every four television households in America are watching your *Big Question* program, Harry. Just thought you'd like to know."

"Thank you for calling, Sid," said the network's vice president of research and development. "That *is* nice to know."

The delighted network veep telephoned the producer in the control room and told him the good news.

The producer did something he rarely did.

He smiled.

In the first round of Game One, each contestant answered the first question correctly. In the second round, Arthur Durch was asked to name the six most common causes of impotence in men.

Durch said, "Let's see, the six most common causes of impotence in men. That happens to be a subject I am extremely familiar with. Okay, here they are: diabetes, alcohol, circulatory problems, some drugs prescribed for high blood pressure, low levels of testosterone . . . let's see, how many's that? That's five, right? . . . and . . . and . . . what the [bleep] is the sixth . . ." Arthur Durch couldn't think of the sixth primary cause of impotence to save his soul.

Time ran out.

Durch missed obesity.

The audience couldn't have cared less. In fact, they thought the braggart's inability to answer the question served him right. Once again the audience gave Durch only a few claps.

Father Brady was asked: "The first Church Council was held in the year 321 C.E. Since then, how many Church Councils have been held?"

He answered quickly, "Nineteen."

"I'm sorrrr-y," said the hammy host, "the *correct* answer is twenty-one."

The audience moaned. They seemed disappointed when a nice contestant missed a question.

Rip Puckett asked Vera Bundle, "Where are the Marang Mountains?"

Without hesitating, Vera answered, "Borneo."

Puckett screamed, *"That is absolutely correct!"*

The audience cheered uncontrollably.

With the score Bundle 2, Brady 1, and Durch 1, host Puckett asked Arthur Durch, "If one suffers from priapism, what exactly is one suffering from?"

Durch looked dazed.

"What the [bleep] kind of a question is that?" Durch asked.

Everyone knew he was angry.

And everyone knew he was going to miss the question.

Time ran out.

A smirking Rip Puckett, glad the contestant who rattled him was on his way off the show, said, "The answer is a large, stiff erection you don't want and can't get rid of. The word is derived from Priapus, the Roman garden god who had a large wooden penis."

The audience laughed uproariously, pleased with the answer and the fact that Durch was gone. Kligman and Siegel, the censors, didn't laugh at all. They wondered how that question had got by them and whether they would catch hell from their boss.

It was time for Father Brady's third and final question. Puckett said, "If you get this question correct, Father Brady, you'll tie Vera Bundle. Ready? Okay, then. Please explain quantum spirituality."

The priest thought for only a moment, then said, "Quantum spirituality is a spirituality that calls us to recognize the holiness of the world and be involved with it creatively, as Jesus did in becoming human with us."

Rip Puckett needed a few seconds to check the priest's answer against the one on his card, completely oblivious to the stage manager, who was vigorously nodding his head and mouthing the word "correct."

After what seemed like an eternity, Puckett yelped, *"You are one hundred percent correct!"*

In the control room, one of the writers whispered in the producer's ear, "The priest wasn't supposed to get that one."

The audience was impressed. Not only did the priest know the correct answer but he said it quickly and modestly. They cheered loudly for Father Brady. The humble priest had become one of the favorites.

Vera Bundle, now tied with the priest, knew she had to answer the next question to win the round. If she didn't, she and Father Brady would each have to answer more questions until one of them broke the tie.

Rip Puckett said, "Vera, are you ready? Get this question right and you win the round. Okay, your question is: We know the Paraguay River runs through Paraguay. What other country does it run through?"

Vera didn't hesitate. She quickly answered, "Bolivia."

Puckett screeched, "You . . . are . . . absolutely . . . *right!*"

The audience cheered for Vera Bundle.

Vera had won the first game. The final score: 3 points for Bundle, 2 points for Brady, and 1 point for Durch.

Rip Puckett thanked the priest. The audience gave him a hearty round of applause. He shrugged his shoulders. He was visibly distraught. He would have to continue thinking of a solution regarding the monumental problem of Rosa Gambino.

Pasty Arthur Durch looked as though he had been condemned to death. As the model Beautiful Monique came to lead Arthur Durch off the stage, he jerked his arm away from her and walked up to a nearby television camera, his eyes filled with tears. He blew a kiss into the camera and said, "Bye, Evie. I love you." The camera was not operating. The show had paused for another commercial.

Durch, devastated beyond belief, returned to the temporary green room with the other losers. He stood by himself off to the side while the show's assistant producers gave the eliminated contestants their mandatory job-well-done farewell speeches and little bags of cheesy gifts for doing the show: tacky men's aftershave lotion, a perfume for ladies that made most people nauseous, several CDs by unknown NBC artists, and a baseball hat that had THE BIG QUESTION printed on the front. Arthur shook his head and put up his hands, warding off the bag of gifts.

"I don't want anything," he muttered.

Arthur Durch suddenly had to leave the repulsively festive scene. He was desperately in need of fresh air.

Durch left the new green room, walked quickly down the long gray hall with all the framed color portraits of NBC stars, past and present, rode the elevator in silence, and pushed himself through the revolving door into the cool evening. When Arthur stepped out onto the pavement, he found himself separated on both sides from the screaming multitude by thick red ropes.

And then he thought he saw her!

In the crowd's front line on his right was his Evelyn. She was holding on to the red rope so she wouldn't be jostled out of her place. There was so much confusion, so many people pushing and pulling at one another, he wasn't sure it was really her. It was either someone who looked just like Evelyn . . . or . . . or . . .

Arthur couldn't believe his eyes. He rubbed each one with a knuckle of his hand and then he looked again. It *was* her. It was Evelyn Lounge Durch! It was his wonderful wife. He ran to her and they hugged and hugged with the thick red rope between them.

"What happened, Evelyn? Why are you here? I thought they'd kill you."

"They didn't."

"I can see that, Evelyn, but *why* didn't they?"

"They said I was an itch."

"You are, Evelyn."

"The kidnapper said I was really annoying and that I got on his nerves something awful."

"You can do that, Evelyn."

"I know. Anyway, it seems the kidnapper couldn't get rid of me fast enough. He even drove me here."

"I love you, Evelyn Lounge."

"Evelyn Lounge *Durch*. I love you too, Arthur."

Father Daniel Patrick Brady also left the NBC building. He walked through the crowds to the street, ignoring the "Way to go, Father" and the "Too bad, Padre" salutations he heard from the screaming crowd that lined the building's entrance.

The priest took a right in the street and walked west on Forty-ninth Street until he could get back onto the pavement. He continued down to the corner of Forty-ninth Street and Avenue of the Americas. He stood on the corner waiting for the red light to turn green.

Only he didn't wait.

He stepped off the curb and into the street in front of an M5 bus.

VI

After the commercial break . . .

After the commercial break, host Rip Puckett said, "And now let's meet our three contestants for Game Two. First, a high school graduate who couldn't afford to go to college. She's now twenty years old and has high hopes of using tonight's winnings to set up a college scholarship fund for underprivileged high school students. Please welcome Miss Retta Mae Wagons!"

Retta Mae Wagons walked across the stage to join host Puckett. Her face had a tense expression and she didn't seem to know what to do with her arms. She folded them over her chest, then uncrossed them and let them hang by her sides, then crossed them over her chest again. And so on.

Rip Puckett, attempting to show what a warm and kindly fellow he was, put his arm around Retta Mae's shoulders and said, "There, there, honey. There's nothing to worry about. You'll be just fine."

Retta Mae shrugged his arm off her shoulders and stepped back.

Rip Puckett's expression signified to one and all that Retta Mae's gesture had rattled him again. After withdrawing his arm, Rip stared at it as if it were diseased.

"You going to just stand there and look at your arm all night, Mr. Host?" asked Retta Mae Wagons with a sardonic smile playing around her lips.

"Ah . . . what? *No!* No. Okay . . . so, Retta Mae Wagons, what are you planning on doing with all that money . . . if you win, that is?"

"I'm going to set up a foundation to help poor high school kids go to college, like you said in my introduction."

Retta Mae Wagons had already tuned out the show's host as she thought about what had just happened to her. The little fat guy with the big ears and the patch over his eye was her savior. A heavenly messenger from somewhere, maybe from the Big Man Himself.

Retta Mae was upset but a different kind of upset. She had been frightened by the noise and temporarily stunned by the blood and brains splattered all over her. It took some doing getting her stomach to settle down. But as for Rasheed Jamal's being dead, as far as seeing the man she had been living with blown away while he sat beside her, that didn't bother her at all. In fact, the event made Retta Mae happy for the first time in years.

Retta Mae Wagons didn't want to die anymore. Quite the opposite. She wanted to *live!* Big-time. Life would be fun again now that Rasheed was dead as a flattened-out racoon after nine wheels of an eighteen-wheeler had rolled over it.

Retta Mae didn't know what she'd use for money and didn't care. Maybe she'd go back to hooking if she had to. As a matter of fact, Retta Mae kinda liked hooking. She'd call Dannyboy Marley that night. Soon as she got back to the hotel. Maybe she could see him tomorrow. She didn't know what she'd do if Dannyboy didn't offer her her job back, or her apartment. She wondered if the great apartment she had had across from the Jackson Hole Restaurant was still available. The one thing Retta Mae Wagons *did* know was this: She didn't want any part of a damn execution.

"Retta Mae? Retta Mae?"

"Uh . . . yes?"

"I think you left us for a moment or two here on coast-to-coast television! Anyway," Rip said, "I understand you're going to give all that money you win, if you do win, that is, to a scholarship fund for underprivileged African-American kids."

"Underprivileged high school seniors," said an obviously irritated Retta Mae Wagons.

"Ha ha ha ha. Speak up, Retta Mae, honey," said Rip, a creaky smile on his face, remembering too late that he'd been ordered not to do those fake laughs. Also he wondered if it was okay to call a colored girl honey.

"I said the money would be for high school seniors," repeated Retta Mae, "who can't afford to go to college. It doesn't matter if the seniors are black, white, green, yellow, or chartreuse . . . *honey.*"

"Certainly. Any color at all. Right. Monique! Monique! Please come take . . . please come and *escort* Retta Mae Wagons to her soundproof capsule. Let's have a nice round of applause for Retta Mae Wagons!"

There was modest applause.

In the control room, the producer said to Ms. Pickle, "Get me a new host by tomorrow morning."

"Anyone in particular?" asked Ms. Pickle.

"Yes. See if that jerk-off that used to do *The Newlywed Game* is available. Not too bright, but he can do a game show. I think. At least he doesn't do fake laughs all the time. Make sure the one I have in mind is not too old. He's probably too old by now. If he *is* too old, get anybody."

Ms. Pickle wrote in her notepad: Get NWG jerk-off.

Onstage, Rip Puckett said, "Okay, our next contestant is a young man from Bowling Green, Kentucky. He loves to hunt and fish and never misses a boxing match if he can see it. *And* . . . he doesn't like grits! My my my, a Southerner who doesn't like grits? Let's give a warm *Big Question* welcome to Mr. Billy Constable!"

Billy Constable walked across the stage and shook hands with Rip Puckett.

"Well, Billy, what are *you* going to do with all that money, that one hundred million dollars, you may or may not win tonight?"

It was Billy Constable's first time on national television and all of a sudden he realized something awful. He couldn't seem to make his mouth work. He wondered if he would ever talk again. He just stood beside Puckett, staring at his ear.

After a horrendous delay, which was again mostly Puckett's fault, Rip said, "Well . . . yes . . . good for *you*! And you're our expert on boxing?"

"Yes," whispered Billy, squinting at Rip Puckett.

"Have you ever boxed?" asked the host.

"Did I ever what?"

"Let's have a big hand for Billy Constable," yelled Rip Puckett as he waved the model over.

While Billy Constable was being led to his capsule by the Beautiful Monique, Rip Puckett said, "And now let's meet our final contestant for Game Two. He comes from a proud American family of industrial giants and captains of industry. He works as director of bones for the Museum of Natural History right here in New York City. His area of expertise will be archaeology, primarily the Mesozoic era, or for dummies like me, the age of dinosaurs. Ladies and gentlemen . . . Mr. Linus Major!"

Linus Major joined Rip Puckett at center stage, grinning from ear to ear.

"You look happy, Mr. Major. I mean Linus. How do you really feel?"

"Happy," answered Linus, and he had been for several hours now.

It was when he hugged Jimmy Joel Jenks in the green room that Linus knew he wanted to see Jimmy Joel, and everyone else he knew, again tomorrow and the day after tomorrow and the day after that. And Artie. And Dr. Bukinberg.

I'm not a kid anymore, he thought to himself. I don't even lisp at all. As a result I don't have to impress anybody anymore. I don't have to do foolish stunts anymore. Ever. Before he signed up for *The Big Question,* Linus had a simple, happy life. The key word there was "happy." He had been happy. He wanted to be happy again.

"There doesn't seem to be a worry in your head, Linus," said the show's host, Rip Puckett, unaware of how prescient he was. "I take it you're not thinking about the consequences of missing the big question?"

"In the first place, Mr. Puckett, I'm—"

"Call me Rip."

"In the first place, Rip," said Linus Major with a modest smile that befitted him, "I'm going to try not to miss the big question. I'm hoping like the others I'll be able to answer all my questions."

Linus Major was lying through his teeth.

The audience applauded Linus. They approved of his simple confidence.

"Good for you, Linus," said Rip Puckett, and it's possible he meant it.

"I don't believe a word that contestant's saying," said the producer to his staff in the control room. "Not a goddamn word. I can tell by the look on his face and his demeanor. The bastard's going to throw it."

In the first round of Game Two, Retta Mae Wagons's general knowledge question was: What was the number one reason given by patients for emergency room visits last year? Retta Mae Wagons knew it was stomach pains. She remembered reading the answer in *The World Almanac*. The number one complaint patients gave in emergency rooms were stomach pains, cramps, and spasms.

Retta Mae pretended to think and think and think. When time was almost up, she confessed she didn't have a clue.

Rip Puckett, who didn't like Retta Mae Wagons, said almost cheerfully, "Not a clue?"

"Not a clue."

The buzzer sounded and Rip said, "Ahhh, too bad, Retta—"

"Retta Mae."

"Too bad, Retta *Mae*. Too, too bad. The answer is . . . stomach pains, cramps, and spasms! I'm *really* sorry."

I'll bet you are, thought Retta Mae Wagons, who wasn't.

In the control room, the producer said aloud, "That black bitch is throwing it. She's just plain chickening out. The possibility of being executed has scared her. I knew the bitch would chicken out. God*damn* it."

"Current estimates," said Rip Puckett to Linus Major in the next soundproof booth, "put the age of Earth at 4,600 billion years. The years from that date up until about 542 million years ago are grouped in one large division of geological time. What is that grouping called?"

Linus Major didn't utter a sound. He knew the answer—the Precambrian age—but preferred to keep his mouth tightly shut. Linus shook his head and dropped his chin dejectedly to his chest. He continued to pretend he was thinking about the question, waiting for time to run out.

It seemed to take forever.

"Time's running out, Linus," coaxed Rip Puckett.

In the control room, a nervous question writer ran up to the producer and said, "We thought that was an easy question for a guy like him. He should know the answer."

The producer ignored the question writer. Looking straight ahead through the control room to the stage and Linus Major's soundproof tube, the producer said, "I *told* you. The bastard's quitting on me too.

He knows the answer. He's just not saying it, either. That's two in a fucking row! Look at that shit heel. Just look at the pissy wimp. Metzger, get over here!"

The contestant coordinator, Elsa Metzger, browbeaten and introverted from birth, spectacles resting on the tip of her nose, dress down to her ankles making her look like the spinster she would always be, ran—not walked but ran—to the producer's side.

"Do not," said the furious producer, "I repeat, do not ever let this happen again! Do not ever give me another contestant who will change his or her mind in the middle of a taping and decide not to go all the way. If you can't figure out what the hell the story is with these contestants of yours in their auditions . . . if you . . . goddamn it . . . if you give me another Wagons or Major, you'll be out of work. You hear? You'll be out on the street. And I promise you, you will never work again in this industry. Now get the hell out of this control room. I can't stand the sight of you!"

Elsa Metzger turned and ran out of the control room, sobbing.

Onstage, Rip Puckett said as sadly as he could, "Sorry, Linus Major, time is up. The answer is . . . Precambrian!"

Linus Major shrugged his shoulders.

The spotlight moved to Billy Constable's soundproof tube.

"Billy, Billy, Billy. Are you ready?" asked the jovial host.

Billy, inside his soundproof tube, adjusted his earphones and nodded yes.

Rip Puckett asked, "Who was the undefeated welterweight from Philadelphia who was discovered to have only one good eye and was banned from boxing?"

Billy Constable grinned a cocky grin and quickly answered, "Gypsy Joe Harris."

"Ab-so-lute-ly correct!" shouted Rip Puckett.

In the control room, the producer turned to his lawyer, Sigmond Levy, sitting behind him, and said, "*That* kid wants to win."

In the second round of Game Two, Rip Puckett asked Retta Mae Wagons, "What age group accounts for the most deaths from firearms: five to fourteen, twenty to twenty-four, twenty-five to forty-five, or forty-five to sixty-four?"

Retta Mae had read somewhere that it was twenty-five to forty-five. She crossed her fingers, prayed she would miss, and said, "Five to fourteen."

The audience moaned.

"See! *See!*" screamed the producer in the control room. "Even the audience knows she's wrong!"

"Oh, too too bad, Retta Mae Wagons," said Rip Puckett, showing blatantly obvious false remorse. "You're wrong again! The correct answer is twenty-five to forty-five."

Retta Mae Wagons smiled and shrugged her shoulders.

"See how thrilled the bitch is she lost?" said the producer in the control room. "Did you see that smile? She's thrilled she lost."

"Linus Major," said host Rip Puckett, "your question is: This reptile was known for its large sauropods and the lengthening of its forelimbs relative to its hind limbs. It had chisel-like teeth—twenty-six on each jaw—to fight predators and an extremely long neck for feeding off vegetation on the tops of trees. It stood approximately fifty feet high and laid its eggs while walking, leaving its young to fend for themselves. What is the creature's name?"

"He knows the answer," said the producer in the control room. "That bastard knows the answer."

The producer was right.

"But he won't say it," snapped the producer.

The producer was right again. Linus Major shook his head back and forth, a baffled look on his face. Time clicked away . . . and clicked away . . . and soon there wasn't any more.

"I . . . I'm sorry . . . I'm really sorry . . . ," moaned Linus, worried that he might be overacting.

"See! *See!*" screamed the producer in the control room.

"Too bad . . . again . . . Linus," said the host. "The correct answer is the *Brachiosaurus*!"

"Bastard," shouted the producer. "I'll *kill* him."

Several members of the show's staff and some of the control room technicians turned to look at the producer.

"I'm only kidding, for Christ sake," he muttered, ignoring everyone, looking through the control room window to the stage.

"That was an easy question," moaned one of the writers, who had tiptoed up behind the producer. "He should have certainly gotten that one."

The producer whirled around and shouted, "Stop pussyfooting up to my ear every five minutes to tell me how the contestants should have answered your goddamned question, you stupid faggot."

"Don't you *dare* talk to me that way," said the writer, jamming his clipboard into the producer's stomach, making the producer say "Oof" and knocking him against a bank of monitors. The writer turned and walked out of the control room, yelling as he left, "You can take your fucking job, Mr. Producer, and stick it up your anal orifice."

The producer ignored the tittering in the control room.

His mind was miles away.

He would have to find some way to prevent a contestant from changing his or her mind on the air. That was the show's Achilles' heel, a far more despicable problem than the immediate loss of Major and Wagons. If Elsa Metzger couldn't sift through the flaws in potential contestants during auditions and get rid of the show's only cancer, nobody could. Elsa would just have to adopt the old adage: When in doubt, throw them out. Elsa Metzger was the best contestant coordinator in the business. Suddenly the producer hoped he hadn't frightened the woman into quitting.

"Okay, Billy Constable," said Rip Puckett onstage, "ready for your second question?"

Billy nodded.

The audience was quiet.

The control room was quiet.

Billy waited in his soundproof booth, wiping sweat off his forehead with the sleeve of his sport coat, the same sport coat he had worn on the bus from Bowling Green, Kentucky, to New York City.

Rip Puckett said, "Who was the first heavyweight champion of the world and . . . in what years was he champion? I'll repeat the question again. Who was the—"

"John L. Sullivan," interrupted Billy. "Sullivan was champ from 1882 to 1892."

"Absolutely correct!" shouted host Rip Puckett.

In the last round of Game Two, Retta Mae Wagons incorrectly answered her third question and Linus Major kept his mouth shut until time ran out. Billy Constable wasn't even required to answer a third question. Rip Puckett declared him the winner of Game Two, and the audience cheered.

Retta Mae Wagons and Linus Major both looked disappointed over having lost and were led off the stage, but though he couldn't see for sure, the producer was certain Wagons and Major were grinning as they left.

Billy Constable stood in his soundproof tube, stunned and amazed and a tad woozy. One hundred million dollars was maybe one question away. He just had to beat the old woman, whatever the hell her name was. Vera something. Billy was sure he'd beat her. Hadn't he had that omen dream where the roulette wheel's little rubber arrow stopped on the $100,000,000 slot? God promised him he'd not only get on the show, but win! He'd gotten on the show. Now all he had to do was answer one more lousy question and hope that the old biddy missed hers.

A hundred million dollars almost in his hands! And all his troubles gone. *Gone!*

God Almighty.

Billy refused to think about the glass of deadly poison.

Meanwhile, in the temporary green room, Jimmy Joel Jenks hugged Linus Major and, even though he didn't know her, gave Retta Mae Wagons a big kiss on her cheek when the two walked back into the green room. Linus, along with Artie Flowers and Dr. Gregory Bukinberg, were all going to Hurley's Bar just down at the corner of Forty-ninth and Sixth Avenue to celebrate Linus's defeat. They asked Jimmy Joel Jenks to join them.

He begged off, saying, "I wanna stay with Rosie to give her support and be here when Billy comes back a rich man." He promised to join the group later.

Linus asked Retta Mae if she'd like to come.

"Give me one good reason why I should," she said, smiling.

"Because I'm in love with you."

"Give me another."

"Because you're in love with me."

Rosie Feinstein was a nervous wreck. She borrowed a piece of paper and a ballpoint pen from someone, sat down, and started to scribble. She said to Jimmy Joel, "JJ, you know what Billy will be left with after he pays off every single penny he owes to Sanseli and Eddie? Ninety-nine million, six hundred and twenty thousand dollars *after* he pays off all his debts! Jesus, JJ, that's a lot of money."

"How much?" asked Jimmy Joel.

"Ninety-nine million, six hundred and twenty thousand dollars."

"Wow!" said Jimmy Joel Jenks.

It was the Championship Round.

Vera Bundle and Billy Constable were listening to the voice of host Rip Puckett on their headsets in their soundproof booths.

"Everything okay?" asked the host.

Both Vera and Billy nodded yes.

Rip Puckett, reading the script from cue cards, said, "You two know the rules. I'll ask you each a question that deals with your specialty, Vera's being geography and Billy's boxing. If you both answer correctly, I'll ask you each another question. The first one to get the correct answer *after the other misses* will be our winner and will go on to try for the hundred-million-dollar grand prize . . . or that dis*gus*ting glass of poison. Our loser will receive ten thousand dollars in cash courtesy of *The Big Question*. Age before beauty," said Puckett. "So Vera, are you ready for your first question?"

In the control room, Tammy Teesdale asked, "Wouldn't it have been nicer if the host had said 'Ladies first' and not 'Age before—'"

"Shut up," said the producer.

Onstage, Vera Bundle nodded she was ready. She stood up straight in her booth, calmly clasping her hands together as if in prayer, her index fingers pressing against her nose and lips, her thumbs under her chin.

"Okay, here it is," said Rip. "For a chance to win *one . . . hundred . . . million . . . dollars,* your question is: In 1554, the Spaniards came to the New World and founded the city of Trinidad. Where is the city of Trinidad located?"

The orchestra started to play the music of time passing but didn't get very far. Vera was waving her hand. She was ready.

"In Cuba," she answered.

"That is correct!" shouted the host.

The audience howled and screamed their approval. Kindly old Vera was definitely a crowd pleaser.

Then Rip Puckett turned to a visibly nervous Billy Constable and said, "Billy, you've got to get this question or you're outta here. Ha ha ha ha. Here's your question: Who did Joe Louis fight and was so convinced he lost that he left the ring only to hear when he was going up the aisle that he—Joe Louis—was the winner by a unanimous decision?"

Billy Constable's color drained from his face.

"Jesus Christ," he muttered aloud. He rubbed his hands together as if he were washing them with soap. He squinted. He prayed. He said, "Oh, Lord, please help me."

Silence.

More silence. Billy Constable's time was almost up.

"I'm sorry . . . Billy . . . but . . ."

"Oh, God, have mercy on me," whispered Billy.

" . . . but . . . time's up. I need your answer," begged a bewildered Rip Puckett.

"Jesus Christ Almighty, my mind's gone empty on me. I . . . I . . . I don't know the answer," said Billy.

The audience moaned.

"I'm sooooo sorry," said Puckett sadly. "The answer is Jersey Joe Walcott." Rip's sadness was sincere. He had grown to like Billy just as the audience had.

Rip Puckett dawdled for a few minutes so the audience in the studio and around the country could feel and see Billy Constable's considerable pain, his arms by his sides, his head and shoulders bent, tears streaming down his cheeks.

Then Billy Constable was history.

"That means," Puckett shouted, "our winner . . . and the one who will try to answer the big question worth *one . . . hundred . . . million . . . dollars* is . . . Vera Bundle!!!"

The band played wildly and the audience cheered. Vera was taken out of her soundproof booth by the model Beautiful Monique and led to center stage. A spotlight followed them, leaving Billy Constable standing in his booth in darkness. The audience, busy cheering for Vera Bundle, didn't notice a stagehand lead the weeping Billy from the stage.

"We'll be back with *The . . . Big . . . Question . . .* ," shouted Rip Puckett, "right after these messages."

As Retta Mae Wagons, Linus Major, and Linus's friends were leaving the studio, the producer stepped out of a small hallway and stopped them.

"Both of you threw it, didn't you?"

"Threw what?" asked Linus.

"Yes, we threw it," said Retta Mae Wagons. "So what?"

"You better watch yourself, young lady. I have ways of—"

"No, Mr. Producer Man, you better watch *your*self. I used to be a bona fide member of one of the toughest and most violent street gangs in this city. I have friends that would just love to dust your white ass for your fancy watch. I'm going to spread the word that you threatened me and my buddy Linus. Our friends here are witnesses. You just keep that in mind when you think of us and any kind of retribution you might have in mind. And when you're finished thinking about that, think about kissing my cute black ass."

The four turned and started to leave when Linus Major stopped, turned to the producer, and said, "You can also kiss my cute white ass."

"And mine too," added Dr. Bukinberg.

Oddly, as soon as the foursome arrived at Hurley's Bar & Grill, Artie Flowers quickly excused himself, saying there was a Mets night game and he wanted to get back to his apartment for the late innings. He hugged Linus and ran for a bus. Dr. Bukinberg said something about catching a cold and thought it best he return to his apartment and try to nip the bug with a hot toddy. He hailed a cab and was gone.

"That leaves just you and me, babe," said a cheerful Linus Major, grabbing Retta Mae's hand and leading her into Hurley's Bar & Grill. They sat on the same side of a banquette, Retta Mae on the inside, Linus on the outside.

"You going to hold my hand all night?" asked Retta Mae Wagons.

"I'd like to," answered Linus.

"What's gotten into you, boy?"

"I'm smitten."

"Smitten!"

"Yes, smitten. No . . . *more* smitten. I was smitten before our little talk in the green room. I was smitten when I first saw you. I'm in love with you, Retta Mae."

"You are one crazy white man."

"Why do you say that? You're gorgeous. You're brilliant. And . . . and . . ."

"And what?"

"And you're shorter than I am. I never wanted to marry a woman taller than me."

"Marry!?"

"Yes. Well . . . the word kind of slipped out, but I'm glad it did."

Silence. Just boring bar music that kept repeating the coda with the bass and lead guitar over and over again.

"Is it such a crazy thought?" asked Linus Major.

"No, Linus, except . . ."

"Except what?"

"Except we're poor. You're an employee of a museum and I'm . . . I'm . . ."

"You're a hooker. So what?"

"An ex-hooker."

"I don't care. As long as you come home to me at night."

"You wouldn't mind me being a hooker?"

"No."

"You're an idiot, Linus. A raving idiot."

Silence.

"I'm an ex–gang girl, Linus."

"I don't care if you were a murderess, Retta Mae. You've changed. You're not a murderess now. Not even close. And even if you are, and you get sent to jail, I'll bring you cakes with little saws in them and—"

"Like I said, Linus, we're broke."

"Okay, so maybe we're a little broke. But we'll make ends meet. We're smart and we're hard workers. We'll get to be what we want to be. You wouldn't have to be a hooker anymore if you didn't want to. I make enough money at the museum to pay the rent and put food on the table. By the way, I happen to live in one of the last rent-controlled buildings in New York. You could go to college and get a degree. Maybe work in your spare time. It'll be hard at first but we'll get it done. You can be anything you want to be, Retta Mae Wagons. You're still young and bright as hell. You can get yourself into college in a minute. You were a straight-A high school student. Believe me, it won't be a problem."

"I'd love to be a doctor," Retta Mae said, sort of to herself.

"See! We can do it, Retta Mae. We can. We can do it together, I know we can."

"I've got some money stashed away that Rasheed never got his hands on."

"And I've got a good job and I'm going places at the museum. You can count on it. And, like I said, you don't have to be a damned hooker anymore if you don't want to and—"

"But Linus, honey, we've known each other exactly twelve hours. If that."

"Listen, Retta Mae, I read somewhere that it doesn't matter if you marry your high school sweetheart you've known since grammar school or someone you met an hour ago. Each marriage has as good a chance of working, or failing, as the other."

"That's what you read somewhere, huh?"

"Yes, that's what I read. I love you, Retta Mae. I know that's weird—not that I should love you but that I should fall in love with you so fast—but I love you. Listen to me. I know you won't believe this, but I'm going to tell you anyway. My nose twitches when I'm in the presence of a woman I will be happily married to, and my nose has been twitching up a storm for the last twelve hours."

"Be serious, Linus. This is important."

"I *am* being serious. If certain things didn't happen, you and I could have been on our way to the mortuary tonight. But neither one of us wanted to die, and we didn't. We're alive, Retta Mae! In some strange way our slates have been wiped clean and we have a whole new life ahead of us. So let's make the most of our good fortune. See! We're two of a kind in more ways than one. So let's get married. What do you say? Worst comes to worst, it won't work. But at least we'll have given it a shot. Each of us felt something powerful toward each other in that green room, didn't we? Well, I did. And I think you did too. Whattaya say, Retta Mae? So?"

"So *what,* Linus?"

"So let's get married."

"Shee-it, man."

"What's that mean?"

"It means okay."

Billy Constable speed-walked out of studio 6E.

He didn't stop at the green room for Rosie or Jimmy Joel but kept walking down the hall, ducked into a stairwell, took the steps two at a time for two flights, then left the stairwell on the fourth floor. He waited for an elevator to the ground floor, patting his pockets to make sure his wallet and money were there, while his eyes watched for a red light. When he arrived at the lobby he literally ran out of the elevator, out of the building, and through the crowds standing outside on the pavement in front of the entrance to the National Broadcasting Company. When he was in the clear, he ran east on Forty-ninth Street heading toward Fifth Avenue. Billy stopped running when he came alongside the ice-skating rink at Rockefeller Center.

An unusually cold October wind blew across the city. It felt as though an early snowstorm might be coming. The ice-skating rink was filled with skaters. Billy stood behind a waist-high cement wall and watched the happy people below going round and round. Some did figure eights. Some held hands and skated in pairs. Others played crack the whip. Quite frequently someone slipped and fell down, stood up, and wiped his or her bottom.

"At least none of them skaters saw me miss my question," said a shattered Billy Constable to himself. "And what kinda question was *that?* It was unanswerable is what it was. They slipped it to me at the last minute. That damn producer didn't want me to win. He wanted to get rid a me. He wanted the old lady to win. I'm sure a that. I never did like that bastard producer. He's an evil man. Maybe I shoulda complained. Maybe if I complained to the NBC company, maybe they'd a slipped me some cash to keep me quiet. Maybe they'd a gave me the four hundred thousand dollars I need to pay off Sanseli and Eddie. Maybe the TV people'll give me the money just to shut me up. But how can I prove they changed the question at the last minute? No way I could prove that."

Billy Constable moaned. A couple standing near him turned and stared.

Billy said, "What the hell you lookin' at?"

The couple turned back to the ice skaters.

Billy wished he'd been able to pick up that ten thousand dollars they gave to the losers before he tore ass out of the building. "Better yet I wisht I'd never left home. New York City's too big and full a too many bad people. How could a couple a hick country boys like me and Jimmy Joel survive here? I guess Jimmy Joel ain't doin' too badly, but he's just—"

"Hey, putzo, too bad you didn't win. Time to stop talkin' to yourself an' take a little ride."

Billy whirled around. Sanseli's huge henchman was standing there chewing gum, wearing his leather porkpie hat and a dark blue overcoat with its collar up. It was the guy he talked to on the telephone, the one who called him "Horse's Mouth," the one who sat next to him in the van. The thug had his hands in his overcoat pockets. Billy saw the dirty gray van with the one sliding door double-parked in the street across from where he and the Sanseli guy stood. Sanseli wasn't in the van but the man named Rothberg was.

Twenty-year-old Billy Constable looked at the thug and said, "Sure," then turned and ran east toward Fifth Avenue. Billy was fast. The out-of-shape thug lasted ten feet. Billy ran in the opposite direction the traffic was allowed to go on Forty-ninth Street, where the NBC studio's entrance was. It was a smart move on Billy's part. The thugs wouldn't be able to turn their van around and chase him. They would have to go all the way around Forty-ninth Street to Sixth Avenue, turn right and go to Fiftieth Street, then come up Fiftieth Street to Fifth Avenue. What with all the traffic, that would take a while.

Billy would be long gone by then.

Billy reached Fifth Avenue and was relieved to see so many people. New York was always full of people, forever crammed with New Yorkers and tourists. It was something Billy never got used to. He was constantly amazed at the number of people crowding the streets at all hours of the day and night. Say nothing of the cars and taxis. Billy Constable had never seen so much traffic at almost nine o'clock at night. My God, thought Billy, there'd hardly be a soul on the streets at this hour in Bowling Green.

Bowling Green.

That's where he'd go. Billy would go home. By bus. Just like he came. He'd grab the next bus out of the Port Authority terminal and go back to Bowling Green. The mob would never find him there. They don't even know I'm from Bowling Green, thought Billy, slaloming through the pedestrians as he ran toward Park Avenue.

When I have that bus ticket in my hand I'll be a free person!

An empty cab passed him. Billy put his fingers in his mouth and whistled. The taxi stopped. Billy got in, said, "The bus terminal at Fortieth and Eighth Avenue, please," and slid way down in his seat.

Billy pulled out his wallet and counted his money. Over three hundred dollars. Good thing he slipped those hundred-dollar bills and twenties out of Rosie's pocketbook before they left for the studio. Something told him to do it. He'd pay her back. As soon as he found work in Bowling Green he'd start sending her the three hundred dollars.

Hell, that'll be easy, he mused. I won't owe anybody anything once I get home. Once that bus ticket's in my hand, I'll be debt free!

When the taxi arrived at the Port Authority building, Billy Constable gave the driver a twenty and said, "Keep the change."

The cabdriver said, "Thank *you!*"

Billy ran inside the building. The woman at the information counter pointed to the row of windows where Billy could buy a bus ticket to Bowling Green. He ran to one of those windows and told the woman clerk, "One ticket to Bowling Green, Kentucky, please."

"Return ticket too?" she asked.

"No, thank you, just one way. I'm never comin' back here, ma'am."

"I take it you didn't like the Big Apple," she said. She was an older woman with white hair done up tight to her head like a nun.

"No, ma'am. Not at all. As far as I'm concerned, that bus ticket you're about to give me is a ticket to the Promised Land."

"That'll be a hundred and thirty-three dollars and fifty cents, please."

"Yes, ma'am," said Billy, pushing two hundred-dollar bills toward her.

The woman took interminably long doing whatever she was doing back there. It seemed like forever before the woman pushed the ticket and Billy's change toward him. He put the bills and quarters in his pocket, kissed the ticket, and held it up in the air.

"Freedom," whispered Billy Constable, looking at the bus ticket.

The bus ticket was yanked out of his hand and ripped in half.

"Not so fast," said the big ugly man wearing the leather porkpie hat. "You won't be needin' this where you're goin', putzo."

The big ugly man grabbed one of Billy's arms. Another thug grabbed the other arm, and the two frog-walked Billy out of the terminal. As the three headed for Eighth Avenue, one of the thugs said to the other, "I *told* you he would head for the bus terminal. You owe me a Twinkie."

VII

"And now . . . the moment we've all been waiting for . . ."

And now . . . the moment we've all been waiting for," said host Rip Puckett with forced drama and solemnity. As Puckett said those words, a huge sixty-second clock was lowered into place. It hung in the middle of the stage, casting a somber shadow like Death's scythe.

"The moment of truth has arrived. The time has come to ask . . . the . . . big . . . question! Are you ready, Vera?"

"Yes!" answered Vera Bundle with spirit, a big smile on her face.

"Before I ask the big question, Vera, how do you feel *right now*?"

"Excited."

"Scared?"

"Not at all."

"Good for you. Okay, Vera Bundle, here is your big question. For *one . . . hundred . . . million . . . dollars* . . . or that goblet of dreadful poison . . ."

The studio went silent.

The audience seemed frozen in their seats.

It was deathly quiet in the control room.

Even the cold-blooded producer felt his throat catch.

"The Great Wall of China was built to protect the capital city of Datong by the Ming Dynasty," read host Rip Puckett from a five-by-seven white card. Puckett had to hold the card with two hands to stop it from shaking. "Some sections of the wall were said to date from the seventh century B.C. The wall did not always work. Often invaders merely ran around its ends. Sections built by the Ming alone are said to be long enough to stretch from Washington, D.C., as far as Wichita, Kansas."

Rip Puckett paused dramatically, as he was instructed to do.

"Vera Bundle, for one . . . hundred . . . million . . . dollars . . . *or death!* . . . how long is the Great Wall of China? You have exactly sixty seconds to give me a correct answer . . . starting *now!*"

Vera's expression was inscrutable.

It was hard to figure out if she did or didn't know the correct answer.

A spotlight pinpointed Vera Bundle. Another spotlight circled the gigantic sixty-second clock in the center of the stage. Fifteen seconds had gone by.

Nothing from Vera Bundle.

The lone arm on the gigantic clock now dropped to the thirty-second mark.

Some of the studio audience had their hands clasped in prayer, their heads bent, praying Vera would think of the answer.

Outside on the street in front of the National Broadcasting Company's main entrance, large speakers blared absolute silence to the anxious crowd standing on the pavement. It was the first time NBC had rigged speakers to the roof of their main entrance so that the large crowd on the sidewalk and in the street could hear what was happening in *The Big Question* studio. At Times Square, bright rolling white lights proclaimed: VERA SILENT . . . VERA SILENT . . . VERA SILENT . . .

Nuns, waiting for Vera's answer, crossed themselves. Right-to-life and anti-death-penalty pickets ceased their chanting and marching in circles, standing still and waiting to hear Vera answer the question. Tourists and hardened New Yorkers alike stopped walking and waited too.

Everyone in the street and in the studio was aware by now that when Vera knew the answer to a question, she said it right away. Vera's long pause caused enormous concern. "She doesn't know," was whispered from one to another inside and outside the building.

The gigantic hand on the clock was at the forty-five-second mark.

"Only fifteen seconds left, Vera," said host Rip Puckett, suddenly worried himself.

And then the orchestra played a chord.

Time was up.

"I'm sorry, Vera. I really am," said the obviously shaken host, "but time's up. I need your answer now."

Vera smiled and said, "I *just* remembered! The answer is a little over two thousand miles."

"Vera," said Rip Puckett, "that is NOT correct."

After another commercial break, the program returned to the nation's TV screens. The stage was barren and completely dark except for a pin spot's circle of light surrounding an armchair. Vera Bundle was led to the chair by two nurses dressed in white caps and uniforms and bright red capes over their right shoulders. Vera Bundle sat down. The TV cameras tightened on her face. There were tears in her eyes. In the past few minutes, Vera Bundle had aged ten years. She now appeared to be a very old woman. She was acutely frightened. She wondered what mystical and circuitous route had brought her, plain Vera Bundle from Steubenville, Ohio, to this soft armchair of death in New York City.

Vera's eyes were wide as saucers.

Her mouth was dry as a bone. She continually licked her lips.

The once rowdy audience had turned silent.

Then someone shouted, *"Let Vera go!"* Others picked up the slogan and a chant began. *"Let Vera go! Let Vera go! Let Vera go! Let Vera go! Let Vera go!"*

Outside on the street in front of the NBC building, traffic was halted to allow the crowd to swell. They too chanted, *"Let Vera go!"*

On the stage, on a table beside Vera's armchair, was a small cordial glass with a longish stem. It was filled with an amber-colored liquid. The two nurses in their white caps and uniforms, their red capes the only color on the morose stage, now moved to either side of Vera's armchair. A woman, dressed in a severe black three-piece suit with a black dress shirt and black tie, walked onto the stage. She stood on the other side of the small table, the side away from Vera Bundle. She was a tall, dour woman in her middle forties. Her hair was cut extremely short and shaped like a man's. She wore no makeup. She and her wardrobe were perfect for the part.

The show's host, Rip Puckett, was no longer on the stage.

The tall, dour woman crossed over to the small table and lifted the glass of amber fluid. She carried the glass to Vera Bundle and said, "Mrs. Bundle, I am Dr. Lizabeth Wax-Dupee, the attending physician. I am in charge of your execution. As you know, your beneficiaries will receive twenty-five thousand dollars in cash, a gift from the producer of *The Big Question.*"

Vera Bundle mumbled some incoherent words.

"Pardon? Did you just try to say something? You'll have to speak up, Mrs. Bundle," said Dr. Wax-Dupee impatiently.

"I said I don't have any beneficiaries."

"Yes. Well. Now . . ." Dr. Wax-Dupee held the glass of poison in front of Vera Bundle's face. "This is Madeira with a rather heavy dose of potassium cyanide in it. I suggest you take three or four swift gulps, then drink as much as you can as quickly as possible."

Vera Bundle's face didn't change. It remained rigid with fear. Her trembling hand reached out as though hypnotized and took the glass of poisoned Madeira from the doctor. She didn't seem to have any control over her appendages. Both arms were shaking, as were her legs. The hand that took the glass shook so much that the liquid contents splashed on Vera's skirt, the dour doctor's skirt, and on the floor. It wasn't done on purpose. Vera had simply lost control of her body functions. Dr. Wax-Dupee watched a gray stain spread across Vera's skirt and onto the seat cushion between Vera's legs. There was also a terribly unpleasant smell onstage. The atrocious stink drifted toward the audience.

Vera looked at the doctor and asked through her tears, "Why are you letting them do this to me? Why are you letting me die? You're a doctor, aren't you? Isn't your behavior against some medical code? Aren't you supposed to heal, not murder? Isn't that what you're supposed to do? Isn't it against the law to punish an innocent, God-fearing, good Christian human being? Don't let me die. Please, don't let me die."

More annoyed than impressed by Vera Bundle's diatribe, Dr. Wax-Dupee refilled Vera's goblet from a nearby decanter. This time the doctor held the glass for Vera as though she were an invalid and force-fed her the Madeira, practically pouring it down the woman's throat. Vera gulped and gulped until the glass was empty. Dr. Wax-Dupee removed the empty goblet and placed it on the nearby table.

Dr. Lizabeth Wax-Dupee's expression and slight sneer expressed triumph, as if she had just accomplished something very special.

Vera cried openly now.

Several members of the audience walked out of the studio.

Vera tried to say something nobody heard. She was already too weak to speak.

Dr. Wax-Dupee smiled as warmly as she could at Vera, which wasn't very warm, but didn't say a word. Dr. Wax-Dupee was a dark-complected woman with a pointed nose that jutted out over an incipient mustache. In profile, her mouth and chinless chin angled sharply downward. Sort of to the southeast. She was apparently devoid of both a chin and feelings. The doctor placed a handkerchief over her nose and walked swiftly offstage.

The doctor's husband, Clifford Dupee, the retired chief operating officer of global computer products, had joined the producer and his lawyer, Sigmond Levy, and the show's staff in the control room. They all settled in to watch Vera Bundle die.

The audience chanting of "Let Vera go" had dwindled to a sparse voice here and there, and then nothing. The chanting was over. The audience couldn't help themselves. They had become tranquilized by the bizarre event taking place in front of their eyes. They too watched, waiting for Vera Bundle to die.

Vera began to twitch.

At first her twitches were relatively far apart. Soon the intervals between twitches shortened until she was convulsing as if she were an epileptic. The spasms became frequent and more violent. Her face was distorted, her mouth pulled downward into a grotesque sneer. Her eyes began to bulge. The veins in her neck were stretched to capacity. She extended her arms as far as they could go. Her fingers opened and closed continually. Her body language begged frantically for help, from someone . . . anyone.

Vera was on fire. Flames burned inside every part of her body. The intensity of the fire was increasing by the second. Her throat felt as though it were filled with broken glass. She couldn't swallow. She knew she had very little time left on this earth. Once again she wondered why she was here, seated in this armchair, and why no one would help her. She forgot about the hundred million dollars she had desperately wanted to win. She forgot about someone rescuing her too. She could think of nothing but horror and death.

Vera Bundle willed herself to be mindful of something sweet, something happy during her final minutes on earth. She wanted her last mortal thoughts to be pleasant ones. She thought of John J. Sughrue's face, as she and her new acquaintance bucked the stiff wintry winds and swirling snowflakes of the February blizzard of '96 in New York City. She remembered how the two walked along icy Central Park South together, her arm in his for support. They trudged quite a few blocks east to the Sherry-Netherland Hotel, but it hardly seemed a walk at all. Vera could have walked arm in arm with John J. Sughrue forever. In any kind of weather. It was the happiest walk of Vera's life.

Inside, the Sherry-Netherland's lobby it was warm and comfy, just like the Essex House. Vera shook the snow off her coat and hat while John walked to the manager's desk and spoke to the man sitting there. Eventually John returned to Vera and told her he had taken a room for her. It was just for the night, he said.

Vera Bundle was ever so thankful.

John led Vera to the drugstore off the lobby to buy her a toothbrush and some paste. He also purchased an extra-large T-shirt with I ♥ NEW YORK printed on the front. Vera was to use the T-shirt as a nightie. Then the two boarded the elevator to their rooms. Vera's room was on the fourteenth floor. So was John's. Vera was sure John had arranged it that way.

When the elevator arrived at their floor, they both stepped off. John helped Vera find her room and opened her door. He gave Vera the room key, told her his room number in case she needed anything, explained how his room was just down the hall, and pointed in its direction. John said good night, kissed her on her cheek, and walked away. Vera closed her hotel room door and turned to face the queen-size bed. She knew exactly what she was going to do.

Vera walked into the bathroom and quickly changed into the T-shirt John bought her. She looked for a robe but couldn't find one.

Vera walked out of the bathroom, crossed the bedroom, and took the room key from the top of the bureau. She opened her hotel room door and looked down the hall first to the left, then to the right. The hallway was empty. Quickly Vera scampered to John's room in her extra-long T-shirt with I ♥ NEW YORK printed on the front. She knocked on John's room door. He opened it and smiled. He put out his hand and guided Vera into his suite. Young, handsome John J. Sughrue closed the suite's door and took elderly, plain Vera Bundle into his arms. They kissed each other softly and gently. Then John walked Vera into his bedroom, his arm around her shoulders, hugging her to him as they walked to the bed.

Vera had put herself to sleep every single night since she returned home from that trip to New York dreaming the same identical dream. Just as she was doing now. Dreaming that dream was always the happiest moment of her day. Of her life.

Even if it was just a drea—

Author's Note

The laws of the land in the year 2012 allowed greedy networks to produce and broadcast highly rated game shows like *The Big Question.* The Federal Communications Commission did nothing to stop the networks from airing horrific television shows for fear of lawsuits accusing the commission of preventing freedom of speech. But the public *did* do something about *The Big Question.* The millions of citizens of the United States, the final arbiters of taste and the true deciders of what should or shouldn't be broadcast—and who generally exhibit extremely poor taste in these matters—rose up on this occasion and picketed the network's outlets across America, protesting the barbaric program. *The Big Question* was canceled after just three broadcasts.

Acknowledgments

I thank my agent, Jennifer Lyons, for engineering my move to the "bigs"; David Rosenthal of Simon & Schuster for giving my book a chance; and my editor, Sarah Hochman, for making my book so much better. I also thank Charles Reilly Jr. and Loretta Strickland for their valuable help. And last but far from least, I thank my wife, Mary, for always being beside me.

About the Author

Chuck Barris is a former television show creator and producer whose credits include *The Dating Game, The Newlywed Game, The Gong Show,* and *Treasure Hunt.* He is the author of several books, including *Confessions of a Dangerous Mind* (adapted into a major motion picture) and *You and Me, Babe: A Novel.* Barris and his wife, Mary, live in Manhattan.